Curse Breaker

KINGDOM OF RUNES

CURSE BREAKER

AUDREY GREY

ISBN: 978-1-7337472-5-7

To my mom, for all your love and support.

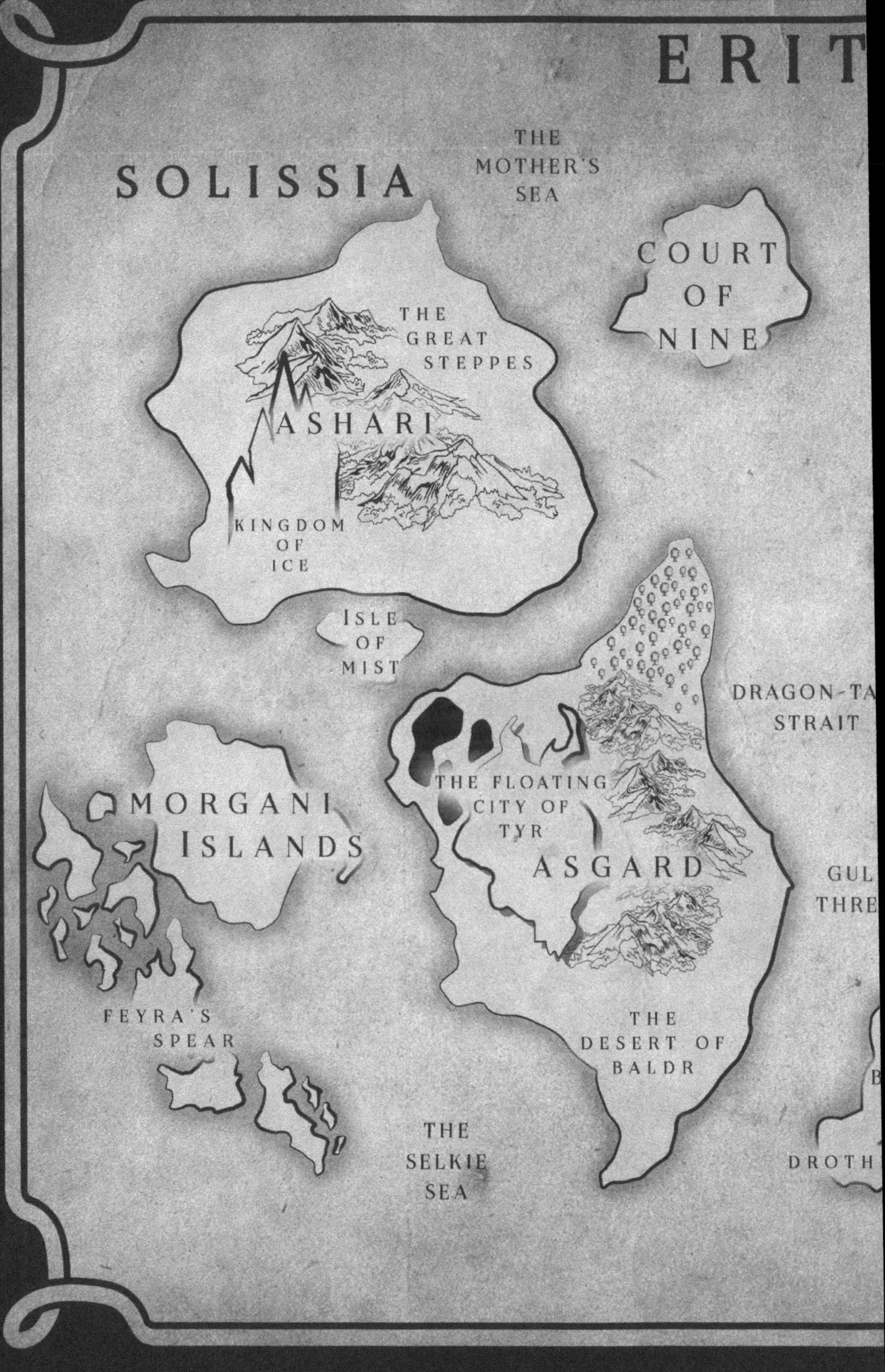

ERIT

SOLISSIA

THE MOTHER'S SEA

COURT OF NINE

THE GREAT STEPPES

ASHARI

KINGDOM OF ICE

ISLE OF MIST

DRAGON-TA
STRAIT

THE FLOATING CITY OF TYR

MORGANI ISLANDS

ASGARD

GUL
THRE

FEYRA'S SPEAR

THE DESERT OF BALDR

B

THE SELKIE SEA

DROTH

EYIA

BAY OF SHADOWS

DARKLING BAY

SPIREFALL CASTLE

SHADOW KINGDOM

THE RUINLANDS

CRED TREE OF LIFE

FEYRA'S TEMPLE

BLOOD BONE MOUNTAINS

THE WITCHWOOD

GLITTERING SEA

KINDOM OF VERDURE

HE SUN COURT

THE BANE

DEVOURER'S CAMP

FFENDIER

MANASSES

DEAD MAN'S STRAIT

ASHIVIER

PERTH

FALLEN KINGDOM OF LORWYNFELL

THE
UEENS

MUIRWOOD FOREST

CROMWELL

DUNE

RUNE WALL

KEN
REE

VENASSIAN OCEAN

KINGDOM OF PENRYTH

VESERACK

THE MORTAL LANDS

THE CURSEPRICE

Forged in heartbreak, set in bone, cast in blood, carved in stone.
A thousand years will my curse reign, unless I have these six things:

The tears of a fairy from a wood so deep.
The fig of a vorgrath from his mate's keep.
The scale of a selkie burnished gold.
The bone of a wood witch a century old.
The midnight sliver of a Shade Queen's horn.
The sacrifice of two lovers torn.

ONE

For the first time in years, Haven was lost. The vorgrath tracks she'd spotted hours ago now seemed an illusion, the musky scent the creature used to mark its territory a figment of her mind.

And yet, she could still smell the foul odor on her finger, swiped from a mossy tree not too far from here.

She spun around, her boots slipping against mud, breath loud in her ears as she searched the treetops for a break in the heavy foliage that veiled the sky. If only she could see the sun's position, she could determine what direction she was heading.

Usually the woods gave her answers—the side of a boulder where moss grew, the direction the clouds were moving; even where a spider hung its web could tell her north from south.

But the dark magick in these woods turned everything she knew about the forest on its head. Massive silver webs of arachnids she prayed never to meet shimmered from high branches on both sides. Moss carpeted everything.

Shifting her newly invoked pack across her shoulders, she ducked under the roots of a huge oak, grimacing as pearl-white larvae dropped onto her head.

She'd crouched beneath the same tree an hour ago, she was sure of it. Only now, instead of one fallen tree blocking her path, three twisting alders sprouted from the ground.

If she'd truly walked here before, there were no tracks. Either the forest was constantly changing, or she was losing her mind.

Oh, Bell. You would love to study this place. She could hear him prattling on about the magickal properties, see him studiously writing it all down. *Goddess Above, I miss you.*

Now that she was alone without the band of Solis constantly distracting her, she had time to consider the hole her best friend left with his absence—his beaming smile, his teasing laugh.

He's why you're doing all of this, she reminded herself. *Don't let him down.*

Thinking about the Penrythian Prince made her redouble her efforts to find the vorgrath. Not only did she need a fig from its keep to satisfy the Curseprice, but if she didn't somehow collect a few drops of venom from one of its famously long incisors, Rook would die.

"No pressure," she muttered, stomping through the brackish waters of a swamp. Mud clung to her boots and made her legs feel heavy while the stench of rancid water filled her nose. Creatures floated along the surface, some type of reptiles with plates of armor jutting from their spines, only the tallest points of their backs and eyes showing.

Fighting the urge to retch, she wiped her forehead, collecting sweat and depositing moss and mud over her skin.

Blasted water! She'd never hated it more. It dampened the air and filled her lungs, making every inhalation a chore. What she wouldn't give for a bath—or ten.

Her eyes strained from searching the boggy soil for the triangular, three-toed tracks left by the vorgrath. As she looked, her mind replayed the second piece of the Curseprice.

The fig of a vorgrath from his mate's keep.

Experience taught her that the male vorgrath was never very far from his mate's keep, guarding the fig trees day and night for his partner. The male vorgrath would kill any creature that came too close, especially during mating season.

Last summer, when she nearly snared the vorgrath terrorizing the Muirwood, she'd counted almost fifty woodland creatures slaughtered within a half mile radius from its keep.

Most of the victims were nocturnal animals, which told her the vorgrath was probably less active during the day. Perhaps it even slept for a few hours—if she was lucky.

By the time she'd found the vorgrath's treasure, a young fig tree hidden near a ravine, orange rays of dusk filled the Muirwood, and she decided to leave and come back in daylight.

When she returned the following day, the fig tree had been stripped of its fruit, and the male vorgrath lay dead on the ground. Killed by its mate, probably after the female smelled Haven's scent so close to her keep.

Apparently, female vorgraths were not the forgiving kind.

Whatever happened now, she couldn't forget that even if she somehow got the fig from a vorgrath's keep, and somehow collected its venom without dying, and *somehow* got away, the female would be close.

Haven discovered more vorgrath tracks near a bog. The day was fading, steeping the woods in deep shadows, a few coral rays of light retreating with every crushing throb of her heart. Here and there, bare patches mottled the trees where something had rubbed away the bark.

Strange, high-pitched shrieks pierced the heavy air along with exotic noises she couldn't place from creatures she would rather not encounter. But the further west she walked, the quieter the forest became.

Most people thought silence in the woods was a good thing, but Haven knew better.

She was now officially in vorgrath territory.

She crept through the latticework of tree-roots and vines, careful to avoid the water-filled footprints she followed. By the depth of the tracks and the length of the toes, this vorgrath was much larger and older than the one from the Muirwood.

And cleverer—it had tracked through streams and doubled back more than once.

Wonderful. Just her luck she'd found a mature, established vorgrath, which meant it would be large, smarter than most, and overly protective of its lair.

How was she supposed to *not* kill it?

But according to Stolas, killing it would doom her. "Don't kill the vorgrath," she mocked, making her voice low and taunting to sound like the Shade Lord's, "unless you want its mate to hunt you to the ends of the earth."

Kicking the worm-eaten stump of a tree, she rolled her eyes. "How does that help me if I'm dead?"

For a breath, the forest stirred, and she could swear an annoyed chuckle trickled from above.

Shadeling's shadow, this place was getting to her. If only Surai were here to complain to. She imagined Rook scoffing as the two tried to find their way through the tangle of woods, Archeron stalking ahead, annoyed at something Haven said or did—like breathing or simply existing.

Still . . . she missed them. *All* of them.

She would have never admitted such a thing a few hours earlier . . . but something about trudging through hideously overgrown forests alone made one appreciate the value of companionship, and there was no denying the truth.

The Solis had grown on her.

Even if they made fun of her and treated her like a pet, even if Archeron had a habit of restraining and taunting her, being around them felt normal. Safe.

Going soft, Ashwood.

Pushing thoughts of the Solis away, she pressed deeper into the overgrowth, growling under her breath as the shadows between the trees seemed to elongate and darken before her eyes.

Tension danced over her sweaty skin, drawing gooseflesh over her arms. She slipped out the dagger generously loaned to her by the Shade Lord. The weapon was heavier than she preferred, weighted down with an intricate gold handle, the onyx hilt a set of raven's wings. Rubies and black diamonds swirled around the handle, tossing stupid sparkles into her eyes.

A ridiculous, tacky weapon, even for the Lord of the Netherworld.

Still, vorgraths were stealthy creatures. By the time she noticed one upon her, her bow would be useless. And she held out a far-flung hope that she would catch this vorgrath sleeping—surely they did that—and be able to somehow incapacitate it without it noticing.

So heavy, garish magickal dagger it was.

The vines and foliage became denser, strangling the light even more. She quietly hacked a path as twigs and thorns gouged her cheeks, ducking and slipping through vegetation that seemed to tighten around her.

Undoubtedly, if Stolas saw how she misused his favored dagger, he would be pissed, but she was beyond caring.

The foliage thickened until she was caught inside the thick mess of brambles and vines. Panic weighed her down, and she forgot to be quiet. Forgot she was supposed to be calm.

Hacking wildly, she clawed her way forward, gasping for breath, for light, for—

A hole opened up, and she tumbled forward.

Blinking against the watery darkness tinged fuchsia by the last bit of sun, she straightened her hat and took in the scene. An enormous tree rose thirty feet in the distance. The massive, gnarled thing was centered inside the hollow of vegetation something had carefully built, a giant nest of vines, branches, and bones glued together with dried mud.

Immense roots swarmed the base of the tree, angry gray serpents half-buried in the earth. The branches were low, thick, and wide-set. And along the smallest branches hung dark, teardrop shaped fruits.

The vorgrath's fig tree.

Haven froze, the breath dying in her throat. Adrenaline narrowed her vision, and her gaze darted around the tree, sifting through the shadows. There were no forest noises inside the vorgrath's nest, no whispering breeze or insects.

Nothing but her ragged, terrified breaths and the low *thump thump* of her heart. A perfume of decay and overripe figs filled her nose and made her head spin.

Her hand tightened around the Shade Lord's dagger as she approached the tree. Sweat trickled down her shoulder blades.

Her soggy clothes made her feel heavy and slow. Hunger and adrenaline and fatigue messed with her vision, making things seem close and then far away. Creating movement where there was none.

As she carefully stepped over the tall, winding roots near the base of the tree, her gaze fell over what looked at first like large eggs. But then, for a blessed moment, her eyesight sharpened.

Not eggs—human skulls.

Pale cracked skulls atop mounds of rusted armor and bone. Fear scraped down her spine as she catalogued the informal graveyard. Human accoutrements were everywhere. A muddy boot here. A mildewed traveler's purse there.

Her breath caught as she spied a brass helmet on its side, vines and other vegetation growing through the visor. The Boteler standard, three black dahlias curving a jagged blade, was visible along its dull surface.

Twelve. Thirteen. Fourteen. Her mind automatically counted the skulls . . . only to stop when she realized what she was doing.

Goddess Above, two grape-sized puncture wounds marred most of the skulls, undoubtedly left by vorgrath fangs. Some had been shattered into hundreds of pieces, and an unwelcome image of the vorgrath smashing a human's skull into the tree trunk flashed inside her mind.

A few had been stacked one on top of the other to form gruesome pillars. A warning to stay away or die.

Good thing she never listened to reason, or she would have fled on the spot.

Instead, she said a silent prayer to the Goddess and toed between the skulls, muscles tense as she waited for her boots to crunch bone and wake the vorgrath.

Clever, she admitted, eyeing the macabre alarm system of bones even as nausea tingled the back of her throat.

How many fools desperate to break the Curse had stepped where she did now, seconds before the vorgrath butchered them?

Deep, deep scrapes were carved into the pale gray trunk of the tree. A last warning made by talons longer than her fingers.

Runes, she wanted to take the warning and flee. Out of this nest of death. Out of the dark, ruined forest. All the way to Penryth.

Except, there was no Penryth without Bell. And if she succumbed to her fear, she could run to the ends of the realm and still never escape the guilt and grief for letting Bell die for her magick and Rook die for her stupidity.

Clamping the dagger blade between her teeth, she began to creep up the tree. She moved slowly, meticulously, aware of every scrape of her boot, every explosion of breath from her lips.

Her heartbeat was a furious drum reverberating inside her skull and drowning out all other sounds.

If the vorgrath caught her now, she would be helpless.

She pulled herself onto a two-foot wide branch and froze, straining to listen. The silence crawled beneath her skin, shivering across her bones.

What if the vorgrath was awake, waiting for her in the upper branches? What if it was biding its time, incisors already drawn and ready to puncture her skull?

Happy thoughts, Ashwood.

She held her breath and scaled to a higher branch. Then another. Each time scouring every tree limb, every glistening leaf, for a fig to steal. But it wasn't until midway up the tree that she found two plump figs hanging at the bottom of a cluster of leaves.

One fruit was still green and hard to the touch. But the other was a deep crimson color, firm yet pliable. It fell away with one cut from Stolas's dagger. As soon as the ripe fig was safely inside her pocket, the urge to leave overwhelmed her.

Releasing a silent breath, she glanced down to freedom. To survival. If she fled with the fig, Bell's chances were a hundred times better. But if she scurried higher, if she met the vorgrath and tried to extract his venom, she would probably die, taking Bell's chances to the grave.

A soft, gurgling rattle trickled from above. Like something rousing from sleep. The dagger shook in her hand.

Run, Run, Run!

She did no such thing. With a heavy sigh—and her promise to Surai ringing in her mind—she shoved the dagger between her teeth and crept higher, her body numb with a potent cocktail of adrenaline and fear.

Netherworld take her, she couldn't break a promise. She wouldn't. Even if this was about the stupidest thing she'd ever done.

A wall of stench slammed into her like rancid meat cocooned in wet dog fur. The odor stung her eyes. The branches above rustled as something stirred, something heavy and large, a hideous melody of guttural grunts and clacking talons clawing her eardrums.

The vorgrath was awake.

Sniffing—it was slowly drawing in the air, tasting it. Tasting *her.*

The inhalations paused, and she went still, a statue of nerves and panic. For an anxious heartbeat, deadly quiet strangled the air, and her muscles contracted, prepared to fight even as her mind howled with blinding terror.

The branch dipped and lifted, leaves rustling and sending her heart into a tailspin as the vorgrath jumped high up in the tree.

Panting, Haven craned her neck to the tallest branches. Where was it? She spied a flash then heard more rustling leaves. She replaced her dagger with her bow and nocked a poison-tipped arrow, following the shimmer of flickering leaves.

But it moved too fast for a good shot. A blur of gray caught her attention, another rustle of leaves, and by the time she swiveled her arrow-tip in that direction, it had moved again.

It was trying to confuse her. To knock her off balance.

The tree was shaking violently. Knees bent, Haven focused on balancing as the vorgrath moved faster and faster.

Again and again, it jumped.

Again and again, she switched her aim.

All at once, the tree branches froze. The noise stopped. Silence rippled over her, intensifying the frantic drumming of her heart.

Where are you?

She felt the tree limb she crouched on waver before she heard the vorgrath's claws click over the soft wood behind her. On instinct, she swung around while simultaneously releasing her arrow.

The vorgrath was a hideous collection of shriveled, scaly gray skin pulled taut over spindly bones. Two twisted and gnarled horns rose from its skeletal head and curled along the spinal ridges of its hunched back. Cadaverous arms, made for swinging across trees and slashing prey, reached nearly to its feet. Black talons, longer than her dagger, sprouted from its lanky fingers.

But its eyes were what shriveled the air inside her chest. Wide, whitish-red discs like blood swirled in milk. There was no pupil, nothing to speak of humanity or connect with.

The vorgrath clawed at the arrow embedded into its gaunt chest, talons clacking. A high-pitched scream turned her bowels to jelly. She'd hit just above where she guessed was its heart.

She nocked another arrow, only to remember Stolas's warning.

Along with the pesky fact that she needed the creature alive to retrieve the venom.

Runes! Everything inside her screamed to put the monstrous predator down. But a promise was a promise.

So the dagger replaced the bow, and she inched forward as the vorgrath screeched at her, revealing jagged teeth that could shred Penrythian armor and sever bone. Drops of poison glistened from the end of two long, curved fangs.

It was said the male vorgrath used its poison to incapacitate the intruder to present, still alive, to its mate. The thought was enough to send bile lapping at the back of her throat.

The vorgrath glanced up at the high branches.

"No!" she yelled, causing the creature to hiss. "Don't you dare jump, you hideous thing."

How did one go about soulbinding a vorgrath?

Its hate-filled eyes dropped to her dagger, and it hissed louder. The webbing over its protracted ribcage vibrated with a warning rattle. Grayish-black goo seeped from its wound.

"Shh," she cooed, stealing another step closer, mirroring the vorgrath's body posture. "Be a good little vorgrath."

The rattle became a staccato of deep growls that curdled her blood. All the delicacies she had scarfed at the Shade Lord's home threatened to come up as she slid closer.

She could do this. She had nearly soulbound a Shade Lord. Surely, she could soulbind this horrid creature.

She was close enough now; one leap, and its fangs would penetrate her neck . . . or her skull. The vorgrath's head ticked to the side. Two translucent membranes shuttered over its hideous eyes as they studied her.

Goddess Above, it was ugly.

Her breathing was in line with its chest; she blinked when

it blinked. The beginnings of a tentative connection formed between them. The bond felt strange, alien, the vorgrath's mind a savage landscape of greed and rage and primal urges, but she grasped onto the one commonality they shared—devotion.

His devotion to his mate became a door to slip through. The vorgrath fought her at first, the tether between them fraying, low snarls churning the air.

But after a few heartbeats, the creature calmed, and she knew he was hers to command.

She approached carefully, slowly, one hand on the glass vial she kept for poisons, the other on her dagger. As she soothed the jagged terrain of its consciousness, gagging on the vorgrath's repulsive odor, she struggled to keep him docile and control her overriding fear.

The dying light glimmered off dead-fish scales riding up the vorgrath's sinewy neck. She held up the vial, slipping the edge just beneath the curved five-inch fang peeking from its upper lip.

Its gray mouth parted.

It was panting in time with her heartbeat, and up close, she realized it did have pupils—tiny vertical red slivers inside a sea of white.

"Good," she whispered, hardly daring to breathe as an iridescent, silvery bead of venom slid to the bottom of the vial. Just one more drop . . .

Clack. Clack. She glanced down to the vorgrath's long talons clicking together. The connection was slipping.

All at once, the vorgrath's murky-white membranes began blinking over its eyes, its bony ribcage heaving faster and faster.

Odin's teeth! She just managed to squeeze out one more drop of venom and slip the vial into her satchel before the connection snapped.

A snarl spewed from the vorgrath as if it was surprised she was there. Its primordial gaze flicked to the arrow still buried deep in its chest, back to her, and it dropped into a crouch, muscles rippling inside bulging thighs.

Dagger in hand, Haven backed away until she was wedged against the tree trunk. In one smooth motion, she traded the dagger for her bow and had an arrow nocked.

"Don't even think about it, dummy," she warned.

That stopped the ugly thing.

It tilted its head side to side, quick, animalistic motions. Then the vorgrath screamed at the arrow pointed at its chest and raked its claws against the tree limb.

But it didn't follow as she hopped to the next limb, then the next. All the while, she never lowered her weapon or broke the creature's inhuman gaze.

Killing the foul thing was tempting, but she didn't want to risk the wrath of the vorgrath's mate if she didn't have to.

Perhaps an arrow in its bony shoulder might slow it down a bit. Or piss it off—not that she imagined the fury raging inside its dead eyes could burn much brighter.

The vorgrath knew that if it didn't kill Haven, its mate would be pissed.

When she hit the ground, arrow still dead center on the vorgrath's chest, it crouched low and began to creep from branch to branch after her, never taking its gaze off her arrow. By the time she made it to the nest's entrance, walking backwards, the misshapen beast watched her from the lowest branch.

Just like that, the last trickle of light dried up, and night came.

Her hand around the bow was trembling and slippery with sweat.

Inside the vorgrath's nest, buried beneath a canopy of vines and leaves and bones, the faint light of the stars and moon couldn't enter, steeping her world in absolute darkness. The only light came from the vorgrath's red eyes, two windows into the Netherworld.

Apparently in the darkness, they glowed bright as Netherfire—which wasn't creepy or terrifying *at all.*

And then, those fiery orbs blinked out, and she turned and ran.

TWO

Bell spent the longest night of his life on the creature's couch. He refused to sleep in one of the many opulent rooms available—every time he entered a chamber and closed the door, the air grew thin, and he couldn't breathe—instead choosing to toss and turn on the same dusty couch as the night before, sweaty from the fire that raged beside him.

When he closed his eyes, he saw Haven falling. Haven burning.

Haven *dying*.

So his eyes stayed open, and he counted the stars that blazed from the open wall near the corner. They were so much brighter than the stars at home, and he wondered if anyone had ever bothered to paint them.

Haven would have tried . . .

Stop thinking about her. She's gone. But Haven was woven too deeply into the fabric of his life for him to extricate with a few harsh words.

For him, she was everywhere. He could see her smile, smell the sticky buns she always had with her, hear her voice ordering him around in his head, her laughter floating down the hallways. Deep down, he knew he would never meet someone as bossy and beautiful and funny and irreverent as her.

She was a fierce star, as bright as the ones above. A light Penryth and the rest of the mortal kingdoms desperately needed.

A world without Haven wasn't something he could think about.

Perhaps if he could finally cry, he could scour away the residue of grief that clung to him like poison. But his tears, which for years came readily at the first hint of emotion, were absent. Depriving him of an outlet for his pain.

Jaw locked, Bell jumped from the couch and headed for the dining room. It might have been morning anyway for all he could tell. Day didn't exist here. Only an endless night full of beautiful stars and horrible creatures lurking in the shadows.

As soon as he entered the starlit dining room, he found another plate of food waiting and a cup of steaming tea.

Bell frowned at the huge table and empty chairs. Any other time, he would have taken a seat and accepted he would eat alone. Any other time, he might have welcomed the privacy to just be himself. But a moment longer inside his head, with his memories of Haven, and he would surely go mad.

Instead, he turned his anger on his host and his lack of manners. Bell might be a prisoner, but he was still technically a guest. Lifting his chin, he turned on his heel and marched out the doors.

Just like last time, there was a spark, and the cold metal handle twisted beneath his palm. Cold air seeped through Bell's clothes and into his bones, but he hardly felt it.

Soon, he would be through the portal and under a sun-kissed sky. Soon, the smell of flowers would replace this musty castle air.

"What are you doing here?"

The stern male voice came from the top of the stairs. If Bell didn't already know who was speaking, he would have thought it came from a boy not much older than himself, not the massive, hunched creature bounding down the stairs toward him.

"I'm going outside," Bell answered, stuffing his hands in his pockets to keep from flinching.

The creature lumbered to block the wall where the portal was, a chuckle rasping from beneath his hood. "Go eat your breakfast."

"I don't want to eat alone."

"Then you will starve."

Bell shrugged. "Fine by me."

"Fine." The creature turned to walk back up the stairs, then paused and glanced back. "Why will you not sleep in one of the rooms I have offered you?"

Bell fidgeted with the pockets of his pants. What would a creature like him know of loneliness, of being afraid?

So he said what he imagined a true prince would say in such a situation. "They are not to my satisfaction."

"And the food I have so graciously offered you? Do you also find that lacking?"

Never in his life had Bell said an unkind word to anyone, but right now, all he wanted was to hurt someone. To spew out the rage and sadness eating him from the inside out.

Less than a week ago, he was happy. Less than a week ago, his best friend was alive. Less than a week ago, he would have never had to deal with a creature such as this.

"It's bland slop not fit for a dog," Bell asserted.

"And I suppose I'm not fit to entertain you, Prince?"

Ignoring the low warning growl in the creature's words, Bell said, "If you were in Penryth, we would have thrown you into the dungeons and chained you up like a beast."

That last word hung in the air. The creature didn't face him, but his rapid, grunting breaths and hands clenched at his sides warned of his fury.

Bell was sure he would turn around and act like the creature he was. Perhaps he would kill him right there. Or roar at him. Or *something*.

Perhaps Bell wanted him to.

But the creature's shoulders sagged. Without a word, he began to scale the stairs.

Guilt tightened Bell's throat. Why had he said such horrible things? He let out a ragged sigh. "My friend . . . my friend is dead."

Silence filled the castle as the creature halted halfway up the steps.

"She was on her way to save me," Bell continued, his voice strangely emotionless, "and they killed her for it. Just snuffed her out, this bright, wonderful being."

The creature tilted his head back. "I don't want to know your troubles."

Bell didn't know why he was telling the creature this, especially since it was obvious he didn't care. But he couldn't stop the words from flooding out. "Haven was the only person who's ever loved me. She was the only good thing in my messed-up life, and they took her away, and now . . . she's dead, and I can't even cry. What's wrong with me?"

"Why would you *want* to cry?"

Through the bitterness in the creature's voice, Bell thought he caught a hint of true confusion, and his throat ached with emotion as he tried to explain. "Because that's what you do when someone you love dies, right?" He kicked at the bottom step. "Your body is supposed to react, to reflect the magnitude of that loss, but I'm a failure at everything, if you didn't know. Apparently, even mourning."

"That's foolish," the creature growled. "Be glad the tears don't come."

"My best friend is gone," Bell said, shaking his head. "She deserves something. Life can't just . . . go on."

The creature let out a dark chuckle. "Oh, but life does go on, spoiled prince. Perhaps it's time you learned that."

Before Bell could respond, the creature stalked up the stairs and left Bell alone in the cold darkness with his grief, wishing he'd stayed in the dining room and eaten alone after all.

THREE

The vorgrath was coming. Haven slammed through wall after wall of thicket, straining her eyes in the pitch black for any hint of a path. Thorns tore at her cheeks, arms, and cloak, but she hardly felt them.

Twigs and vines snapped behind her, close enough to flood her limbs with adrenaline to keep twisting, keep hacking and stabbing at the foliage that was going to get her killed.

Move your ass, Ashwood!

As if in response, a snarl split the air. She lurched forward. Somewhere along the way, she'd traded her bow for Stolas's stupid dagger.

Thank the Goddess it was honed to a killing-edge because she was slashing wildly, cutting into the shadows, into anything and everything that touched her or moved.

Her lungs felt shrunken as her legs pounded the springy ground, and she devoured giant, greedy breaths of air. Every sound had her spinning backward, carving shadows until she had no clue which direction she was headed.

All she knew was the breaking branches were coming from behind her still, and they were closer—too close.

She broke free of the thicket, gasping with relief at the pearlescent wash of moonlight filtering through the wood. After glancing over her shoulder, she darted through the forest, her mind whirring to formulate a plan, a place she could go to evade the vorgrath.

Not the trees. Her head swiveled left to right, searching for something to mask her scent, a place to hide.

Not enough time. She leapt over a stream and broke right, heading down a steep hill. Mossy rocks and fallen birch snagged her boots.

At the bottom of the hill, her gaze flickered over a dead sycamore. Most of its thick trunk was submerged in a shallow pond of silvery water. Something moved just above . . .

Her body went rigid. The vorgrath dropped gracefully from the thick canopy of trees above onto the fallen sycamore, landing quietly. It chirped once, its hairless skull canted to the side, eyes burning inside its skeletal sockets.

Its long neck heaved as it made another strange and eerie chirp.

Once, twice, three times.

Calling its mate, perhaps?

There was no warning before it attacked. One second it was crouched on the tree. The next, it leapt at her, fangs bared and glistening with poison.

The vorgrath crashed into her. Red stars burst across her vision. She tasted mud and moss and blood. She rolled on instinct, dodging the incisors punching down at her skull, and rammed hard into a log. The impact nearly knocked her out.

Before she could grab her bearings, lightning rods of pain shredded through her cloak and tunic and into her back.

Oh, Goddess save her. The pain . . .

The fiery agony burning her flesh propelled her to her feet. She screamed as the vorgrath's talons caught in her skin before wrenching out. The torment blacked out her mind, and she barely fought her way back to consciousness.

With a wild growl, she lurched over the log to run, but the vorgrath's claws were everywhere. Cutting. Tearing. Carving furrows down her cheek, her neck. Shredding her flesh into ribbons.

Blood—blood was everywhere. So much blood.

The pain scorched her body. Her dagger found its mark, once, twice, but only grazed those slimy scales. That gray, sinewy flesh.

A blow caught her in the temple. Darkness. Agony ricocheted around her skull as she crumpled.

She was on her back. She flung up her hand. The knife—the knife was gone. Runes! She scrambled to her feet, scouring the shadowy ground for the dagger, but the vorgrath found it first.

With a guttural shriek, it grasped the blade between its elongated fingers and chucked the dagger into the water.

Nethergates! Her bow.

It was in her hands as soon as the thought hit her. When did she grab it? Her mind was missing pieces. Her senses all mixed up. Adrenaline blurred everything to choppy half-second scenes.

Arrow—she needed an arrow.

She spied the glint of iron arrowheads littering the ground. Only one remained in her quiver.

Taking hold of the thin bolt, she steadied the arrow against the string, habit taking over as she squinted down the arrow's shaft. Her breathing slowed. Her chaotic pulse steadied.

A sense of calm washed over her, numbing the mortal wounds ravaging her body.

Two heartbeats passed. Two whole heartbeats for her to decide to move the arrow half an inch to the left, away from the monster's shoulder. A kill shot.

Stolas's warning whispered through her, but it couldn't compete with the rage, fear, and disgust surging through her.

Kill the sonofa—

The vorgrath leapt—and she released her arrow.

Moonlight sparkled off the spinning metal tip as it shot through the watery darkness. The arrow hit the vorgrath right as the creature came down on Haven. The vorgrath fell just short of its target, smashing into the muddy earth with a resounding thwack.

I don't want to be here when the mate arrives, she decided. She took one pitiful step . . . and then collapsed beside the beast. Monster and mortal, both wounded beyond help.

She forced her head sideways and her gaze on the vorgrath, only letting herself sink into the moss-laden forest floor when she spied her arrow sunk fletching-deep into its monstrous heart.

Before the dying creature succumbed, it let out a warbling scream. The cry was so human that she thought for a second it was her who made the sound.

Then the vorgrath died.

Somewhere deep in the forest, a similar cry shuddered the trees and echoed inside her skull.

Its mate.

Her head fell back, and she released an agonized breath. She wasn't safe yet. Far from it. She was *dying*.

Maybe not immediately. But bleeding out in a forest of hungry predators didn't leave much in the way of hope. And that was if the vorgrath's mate didn't get her first.

So many ways to die, she thought bitterly.

She could only pray the Solis found her body and the vorgrath venom before Rook perished too.

A little smile, part agony part irony, twisted her lips. The Sun Lord would have to respect her then—he wouldn't have a choice.

For a pained breath, she thought she caught a shimmer of something in the trees above, watching her. The form of a man, his head canted to the side in disappointment. Perhaps even the silvery outline of wings flickered in and out of her vision, and a single raven circled above—but she was dying, after all.

One would expect a few hallucinations.

The girl was dying. Stolas shifted on the branch above where he had watched the entire battle—if you could call it that—unfold from the mirror realm.

If she knew how to harness her magick, she could have ended the fight before it began. Thanks to her skill with weapons, she outlasted most mortals who went up against the wicked, territorial creatures—but in the end, weapons and skill weren't enough.

Not against a vorgrath.

The dead shadowling's mate called from across the ravine flanking them, her plaintive shriek laced with fury. He'd already forbid the vengeful monster from coming near Haven—at least he could let her die peacefully—but the creature wouldn't stay away for long.

Out of all the shadowlings under his reign, vorgraths were the hardest to control.

He turned his attention back to Haven. Death surrounded her, a ravenous beast gliding along her exposed flesh, marking her as its prize. Ever the patient specter, it waited for the last of her blood to spill into the earth and her mortal heart to quiver its final beat.

Then and only then would it enter her fleshly body, claim her soul, and present him with it like a proud dog with a dead fowl in its jaws.

Only Haven wasn't a bird to be dropped at his feet.

An inexplicable tug of emotion stirred inside him as he watched her try to get up, clawing at the ground, fingers digging into the mossy carpet.

She lay on her side facing him. Her warring powers—one light and one dark—churned around her, fiery serpents of gold and blue. Strands of her beautiful hair, darkened with dirt and blood, fanned out around her.

It was the first time he'd seen it loose. She looked younger with her hair down. Softer and less ferocious. Like a jagged shard of onyx buffed just enough that one could handle it without drawing blood.

"You lose," his companion purred, her gloating voice digging under his skin. "If only she turned around after she took the fig." She pulled her wings tight to her body and sighed. "Why do you suppose she went back for the venom?"

"Mortal stupidity," he snarled, wishing he could drop down and scold Haven for her rashness.

Even so, something about her courage had impressed him. When she approached the vorgrath's lair, she'd been terrified, her scent laced with the metallic tang of fear. And after she found the fig, he read the doubt in her expression.

She wanted to flee—yet she didn't.

As Lord of the Netherworld, he had watched humans for

centuries, long enough to understand them better than they did themselves. Any other mortal would have left the warrior Sun Queen Rook to die.

As if Haven could feel his presence, she drew up enough strength to lift her head in his direction. Their eyes met, and even though he knew she couldn't see him, he felt a pulse of connection.

She laughed—actually laughed—and then her energy drained, and she fell back into the mossy carpet.

Shock. She was going into shock.

"This is my favorite stage of dying," his companion said. "They always do the silliest things."

Having spectated thousands of deaths, he knew what came next. The stages were simple: panic, denial, shock, and then a calm sense of acceptance at the end.

Afterwards, their spirits escaped their fleshly bodies. Sometimes they slipped away quietly. The act almost serene. Sometimes the souls jerked from their mortal vessels as if being ripped out by an unseen hand, the person looking quite shocked at their new corporeal state.

But always, always, they came to him, unwillingly and terrified. Their new master.

"She'll be ours soon," his companion said. "First dibs?"

The growl that erupted from his chest sent her hopping back on the branch, her wings fluttering behind her and stirring the few leaves left on the trees.

"No one touches her," he roared, surprising even himself. "Understood?"

Her mouth parted, and she let her gaze flit from Haven's dying form back to him. *Since when do you care?* she seemed about to reply before she wisely thought better of it.

He had the same thoughts. *Losing your temper now? Over a mortal?*

Pulling his wings in close to his body, he tried to turn away from Haven, to block out her uneven breaths, so small and helpless. The pain he sensed in her. The fear.

Let her die. You have done enough.

Against all instincts, his gaze circled back to the scene. To her. And something in her face, the ferocious twist of her lips as she stared down death, the fight in her eyes, made him want to help her.

"No," his companion said, though her voice trembled—she was still wary after his last outburst. "You promised you would not intervene."

His talons erupted from his fingertips, the dull pressure and then release almost pleasurable. He knew in his mind he'd already made the decision to save her, but he didn't understand why, so he fought it.

Plenty of mortals had died worse deaths. Why did this one affect him so deeply? He needed her for his plan, but that didn't explain the way her agony sent a raw, visceral protectiveness surging through him with her every dying breath.

Her lips parted, a soft moan slipping out, and he lost it. Snarling, he spread his wings and prepared to swoop down to help her.

In that moment, he would have moved the Nihl and the Netherworld to make her pain stop—

The scent hit Stolas first, breaking the hold Haven had on him. A Solis was close. He growled as his natural enemy appeared, his magickal aura a pale golden essence that lit up the trees around him.

Archeron Halfbane, son of the Sun Sovereign of Effendier and slave to a mortal king. His magick flared and guttered, trying to escape the darkness that fed off its flame. But even the powerful son of the Sovereign couldn't escape the Curse, and his magick was a mere whisper.

Stolas felt his lips tug into a half-smile. The pretty boy Sun Lord would hate having his magick smothered almost as much as he would despise knowing he was being watched from the Netherworld.

"Poor, failed hero," his companion teased as Stolas's wings slowly relaxed, his breathing evening out. "Seems a Solis will claim that title instead."

"Good," Stolas muttered, settling uneasily back into the tree to watch. Now that the spell was broken, he was just as surprised by his drive to help the wounded mortal girl as his companion was. "Let the idiot Solis deal with her."

"You say that, but your face . . ."

"My face what?"

"Perhaps," his companion persisted, her tone changed from taunting to concerned, "the blood you tricked her into ingesting connected you somehow."

Slowly, he lifted his upper lip and bared his fangs. His chest rattled with a low growl. "I only did so to awaken her powers. Now, enough chatter about the mortal. I am not in the mood."

Lowering her head, she slunk a few feet away before leaping to the next tree over, where she cut her eyes warily at him. Normally, he would have already put her in her place, but he was distracted tonight, and ever the cunning Noctis, she'd picked up on it.

She was testing the boundaries of their relationship, seeing how far she could push him. "Have you ever considered," she said, "that you have completed two of the three acts necessary for the mating ritual?"

He had considered such a thing, not that he would admit as

much to his companion. "For a Noctis mating ritual to be valid, the participants must drink each other's blood and share a dream bond," he pointed out. "But the girl does not have access to my dreams, nor has she willingly given me her blood to drink."

Unsatisfied, his companion tangled her arms around her chest and glared down at the dying mortal. Against his will, Stolas followed her gaze.

Ever the gentleman, Archeron was covering Haven with his cloak. They were speaking. Stolas canted his head, straining to listen.

Did she call out his name? And Archeron . . . why did the fool sound so . . . affectionate?

He'd known Archeron for centuries, and he was a lot of things—arrogant, preening, a bastard—but affectionate wasn't one of them.

A prickle of anger gathered between his shoulder blades, and his talons lengthened. Frowning, he released a long breath and tried to be grateful that Archeron had appeared to save the girl and keep his wager intact.

And yet . . . he couldn't escape the impulse, the *need* to be the one to save her. To be the one she saw when she awakened. To mend her flesh and drive out her pain and see her amber eyes bright again, appraising him with that same courageous stupidity he should have killed her for the first day he met her.

His companion tsked from her newfound branch, glaring at him above a pout. "I only mention the blood because . . . the way you look at her . . ." Before continuing her statement, she retreated a few more steps, her wings flaring as she prepared to fly to safety—if necessary. "Do you think she would ever look at you the same? To her, you're a monster just like our shadowling she felled."

His palms prickled; his hands had curled into fists, talons digging into his flesh. His companion watched him unblinkingly as she waited for his response, hardly daring to breathe, holding the sleek blue-black feathers blanketing her wings perfectly still.

"The girl means nothing to me," he said, forcefully, trying to will the statement into existence.

"Then prove it."

Normally, any demand to prove himself would be ignored . . .

"When she has served her purpose, we will drink from her magick," he said. "Together." He shifted, and she flinched slightly, feathers ruffling and ridging, but his movement was only to unfurl his clenched fingers. He was glad to see his talons had retracted. "Does that satisfy you?"

She nodded, slowly. But concern tugged down the corners of her lips, and more than once, when she thought he couldn't see her, she studied him carefully.

Lowering his eyebrows, he forced his attention back to the scene unfolding below and made a vow. If Archeron saved the little fool, he would treat her with the same indifference as every other Goddess-forsaken mortal until he could be rid of her.

FOUR

Archeron's head whipped up at the sound of the dying vorgrath, and he darted faster through the trees, snarling under his breath. He'd heard Haven's cries a mile back. Plaintive, scared wails that stirred up ancient feelings of protection and fury and forced him into a sprint.

He cleared the hill, his runesword held high, and froze. The vorgrath was sprawled on its back, an arrow sticking from its chest, another broken off at its shoulder. Beside the shadowling was an unmoving bloody mass, tiny and frail in comparison.

The vibrant hue of her hair was familiar—as was the scent beneath the tang of blood.

"Haven." The mortal girl's name came out a whisper, and he loped toward the scene, his head on a swivel as he watched for the mate.

Even with the predator dead, Archeron's body reacted, muscles tensed and eyes sharp. He quelled his instinct to part the shadowling's head from its body, the kill method he preferred for such abominations. The mortal girl had seen enough blood today.

More than half of which looked to be hers.

Tearing his focus from her injuries, he shrugged off his cloak and dropped to one knee beside her. As he draped the dark silk over her broken body, the fabric stuck to the blood that seemed to come from everywhere. He'd barely set it down before the entire garment was soaked.

His jaw clenched as her injuries became clear, the deep red furrows marking her pale skin, the white bits of exposed bone.

The monster had toyed with her. Flaying her delicate mortal skin when it could have easily offered a killing blow.

Rage surged through him, hot and blinding, and he had to focus his breathing to regain control. *Why was he reacting so strongly?* He'd seen soldiers injured just as badly in battle, and his response, though empathetic, had never felt so visceral, so out of control.

Burying his emotions beneath a hard mask, he demanded, "Can you walk?"

Moaning softly, she glanced his way as if just now noticing him, her pale amber eyes distant and glazed. Shivers wracked her body and sent fresh anger coursing through him.

Thank the Goddess, shock was masking the pain.

"If I pass . . . pass out, check my satchel." She blinked wearily, but surprisingly, even in such a state, her eyes glimmered with . . . pride. "I have a present for you." She licked her dry lips, and her gaze wandered to the dead vorgrath. "The bastard's dead?"

"Yes." He scooped her up with one arm, surprised by how light she was, his sword ready in his other hand. The vorgrath's mate would be close by. "It was a good, clean shot straight to the heart."

"How hard was it . . ." she panted. "To admit that?"

"I have no problem admitting when a mortal does something worthy of praise," he growled as he slipped through the forest, Haven tight in his arms. "It just doesn't happen very often."

"Hmph." A tiny, rasping laugh slipped from her lips, but then she moaned and squirmed against his chest. Blood, warm and sticky, smeared over his tunic and neck.

In contrast, her small body was ice cold.

"I can walk," she stubbornly insisted.

He grunted. "Even near death, you argue."

"Please . . . can't owe more . . ."

"It is nothing. You weigh less than a sack of grain despite eating more than ten Sun Queens." *Not helping*. He lowered his voice and tried a gentler tactic. "Let me carry you, Haven Ashwood."

Archeron had never used her given name. He was not aware, actually, that he knew it. Perhaps he overheard it at court or during one of the few times he watched her in the training arena at Penryth, battling clumsy mortal boys who thought they were men.

But as soon as her name slipped over his tongue, she became something more than just the infuriating mortal who tested him at every step.

Someone more.

Maybe, as Surai said, she had been for a while, and he'd just been too stubborn to realize. Maybe it took her being halfway between the living realm and the Netherworld for him to acknowledge that he didn't want her to slip away.

But now, sprinting through the trees with her bleeding out in his arms, the thought that she could die—that she probably would die—hit him hard. The emotion felt as real as the blood pouring over him and the gibbous moon lighting their way above.

For reasons he couldn't fully explain, he cared about her. A mortal. More than he'd cared about anyone in a long time. And a sudden, wild fury filled him at the thought of her being taken away.

She beat a tiny fist against his chest. Once. Twice. Then her eyes closed. Rose gold eyelashes fluttered and went still. Her matching dusky pink hair, near iridescent in the moonlight, was soft against his neck as she rested her head in the crook of his collarbone, her breath coming out warm and fast.

Every hot pulse of air against his flesh assured him she was still alive.

He shifted his focus from the girl to their surroundings, quickening his pace. His ears tuned in to the song of the woods, straining to pick up anything worthy of his sword. Something watched them; he could feel their presence. But locating the dark entities was another matter. Other than the usual noises of running water and rustling leaves, the forest was quiet.

Perhaps the feeling simply came from the insidious dark magick permeating this blasted forest. Archeron wasn't one to run anywhere—but he forced himself into a sprint, in a hurry to save the girl and be rid of this place.

Haven stirred, groaning into his neck. The sound struck him like a blade.

"You're okay now," he whispered protectively.

Plunging his sword into the scabbard at his hip, he slipped his other arm beneath her legs, pressing against the leather of her pants stiff with partially dried blood. He tried to shift his focus once again to the forest, but something drew it back to the bloodied bundle in his arms.

Part of him wanted to dump her on the ground and give her a tongue-lashing for her impulsiveness.

How could she be so naïve? So reckless! Going after the vorgrath alone. Doing things her way with no advice, no help.

But then, she stirred in his arms, a ragged sigh slipping from her parted lips, and he wanted to tighten his arms around her until he somehow took away her pain.

A low growl rumbled from his throat, and he let his gaze slide over her face. Her forehead seemed the only part of her not bloodied. As he ran below gaps in the treetops, moonlight flickered over her face, illuminating tiny freckles dotting her fine cheekbones—faint stars inside a porcelain sky.

As if she felt his gaze, her eyelashes fluttered, her lips working into a frown.

Please, he prayed to the Goddess. *Take away this foolish mortal's pain. Let her awaken to . . . to eat again—she enjoys that—and to drive me crazy. She especially enjoys that. And whatever other mortal pleasures she possesses.*

He lifted his face to the sky, surprised that he'd called on the Goddess. How long had it been since he'd invoked her? Months? Years? After having his prayers go unanswered for so long, there didn't seem much point to prayer . . .

Focusing on the patches of stars through the trees, he willed the Goddess to hear him. *Don't take her yet,* he pleaded. *I know she's only a mortal, but she's as brave as she is foolish, enough to rival any of your Sun Queens. She deserves another chance at life.*

It was partly a selfish request. Every moan, every gasp from her lips filled him with rage . . . and helplessness . . . helplessness so deep, so overwhelming that if he could, he would cut it out of his heart with the tip of his sword.

The Goddess must have been listening because Haven stopped writhing and moaning with pain. Her ragged breaths smoothed out. The rigid muscles of her body softened.

"See," he whispered. "You're okay, Little Mortal." And for the briefest of seconds, the Heart Oath amulet at his neck pulsed searing heat before cooling to an icy pebble against his flesh.

Then he was slipping between the tangle of vines, sycamores, and oaks with her tight to his body, her slow heartbeat drumming against his chest as he counted her breaths and willed her to live.

FIVE

"We should have married," Rook rasped. It was the first coherent thing she'd spoken in hours. The Sun Queen's head rested in Surai's lap, the intricate design of braids wrangling her hair tangled with leaves and dirt. Her eyes were closed, her lips pale and cracked, parting slightly with each shallow breath.

This cursed land's gibbous moon hung low and heavy, casting a gray pallor over her normally sun-kissed skin.

It's not just the moon to blame, Surai admitted as she gazed down at her mate. Death's shadow had crept over Rook while Surai succumbed to sleep. She'd curled up next to Rook's feline form, promising herself it would only be a few minutes—but then, half the night had passed.

When she jerked awake, Rook was curled on her side, in her fleshly body, shivering and moaning.

How could she have left Rook alone to struggle while she slept?

Biting her cheek until she tasted the metallic tang of blood,

Surai forced her weary eyes open. *I'll stay awake as long as it takes.*

A far away shriek from some night creature sent adrenaline surging through her veins. How long had Archeron been gone? She'd lost track of time, her entire focus on Rook, willing her chest to rise, her mouth to breathe, her eyes to open. *Don't give up, my love.*

"A little longer and then we'll have the antidote, and we can marry right here," Surai promised. Her eyes prickled, but she kept the tears from falling. Rook would hate that.

"Why?" Rook croaked, her voice so soft that Surai nearly missed it.

"Why marry you?" Surai asked, brushing a hand over Rook's clammy cheek. It was startlingly cold, and she quickly tried to joke to hide her alarm. "I ask myself that daily."

"No," Rook said. Her voice was breathless and weak, a stranger's voice. "Why . . . trust . . . her?"

Surai shook her head. She didn't have an answer for why she put so much faith in Haven other than her heart willed it so. But her warrior mate had never understood Surai's reliance on her heart. Rook preferred to govern her decisions using the cunning she'd learned in her mother's court and her soldier's instincts instead.

"I'm afraid," Rook whispered. Her pale eyelashes fluttered, contrasting against the dark red band tattooed around her eyes.

Afraid?

Surai clutched Rook's hand, aware that any other time, she would have relished holding Rook's fingers instead of her paw. The pads of her hand just below where her fingers met her palm were calloused from a lifetime of swinging a sword, the lines below deep and furrowed.

How had she never noticed such details?

"What are you afraid of?" Surai asked. She'd never heard Rook admit to being afraid of anything, and the declaration unsettled her.

Rook's eyes fluttered opened for a moment, the tawny gold irises faded and dull, flecked here and there with brown. "I'm afraid that when I'm gone, your kind heart will make you a target."

Surai's throat tightened. "Then don't leave me."

"I won't. Not . . . yet." Rook relaxed in her lap, a sigh leaving her body. After a desperate check to ensure her mate's chest still rose and fell, Surai smoothed Rook's forehead, pushing a few sweat-damp braids off of her face.

"Not yet," Surai repeated. "And not for a long time. Do you hear me, Morgani Princess?"

Rook had the silly belief that she knew how she would die. Every Morgani child was given the details of their death—supposedly—so they wouldn't fear it. But that was superstitious crap meant to lessen their fear of dying. Just another way for Rook's mother, the Morgani Queen, to control them.

Fate was what you made of it. And Surai was determined to live to see Rook an old, cranky woman.

Surai was about to slip away to brew Rook some broth when thundering from the trees behind them drew her attention. Gently setting Rook's head aside, she leapt to her feet, her katanas steady in her hand.

Archeron burst through the brush. It took a moment to realize the dark smears covering his tunic and arms were blood and another second to understand that he was carrying something.

Not something. Someone. A small, fragile girl bundled in his cloak. Both girl and cloak were soaked in blood. A long stream of hair, dark with blood and ashen in the moonlight, fell over

Archeron's shoulder. The riot of wavy locks was a strange color, tinged almost pink, and fell to the hilt of his sword—

"Haven?" Surai sheathed her blades and rushed to them, prepared to help Archeron carry her—but as soon as Archeron's gaze flicked to her, she gasped.

There was a wildness in his eyes, a raw possessiveness that made her wish she hadn't buried her steel.

Growling, he shifted Haven on his chest and reached for his sword. She froze when she took in his dark expression, his lips bared like a mountain cat's in a warning snarl. Angry serpents of gold flickered around him, and for the first time since they'd entered this horrible place, she was grateful for the dark magick that bound their powers.

Surai flung up her hands. "Archeron, it's me!"

He blinked, green eyes flaring with magick. The mortal's head rose and fell with his heaving chest. His hand stilled over his sword hilt before returning to cradle the girl. As he tightened his arms around her body, some of the fierceness left his face.

But Surai still walked slowly toward them, arms held high, keeping her steps measured until the savage inferno in his eyes had become a guttering flame.

"We need to set her down," Surai said, speaking softly and hoping her voice elicited some sort of familiarity. "Last I checked, mortals only have so much blood, and by the look of it, she doesn't have much to spare."

When she caught a flicker of recognition inside his expression, she dared lift a hand toward Haven. But it was too soon. Archeron reacted, his arms encircling Haven, a low growl rumbling from his chest.

"Don't touch her," he snarled, his tone more beast than Solis.

Surai froze, unsure what to do. She'd never seen him like this.

Because of their deep well of magick, all Sun Lords cultivated primal parts of themselves that, when unlocked, could become wild and dangerous.

But Archeron had never lost control. He'd come close when Remurian died, but never like this . . .

"Archeron, look at me," she urged.

His breathing slowed as he took her in.

"I am your friend, Surai," she continued in that safe, warm voice. "I want to help."

Releasing a ragged breath, he relaxed, the muscles in his neck and jaw softening as he slid his gaze to the girl in his arms. Something close to agony passed over his face. "We cannot let death take her. Not her, too."

Surai felt a shock of anger pass through her. First death claimed Remurian. Now it threatened both Haven and Rook.

She was done with death hurting those she loved.

Her fear of Archeron faded as she reached for Haven, her mind suddenly of one purpose. "No one is dying tonight. Death will just have to wait. Now, I'm going to touch Haven, and if you hurt me, Archeron Halfbane, I'll curse you to the Netherworld for an eternity."

The moment Surai's hand made contact with Haven's arm, Archeron snapped out of his trance. After that, they worked together to lay the mortal down on a pile of blankets next to the fire. Bjorn appeared, not bothering to look the least bit surprised by what was happening as he wordlessly stoked the fire.

Afraid that once she lifted the cloak and exposed Haven's wounds, Archeron would return to his primitive state, she used all of her wiles to convince him to leave Haven and search the woods for healing herbs. Once his footfalls disappeared, Surai peeled back the silk cloak.

A gasp spilled from her throat as she took in the damage. The pain must have been unbearable.

Surai did what she could for Haven, but her injuries were severe. As Surai assessed the deep furrows along her belly, she knew only one type of shadowling that could have done this.

Vorgrath.

Surai took shreds of silk from what was once Rook's favorite scarf and pressed them into Haven's side. As she did, Haven groaned. Then her lips pressed firmly together, her face schooling into a stubborn grimace as she fought the pain with a warrior's heart.

"Tough little mortal," Surai murmured.

As she dressed the many cuts and rents in Haven's flesh, warmth fluttered beneath her hands. It was a different sort of heat than from a body. The sensation prickling and electric, like miniature lightning bolts danced beneath her palm.

Her magick had returned, if only partially.

Surai's magick wasn't as powerful as the others', but years of soldier life had taught her proficiency in the healing arts. For whatever reason, her magick was working, at least enough to cauterize the girl's wounds and perhaps, if she concentrated hard enough, stop her bleeding.

Brushing her hair from her forehead, she hurried to mend the mortal's flesh before her magick fled, ignoring the disappointment that filled her.

Haven had obviously failed to get the venom, which meant . . .

Surai glanced up at Bjorn, who was standing near the fire. Even though she knew he could not actually see, his gaze bored into her, awakening that familiar uneasy feeling she sometimes had around him. "If you're done with the fire, can you help me with her?"

Firelight gleamed off of his teeth as he grinned, infuriatingly silent.

"Are you just going to stand there smiling while our friend bleeds out?" Surai demanded, biting back tears.

But they were guilty tears, her fury directed inward. Why did she put such faith in a mortal? Haven had tried—that was clear—and she loved her for it. But a mortal gathering venom from a vorgrath?

She would never forgive herself for such a lapse in judgment.

"It seems," Bjorn began as he strolled toward Surai, his dark red cloak trailing behind him, "that your judgment was sound."

Cracking her neck, Surai lifted to her feet. Blood stained her hands. Her body ached, and her eyes burned. Quite frankly, she wasn't in the mood for Bjorn's tricks.

"Seer, what have I told you about entering my head . . ." Her words caught in her throat as his statement sunk in.

"Then you do not want to know what the mortal found?" Bjorn asked. He wasn't smiling anymore, but one corner of his lips was quirked.

Found? Her heart punched sideways into her ribs. "Enough cryptic speak, Bjorn." Surai held her breath as she studied his face, looking for signs of teasing. She didn't dare hope. Not yet. "What are you saying?"

But Bjorn, as always, refused to give her a straight answer. Instead, using his magick, he flicked his wrist and drew open Haven's sad little pack laying in the grass to her right.

"How is our magick breaking through?" Surai murmured.

Bjorn shrugged without glancing her way. "These things are for the Goddess to know; I don't question fate."

She would have rolled her eyes at his vague answer, but her attention was glued to Haven's pack as it rustled and shifted.

Bjorn twirled his fingers—like methodically wrapping ribbon around a spool—and something small and shiny emerged from Haven's pack.

She watched, hardly daring to blink, as a tiny vial of something floated on a stream of golden magick, and sparks rained down on the ground below and reflected off the rectangular glass bottle.

Bjorn's magick carried the vial ever so slowly over rocks and grass until it was resting in Surai's trembling palm, the delicate glass hard and cold and *real.*

Only when she saw the iridescent liquid inside, clear and viscous, did she finally allow an ember of hope to light inside her.

"Is this . . .?"

Bjorn nodded.

"Haven did it?" Surai locked her knees to keep from falling as the ground seemed to sway. "She did it," she repeated before finally uttering the words she'd wanted to scream for the past four days. "Rook . . . Rook will live."

Bjorn nodded again, but Surai was already rushing to Rook to give her the vorgrath venom antidote, rebel tears streaming down her face.

SIX

Haven knew she was dreaming because the pain was gone, and she had new skin where her ravaged flesh should be. She stood in a sweeping meadow enclosed by birch and pine, the grassy carpet swaying around her knees. Brilliant bursts of wildflowers painted a canvas of pastels across the glen—milkweed, trillium, daisies, and jessamine.

A yellow and powder-blue checkered quilt was spread beneath a giant oak. It was there Haven and Bell had found refuge when the library was too crowded. There, they would watch the violent Penrythian storms cross the western sky at dusk.

And it was there, apparently, that her dreams took her.

Except now, a midnight sky, encrusted with stars, hung heavy over the glen, and countless ravens blackened the oak's boughs. Below Haven and Bell's sacred oak, the dark-winged Shade Lord waited for her with a dour expression and pearlescent skin that rivaled the daisies' snowy petals.

She'd almost forgotten their deal to train, and she hid her shock behind a glower as she studied him in this strange dreamscape world.

He seemed . . . different somehow. His usual regalia—the raven's cloak and crown—were missing. Instead, a sleek but simple black tunic of silk fell to his thighs, and his ashy-white hair was wilder than normal, wavy and tousled instead of neatly held in place.

Two steel-gray irises made up his eyes, the yellow ring of flame encircling them highlighting their unusually dark color.

But it was the way he looked at her that had changed the most. Before, he seemed hardly aware of her presence. Barely sparing her more than a glance.

Now—well, now his gaze followed her every move. His eyes drinking in her every detail the way she did him as if something about her was different too. But what?

Feeling self-conscious, she almost patted her back to see if she'd sprouted wings or something.

Speaking of . . . she let her own gaze feast on the purples and indigos in his massive display of feathers, coaxed out by the delicate silver light from the moon above. As opposed to their usual place tucked against his back, his wings were loose and flared, showing off their stunning, otherworldly beauty.

Something changed in his face, and he tore his focus from her as he jerked his chin in an impatient demand for her to hurry.

She did no such thing, sauntering across the field toward him while switching her attention to the stars.

It was her dream, after all. She could do whatever the Netherworld she wanted. And it felt like years since she'd looked upon proper stars.

As soon as her toe touched the quilt, she called, "Where's your raven cloak?"

Instead of answering, Stolas hurled a white-hot ball of blue lightning at her.

Icy pain wracked her body, freezing layer after layer of skin and muscle, penetrating deep down into her marrow until she thought she would die from the cold.

All of this happened in the span of half a second.

Growling, she pulled herself up from where she'd fallen in the grass, her body aching as it thawed. "Runes! Why would you do that?"

"Well, Beastie, we are not here to sip tea, are we?" he drawled. He twirled his fingers while sizzling blue charges skipped between them. "Tonight, we build up your defenses seeing as you have exactly none."

She would have argued, out of habit if nothing else, but something about his expression, the darkness in his eyes, made her comply.

They worked on a few evasive maneuvers. Easy techniques, like creating a temporary shield. Then they moved on to what Stolas called the three lines of defense against dark magick: distraction, countering, and nullification.

"Distraction," Stolas explained, "works with dark magick too powerful to counter or nullify. It is only used as a last-ditch effort because the magick will quickly learn it is a trick."

He swirled his hand in a tight circle, forming a gold ball of churning fire. Inside his other hand grew a bright sphere of dark magick. When the bluish flame was as large as his head, he nudged the golden ball toward her.

It floated through the air slowly and paused just to her left, hovering.

"Most strong magick is brutish, unsophisticated, because its wielder does not have a clue how to properly harness it. Since dark magick feeds off light magick, it cannot tell the difference between you and that shiny distraction by your head."

With a flick of his wrist, he sent the dark magick streaming at her—but at the last second, it veered and consumed the golden orb in a silent explosion of light that lit the meadow.

"Now," he said, "you try."

Haven tried. Once, twice, a hundred times beneath that oak tree, the dream stretching into what felt like an eternity as she failed over and over again. Stolas was merciless, hardly giving her any time at all before lobbing the stupid magick at her.

"I don't know what I'm supposed to be doing," she grumbled, teeth clacking together as she dragged herself back to her feet.

"It's simple, Beastie," Stolas purred as dark magick danced between his fingertips, throwing blue light over his face and horns. "Conjure a bit of your light magick. You've done much more than that before."

She glared down at her inept, magickless hands. "But I thought I couldn't make light magick in the Ruinlands."

Stolas huffed out a long, aggrieved sigh as he spread his arms wide. "Are we in the Ruinlands? Or are we inside that nebulous landscape of dreams? Hmm?"

"For that matter," she said. "How can you wield light magick? I thought . . ."

"Beastie, magick is in everything. Both kinds. I might not be able to fling open the door to the Nihl like you do, but I contain enough light magick to create a tiny orb of light."

"But—"

The words shrank back down her throat as he took two steps toward her. His pointer finger poked hard into her forehead twice. "This. This is your problem."

"My head?"

"Your mind." He tapped again. "What little mortal troubles are running around your brain?"

Uncomfortable with being so close to a predator, even if only in a dream, Haven took a step backward. "For one, I'm a bit concerned I might be dying on the other side."

"You are not," he said matter-of-factly, elaborating only when she scowled at him. "I put a temporary shield over your foolish Solis friends' encampment to ensure they can access enough of their magick to heal you. I also made sure that pretty, arrogant Sun Lord found you some bog root. Hideous stuff, but it will mend together what the vorgrath destroyed and restore the lifeblood you so foolishly gave away."

"I didn't willingly bleed," she hissed before realizing the implication of his words. "You were watching?"

"Cringing, more like it. That poor attempt at soulbinding you tried on the vorgrath? You are lucky it did not kill you right then. And lucky I retrieved my dagger from that pond before a selkie claimed it, I might add."

"Sorry, I was a little busy trying not to be eviscerated to worry about your ridiculous dagger." She kicked at the grass. "And for my first time soulbinding, it seemed to go relatively well."

"No." She trembled at the hushed tone of his voice, the space Stolas entered without her knowing. Once again, they were inches apart, and he tapped the middle of her forehead. "You are trying to think the magick into being, but it does not work that way. The magick already exists. Your thoughts? Your mind? Let those go."

"If I can't?" she asked, crossing her arms over her chest.

"Then your friend will die, the Curse will take over your mortal lands, and everything you hold dear will cease to exist."

No pressure. Haven forced out an angry breath, her face twisting into a scowl.

"Stop." The command was smooth, almost soothing. Stolas took her by the arms, his fingers icy bones around her flesh—but they held her gently, unlike before. "Close your eyes."

She obeyed, pressing her eyelids shut.

"Now, focus on your breaths. In, out. Yes? Good. Find your heartbeat, that slow, gentle rhythm. Let your thoughts melt away. Just be."

At first, her mind raced with even more thoughts. But she concentrated on her body, the feel of the air rushing down her throat and into her lungs, the soft whoosh of blood pulsing through her veins . . . and soon she was nothing but energy.

Deep, throbbing energy.

From far away, she felt warmth cocoon inside her, the trickle of light in the darkness.

Soft heat tickled her palm. She opened her eyes to a perfect little golden sphere hovering inches above her hand.

Blue light flashed as Stolas slung his dark ball of magick at her.

At the last second, she tossed her light magick into the air. Inches from her face, his magick brushed frigid air over her cheeks as it veered up, colliding with her orb.

A pulse of light spread over the glen, turning night to day for the briefest of seconds.

Stolas was smiling at her. A soft smile that tempered the feral look inside his eyes and made her a little less afraid of him. "Very good, Beastie. Very good."

Pride filled her chest. She knew they weren't friends—they would never be that. But they had just shared a victory, however minor. She leaned into him without thinking. Her arm brushed his.

Their eyes met, and she became aware that she was purposefully touching him. *What the Netherfire are you doing, Ashwood?*

At the same moment she was thinking this, he flung a sphere of magick at her, the prickle of it on her skin like wintry fire. Cold and burning and all powerful. The force was a gust of icy daggers that slammed her on her back hard enough to knock the breath from her lungs.

Droob! Confused and disoriented, she whipped up to her feet, ready to fight, but the Lord of the Netherworld was gone.

SEVEN

Haven jerked from her sleep, chest heaving, to find herself beneath a cobalt night sky and Surai's too-thin blanket. The dying remains of a fire smoldered a few feet away. Beyond, a wall of sycamores stood sentry over the camp.

She ran a hand through her sweat-damp hair—and paused. Her body felt bulky and strange as if she'd grown an extra layer of skin.

Biting her lip, she peeked under the blanket. A thick, crusty layer of something black, something *foul,* encased her torso all the way down to her legs, cracking and itching as she shifted. Before she could get up, the smell hit her.

Like excrement, only worse. Bog root.

She was up in a heartbeat, slimy bits of bog root sprinkling the ground by her feet.

Wrapped in nothing but the blanket, she scurried over rocks, halting at the edge of a cliff. Two dark silhouettes huddled in the shadows below. As her eyes adjusted, she made out Archeron and Bjorn.

Why would they venture away from the fire?

It was curiosity, perhaps, that made her drop flat on her stomach and wiggle to the edge of the cliff. Every movement sent dull shivers of pain darting through her joints, but not the kind of agony she should feel after the vorgrath's talons shredded her flesh to the bone.

And her back—her back had been rent apart by the creature. Destroyed.

Goddess Above, she shouldn't even be alive, much less well enough to spy on the Solis. But whatever magick in the bog root had saved her, she wasn't complaining . . . much.

Archeron's velvet voice drew her attention back to the cliff's base.

"Your vision has not changed at all?" Archeron asked, leaning closer to Bjorn.

She strained to hear. There was something about the way he asked the question, the way he put emphasis on the last word and held his breath, that made her think the answer was important to him.

"I'm sorry, if I could tell you a different answer, I would. The girl . . ."

Bjorn dropped his voice to a whisper only Archeron could hear. A second later, Archeron murmured something she couldn't make out, an angry, frustrated sound, and his movements became rapid instead of displaying their usual smoothness.

"Are you sure, Bjorn?"

Haven heard that time because he practically yelled it.

She dropped her head over the cliff, for some odd reason willing Bjorn to say he wasn't sure. That he was wrong—even though she didn't know who they were talking about. Only that Bjorn's answer hinged on Archeron not being angry.

Bjorn's head lowered. "You know I am."

Pebbles clattered near her head, and she glanced up in time to see a slim, cloaked figure settle down cross-legged beside her.

"Are they saying anything interesting?" Surai asked, yawning through her words. A dark messy braid snaked down her shoulder to her lap.

Haven shoved off her elbows, landing on her rear, and felt heat bubbling under her cheeks. "I didn't hear . . . much." A grin found her lips. There was no condemnation in Surai's face—only a red crease across her forehead from sleeping on rocks. "Not that I wasn't trying."

Surai laughed, a tinkling sound like breaking china. "It's okay. We must seem so foreign to you."

"A little." She picked at the gummy flakes coating her arms. "Actually, a lot. So . . . is Rook okay?"

"Yes." Surai's voice wavered, and she glanced back at the sleeping form of Rook on the other side of the fire. "The vorgrath venom you procured worked immediately. Although, she will undoubtedly use this excuse to sleep until sunrise."

"Almost dying is a good excuse—"

Haven froze as Surai's forehead pressed against hers. Surai's flesh was warm and smooth, and Haven could see the faint outline of Surai's runes shimmering beneath the almost-dawn. The delicate scent of lotus clung to her dark hair.

"My people, the Ashari, believe that the soul is housed in the forehead," Surai said. "By placing our foreheads together, we are joining our souls as sisters."

Haven's throat ached with emotion. Except for Bell, she made a practice of keeping everyone at a distance, but somehow Surai had snuck in.

Trying to brush off the intimacy, Haven joked, "So this is like a hug, only less annoying?"

"No, this is a thank you," Surai whispered, her normally whimsical voice heavy with purpose. "For Rook. For repairing the bridge so we could cross. You could have used your magick on the Wyvern or to save yourself, but you did not. I knew I was right about you, mortal. Now our fates are entwined just as our hearts."

A part of Haven wanted to pull away. She didn't know how to accept such closeness, nor did she feel deserving of praise. Not with Bell a prisoner because of her and the Curse unbroken.

Still, she would never leave such a heartfelt compliment unanswered.

"It was my honor," she whispered in Solissian, hoping Surai felt her sincerity.

They stayed that way for five whole heartbeats.

Then Surai let out a laugh and leaned back. "Goddess Above, you stink worse than a Lorrack's arse."

Frowning, Haven thrust out an arm. Something told her the Solis would not approve of her nightly training with Stolas, so she feigned ignorance about the bog root. "What is this stuff?"

"Paste made from the root of the most disgusting plant in the Ruinlands," Surai said, not even trying to hide her amusement. "Smells like the Netherworld, but it's the reason your wounds have nearly healed." Surai settled back. "After we gave Rook the vorgrath venom, I used some in her wound too. We are lucky to have found it so quickly. It is very rare."

"Glad I'm not the only one to stink."

"Oh, there is no comparison, believe me." Her eyes brightened to lavender. "We're to get married once the Curse is broken.

Rook would invite half the Morgani Islands if I let her." Her hands dropped to her lap. "I just want to have a wedding together in our true flesh. I want to hold Rook with hands, not claws, and use all the words I cannot say as a wordless beast to speak our vows."

Haven chewed her lip. "Forgive me if this is personal, but how did . . ."

"We end up as a raven and a lynx at opposite times of the day?" She glanced over her shoulder at her mate's sleeping form. "Rook and I were both born with shifter runes. As the eldest daughter of the reigning queen of the Morgani Islands, Rook's shifter form was considered regal and majestic while mine was deemed lowly. A clever bird with black feathers reminds my people too much of our ancestral enemy, the Noctis, and I have no royal line to fall back on."

Haven's gaze drifted to the faint, elegant lines that curved over Surai's lean forearm before disappearing inside her wide black sleeve.

"Even so," Surai continued. "I transformed whenever I could just to feel the wind ruffle my wings."

"I would too," Haven said, remembering the way it felt to fly in Stolas's arms.

A smile flickered across Surai's face and then quickly died. "There is a tale in Effendier about the brave lynx and the clever raven, two animals from different worlds. One lived in the sky, the other in the mountains. Despite their differences, they fell in love, but of course, it was doomed from the start."

"Your love isn't doomed," Haven declared, immediately feeling silly for the emotion behind her words. But she meant it. "I've seen a lot of mortals yoked together through marriage, but none have ever had the special bond you and Rook share."

"Perhaps if not for our curse . . ." Surai released a heavy breath. "Our punishment could have been worse. The ruler who meted out our judgment thought it befitting to ensure we only spend an hour together in our true form beneath the sunlight and an hour together beneath the stars. It could have been worse," she repeated.

What ruler punished them? The Shade Queen?

But Surai's fine-boned shoulders curved inward, her body shrinking a little. There was no escaping her private torture, so Haven didn't question Surai further.

If Surai wanted to say more, she would.

Scooting forward, Surai cast a glance over the cliff. "Tell me, Haven. Were you and Archeron friends in your mortal kingdom?"

"Penryth?" Haven half-snorted. "No. I mean, the Sun Lord kept to himself. I don't think mortals are his thing."

Surai's fingers fluttered over her long neck, her gaze still on the shadows below. "How did he seem to you?"

"Bored." Haven shrugged as she tried to recall the few times she was around Archeron in Penryth. "Annoyed. Angry. Maybe . . . maybe lonely."

Surai's head snapped up at the word, a sharp breath escaping her lips. "Of course, he would have been," she said, speaking more to herself than Haven. She'd mindlessly switched to Solissian. "Of course," she repeated.

Haven's curiosity flared. "Why was he—*is* he enslaved to King Horace?"

Surai jumped to her feet, brushing off her pants and refusing Haven's questioning stare. "Hungry? I'll see what Bjorn can make us."

"Wait," Haven called as she stumbled to a stand, fidgeting with her blanket to ensure it was still tight around her body. She held out a crusty arm. "How do I get this crud off?"

"I'll take you."

Haven whipped around at the velvety voice to see Archeron not two feet away. Arms crossed over her chest, Haven retreated a step, the flesh under the bog root paste burning as his gaze shifted to her arms and chest before flicking over her exposed calves.

"Take me where?" she demanded, lips twisted in a sneer. She could still feel the burns on her wrists from being restrained upon his order. Twice.

Archeron shifted on his feet, hands plunged deep in his pockets. "There is a pond below"—he jerked his tight jaw down the cliff—"if, that is, you would like to be clean?"

Of course, I want to be clean, she almost shouted. Except, for once, any trace of Archeron's arrogance had vanished.

If she were being bold, she might even say he appeared vulnerable.

A wry smile graced Bjorn's face as he stared at the ground, pretending not to listen. Out of the corner of Haven's eyes, she caught Surai with a hand cupping her mouth, silent laughter wobbling her shoulders.

"I don't know," Haven said, fixing him with a ruinous stare. "Does it involve tying me up? Because that happens when I'm around you."

Anger flashed inside his emerald eyes, and he glanced at Surai beneath lowered brows before huffing out a breath. "No binds."

"Fine then," Haven murmured through clenched teeth.

"Fine?" Archeron said quickly as if he couldn't quite believe it was that easy. "I mean . . . good." He pivoted to leave then paused, his wide, muscled shoulders lifting as he released a heavy sigh and turned back around, a hand held out. "Would you follow me, please?"

Haven tightened the blanket around her body, let out a huff, and traipsed past him down the trail despite having no clue where she was going.

She might allow the Sun Lord to escort her, but she certainly wasn't going to hold the hand of the man who almost sold her to the Devourers.

Even if his repentance seemed genuine and his newfound manners made him somehow more gorgeous than before.

EIGHT

Haven thought the Penrythian sun was merciless, but the burn from a Sun Lord's stare was a thousand times hotter. She paused at the bottom of the cliff to let him pass, and he ran that emerald gaze over her skin again, her face, drinking her in for the first time since the journey began.

Her body froze beneath his assessment.

Before, he hardly seemed to notice her. Now, it was as if he found every crack and pore of her flesh, every curve of her body, interesting. Now, it was as if he realized she was female.

Except his stare wasn't like the leering looks she received from the Penrythian men. It wasn't meant to humiliate her or make her feel small and weak. If anything, there was appreciation inside his too-green eyes.

"I can go alone, you know," she said. "You don't have to come."

"True. But Surai would send me to the Netherworld in pieces if I let you become breakfast for one of the hungry creatures lurking in these cursed lands."

"I haven't seen that many," Haven quipped even as her gaze flitted over the forest, searching the shadowy thickets. "And I'm rather good at taking care of myself, if you haven't noticed."

"Oh, I noticed," he chuckled. "But unless you plan to bathe with a dagger in one hand and a bow in the other, you need a spotter. Especially since every drop of water in this wretched land belongs to the Selkie Queen."

The word conjured images from the book in the library of slippery bodies glinting with amethyst and gold scales, large black eyes, and rows of needle-like teeth.

After that, she stopped protesting Archeron's presence.

Instead, she watched him as his long, corded thighs gobbled the earth with smooth strides, leading her through a dense wall of towering oaks. The moist air thickened with each step into the forest. He swung a short sword over the curtain of vines and branches ahead, the muscles of his shoulders and back shifting and bulging through his thin tunic.

The golden threads that ran along his collar sparkled in the sunlight, similar to the antique gold of his unbound, shoulder-length hair.

A glimmer of turquoise water popped between the bright vegetation. Archeron glanced back at her, a half-smile on his lips as he jerked his head toward the water. "As promised, Little Mortal."

"Haven," she murmured, drawing up beside the mossy rocks rimming the shore. "My name is Haven."

"*Haven.*"

Perhaps it was the way he said her name in his deep, sensual voice, or the way his lips curled at the corners afterwards, but a shiver slammed through her body.

She cleared her throat. "I need to disrobe."

He flicked his brows up. "By all means."

"Alone."

Since their little trek began, the Sun Lord's lips had toyed with a smile. But now—now the grin that carved into his square jaw was feline, predatory even. "Who do you think covered you in the bog root, *Haven*?"

Every drop of moisture shriveled in her mouth, as much because of the way he practically purred her name as his implication. "Surai?"

"She was busy attending to her mate. And you were busy dying. I rubbed that disgusting paste over every inch of your ravaged flesh."

"What about Bjorn?"

He arched an amused eyebrow. "The *blind* seer?"

She smooshed her toes into the greenish-black mud, arms crossed over her chest, clutching the blanket. "Then, thank you. But I would still like to be alone."

He took a slow, roving look over her, his grin transforming into something else, a primal flicker, and then turned around.

Without his intense gaze to deal with, she could finally breathe. She glanced one last time to make sure he wasn't peeking, then slipped into the clear, warm water, her feet stirring up the mud into dark clouds around her thighs.

When she was waist deep, she turned to face the Sun Lord's back, trembling as a faint current of energy zipped down her legs.

Dark magick was in these waters. Lots of it. The Curse was powerful here.

Her breath caught as she unraveled Surai's blanket from her body and the water caressed her skin. The bog root paste caked onto the woolen fibers of the blanket came away beneath her massaging fingers.

She squeezed the fabric out, drops rippling over the pond's surface, then chunked the balled-up blanket onto the shore . . . and caught Archeron leaning against a split oak, still and quiet, watching her the way a hungry mountain cat would watch fish darting below the water's surface.

She froze. The water lapped at her navel, the rest of her torso hidden behind a blackish-gray paste. But still. The naked outline of her body was clear as day, so she crossed her arms over her chest as her stomach did somersaults.

"Why are you ashamed of your body?" His soft voice caressed her bones.

"I'm not," she said, and it was true. She loved the hardness of her thighs, the tautness of her belly, the powerful clench of muscles in her back when she drew back her bowstring. "But in my culture, a female's body is . . ."

What? She couldn't remember the words ever being said, just that it was implied. A woman's body was shameful. Something to be both ogled and denigrated. Something to hide along with her hair, a possession that could be stolen if she wasn't careful, taken without her consent.

"In my culture," Archeron said, emerald eyes twinkling, "the female form is the truest expression of beauty and strength. Our Sun Queens display their bodies without remorse or shame, and any male who tried to make them feel otherwise would quickly lose his head."

Haven grinned at the idea. "Do they walk around nude in Effendier?"

A long pause ensued. "When we go without clothes, there is usually not much walking, no."

Goddess Above and everything holy.

Heat sizzled beneath her skin at the implication, and she looked away from the feral gleam in his eyes, wading deeper into the water. She worked her hands over the gunk glued to her flesh, softening the paste, working bits off here and there.

It darkened the water and gave off a stagnant smell.

Beneath the water, her flesh glowed rosy and fresh. Faint red streaks were all that was left of the vorgrath's work.

She longed to stay there for hours. Longed to slip below the surface and feel the water gliding over her skin, cleansing the dirt and grime from the last few days.

But she couldn't enjoy herself when Bell was still trapped, afraid, possibly hurt.

She forced herself to slowly wade back to shore.

When the water hit just below her sharp hip bones, she hesitated.

Archeron's gaze had lost some of its intensity, but he never really stopped watching her.

Her belly tightened. She thought about his words. About not being embarrassed or ashamed. After all, her body had gotten her through more than most men her age could survive.

Why would she be ashamed of something so powerful? So alive?

Swallowing, she released a long breath and strode proudly to the shore, hardly breathing, her skin aware of the water as it swirled around her thighs, followed by her knees, her calves, and finally her feet.

Archeron still watched her, but perhaps he hadn't actually thought she would do it because he seemed to have stopped breathing as well. His chest was still, his lips tight. His eyes were glinting feverishly as they followed her—without apology, without remorse—gliding languid trails from her body to her face.

Then she stood, completely bare, on the shore. Sunlight trickled through the green carpet of leaves, warming her skin. Water trailed like rivers down her belly, her legs. Every muscle in her body tightened beneath her flesh.

Never in her life had she bared her body and felt this way. This . . . strong. An emotion layered in both vulnerability and power.

This is me, she seemed to be saying. *And I'm not ashamed.*

Without a word, Archeron left the tree and glided to where she stood. As he did, his gaze raked up her body and met her stare, his lips parting slightly, hands curled into loose fists at his side.

He stopped within inches of her, a sharp breath escaping his lips.

Then he was stripping off his cloak and sliding it around her shoulders. Numbly, she pulled the cloak tighter; it was still warm from Archeron's body, his heat hotter than the sun's kiss on a Penrythian afternoon.

Grasping his tunic from the bottom, he slipped it over his head, revealing tawny skin and ropy muscles that danced with his every movement. The morning light swam along the silver runemarks engraved in his flesh, a latticework of complex runes she didn't recognize.

He shook his golden hair out, folded the tunic, and handed it to her.

The muslin shirt felt like clouds beneath her fingers, soft and light. "Thank you," she said.

She walked a few feet and hung the cloak on a branch, ducking into the Sun Lord's tunic. The garment fell to her thighs, the muslin delicate against her skin.

She forced back the urge to inhale the bouquet that clung to the shirt, an intoxicating mixture of leather, magnolias in the summer heat, and rich, loamy earth.

Did all Sun Lords smell this divine, or was it just Archeron?

Or, perhaps, the dark magick of the woods was messing with her mind.

Dizzy, she turned around, but Archeron was bent over the water, the muscles of his back feathering as he swirled her clothes in the shallow water, kneading the caked layer of grime from her leather pants. She didn't tell him she could invoke fresh pants.

It was too much fun watching him be domestic.

From his profile, she could see his eyes flick upward. She followed his gaze to the far side of the lagoon.

Three sleek heads bobbed in the water, silvery manes of hair fanning out around them. From their pearly faces blinked large black eyes so dark they swallowed the light.

Just below, golden sunlight filtered through the translucent water and illuminated jewel-toned scales and long cerise-colored fins swirling like seaweed caught in a wave.

The scale of a selkie burnished gold.

The Curseprice. Three heartbeats passed before she had a bow and arrow invoked and in her hand, magick tingling her fingertips.

Before she could even lift the arrow, the selkies disappeared into the water, sending little ripples toward the shore.

"Selkies are too cautious for that," Archeron said as he stood and wrung out her clothes, the muscles of his arms jumping with every twist. "Besides, if you kill one, you can never enter the water again. They are vicious, vindictive creatures."

Haven gathered her clothes, unable to take her eyes off of the ripples slowly cascading across the surface. "Did you have selkies in Effendier?"

He scratched his neck. "They were rare, but yes. A few frequented the coast. Once, when I was a boy, my uncle caught one in his fishing nets and decided to let it live in the moat outside his castle. The creature was the most beautiful thing I had ever seen with skin like the inside of the seashells that washed up on shore and hair like liquid gold."

"What do they like?" she asked, slipping on her wet pants as she wondered how to trap one.

"Males." Archeron said the word so softly that she shivered. "The prettier, the better. We found that out when four of my mother's soldiers went missing after she visited her brother. By the time my uncle searched the moat, all that was left of the young men were bones, picked clean by the selkie's teeth. They even kill and eat their mates after copulating."

Another shiver barreled down her spine, but Haven's attention had gone to something else. "You said your mother's court. Is she some sort of royalty in your world?"

His lips curled into a wry smile that didn't reach his eyes. "Okay, curious mortal. You answer my question, and I will answer yours."

Haven swallowed, shifting on the balls of her feet. Yet, what could he possibly ask that she was afraid to answer?

Huffing out a long sigh, she nodded.

He straightened, and she had to pry her gaze away from the muscles shivering beneath his golden flesh as he pulled at his chin, assessing her. "Why do you hide your hair?"

"You mean besides the strange color?"

He nodded.

She ran a hand over her hair tangled in a wet knot at the base of her skull as her heart fluttered against her sternum. "I suppose I wanted men to stop looking at me." But that wasn't the whole truth. "No, more than that. I wanted to be invisible for a while. To disappear from the world of men."

She didn't dare bring up Damius or the terror she endured. But somehow, she felt like Archeron understood, like he had pieced that part together already from the memories she sent him in the Bane.

Even though his eyes glinted with violence, his voice was gentle as he said, "It is unforgivable for your males to keep you weak and then prey on you."

"They couldn't *keep* me weak," she said, bitterness tingeing her voice as she remembered how much harder she had to fight than the men in her academy. How many more times she had to prove herself to become Bell's royal guardian.

"I know."

She blinked at him. Why was he so different now? What had changed? "I want to switch my question. Is that allowed?"

He ran a thumb over the runesword hilt at his hip. "Depends on the question."

"Why are you being nice to me? The last time I saw you, you had me tied to the back of a horse and called me a chinga."

He shrugged. "Yes, but then I released you."

She flicked up an eyebrow.

"And chinga isn't always a negative term."

"No? So I'm a pest that burrows under your skin and lays eggs inside your heart before killing you?"

Sighing, he moved closer before his gaze collapsed to his boots. "I'm sorry I treated you unfairly." Her mouth fell open, but he continued. "Your kind betrayed me on the eve of a very important battle. Because of their actions, my brother-in-arms died, and my betrothed and friends were cursed for eternity. That is why I took my rage out on you." His eyes met hers. Repentant eyes. "I hope you can forgive me."

She wasn't expecting such honesty or sincerity. All the words she wanted to say clumped together, but she managed to nod.

His stare lingered for a moment longer, his jaw tight, and then he turned to leave.

"I'm sorry, too," she blurted. Maybe because she knew a Sun Lord apologizing to a mortal was almost unheard of. Or maybe because she was truly sorry. "Sometimes, I let my emotions cloud my judgment."

"Sometimes?" she heard him mutter under his breath before he cut his gaze back at her, causing his golden hair to slip over his forehead. "Apology accepted, Haven Ashwood."

After that, he seemed contemplative, staring into the trees as he led the way back through the dark green forest without a word, their footsteps the only sound.

Even though he didn't say anything, she could tell by the inward curve of his shoulders and the flexing of his hands that something was bothering him.

When they broke through the trees and the cliffs came into view, Archeron whipped around to face her. "You might have thought hiding your hair made you invisible, but all it did was highlight that elegant neck of yours. And someday, Haven Ashwood, you will want someone to kiss that neck . . . and other places."

She tried to speak, but he held up a hand. "Stop longing to be less, Haven, and accept that you are more. Stop apologizing for the fire inside you. Instead, burn and burn like the sun until you set the world ablaze."

He turned and strode toward the cliffs before she could reply. Not that she could have—she was literally too shocked to speak.

NINE

Haven was reaching out for Bell as flames licked over her cloak. She yelled his name from her perch on the burning bridge. He tried to grab her hand, but he couldn't quite reach her, and every time his fingers got close to hers, she would somehow become farther away.

All at once, the bridge gave out, and she slipped into the void.

Bell jerked up to sit, kicking at a pale sheet tangled around his legs, and tried to catch his breath. He had fallen asleep on the hard stone floor near the open wall.

Just like last time, it took a moment to remember where he was. He scraped his gaze over the obsidian mass of Spirefall silhouetted against the midnight sky.

Stomach rumbling, he dragged to his feet and found the dining room. Pale flames danced from the chandelier, and torches lined the wall. The gossamer curtains were drawn back from the arched windows, revealing a night thick with stars.

A plate of bread, cheese, and an assortment of shaved meats heaped the usual solitary plate, meaning it was lunchtime. By now, he'd learned to tell time by the food served—if time truly existed here.

He couldn't be sure.

The chair squeaked against the floor as he sat. In the corner of his mind, he could hear Haven scolding him for giving in so easily.

If you threaten not to eat, she would say, then you had better starve.

Not that Haven would ever threaten such a ridiculous thing. The girl was a bottomless pit. Bell chuckled and started shoveling food in his mouth, ignoring the silverware tucked neatly into his napkin.

What did he care for manners and decorum now?

A door creaked open down the hall, and Bell's head snapped up, cheeks swollen with bread, to see the creature standing just outside the dining room.

"May I join you?" the creature asked, his voice lacking its usual gruffness.

Bell scowled and stuffed a slice of ham in his mouth then swept his arm out. "It's . . . your . . . table."

The creature grumbled as he pulled out the seat on the opposite end and readjusted his cloak before sitting. His massive girth spilled from the chair, his knees coming to the top of the table.

Bell took a long sip of warm tea, ignoring him.

The creature cleared his throat. "Did you sleep well?"

Wiping his mouth on his sleeve, Bell gave a quick nod.

"And, um, the food is to your liking?"

Bell shrugged. His cruel words to the creature earlier still bothered him, but not enough to apologize—and certainly not enough to acknowledge the creature's presence.

After all, he had explained why he said those hurtful things, and the creature left him there to grieve alone. Bell would have never done that even to his worst enemy.

Somewhere, a clock ticked as the silence stretched out. Another plate of meats and bread appeared in front of the creature, but he didn't touch the food.

"I'm sorry," the creature began, clearing his throat. "About your friend."

Bell froze then set the bread he was about to bite back on his plate. He tried to swallow, but his mouth had gone dry. "Thank you."

"Her name was . . . Haven?"

Blinking back his grief, Bell nodded. "Haven Ashwood. That's what I named her, at least. Haven, because that's all she could say when we met. Her only belonging was an ash-wood bow. It seemed fitting."

The creature nodded from behind his dark hood, and Bell was surprised by the feeling he was actually listening.

"She came to Penryth when she was young," he continued. "We guessed only nine summers, but only the Goddess knows for sure. Runes, she was a savage, filthy thing, caught stealing in the market by my father's men. I chose her as my birthday present, mainly to piss off my father, who wanted me to pick a hunting bow instead. What he didn't know at the time was that she was a more effective weapon than a bow could ever be, even at nine."

Bell went on, describing the nightmares that woke her screaming and the past he knew she hid from him. How they began to sneak her from the servant's quarters into his room at night.

Soon, he had told their entire story, down to the minutest of details. When he was done, he felt a bit of the weight on his shoulders lift.

They talked casually after that. The creature explained how the Curse kept the Ruinlands stuck in permanent half-night. How all of Spirefall used to be a beautiful castle made of moonstone, ruled by the most powerful mortal house in the north.

The part of the castle they stayed in now was the only piece left untouched by the Shade Queen's dark magick.

A lull in the conversation threw the room into casual silence, and Bell glanced out the windows to his left. Snow was falling in the silver half-dark world outside, and a thin layer of frost framed the glass windowpanes.

When Bell turned back around, he found the creature watching him quietly.

Creature. The term no longer seemed to fit with the figure sitting across from him, running one gloved finger over his fork.

"I'm not sure what to call you," Bell admitted. "Do you have a name?"

Beneath his cloak, the creature stiffened, his hand gripping the fork. "Please, call me what they call me . . . creature."

"But you're not—"

"Anything else is a lie." His words were gruff, final.

"If you insist." Bell fiddled with his soup spoon. Now that he saw the creature was capable of human emotions, he couldn't escape his curiosity about him. "How did you come to live here? What are you?"

An eternity seemed to pass as the creature studied him from his veil of cloak and shadows, the howl of the wind against the window panes suddenly deafening.

He stood with a grunt. "If you refuse to use the bedrooms, at least bathe and accept clean clothes." Bell got to his feet, ready to protest, but the creature held up a hand. "When you are ready, you may join me in the portal."

His dark, ragged cloak slithered along the stone as he stalked away, and Bell was left wondering if he did something to upset him.

But the creature was right; Bell was starting to stink, and fresh clothes would cheer him up.

He wandered into one of the chambers where, magickally, a folded silk tunic of ivory embroidered with green waited atop the bed along with pants Bell's exact size. The room was sectioned into a bedroom, a sitting room with colorful pillows, and a bath chamber behind dusty chartreuse curtains.

After a hot bath in a claw-foot tub, which could fit three of him and held water that never cooled, Bell slipped into his gorgeous new clothes, wishing his magick could at least make attire like this.

Then he left his room and found the portal, feeling better.

He sighed with pleasure as the sunlight on the other side greeted him, running along his cheeks like silken tongues of fire.

Who knew a few days imprisoned in a night realm could make him miss the sweltering Penrythian summers?

But the sun in this place was warm without intruding, a gentle kiss upon his dark skin.

Bell spent the next few hours helping tend the garden of flowers—pruning and weeding, collecting fallen petals. Perspiration trickled down his back and dampened his temples.

The scents of earth and dewy grass soothed the jagged parts of his mind, allowing him to forget his situation for a little while.

This—This was the closest he had gotten to peace in a week.

When they were done, dusk had fallen over this other-world, a tangerine glow hovering near a forest in the distance.

Where was this place?

Bell didn't dare ask. And it wasn't important, not really. All that mattered was that Bell could escape the chill of the Shadow Kingdom and Spirefall for a few hours.

The creature joined Bell for dinner that evening, wearing a new forest-green, satin cloak trimmed in white ermine. All of the cobwebs had been scrubbed from the marble walls and the chandelier, the thick layer of dust swept away, and the table gleamed as if freshly polished.

A porcelain vase of red roses so perfect they looked fake crowned the table, filling the air with their sweet scent. And when dinner was over, Bell found he could sleep in the largest chamber where he bathed earlier without panicking.

The next morning, the creature met Bell for a breakfast of biscuits, fruit, and cheese, making pleasant conversation.

Afterwards, they went outside to the other-world, toiling in the garden until lunchtime, when the creature summoned a blanket and an assortment of meats and more fruit.

Bell spent two days that way. Dining with the creature who, although not much for conversation, listened politely as Bell talked of Penryth and Haven and his mother, and anything else, really, that came to mind. They continued gardening beneath the other-worldly sun, tilling soil and lifting rocks until muscles Bell never knew existed ached.

He bathed every night in that monstrous tub and fell asleep to beautiful stars. His dreams of Penryth and Haven were pleasant, no hint of burning bridges or wyverns. No images of his best friend falling to her death.

For a few days beneath that impossibly-blue sky, he tricked himself into pretending things would be okay. He could be, if not happy, then unafraid. His nightmares were behind him.

And then, on the third day in the garden, everything changed.

TEN

Haven felt as if they had been tramping through the dense forest for years, not days, lost inside the moving labyrinth of shadows and fog. She wrapped her arms around her chest, fighting the deep chill that hung in the air, regardless of temperature.

Grunting, she whacked at a vine that had slipped around her arm, the thorns as big as her pinky. Blood seeped from where they gouged into her flesh.

The tangled canopy of branches and vines above strangled the already faded light, so they hiked in a watery semi-darkness that muddled her days and made her feel like she was stumbling through a dream where plants clawed at her and the sun was dying.

Every time Bjorn thought they were close to the Witchwood, the land would shift, the trees would change, and they would have to find the right paths again, which took hours, sometimes days.

Days they didn't have.

They would have made better progress if Haven didn't have to rest at night. When dark fell, Archeron would make some excuse for them to stop, and none of the Solis pointed out that it was for her.

Haven despised being the reason they were lagging behind even if she'd come to look forward to sleep. Sleep meant escaping the horrible, damp, dreary forest for a few hours to dream—and dreaming meant Stolas's lessons on magick.

So far, she'd blown through the three main defenses to dark magick, and they had just begun offensive maneuvers. Just thinking about training made her heart speed up in anticipation.

Besides being a much-preferred occurrence to her usual nightmares, her training with the Netherworld Lord meant every day she became more useful, her magick less of a liability and more of a weapon.

By the time they stopped for lunch, Haven was famished, cranky, and sopped with sweat. Frustration showed in the others as well. Rook and Surai, in their true forms, were arguing over the Curseprice.

"The bone of a wood witch a century old does not make sense," Rook insisted, picking twigs from her light braids. "Everyone knows a wood witch is in spirit form."

"Yes," Surai muttered, more snappy than usual, "but everyone also knows a spirit once owned flesh and bone. We just have to find it. Archeron—"

Before Surai could finish drawing the Sun Lord into their argument, Archeron disappeared into the forest, muttering something about firewood.

Both girls looked to Bjorn, the only person in the group who had ever been to the Ruinlands, but Bjorn focused on his pack, pretending not to notice their attention had shifted his way.

Haven didn't blame him. She wouldn't want to get in between

the two arguing girls either.

As she began helping Bjorn unload the campfire pots and supplies, she handed him a ladle and whispered, "Wise move."

"Indeed." His jaw tightened. "It is the dark magick here. We can feel it slithering deep in our bones, in our minds. Right now, our light magick fights it, weakened as it is. But eventually, despite the wards and runes we have completed, our magick will be drained, and we will succumb."

"And then?"

Bjorn rubbed two fingers over his jaw. "Everyone is different under the influence of dark magick. Some go mad. Some change over time into beastly creatures. Some weaken until they are no more than a statue, unable to move as the forest eventually entombs them."

Haven shivered. "Is there anything we can do to stop it?"

"I've already given the others a potent mixture of blooms straight from Effendier to slow the change."

"I haven't gotten anything," Haven pointed out, trying not to sound too pouty.

"My dear mortal," Bjorn said, looking at her for the first time since they started talking, "darkness already lives inside you."

Touché. Frowning, Haven decided to change the subject rather than talk about a topic that unsettled her. "So, their argument. Do you know the answer?"

Bjorn released a dramatic sigh, something he was prone to do when she was around. "So many questions, mortal. Can a Solis not find peace around you?"

"No. Not when I know so little about this place, and you know so much."

His sightless gaze drifted to the dark shadows between the trees. "I would rather not know anything about this place."

"But?"

"Years ago, when I was imprisoned here," Bjorn said, a dark shadow falling over his expression, "the Noctis caught the scent of a wood witch haunting the nearest wood. A wood witch is not a shadowling; it is something worse, a once mortal demon who was pledged to the Shadeling. They can neither be bargained with nor controlled. So Morgryth ordered the wood witch caught, and several Noctis marched into the wood, never to return.

"After a few months of this, a clever Noctis figured out a way to track the wood witch's bones to her burial site deep in the forest. He burned them, and that particular wood witch was never seen again."

Haven bit her cheeks to keep from rolling her eyes. "You forgot to mention how he tracked the bones."

"I did not forget," Bjorn amended, taking a sip of whatever was in the cauldron over the fire. "It is not relevant at the moment."

Growling under her breath, Haven swallowed the surge of questions she had, knowing Bjorn was not in the mood to answer them.

Cryptic Sun Lord!

She glanced sideways at the seer. Out of all the Solis, he was the only one she couldn't figure out.

Archeron was, well, Archeron. Arrogant, a bit vain, stubborn, honorable to a fault. But in the last few days, she'd seen another side to him as well. Loyal and caring, he would die for any of his friends.

Rook and Surai were the same. They weren't perfect, but they were honorable and good. And all of them embarked on this suicide mission for clear reasons.

Freedom. Honor. Love.

All except Bjorn. Why was he trying to break the Curse? What wish would he ask for? His sight? She doubted he would go to all of this trouble for his vision seeing as his blindness hardly hindered him.

Haven rocked onto the toes of her boots, trying to pinpoint the thing about Bjorn that bothered her.

A twig snapping drew her focus to the forest. Archeron stood four feet away, a bundle of firewood inside his arms, watching her. His emerald-green tunic matched his eyes, both the vibrant color of the evergreens of Penryth.

A pleasant shiver barreled down her spine all the way to her toes as she held his intense stare, wondering how long he had been there.

They had played this game for days, ever since the water.

It started with a look that lingered a second too long. A brush of fingers over her hips as he passed.

Perhaps he expected her to be timid. But timid was the last thing Haven was, and she met his looks with her own. Stolas even commented on their harmless flirtation in her dreams last night, and Haven had laughed off the idea along with the unhappy downturn of Stolas's lips as he said it.

Archeron was engaged to a gorgeous queen. And Haven had no interest in an affair with a man promised to another—even if that other person was currently cursed as a skeleton.

Their playful looks were to pass the time in this dreadful forest, nothing more.

Suddenly, Archeron's head snapped up, and he dropped the firewood, unsheathing his sword. The scrape of metal drew Bjorn's attention. A split second later, his axe replaced the ladle in his hand. Haven found her bow and arrow and had an arrow nocked by the time Rook and Surai had their weapons out.

Something was here.

ELEVEN

"The vorgrath's mate," Archeron snarled as he entered the small clearing. "She has been following us for days, but this is the first time she has come close."

Haven felt the blood drain from her face as she scanned the forest. "What? Why am I just now hearing about this?"

"I did not want you to worry unnecessarily," Archeron said without a trace of remorse. "Your sleep was already restless."

She swallowed down the string of obscenities on her tongue. She must move in her sleep when training with Stolas, and Archeron thought she was having nightmares.

"I can handle anything except having things kept from me." Her voice was tight, and Archeron's eyes widened even as his lips curled into a pleased smile. "Understood?"

The others were all tending to their weapons and pretending not to listen.

Archeron gave a small nod, his eyes never leaving hers.

"Understood."

Cooling the anger in her voice, she said, "How close is she?"

"Too close," he answered, shifting back into warrior mode, his gaze tearing from her face and gliding over the forest edge. "Haven, stay here with Rook. When—"

"I'm not helpless, and I refuse to stay here while you—"

"You are bait." Archeron's eyes twinkled, but she could tell by the way they studied her that he was wondering how she would take that revelation.

Surprisingly, it filled her with pride. He thought she was capable of handling herself. And, considering Archeron, it may have been the highest compliment he could give.

"Okay," she said, slipping her arrow back into its quiver.

Her breath halted as he abruptly leaned in, his warm hand resting lightly, so damn *lightly*, on her hip.

But behind his amused expression was something else. Concern. "Stay sharp, Mortal."

On some command Haven couldn't hear, all of the Solis but Rook broke off into the woods in different directions. Although Haven had only ever hunted alone, she knew enough about pack hunting to understand they were trying to outflank the vorgrath.

As soon as they were gone, icy dread prickled across her skin, and she joined Rook in the center of camp near the fire though the heat did nothing to thaw her unease.

The parts of her flesh once ravaged by the vorgrath's talons tingled; she could still feel her body drenched in her own blood, still smell the coppery tang.

Releasing a ragged breath, she sank next to Rook on a fallen oak and rested her bow on her thigh along with her red-tipped arrow.

Rook ran her gaze over Haven's weapon. "Poisoned?"

Haven nodded, swallowing despite her mouth being dry.

"Oleander."

Rook raised an eyebrow. "Do they teach you that in your mortal lands?"

"No," she scoffed. "Trial and error. I hunted shadowlings in the woods outside Penryth's runewall. My regular arrows had little effect, so I experimented. One day, I was tracking a shadowling and noticed it avoided some belladonna in the middle of a path. After that, it just took finding the right flowers."

Rook was studying her, really studying her, as if seeing her for the first time. "I've heard the mortals deprive their women of fighting skills, so how did you learn?"

"The Prince of Penryth and I were . . . are friends. I tagged along for his sword lessons, and one day, the master of swords let me try. He said he hadn't seen natural talent like that ever, so he agreed to train me after hours. The rest is . . . a long story."

Rook's golden eyes sparkled behind her red tattooed band. "I see it now."

"See what?"

"Why Archeron is smitten."

A laugh escaped Haven's lips. "Smitten? Archeron?"

"Yes." Her expression had gone from teasing to solemn, her lips tight. "You may think he's just being playful, and maybe he is. But I've never seen Archeron like this."

"Not even with Avaline?"

"Oh, that was different," she insisted, tossing her thick tangle of pale golden hair over her shoulder. "They were friends practically since birth and engaged nearly as long." She shrugged a muscular shoulder. "It was a good match. He's the bastard son of the reigning Sun Sovereign of Effendier, and Avaline was the heir apparent to a large, pivotal kingdom in the mortal lands.

"Because of Archeron's bastardy, he would never marry the

daughter of a Sun Sovereign from across the Sea, but Avaline is half-Noctis, half-mortal. Their marriage would ensure ties to the mortal lands and a chance for an alliance with a few of the less wicked Noctis families—if such a thing exists anymore."

Haven curled her hands into fists in her lap. "So, he's a pawn?"

"A willing pawn," Rook amended. "Archeron will do anything to ensure Effendier's reign."

Haven knew she shouldn't be disappointed. Of course, Archeron had responsibilities to his kingdom just like Bell. Of course, he wouldn't risk his kingdom and honor for her. A commoner with no family and forbidden magick.

"Does this upset you?" Rook asked.

"It just seems pointless." She shrugged. "Whatever this is between us."

"Pointless? You are attracted to each other. That is a beautiful thing. Besides, Archeron can have any woman he desires, even once married. As long as you don't produce offspring."

Heat flooded Haven's cheeks, and she fiddled with her bow. *Have* any woman he desires? The word made it sound like he was choosing what to *have* for lunch.

"Oh." An amused grin lit Rook's face. "You have never made love?"

Haven shook her head even as the thought sent waves of warmth crashing through her body. "I mean, there have been men, but never . . . it was never with someone I cared about."

"Well, Little Mortal, Archeron Halfbane could teach you a lot."

"Teach?" Haven snorted, wishing her voice didn't sound so giddy.

"Yes. How do you learn to make love properly in the mortal world?"

"We don't. At least, we're not supposed to until marriage. A woman's virginity is considered—I don't know—a prize for her husband."

Rook frowned at this. "A prize? Like you are an object to be won? Does the man wait too?"

"No." Haven remembered how the king had laughed proudly at Renk's penchant for sleeping with the serving girls.

"Well that doesn't seem fair to me," Rook pointed out.

Haven agreed. She opened her mouth to say as much when Rook's gaze darted to the forest, and she held up a hand.

Silence—a deep, terrible silence had fallen.

A second later, both girls had their weapons ready in hand. Haven's heartbeat reverberated inside her skull as she pulled her bowstring taut with one eye closed, the other focused on the end of her arrow point.

Beside her, Rook had her whip in one hand and a sword in the other.

Still, Haven didn't feel safe.

"She must have somehow thrown them off her trail," Rook whispered. "Clever girl."

Haven shivered. The quiet wormed under her skin, and an ancient, primordial instinct felt something watching her. Sweat slicked her palm around her bow, and her shoulder trembled as she pulled the string tighter.

Rook lowered her weapons, her stare locked on the trees. "Save your energy. She will not attack now. She's studying you. Seeing if you scare; what weapons you use."

"How do you know?" Haven breathed, refusing to lower her bow.

"Because she's smart. There are too many of us, and we are alert. She will wait and pick a time when we least expect."

A ragged breath poured from Haven's throat. "Maybe she'll just give up?"

"Maybe." But Rook's skeptical tone didn't leave much room for hope.

All at once, the forest seemed to come back alive with birdsong, the wind once more rustling the leaves. The tension in Haven's shoulders eased, and she dropped her bow in her lap.

Archeron and the others burst from the trees, weapons ready. Archeron loped over to them, his body stiff. Sunlight ran down the length of his outstretched blade.

"We lost her for less than a minute," he explained, "and headed straight back here. Did she show?"

"No," Haven said quickly before Rook could answer.

Archeron wasn't the only one who could keep things hidden, and the last thing Haven wanted was for Archeron to start treating her differently because he thought she needed protection.

"No?" Archeron sounded unconvinced, and he glanced sideways at Rook.

"She did not appear," Rook answered, her gaze slanting to Haven, lips curved ever so slightly.

It was a half-truth. And their secret.

Just hopefully one that wouldn't cost Haven her life.

Archeron's tight jaw softened, and his warm gaze lingered on her for a second before he said, "While we were searching, Bjorn found the path to the Witchwood. If we hurry, we can make it there before dark."

Haven's palms were still sweaty as they packed camp and prepared to plunge back into the forest. And even though she knew the vorgrath's mate was gone, even though the forest told her it was now safe, she couldn't quite extinguish the fear that smoldered inside her heart.

Before she entered the wood, she replaced her bow with her two scythes, better for close quarter fighting.

Although, deep down, a part of her knew she would never see the attack coming.

TWELVE

The Witchwood was unlike any forest Haven had ever traveled through. Charred tree trunks the size of ten large men sprouted to the sky, gnarled and twisted as if over time, the dark magick seeped into their roots and poisoned them. There was no other vegetation, no tracks or markings or any other sign of woodland creatures.

But it was the dead silence that permeated the dark shadows of the forest that sent adrenaline raging through her body.

They walked single file, Haven following Archeron. Surai, in raven form, was perched on the hilt of the sword strapped between his shoulder blades. The other Solis were behind Haven.

If she wasn't so focused on her environment, she might have smiled at how gentle their footfalls were, how they moved soundlessly and breathed in a soft, noiseless murmur.

They could be quiet, too.

But it wasn't just the stillness that scraped along her bones and settled deep in her gut. Ancient, evil magick resided here, a cold, detached presence lurking in the darkness, drenching the air, pervading everything that was once green and good and alive.

A shudder wracked her chest; that same dark magick hid inside her.

And every few cloudy breaths, she could feel that part of herself welcoming whatever it was that watched them. Calling to it. The voice changing from an imagined echo to a plaintive, undeniable whisper.

Set me loose, it urged. *Become what you are meant to be.*

Archeron glanced back, locking eyes with her. Behind his casual gaze hid concern.

She gave him a slow, irked smile that died as soon as he turned around.

It had only been a few days since she bathed in the water while he watched, and yet somehow, he was now attuned to her every mood.

Runes, sometimes she thought he could read her mind.

Then, of course, she remembered he actually *could,* and she gritted her teeth, determined that tonight, she would have Stolas teach her how to prevent soulreading.

Archeron halted suddenly along the narrow path they traveled, his back stiff. A second later, the unmistakable caws of a raven trickled down from above, the sound echoing in the silence.

That was their signal.

Without a word, they slipped off the path and hid twenty feet back; everyone but Rook, who was glaring at them from the path, hand on her hips.

Surai took flight, swooping down by Rook's head and chirping in quick, angry bursts. Shoulders slumping, Rook ripped a golden bangle from her arm and tossed it onto the path.

Then she stomped toward them, grumbling beneath her breath, "This had better work, Seer. That's a royal heirloom that could have bought us a small kingdom."

"And now," Bjorn said, not unkindly, "with the Shadeling's luck, it will buy yours and Surai's freedom."

Rook made the sign of the Goddess: a tap to the head and tap to the heart. "May it buy all our freedoms."

Rook ducked behind the tree with Bjorn and Haven, her gaze pinned to the golden bauble in the dirt, while Surai settled on the Morgani Princess's shoulder. Archeron, as usual, leaned casually against the tree, picking his nails with a knife as they waited for something to happen.

"Tell me again, Seer," Haven said. "Why Rook had to give up her jewelry?"

Bjorn heaved an indignant sigh Haven knew all too well. "Legend says that ravens will bring jewelry to the gravesite of a wood witch's bones in return for her favor."

"And what does a wood witch's favor get you?" Haven asked even as a part of her said she didn't want to know.

The seer flashed his teeth. "If you are a raven, it gets you a bite of flesh every now and then from a wood witch's victim. I hear their favorite treat is the eyeball."

Haven swallowed down a surge of bile and looked at Surai. She would have to ask her later if that were true.

Goddess Above, let it not be.

Something touched her shoulder. She looked up to see Archeron staring down at her, one hand resting with a finger alongside her collarbone.

He sunk down to her level, his knee pressing into hers, the hand on her shoulder sliding down her arm to rest at her elbow. "Remember what to do if you run across a wood witch?"

The flash of pleasure from his body touching hers made focusing hard, and she pulled away slightly, trying to recall his instructions. "Close my eyes and say the Goddess's Prayer."

"Never look at one, Haven, no matter how afraid you are. Now, recite the prayer."

Haven frowned. *Goddess Above.* He ordered her about like it was the most natural thing in the world. And yet, his concern was strangely welcome even if it came off a bit too bossy for her liking.

From the corner of her eye, Haven saw Rook watching them with a knowing smile. But Archeron wasn't smiling. His eyes held an intense look that halted the objection on her lips.

"The prayer, Haven," he persisted, the soft, lethal tone of his voice ending any chance of refusal.

"Goddess Above, keep my fire burning," she began, "my mind sharp, and my fear away. Keep courage in my heart and the darkness at bay."

"Good." He got to his feet, leaving a cold spot in his absence, and pulled his cloak tighter over his chest as he turned to watch the bangle. They all watched it. Their breaths coming out in frosty clouds, their hopes and dreams resting on this one tiny piece of gold.

A dark shadow flickered. Haven blinked and almost missed the raven as it swooped over the path and plucked the bangle into its claws. There was a fluttering of wings as Surai took off after the raven.

They followed, bounding silently through the woods.

The raven cawed and flew high into the treetops, Surai a few feet behind. When the birds disappeared from sight altogether, Haven listened for the crash of leaves or the occasional squawk to lead her.

She bolted over a downed tree, ducking and weaving through the quiet forest, keeping her breaths low and her footfalls soft.

A bird's cry came from her left, and she zagged after the sound, stealing quick glances at the shadowy treetops. Her heart pounded out of her chest as she pushed herself faster even as it became harder to avoid colliding with the trees.

Darkness had fallen at some point, turning the air blue-black, and she instinctively conjured a small flame of light magick to illuminate her path as she sprinted.

Up ahead, she caught sight of Archeron darting through the forest, a pale shadow flickering in the dark much like the flame in her hand.

The Solis were fast. Probably faster than her mortal body could muster. Yet she had a flame, which meant she could navigate the dense woods with lightning-quick reactions.

Duck. Dive. Left. Right.

She fell into a rhythm of movements and controlled breaths, her strong heartbeat matching the cadence of her footfalls. Nothing else mattered but following the raven and finding the bones.

It wasn't until she had to pause and catch her breath that she realized she hadn't seen the others in a while.

And then, from the far side of the trees, she caught a glimpse of the raven from the wood dropping low into a clearing. She approached slowly, working to soften her panting, her ragged breaths pluming out in a milky fog that nearly matched the mist gathering around her boots.

The air here was achingly cold. Her teeth chattered loudly as claws of ice reached through her cloak and scraped her bones.

I'm here, something whispered. *All around you.*

The flame inside her palm was sputtering, shrinking.

She forced the fire to grow until stinging-hot heat licked her cheeks. A second later, it dimmed again, sinking low into her hand.

I have not tasted such strong magick in years, the voice continued—a beautiful, ancient sound like the wind whistling through cliffs. *Do you feel me inside you? Let me help you.*

Haven's mouth tingled with the warm tang of blood, and she realized she'd bitten through the sides of her cheeks. Pushing forward, she focused on the clearing, straining to pick up any sounds as she entered the small circle of space.

In the middle of the grass was a four-by-four mound of earth covered with the ornaments of man. Golden brooches, silver bracelets, the hammered steel of a breastplate.

She shivered as she tried to count the adornments piled over the grave, relics of the soldiers who entered here years ago to break the Curse, she assumed—and never made it out.

A sound rang through the still forest, and Haven turned her head. It was a boy's voice.

Recognition shot through her. *Bell.*

"Haven, help me," Bell called from the woods.

She glanced back down at the grave, fighting the panic that raged inside her. This had to be a trick of the mind. Bell was a prisoner in Spirefall. It couldn't be him.

But then, why did it sound exactly like him?

"Please, Haven. I'm cold, so cold."

Her mind told her it wasn't Bell, but his voice . . . his voice was so real.

"Haven, help me! She's coming. Please, hurry!"

Her gut clenched, and she spun around, her gaze darting around the black trees. Maybe it was Bell. Maybe the Shade Queen brought him here. Could she take the chance?

"Haven—"

The terror in his voice made her gasp. *He was hurt. Calling for her.*

A split second later, she was charging through the dark woods toward the sound, her scythes by her side.

"Bell!" she screamed, scraping her shoulder against a tree. A crying noise came from just beyond. "Bell!"

She stopped dead in her tracks at the sight of Bell a few feet away. His back was to her. Silvery moonlight glinted from a rare break in the canopy above, turning his ragged and torn Runeday cloak the color of old blood.

"Bell?" she whispered as cold dread pooled in her belly. "Bell, it's me."

Her heart lodged in her throat. Why wasn't he turning around?

She halted, close enough to touch him if she wanted—yet something made her hesitate. By now, she could recognize the cold tingle of dark magick, and every step closer to Bell felt as if she was plunging into an icy lake of evil.

Her hands tightened around the handles of her scythes.

This wasn't Bell.

THIRTEEN

The second the thought came to Haven that the figure wasn't Bell, the figure turned around. Haven froze. The smoky, translucent form of a beautiful young woman with flowing hair and glowing eyes floated in front of her.

Wasn't Haven supposed to say something?

A cool fog of acceptance rolled over her. Suddenly, she was paralyzed. Unable to move or think or do anything except watch the lines of smoke swirl like slow-moving threads of spider silk caught in the wind.

They were mesmerizing, so pretty . . .

"Don't be afraid," the woman murmured as she glided closer, her gentle voice echoing inside Haven's mind. "I want to help you. Let me ease your troubles, mortal girl. Let me inside you."

The woman's long, wispy fingers ran down Haven's arm, spewing hoarfrost wherever they touched. The insidious cold plunged straight through her mortal flesh and muscles and lodged marrow-deep.

"There," the woman whispered. "See how nice it is to accept the darkness? Feel how it coils through your veins, how it burrows into your warm, beating heart? Accept it. Welcome it. Let it *inside.*"

Fight. The voice came from a primordial part of her being.

Close . . . your . . . eyes.

As soon as her eyelids pressed together, the wood witch's control was severed, and Haven remembered what to do.

"Goddess Above, keep my fire burning," she choked out even as the cold took over her body. "Keep my mind sharp and my fear away."

The wood witch screeched with rage and scraped her nails across Haven's chest, icy daggers piercing to the bone.

Haven gasped as the cold pooled beneath her breastbone. "Keep courage in my heart," she whispered, "and the darkness at bay."

This time when she looked upon the wood witch, she saw her for what she truly was, a crooked hag with hideous, blackened skin stretched over a skeletal face, black hair flowing around her like ink. Her bones peeked from her tattered cape, patches of skin clinging to them, and her too-long fingers ended in talons.

Jagged teeth flashed as her mouth opened in a gut-curdling shriek.

The wood witch lunged at Haven with those wicked claws, and Haven retreated, swinging her scythes at the witch . . . only, the curved blades sliced straight through the smoky apparition.

"*Nethergates*!" Haven hissed, leaping backward.

Her back rammed so hard into a tree the air fled her lungs, and she nearly lost one of her useless scythes. She pivoted sideways as the witch slammed into the trunk, dispersing into a black cloud that regrouped on the other side and barreled toward her.

Haven dropped her scythes and conjured a ball of light magick. The witch screeched.

In a dark flash, she swerved behind Haven and shot into her back.

Icicles of pain pierced Haven's flesh. She was on her knees, her energy draining, the cold coming in freezing waves until she feared she would turn to ice and shatter.

The witch swarmed above her, a storm cloud of evil. "Foolish girl," she hissed. "I've slaughtered legions of your kind and feasted on their essence with that one simple trick."

"It was a trap?" she whispered, her body arching to escape the cold that kept building inside her. "But the—the raven . . ."

"All the ravens in the trees," the hag sang in a horrid voice, "they split you off as I please. And then I take you one by one before the dawning of the sun."

Haven's heart sank. The birds were a distraction, a way to separate them.

"And you," the witch said, her black form slowly surrounding her, closing in. "You were promised to me by the Shade Queen."

The Shade Queen?

In a last attempt to fight, Haven summoned another fiery ball of light, wincing as it began to shrink immediately.

Cackling laughter tore from the witch's throat. "Your light magick has no power here, girl."

And then the wood witch's laughter died, and a flicker of surprise ran across her face. Haven glanced at her magick, surprised to see tendrils of blue fire spiraling through the orb.

It pulsed bigger, the dark feeding off the light, surging outward.

She didn't know how her dark and light magick were mixing, and she didn't care. Her veins burned with power, a different kind than she was used to, her body humming with it.

A fiery, raw power, both hot and cold. Fire and ice. She could feel the strength in it, the absolute destruction at her fingertips.

It was both terrifying and beautiful.

"Looks like my light magick has power here after all," Haven said, taking pleasure in the way the wood witch shrank from her.

"No," the wood witch hissed, shielding her eyes from the glow. "Impossible. The Shadeling killed you."

Haven grinned. "Then I am a ghost, and this shouldn't hurt at all."

Clenching her ball of magick, which was the size of a dragon's egg, Haven hurled it at the witch. A second later, she was screaming as bright golden fire consumed her.

The fire felt brilliant on Haven's frozen skin.

She didn't even glance at the witch as she popped to her feet and ran, bouncing off trees in the darkness until she fought her way to the clearing. She fell to her knees by the grave and knocked the trinkets aside.

Her hands were too numb to feel anything as she clawed the mound of earth. Beetles, snakes, and maggots slipped between her fingers.

She shuddered, digging deeper and deeper.

Panic shot through her. *Where were the bones?*

The wood witch's screams grew louder, angrier, as if she could feel Haven desecrating her grave.

Hurry. A few feet in, her hands hit something hard. Slipping her fingers into the soil around the bone, she pulled. A yellowed jawbone sprang from the earth, and she shoved it into her pocket.

Then she removed the rest of the soil around the bones, revealing a twisted skeleton amid the decayed remnants of dark clothing. Odd runes were carved into the malachite and pyrite stones scattered among the remains.

As curious as Haven was about the ancient runes, she knew disturbing such death stones would invoke a curse, so she carefully removed the soil around them.

Another curse was the last thing she needed.

A shrill, unearthly howl split the air as the wood witch streaked toward her, still burning, eyes bright red with fury.

The flame Haven conjured was small, barely large enough to brighten the grave. But when she threw it over the bones, there was an explosion of light and the bones went up like kindling, burning to ashes before she could blink.

The shrieks died. The wood witch turned to ash in front of Haven, and floating bits blew into her mouth and eyes.

Gagging, Haven tried to stand, but her body was weak from the witch's attacks and from using magick.

She stumbled, nearly falling into the grave.

Her mind was reeling, and each step was wobblier than the last, but she had enough sense to find her scythes and head back the way she came. She had killed this wood witch, but there were hundreds more in these woods.

And with the jawbone in her pocket, it wouldn't be hard to determine who killed their sister.

Where were Surai and the others? She glanced up, searching for the raven, when a series of ghastly shrieks filled the forest all around her. Had the other wood witches felt their sister's death?

She'd rather not find out. Head spinning and vision blurry, she ran.

FOURTEEN

Prince Bellamy Boteler had never done a day of hard labor in his life, but he found the work surprisingly pleasurable, enjoying the powerful ache of his back muscles as he swung a hoe, the clench of his thighs while he bent down to pluck a petal from the dirt, even the feel of sweat streaming down his shoulder blades and drenching his shirt.

All of it filled him with, if not pleasure, an elusive calm that allowed his mind to be still.

He wiped the sweat from his forehead and squinted against the afternoon sun. A cardinal landed on an apple tree, chirping, its red feathers as bright as the roses Bell tended.

The creature was applying some sort of antifungal mixture to the rose bushes near a large stone birdbath, and a small yellow butterfly flitted to the closest flower.

Unaware that Bell was watching, the creature stopped his work to watch the butterfly.

Bell found himself smiling as the butterfly left the flower and found a perch on the cuff of the creature's sleeve. As the butterfly opened and closed its wings, the creature went still as a statue.

Bell couldn't help but think beneath his hood, the creature was smiling.

All at once, the butterfly took to the sky. The creature whipped around, his cloak tangling in the rose bush and his body tense.

Whatever the creature heard, it must have scared him because he rushed to Bell and herded him toward a circular courtyard, half-hidden inside a circle of hedges. A marble structure rose on the other side. Bell's heart raced as he ducked low and ran toward the building, their boots crunching loudly over gravel.

The creature was too big and clumsy to master the art of quiet.

Luckily, whoever they were running from was much louder. Laughing voices trickled from behind them just as they reached the ivory temple. The marble dome was small with dusty, stained-glass windows that colored the spears of light green and red.

Benches lined the walls, all facing the naked statue of the Goddess Above holding a sword in one hand and a swaddled baby in the other.

They ducked onto a bench by a broken window. Bell ran a hand over the silver veining the marble wall and tried very hard to ignore the creature's body so close to his. He smelled of earth and flowers, a scent Bell was beginning to love.

"Be quiet," the creature said between pants, his gaze riveted to the courtyard. "They should be gone soon."

The irony of the creature asking *Bell* to be quiet made his lips quirk. "So they can see us?"

"My magick has been weakening. I cannot say for sure that we are hidden."

Bell peeked through the hole in the glass. A girl around Bell's age rounded the corner, her skin and hair dark like his mother's. She wore a fine scarlet dress with belled sleeves, and her light gray eyes crinkled with laughter as she twirled to face whoever was behind her.

"Ephinia," a boy teased, following in her footsteps. "I know you want to play."

Bell's breath caught inside his chest; the boy was strikingly handsome with high cheekbones and golden eyes, and the sunlight brought out a whisper of red inside his fair hair. He wore an expensive blue jacket and crisp pants that screamed of wealth.

Another boy strolled behind them, taller than both, his midnight skin the same as the girl's. His head was held high in a regal manner Bell wished he could emulate. "Leave my sister alone, Renault."

"Or?" The boy, Renault, teased. He flung out his hand, spewing a ball of fire. *Magick.* Bell felt himself leaning closer as the orange flames unspooled to become a wyvern with wings and a long, barbed tail.

Ephinia squealed and tried to run, but the fire dragon stretched out its great fiery wings and circled her. "Stop, Renault!"

But she was laughing. And the other boy created a wyvern of water to chase the one of fire. Round and round the magick creatures went, flashes of blue and orange that left Bell mesmerized and giddy.

Beside him, the creature was hardly breathing as he watched with his hands clenched over the back of the bench.

"Who are they?" Bell whispered.

The creature just stared through the shattered glass. If he heard Bell, he didn't show it.

All at once, the water wyvern fell to the ground in a puddle, and the fire wyvern turned to smoke that drifted in the air between them. A split second—that's all it took for their faces to go from smiling to stiff with fear.

A sharp grunt escaped the creature's chest as a woman entered the courtyard. Bell felt his body go cold as he took in the plaited pitch-black hair and alabaster skin, the cruel turn of red lips.

He'd seen plenty of portraits of the Shade Queen's daughter to recognize her now.

Ravenna. Her onyx, skin-tight dress shimmered beneath the sunlight, and as she got closer, he could make out the scales from whatever unknown creature the dress was made from. Inky shadows followed behind her, swirling around her wings and darkening the sun.

Bell blinked. That meant . . . This was in the past.

Ravenna lay somewhere in Spirefall, undead and awaiting the completion of the Curseprice to come back to life.

"Leave us," she hissed, and the boy and Ephinia fled—but not before he saw Renault slide his fingers over the back of the boy's arm, a comforting gesture, and flash him a quick *I'll be okay* look.

Once they were gone, Ravenna turned to Renault, her lips bared in a smile. "How do the preparations go, sweet, lovely prince?"

Renault stiffened, a muscle in his neck tensing as he raked a hand through his hair. "I . . . I'm not sure I can do this."

"No?" Her grin stretched wider even as her eyes tightened. Her black, membranous wings folded close to her back. "You summoned me from the Netherworld, Prince Renault. Yet, now you tell me you don't want your father's kingdom anymore?"

There was a warning in her soft, mannered voice, and Renault glanced behind her to the path. "I've never wanted his kingdom! I told you—"

"You told me . . ." She stroked her fingers down his neck,

her wings slowly fluttering. "That you wanted freedom. That your father and brothers would make you marry a hideous mortal princess you do not love. You told me, sweet, handsome prince, that you would do anything to escape being married off. *Anything.*"

"And in return?"

"In return, I only ask the smallest of favors."

"A favor you refuse to specify."

She ran a finger over her low-cut bodice. "A favor you can easily give, my sweet. And then you can be happy, truly happy to live your life."

He shifted on his feet. "Promise me they will not be hurt. My family. And my friends, the Solis, Ephinia and Bjorn."

"Of course not, my lovely prince. What sort of wicked creature do you take me for? Hmm?" A shudder of revulsion twisted his face as she leaned forward, brushing her lips over his cheek, and whispered into his ear something too low to hear.

The Shade Queen's daughter then wrapped her clawed hands around Renault's back and yanked him into her. He went rigid but seemed powerless to move away.

Bell's stomach churned as her hands explored their way down his back until they cupped his ass. All of the boy's arrogant confidence was gone, and his eyes stared off at something in the distance as she whispered more things to him.

Horrible, horrible things, from the disgusted turn of his lips.

Bell finally had to look away. He felt like he was watching something he didn't quite understand, but the revulsion and powerlessness inside the boy's face made him sick to his stomach.

He'd felt that powerlessness before . . . many times.

With a low growl, the creature turned and stalked across the temple. Bell followed him out another door, barely able to keep up as the creature tore through hedges and thorny rose bushes to get away, shredding his new cloak.

When Bell caught up near the portal door, he grabbed the creature's arm. "Who were they? And why was the Shade Queen's daughter there?"

The creature's muscles tensed beneath Bell's fingers, and he growled, "Leave it alone!"

Then he left Bell standing there beneath the sun, trying to figure out what had just happened.

FIFTEEN

Haven staggered through the darkness of the forest, shivering and swaying with each step. Every part of her ached with cold. The wood witch's ancient magick lingered in her body, slowly draining her warmth.

Her life.

She lifted a half-frozen hand and willed a flame, only to be disappointed by a wisp of smoke.

Her magick wasn't working.

Despite her foggy mind, she knew it was because she'd overused it earlier, killing the wood witch. Just as she knew that if she didn't find the others before she faded, she would die.

A moan slid from her icy lips. She tried to call Archeron with her mind the same way she'd sent him her memories, but nothing seemed to happen.

The darkness was closing in. The wood witches' shrieks were growing louder. *Closer.*

She didn't remember falling to her knees or curling on her side on the ground, but there she was, mist rolling over her.

Dying. Again.

Goddess Above, she was tired of dying.

She couldn't die. Bell needed her. The others needed her. For some reason, her mind went to Stolas. The way he became angry when she touched him . . .

Stolas! She'd been too out of her mind with pain the last time she nearly died to remember his promise to help her, but now her brain was functioning just fine.

"Stolas." The word was a broken plea. Two more times she uttered the Shade Lord's name as instructed for emergencies, which this definitely was. "Stolas. *Stolas*."

She'd hardly gotten the last word out when wings of darkness appeared from the shadows, scooping her up inside a cold cocoon. Her mind was dimming, her pulse slowing; she was about to pass out.

But then, waves of calm washed over her, a gentle euphoria of love and happiness. Everything would be okay. She felt the violent chills wracking her body ease as heat sparked in her core. A heartbeat later, the warmth was raging, and her body shuddered as her flesh thawed beneath the delicious flames of magick.

She sighed, never wanting the warm, joyful feeling to end.

Then, they were in a clearing near a huge bonfire raging close to a wide oak she recognized. As Stolas gently set her on her feet, she realized this was her clearing. The one she took Stolas to in her dreams.

Drawn to the fire, she spread her fingers as close as possible to the flames.

"How?" she began, glancing around a second time. Her tree was there along with a sky full of stars. "Am I dreaming?"

"No." His usual sulky voice was an ominous rumble that chased away the bubble of calm surrounding her.

"Then how—?"

"No questions!" he growled, prowling around the clearing as he assessed it for danger.

"If you were going to yell at me, why bother using your magick to make me feel calm?"

"Because I . . ." He raked a hand through his snowy hair and growled. "Enough questions unless you want me to finish what that witch started."

Haven scowled at him. "Why are you so moody? I did exactly what I was supposed to!"

"If," he countered, drawing up beside her, "you mean leaving the protection of your group and falling right into the wood witch's trap, then yes, you did."

"Not fair. And I got the second piece of the Curseprice. That makes two, by the way. If you're counting."

He raised an eyebrow. "I am not. And it only takes one time to die, Beastie."

Averting her face from his gaze, she flipped around to warm her backside. "If I had known your help meant a tongue-lashing and sulky stares, I would have—"

"What?" He prowled to a stop inches from her face, his shoulders tight and wings snapping out to blot the sky. "You would die? Are you so eager to do that, Beastie? Because I'm starting to wonder. You are rash. Impulsive. You threw your dark and light magick together, damn the consequences! You are a mortal, easily broken, easily killed, and yet you roam my lands as if you are invincible."

"I would be if you helped once in a while!" she yelled, ignoring his smoldering glare. "You were obviously here! You knew I was seconds from death! Or is that your thing?"

The flames inside his eyes grew to match the bonfire, so bright with rage she thought they would erupt. "If I could break this Curse myself, I would have done it years ago. And, yes, I was watching, but I could not leave."

"Then why are you here now?"

"Because you called my name three times, and a promise is a promise. So I left Morgryth's presence immediately."

Icy fingers clawed down her spine at the Shade Queen's name. "Did she visit you in the Netherworld?"

"No, she beckoned me to Spirefall. And when she calls, I have no choice but to come."

"Won't she ask where you went?"

"Yes, Beastie, she most certainly will." His voice was resigned.

She actually felt a hint of remorse for what she said as she eased away from the fire burning her back.

She closed the tiny bit of space left between them, the cold of his body welcome, and glanced up at his face. "I'm sorry. I wish I hadn't called you."

"Then you would be dead, and the Curse would remain unbroken." His breath was a gentle gust of snow on her cheek, but for once, she didn't mind. "The death frost of a wood witch spreads quickly, and you were ice when I found you. Let us not discuss it further."

"Okay," she said, rubbing her hands together. Now that her blood was pumping in her fingertips, they burned something awful.

For the first time since Stolas found her, she thought about how close she'd come to death. Why had she run after the raven like a fool? She was smarter than that.

"Ah," Stolas drawled, lifting her chin. "Now, that is the look of someone who nearly died. Remember this feeling, Beastie. And try not to repeat it."

"Don't be absurd," she grumbled, trying and failing to dislodge her chin from his fingers. "That's all we mortals do—try not to die. You have no idea how exhausting it is."

Chuckling, he tilted her head side to side, appraising her. "You do look rather fragile."

"Why me, then?"

Her question hung in the air between them. He released her chin but didn't answer.

"Why choose me?" she repeated. She held up her tingling hands as if he needed reminding she was a mortal. "Like you said, I'm a mortal. There are thousands of ways to kill me. *Nethergates*, you probably have a thousand spells to kill me. So why put your faith in me?"

"We have been over this—"

"I know! I know! You don't answer certain questions. It's just, it doesn't make sense. Do you know something about my magick? Why I have both light and dark?" She put a hand on his arm, ignoring the way he stiffened. "Are there others like me?"

His fingers were like ice as they wrapped around her wrist and carefully plucked her hand from his arm. At least this time, he didn't slam his magick into her. "Those are questions for another day. But since you are so full of inquiries, ask others, and if I can answer them, I will."

A grin found her face; she assumed being questioned by a mortal girl wasn't top on his list of pleasures. "Okay, why are your wings feathered, but the few paintings I found of Ravenna, your wife, shows her wings membranous, like the gremwyrs?"

He paused for a heartbeat and then flicked his gaze to the stars. "There are two kinds of Noctis. I am a Seraph, from the Seraphian race, while they are Golems from the Golemites."

"And both kinds of Noctis intermarry?"

Although his face was a cold mask, something dark flashed just beneath its surface. "They do now, yes."

"But you didn't used to?"

He sighed. "I can see you are not going to give up until I explain. Long before the Curse, the Seraphians ruled Shadoria peaceably beside the mortal and Solissian kingdoms while the Golemites ruled the Netherworld. But then, the Solis gave the mortals magick, infuriating Morgryth and her kind, the Golemites.

"The Seraphian Empress tried to calm the Noctis. She was no champion of the mortals—and they, no friend of ours—but she was wise beyond anyone I've ever met, and she knew war was not the answer.

"But the Golemites wanted nothing more than to escape the Netherworld and take Shadoria as their own. Being the trickster that Morgryth is, she used our people's anger and distrust of the mortals to make them think war was inevitable. Fear is an effective tool and Morgryth an expert at wielding it. It wasn't long before Morgryth turned the Seraphian people against their Empress, claiming she was a coward and a traitor."

Haven felt chilled all over as she asked, "What happened to her?"

Pain glinted in his eyes, which had turned the palest silver. "The Shade Queen waited until she had enough support, and then she orchestrated a coup, taking the Empress and her husband hostage. When she claimed dominion over the Seraphians, our people were already too divided to resist the Golemite forces. And then—well, then she could do whatever she pleased."

"That's terrible," Haven said.

"You have no idea." His eyes were distant as if he were reliving the moment. "The Seraphian Empress had ten children. For sport, Morgryth had her husband and all but two children torn apart in front of the Empress and the entire court. Then the Shade Queen soulbound someone very dear to the Empress and had them put a blade through her heart, slowly, so that she felt everything." A deep shudder wracked his body, and when he resumed speaking, his voice was painfully soft. "By then, the Seraphians realized they had made a mistake, but it was too late. She took the wings of every Seraphian save a select few and then enslaved us."

Haven released a breath. She'd known the Shade Queen was terrible, but this . . . the Noctis he described was a monster. A monster that had Bell.

And it was all her fault.

Her focus drifted back to the Shade Lord. Perhaps it was the way he spoke with raw emotion, a sharp change from his normally guarded tone, which got to her. Or how young he suddenly seemed, not much older than her.

"You were close to the Empress?" It was less a question than a declaration.

Anger rippled over his face, and he touched a feather from the cape cascading down his back. "Whose feathers do you think I wear?"

She felt sick. The grief in his voice, however well hidden, sounded like her own. "Why would you wear a cape made of the Empress's feathers?"

"Because Morgryth thought making me wear my mother's famously beautiful wings would keep me docile and afraid."

"Your mother?" Haven whispered as it all suddenly, *horribly* clicked into place.

But it was as if he didn't hear her, his unfocused gaze aimed over her shoulder. "I was the equivalent of a mortal's ten years.

Afterwards Morgryth kept my sister and me imprisoned in the Netherworld as pawns until I was old enough to marry Ravenna."

"Why?"

"Our *union*"—his lips curled with disgust at the word—"strengthened Morgryth's claim to the Seraphian throne. We are hostages, in a sense. As long as my people remain compliant, Morgryth keeps us alive."

Haven felt tears wet her eyes, and she quickly blinked them away. No one deserved to have their family ripped away like that.

"And your sister?" she asked despite dreading the answer.

"Dead." His voice was a detached whisper. "Killed trying to escape."

All at once, she wished he hadn't told her the story because now . . . now she saw him as less of a monster. As less of a Noctis and more of a regular being like her. He was a kid when his parents were murdered. He watched most of his siblings die brutally.

And that kind of thinking would get her killed.

"I'm sorry," she said, drifting away from Stolas and toward the tree. She needed to distance herself from him and the emotions she felt. "Another question if the offer still stands?" Before he could refuse her, she blurted, "Are we inside my dream?"

"Not quite." His wings, which had been spread wide, drew together and curled into his back as he relaxed. "When I found you, you were already surrounded by wood witches, and I only had a few seconds to create a rift between our world and the Netherworld. I made this little pocket of space using your memories."

"And they can't find us here?"

"No. It is hidden and warded from anything that would do you harm. But my magick cannot sustain the rift for long."

Haven didn't relish going back into the Witchwood, but at

least now, she was strong enough to defend herself. "The mix of dark and light magick I created. Why did it work when the light magick alone did not?"

He swept his cape back as he walked, and she shuddered at its origin. "I assume the dark magick was able to mask the light magick and prevent it from being siphoned. Or possibly, the dark protected the light somehow."

"But," she reminded, "you said it could be dangerous?"

"Magick is always dangerous, Beastie. Mixing two kinds of magick, well, I'm not sure of the consequences, but it was a risk a wiser, more prudent person would not have taken."

She grinned; no one had ever accused her of being either of those things. "Well, wisdom and prudence won't break the Curse, will they?"

A rumble grew in Stolas's chest as he glowered at Haven. "Possibly not. But they will keep you alive, and last time I checked, Beastie, you cannot break the Curse from the Netherworld. So perhaps a compromise is in order."

If he actually knew her, he wouldn't have suggested such a thing. But she didn't dare contradict him. Instead, she decided to make the most of their time together. "Can you hold the rift long enough to train?"

"No." His voice was decided.

She released a disappointed sigh. "Just one trick? Anything. Please. There's so many hours between my dreams, and I want to know everything."

"Darkcasting cannot be boiled down to one trick," he growled, but she could swear one side of his lips curled upward with pleasure at her eagerness.

"You're right. But can't you give me something to keep people from soulreading my mind?"

Stolas regarded her the way one would a child, his ashy-white eyebrows drawn together in an angry line. "Protection against soulreading takes centuries to perfect."

"I'll take anything. Please." She forced a coy smile. "I'm afraid the others will discover our deal, and I don't think they'd take well to you invading my dreams. Do you?"

He regarded her coldly even as his eyes danced with amusement. "I am thousands of years old. Do you really think you can manipulate me into getting what you want with a grin?"

Thousands? Goddess save her. He was ancient.

"I prefer the term 'experienced,' or even 'well-lived,'" he answered coolly.

Of course the bastard would soulread her. "You should add *droob* to that list of descriptions."

He arched an eyebrow. "I don't know what that means, but I suspect you are correct."

Enough of this. His smarminess had killed any newfound enjoyment she'd taken in his presence.

Ignoring his smirk, which promised the feeling was mutual, she straightened her cloak and held out a hand. "Ready?"

"Are you sure you're well enough?" He ran a skeptical gaze over her body. "If even a shard of the witch's magick is left inside you, it could fester and spell your death."

"I think so." She massaged her chest, remembering the horrible cold. "Before you healed me, you somehow filled me with a sense of euphoria. Do all Noctis have that skill?"

Stolas's eyes flashed. "I thought you couldn't wait to be rid of me."

She lifted a shoulder in a shrug. "It was just a question."

His lips parted as if he were about to scold her again. Then he glanced at his fingertips. "Not all Noctis have my soothing ability, but a few of the more powerful do. It helps us keep you calm while we . . ."

"Drink our magick," she finished, holding his stare.

He watched her carefully, searching for any signs of squeamishness, but she refused to look away.

"Does that scare you?" he asked softly.

Still holding his stare, she shook her head. "You haven't fed off me yet, which means you aren't a total monster."

A wolfish grin curved his jaw. "That you know of."

He moved like smoke. Before she could react, he pulled her to him, brushing his cold, smooth flesh against hers. Despite his teasing, she wasn't afraid of his closeness—even when his nose brushed along her neck.

"If you're trying to scare me," she hissed, squirming against his firm hold, "you're failing."

"Right," he chuckled. "That must be why your scent is laced with fear. Because I *don't* scare you." Then his wings spread wide, and he snarled into her ear, "Hold on tight. If you fall, I won't come back for you."

His sudden change in mood had her rolling her eyes, and her mind went back to the delicate silver brush in his bathroom. What sort of woman could put up with his mercurial temper? What woman would want to?

One of these days, she decided, she would find out.

Right before they crossed the veil back into the now-world, she felt his chin press into the curve of her neck as he said, "If that puffed-up Sun Lord tries to soulread your thoughts, think the word 'foetor.'" She could tell his face held a wicked grin. "That should keep that pretty bastard out of your head for a while."

"It won't . . . seriously hurt him, will it?" she asked.

"Hurt, no." Amusement tickled his voice. "But I would keep a few feet between you and him when you do."

Thank you, Shade Lord, she thought.

Around her waist, his arms squeezed in reply.

SIXTEEN

Stolas dropped her at the edge of the Witchwood near where the Solis were grouped. She waited an entire minute after Stolas disappeared before leaving the cold shadows of the wood.

Orange sparks drifted from a blazing fire by a stream. Surai was positioned close to the flames with Rook and Bjorn tending to her.

Archeron stood a few feet away, his body tense.

Archeron's head whipped up as soon as she left the cover of trees, and even though his face remained a guarded mask, his shoulders relaxed, and he let out a breath.

When Surai saw Haven, she flung her arms around her, squeezing so tightly Haven could barely breathe. Half of her body, Haven noticed, was frigid against her flesh, and it felt like hugging a block of ice.

She shivered, knowing the agony Surai must feel.

The Sun Queen finished fretting over Haven and pulled

away, her frown mirroring the stern expression on Archeron's handsome face.

"What happened?" Surai demanded.

"I must have lost my way following the raven," Haven explained, trying to decide how much to tell them, "and I got separated from the group."

She hated lying but couldn't figure out how to properly explain the rest.

So, I nearly died and summoned the Lord of the Netherworld, who I also just happen to dream of every night, and oops, I might have struck an ironclad deal with him to train in dark magick . . .

"Well," Surai said, squeezing Haven's shoulder, "thank the Goddess you are okay."

Rook came up beside Surai, slipping an arm around her waist. "This one flung herself at a wood witch—"

"Trying to save you!" Surai protested.

". . . and ended up nearly dying," Rook finished. "If the wood witch hadn't suddenly left, you could have ended up much worse than this."

Surai cut her lavender eyes at Archeron. "The way she screamed and fled, she must have seen your ugly face, Archeron."

"Okay," Rook said, her voice gentle this time as she touched Surai's shoulder. "Back to the fire, *herois*. You still need to thaw."

Herois was basically *my hero* in Solissian.

Settling by Surai near the fire, Haven bit back her smile as Archeron's gaze found her. Orange firelight played off his high cheekbones and shimmered inside his pupils.

By the way his lips tugged downward, she assumed he was angry with her for making such an amateurish mistake as getting separated from the group.

But when he approached her, there was something in his

eyes—relief, maybe something more—and he lightly brushed his hand over her arm as he passed to feed the fire.

"Glad you're okay, Mortal," was all he said.

And yet, it was the way he said it—his uneven breath and lingering touch—that left the words hanging in the air and etched into her mind. She'd done something dumb, yet he hadn't yelled at her.

That was *huge.*

Bjorn came over with a tin mug of steaming broth for her and Surai.

As soon as the warm cup found Surai's hands, she sighed. "I lived near the mountains in Asharia where winters last half the year and water freezes the second it hits the air. Yet, I've never felt cold like that."

"That was the dark magick," Bjorn explained, rubbing his hands together over the flames while discreetly assessing Surai. "Will you be okay to enter the Witchwood? We have to try again before daybreak."

The jawbone! Haven had almost forgotten.

She broke into a grin as she pulled it from her pocket. "Actually, we don't."

Surai's lavender eyes widened at the sight of the jawbone inside Haven's fingers. Rook made a surprised squeak and came up to examine the hideous bone, her golden eyes bright against the painted red band as they examined the relic.

Even Bjorn sported what Haven assumed was his form of an impressed grin as he took the jawbone from her, turning it over inside his hands.

Archeron, however, gazed through half-slitted eyes at the thing as if it wasn't another item from the Curseprice and another step closer to freedom for them all.

"How did you kill the wood witch?" Barely veiled temper laced Archeron's voice.

"With my magick," she said casually—too casually by the way they all stared.

Bjorn stopped examining the jawbone with his fingers, his head canted toward her. "Yet, you would need light magick, not dark, to subdue a wood witch."

"I'm aware, believe me."

"And how," Bjorn asked, taking a step closer, "did you keep the dark magick inside this forest from extinguishing your light magick?"

Again, she wondered how much to say. Possessing light magick as a commoner was enough to have her thrown in jail by her own kind.

But wielding both light and dark magick together?

Something like that would definitely interest the Solis. She could be hunted and killed. Or worse.

"I'm not sure," she said. It wasn't a lie, not exactly. Stolas had theorized that her dark magick somehow masked the light, but that wasn't knowing. At least, that's what she told herself as she shook her head and repeated, "I'm not sure; it just . . . happened."

A long stretch of silence fell over them. Haven didn't know if that was a good thing or a bad thing, but at least she didn't have to talk about it anymore.

"Who would have thought," Rook muttered, her tired voice shivering with hope, "we would ever get this far? A band of cursed Solis and a mortal girl. If my mother could see me now . . ."

Haven felt the Sun Queen's focus shifting toward her, and she dared to imagine there might be pride in that gaze.

After that, the mood transformed back to excitement, especially between Surai and Rook who joked with each other as they all gathered their stuff and prepared for the next item on the Curseprice list: fairy tears.

A golden smear of light painted the treetops as dawn crept over the land. With the promise of day lifting their spirits, they set out for the Emerald Glen, a small fairy kingdom inside the Ruinlands, according to Bjorn.

Archeron slowed to speak to her as the others continued up a ragged hill that led to a promontory, and her heart stopped when he brushed his lips over the shell of her ear and whispered, "You seem intent on getting yourself killed."

"Would that bother you?" she asked, sliding her gaze to him.

"It would. Immensely."

She flicked her eyebrows up, unsure of where this was going. "Why is that, Sun Lord?"

"Because . . . I would miss you."

She watched Archeron strut away, hands in his pockets, his golden hair catching the pale light, and it wasn't until he was out of sight that she remembered to breathe.

SEVENTEEN

The Emerald Glen was nestled in a valley between snow-capped mountains shrouded in clouds. As they crossed between a low pass, shivering beneath the cold shadow of the tallest peak, Haven was sure they were the same ones she'd looked down on from Stolas's hidden estate.

Even though she knew the mountains would be mirror images, she studied the sky for gremwyrs or any other sign of Stolas and the Netherworld that paralleled their own.

Strangely, she yearned to revisit that shadowy mirror world of the dead. To explore its depths and understand how it all worked . . .

Rolling her shoulders, she tried to shake off the memory of Stolas, but it clung to her. Despite everything she had to worry about—the upcoming mission, the vorgrath's mate, Bell's safety—her mind kept going back to the Lord of the Netherworld.

Surely, he was clever enough to find an excuse for the Shade Queen?

And yet, when she slipped into her dreams after the Solis had stopped earlier for a few hours, he hadn't shown.

She chewed her lip. The disappointment she'd felt at not training was laced with worry. Was Stolas okay?

Sighing, she buried the emotion as quickly as she discovered it. It was silly, even pointless for a mortal like her to be concerned about a creature like Stolas.

He could take care of himself just fine. Odds were he'd grown tired of her mortal deficiencies and abandoned their deal.

Picking up her pace, she finally purged her mind of anything Stolas related. She had enough troubles, after all. And adding a mercurial Shade Lord to that list was the very definition of stupid.

But before she did, she said a little prayer to the Goddess for him. Just in case.

Even the Lord of the Netherworld deserved mercy now and again.

The sun warmed their faces by the time they reached the glen—a long stretch of verdant land carved into the valley, blanketed with violets, white trillium, and daisies. The air thrummed with the sound of rushing water. It came from countless waterfalls feeding into a large stream that cut down the middle. A gentle breeze rustled the birchwoods and alders that grew around it.

As if awakening from a long slumber, her light magick stirred inside her. It ran sluggishly through her veins and tingled her fingertips, begging for release.

This place has light magick.

But how could that be when the whole of the Ruinlands

possessed dark magick? It should have bled this place dry long ago.

She'd have to ask Bjorn, she decided.

But her focus quickly shifted to Rook as she bounded through the glen in her cursed beast form, her golden tail switching back and forth in the tall grass.

After days tromping through the dark wood, the brightness of the glen lightened their moods. Rook and Surai chased each other through the meadow while Bjorn hummed a soft tune before disappearing somewhere presumably to scour his visions.

Even Archeron hopped onto a large boulder and leaned back, sunning himself like a cat, one alert eye still open of course. It rolled to her as she joined him, relishing the warmth from the rock against her back.

"Mortal," he said by way of greeting. Which was arguably better than chinga . . . although not by much.

"Sun Lord."

They hadn't said a single word to one another since his admission near the Witchwood half a day ago, yet it felt as if they were picking up the conversation minutes later.

"I am no one's lord," he drawled, closing both eyes again. "Call me Archeron."

"And I am no one's mortal pet," she countered. "Call me Haven."

"Haven." He rolled her name around his tongue as if it were a drop of chocolate to savor, sending shivers coursing down her spine. The sound was hallowed, sacred. "*Ha-ven.*"

Part of her hated the way her name in his mouth curled her toes with pleasure. Yet, a substantially larger part of her enjoyed the feeling. It was a welcome emotion after all she'd been through recently.

Why not play this game and see where it led?

"There is light magick here," she began, arching an eyebrow. "How?"

His lips curved upward as he slipped his hands behind his head, and his golden scabbard scraped the rock. "The fairies were just one of many light magick creatures that used to live in the mortal lands, but they caused mischief and trickery for you mortals. So when the Solis banished the Noctis to the Netherworld, you insisted the Solis include all magickal creatures, not just shadowlings.

"When the Netherworld was rent open by the Curse," he continued, "the fairy folk struck a bargain with the Shade Queen." He glanced over the glen. "The valley stays warded from the surrounding dark magick, and the fairy folk are left alone."

"In return?" Haven asked.

"In return, they deliver unsuspecting mortals like you to the Shade Queen."

A loud splash of water from the stream sent Archeron's eyelids flicking open although his body remained still. It was only when he spied Rook in the water that he seemed to relax.

His calm was all a ruse. The realization sent her heart racing. Beneath his casual demeanor, his muscles were taut, his chest quivering with fast breaths.

Haven glanced at the stream. Rook pawed at orange flashes of fish beneath the water, but her dark-tipped ears were pointed toward the trees as if listening. And when Surai joined her in the water, the stream catching her crimson tunic and swirling it around her body, she paused amid splashing water to dart her gaze around the glen.

"So, once again, I'm bait." It wasn't a question, and Haven took another look at the glen as the feeling of being watched pricked her skin.

"You are," admitted Archeron, not sounding the least bit repentant.

Haven shot him a skeptical look. "And what are we supposedly doing here, hmm?"

Slowly, Archeron's eyes opened and slid to her. "All of us? Or . . . you and I?"

Before she could respond, he rolled over her, his hands planted on either side of her head. The weapons adorning his body prodded her waist, but beneath that, she felt his flesh, firm and hot and alive, pressed into hers.

He lowered his head until their noses nearly touched and his golden hair hung like curtains on either side of their faces.

"They will assume we are lovers," he purred, his soft lips flicking over hers with every word. "Lost on some journey. And this place has lulled us into letting our guard down."

She started to snort, but right now, with his breath warm and sweet on her face, the heat and weight of him pressed into her body, it made *perfect* sense.

"They think," he continued in a low, syrupy voice, his words dribbling out like melted sugar, "that tonight, after our bellies are full of wine and food and we dream, they can sneak up on us and steal you."

"Hmm."

"Just like they think this is a lover's kiss."

Her lips parted. "So . . . we are . . . pretending?"

"We are, unless you would prefer something more . . . authentic?"

The question hung heavy in the air even as her lips yearned for his mouth to cover them. Most of his weight was supported on his hands, and she fought the urge to wrap her legs around his waist and yank him down until his weight pinned her to the rock.

A tiny noise escaped her lips, and she felt him grow hard above her.

"Is that an answer," he asked, his voice a quiet purr. There was something inside his tone. A veiled question of consent.

Things had become serious, and he wanted to make sure she agreed.

The game had changed, had become real, and her stomach clenched even as the rest of her body shivered with need.

Confusion set in. How could she enjoy herself when Bell was imprisoned and terrified? What type of person did that make her? She'd let a pretty face and the promise of a kiss make her forget him, and the pleasure she felt became stabbing pains of regret.

Besides, Archeron was promised to another, and even if the Solis had rules that allowed his and Haven's union, she had other rules.

"I'm sure, Sun Lord," she said in a voice colder than intended, "that Avaline would prefer us to pretend."

Archeron's eyes tightened, and his body stiffened as he studied her. She could swear, for a moment, hurt flickered across the Sun Lord's face. "Avaline would understand as she has taken many lovers since our engagement began . . . when I was barely nine." The tight skin around his mouth relaxed, and a hopeful look sparked inside his emerald eyes. "I can explain our customs to you if that would help?"

"No . . . I . . ." She didn't have the words. How could she explain the guilt she felt at being happy? At feeling desire and affection when Bell was locked away by a monster for Haven's forbidden magick?

His jaw clenched, his body stiffening above her. Then without a word, he lifted up, careful not to touch her, and strolled toward the water, leaving cold air in his absence.

Haven let her head fall back to the rock with a thunk and glared at the sky. Sometimes she felt wholly incompetent dealing with anything other than swordplay and fighting.

Stabbing things that needed stabbing was easy; understanding how to navigate the heart was so much harder.

With a groan, she left the boulder and busied herself preparing camp in an effort to ease her mind. She gathered dead branches for the fire, water from the stream for Bjorn's pot, and even tried her hand at fishing for the orange and silvery fish that frequented the stream.

And all the while, she was aware of the sharp, hungry gaze of the fairies—and the nonexistent gaze of the Sun Lord.

She hadn't realized how used to his focus she was. Now, though, whenever they passed, it was as if she didn't exist. Even when he nodded to her or smiled to keep up the ruse, it was as if an icy wall separated them.

It's for the best, she decided as she finished packing the fish she'd caught into a wire basket, the sun glinting off their delicate turquoise and coral scales.

It was a game, a stupid, silly game. Anything more than that would be selfish.

She would never allow herself to be happy until Bell was free.

A soft *whoosh* drew her gaze to the other side of the stream. A shimmering canopy of pale gold fluttered in the breeze; citrine-yellow roses twined along the beams and hung from the gossamer drapes. As she watched, Surai flicked her hand, and a long table of knotty pine appeared. Another flick summoned silverware and napkins.

So much time had passed since she'd witnessed the Solis use magick that she'd nearly forgotten they possessed it, and she watched the Sun Queen conjure things from thin air with a tinge of jealousy.

Perhaps someday she would be able to use her magick without it draining her. Although, once the Curse was broken and she was back in the land of mortals, she could never perform magick publicly.

"Haven," Surai called. "Come try."

By the time Haven crossed the stream to meet them, Surai had added hammered silver chalices and delicate, gold-rimmed porcelain plates.

"Anything else?" Surai questioned as Haven inhaled the sweet hint of rose that perfumed the air.

Haven frowned at the fully set table. "Did you invoke these from items that already exist?"

"Very good," Surai answered. She twirled a gold panel inside her fingers, not bothering to ask how Haven knew about the art of invocation. "This exact setup came from the bridal feast the night before Rook's failed wedding."

Rook, who was in her true form, ducked through the flowing canopy and flashed her teeth in a grin. "She's doing it to remind me what a mistake I almost made."

Surai plucked a rose from the fabric and slid it behind Rook's ear. "No, I'm doing it because that was the most divine celebration I had ever seen, and I thought we could recreate it tonight." She glanced back at Haven, almost sheepishly. "I won't be here, of course, not in my true form, but I'll act as watch while you have this night to live."

She didn't say the thing that hung in the air: If they succeeded tonight, the remaining challenges would be much more dangerous. The next item on the list after fairy tears was a selkie's scale.

Even if they all somehow managed to survive that task, the final item was a sliver of the Shade Queen's horn.

That was an impossible task that none of them had found the courage to discuss yet.

Tonight might be their last chance to have a nice meal . . . *ever.* And it would serve the dual purpose of keeping up the ruse that they had no idea the fairies were here, hiding and watching.

"Anything you want to add?" Surai repeated, dragging Haven away from her thoughts.

She studied the setting, her mouth watering as she recalled the three silver platters from the morning of Bell's Runeday. Then she imagined the way the fresh pears and candied hams smelled, the way the light refracted inside the engravings curving the trays, the way the sticky bun melted into a pool of sugar in her mouth.

A tingle pulsed inside her fingertips, and the three trays appeared on the table exactly as they had that morning. A proud smile found her face. The invoking was simple and clean. No burning ash or crumbling material.

Take that, Shade Lord.

The two girls were wide-eyed as they dragged their gaze from the food to Haven, and Rook said, "Where did you learn to invoke like that?"

Haven hated to lie, but there was no way she could tell them about her lessons with Stolas. So she answered, "I read a lot about magick when I was in Penryth."

Not a lie, exactly.

"Well there's no doubt the fairies will try to steal you now," Rook said in a casual voice as if being taken in the middle of the night by fairies happened every day, and Haven realized her performing magick was just another part of the plan to lure one into camp. "You would make a fine gift to the Shade Queen, and

I imagine it's been a while since they had any mortals to offer."

Haven scoured the craggy cliffs and hills with her gaze, shivering at the thought of being watched. "Are we sure they're here?"

"Does Freya love steel?" Surai said. "Of course they're here, the sneaky sylph bastards." She flung her dark hair over her shoulder. "I nearly died from one of the wicked creature's bites during our last campaign against the Noctis."

Rook laughed. "We thought her arm would rot off, and every day, I had to dress her wound. Goddess Above, she whined like a mortal." She cut her gaze to Haven. "No offense."

Surai clicked her tongue at Rook. "I was wounded trying to make you happy. There we were, Haven, surrounded by half the Noctis army, and she was complaining about the conditions of her tent. So—"

"They were deplorable!" Rook interrupted.

"So I picked her some gorgeous lilies," Surai continued, "but unbeknownst to me, they belonged to a coven of woodland fairies."

Haven's eyes narrowed slyly as she remembered the wildflowers near the pass, and before they could talk her out of it, she invoked a heart-shaped glass vase from the great hall of Penryth and filled it with the wildflowers along the hill.

When the vase was filled with water and a vibrant mixture of purple, white, and yellow flowers, she placed it in the middle of the table, satisfied.

"There," she said. "That should rile the fairies up a bit."

Rook clapped a hand on Haven's shoulder. "I see why Surai likes you so much." Then she plucked a violet from the vase, twirling the delicate stem between her fingers. "Bjorn is taking his time seeing. I think I'll check on him."

The offhand way Rook said it couldn't hide the concern lining her forehead, and Surai chewed her lip as she watched her lover go.

"Is Bjorn okay?" Haven asked.

"I'm sure," Surai said. "He has the lives of a wyvern."

Haven raised her eyebrows.

"Legends say wyverns were granted seven lives for helping the Goddess escape the Noctis during battle." Surai shrugged, her gaze still drawn to where Rook had disappeared. "Bjorn's visions have never taken this long before, but I'm sure he's fine," she repeated.

Haven let the lie go. They all had their secrets.

Some just had more than others.

EIGHTEEN

While Rook went to check on Bjorn, Haven and Surai found a pool of sluggish water downstream to bathe in. Dark red flowers Haven didn't recognize flanked the mossy shore, and she made a note to gather some later—even if it meant the fairies' wrath.

"I thought flowers didn't grow in the Ruinlands," Haven remarked after she was clean and dressed in fresh leathers and a silver tunic she invoked. "But here, they're everywhere."

Surai peeked her head from the water, her black hair fanning out around her. "Flowers? The fairies harvest them for the Shade Queen. There's a huge meadow of them on the other side near the cliffs. We should see them before we leave."

"What does she do with them?"

"Bjorn once mentioned she makes poisons to torture her own Noctis. For petty infractions, too, such as not bowing low enough or walking in her shadow." She shrugged. "But Bjorn rarely talks about his time there unless he has to."

Surai emerged from the water, waving a hand over her body to dry it with magick. Soft flickers of golden light swam over her slim thighs and up her lithe stomach, causing glistening drops of water to disappear in the magick's wake.

Normally, Haven would look away, but she was drawn to Surai's confidence. The way she moved with ease despite being completely naked.

As she wrangled her glossy black hair into a limp braid, Haven's eyes fell to the iridescent runes covering her flesh. Runes that harnessed her magick and allowed her to use specific powers without wasting energy and tiring.

"Have you ever heard of a mortal who had runes like yours?" she asked, wondering if there would ever be a way for her to have the same.

Surai froze, tunic in hand.

Then, she turned to Haven. "Mortals cannot be runemarked; that is blasphemy. The Goddess Above gave your kind runestones, nothing more. I'm sorry, but that is the Goddess's Law."

Haven slackened her gaze and pretended to tie her tunic to hide her disappointment.

But Surai noticed anyway, and when Haven was done dressing, she took her aside. "I know that's not what you wanted to hear. But this is probably for the best. Right now, your inexperience and lack of runemarks is the one thing keeping you unnoticed and safe. Far as I know, fleshruning a mortal is impossible, but if you ever found a way, you would never be able to hide from my kind."

"Or mine," Haven admitted.

"See, it is for the best. You're my friend, Haven Ashwood, and I want you safe. Not hunted across the kingdoms."

That makes two of us, she thought as they grabbed their dirty clothes to leave.

And yet, as the light skipped across the pale hairs along her arm, she imagined runemarks running beneath. Could nearly feel them. Hot and tingly and powerful.

And in the back of her mind, she knew that someday she would have her runemarks, to the Netherworld with the rules.

On the way back, she plucked a shirt-full of red petals from the flowers sprouting from the muck along the stream. As she rolled a velvety petal beneath her fingers, one question refused to go away.

If the Shade Queen poisoned her own people, what would she do to someone like Bell?

But more presently worrying was the anger she felt all around her from the fairies after she took the flowers, and she scurried through the grasses to the camp, glad it was not yet time for them to come.

Magick kept the campfire blazing. To keep the fairies away for now, Surai explained as they slipped beneath the canopy of gold. The strange spices of the Solis food Rook must have invoked while they were gone tingled Haven's nose. Surai, in her raven's form, perched atop one of the overhead wooden beams.

Her head cocked as she watched them, and Haven thought she saw sadness and longing in her eyes.

To be trapped in creature form, unable to live most of your life with your partner and loved ones—that was a curse indeed, and Haven decided whoever this Effendier Sovereign was, she wasn't a true queen. Because a true queen would never be so cruel.

Haven took a seat next to Rook. Except for the prickling feeling running along her skin from the fairies' gaze, she could almost pretend she was in Penryth beneath one of the pavilions they sometimes set up along the courtyard in spring. Could almost pretend Bell sat to her right, waiting to tease her about her love of sweets.

Speaking of sweets . . . pastries and delicacies of every kind greeted her. Some were foreign to Haven, but most she recognized from King Horace's appetite for rich, exotic foods. His only redeeming quality.

A second later, Archeron joined them, setting his sword belt and sword against a post. As he took his place to Rook's right, his gaze flicked over Haven.

Silence followed, and Haven squirmed in her chair.

Without Surai and Bjorn, the meal had already descended into awkwardness—and they had yet to actually eat. She placed her napkin in her lap and was about to reach for the glazed bread bowl when the two Solis began their feast prayers.

Choking down an impatient sigh, she sat quietly, her stomach growling in protest. Surely the Goddess didn't need five minutes of thanks for food that was already spoiling beneath the sun?

Prayers over, Haven filled her plate, not even bothering to touch the fine silverware by her elbow. Rook, who slowly chewed her food with the grace of a princess, watched Haven with curled lips.

Archeron scooped candied beets and glazed carrots onto his plate and stabbed the pile with a fork, taking quick, mechanical bites—as if trying to get this charade over with.

Haven was the only one who seemed to be hungry. Dumping a second helping of food onto her plate, she paused. "Where is Bjorn?"

The question hung heavy in the air. Rook's jaw tensed, and then she stared down at a pile of untouched vegetables. "I couldn't rouse him from his visions."

"Should I take him some food?" She held up a fine roll, its golden-baked skin glistening with honey butter.

A sour look twisted Rook's tanned face, and she set her fork down beside her plate. "If he's trapped in his visions, Haven, how do you suppose he will eat?"

Oh. She fought down the blush creeping up her neck. "Right."

Rook picked her fork back up then set it down again and sighed. "I didn't mean to snap at you." Her golden gaze slid to Haven. "It's just . . . we are all tired of these lands, the darkness. There is something bent and twisted waiting close by, and it feeds off our hope along with our magick."

Haven shivered, but she couldn't deny Rook's claim. Although they were ensconced inside a bubble of protection from the Curse, she could still feel the icy claws of darkness waiting for them outside this glen.

After that, the only sounds were their chewing and the occasional scrape of a fork over porcelain. If they were trying to fool the fairies into thinking they were having a good time, they were failing.

Haven examined a lumpy yellow fruit on her plate, prodding the hard skin with her knife. "What's this called?"

Rook's lips twisted to the side as she regarded the strange item. "I believe it's a type of bitter gourd from the Diamond Isles of Effendier. Archeron?"

He darted his pouty gaze over the fruit but didn't meet Haven's stare as he said, "A kwamlee," and went straight back to his mindless chewing.

Rook looked from Haven to Archeron then stood, a knowing smile on her face. "I think I'll check on Bjorn again."

Rook was gone before Haven could protest. Her gut clenched as she frowned down at her plate, tempering her desire for an extra helping of the custard.

Instead, she poured herself a thimbleful of elderberry rum, not because she particularly liked it but because that was the only spirit she remembered from Penryth when she'd invoked it.

The syrupy liquor burned down her throat and warmed her belly, loosening the tension enough that she could breathe at least.

All at once, Archeron kicked back in his chair, arms behind his head as he stared at her, his gaze like a sudden blast of fire over her skin.

Slowly, she turned to meet his focus and raised an eyebrow.

"You were right," he said, his face a hard mask she couldn't break through. "Anything other than pretend would be wrong. I will enter your tent tonight before sleep but only for appearance's sake. Ten minutes, and you will be rid of me."

She crossed her arms over her chest, annoyed by the arrogant gleam in his eyes. "Good. If ten minutes is all it takes . . . are you sure five would not be more appropriate?"

His eyes narrowed to emerald slits. "You know what? Make it an hour . . . for authenticity."

"A whole hour, huh?"

"If I'm being quick."

"Fine."

"Fine."

Rook appeared just inside the tent, Surai perched on her shoulder, and paused. Rook looked from Haven to Archeron before taking her seat. Bjorn was a quiet shadow behind her, and the moment Archeron pulled out a chair for him, he collapsed into it.

Haven clenched her hands at the sight of Bjorn's dull eyes, slackened face, and disheveled tunic, but it was the way he tilted his head at everyone except her that churned her stomach.

Blind as he was, he always acknowledged her in some way.

But now—now it was as if she wasn't there at all.

Silence swelled the air as Archeron filled a chalice full of dark liquor from a crystal decanter. Bjorn drained it in one gulp, and Archeron frowned. Another pour. Another empty cup.

Archeron and Rook traded worried looks while Bjorn ran his finger over the rim of his golden chalice, lost somewhere faraway.

Then, at last, he focused his haunted gaze on Haven. All the air seemed to flee her chest as he rasped, "Haven Ashwood, you are going to die."

NINETEEN

After the strange encounter in the other-world garden, Bell and the creature worked for another hour close to the portal door in silence, pruning the nest of climbing lilacs over an arching trellis. Bell knew most of the flowers' name's now, and every time he got another name right, his first thought was of Haven.

How she would have laughed at his new hobby. Laughed and teased him even as she listened to his musings about which flower bloomed at night, which buds the butterflies were drawn to most.

He could have talked for hours about his observations, and she would have half-listened because she loved him. He'd taken that love for granted, and now he wished he'd told her how much he appreciated her.

You'll get your chance soon, he reminded himself darkly.

Unless, of course, Haven traveled to the Netherworld instead. Despite the grim possibility, Bell smiled at the thought of the Lord of the Netherworld trying to deal with her.

If she did go to that underworld hell, the Dark Lord would send her to the Nihl soon enough just to be rid of her.

Pushing thoughts of his dead friend away, he put all his efforts into the lilacs. When they had clipped and gathered most of the dark purple blossoms, the creature stood and gestured Bell toward the portal.

The second they were back inside the dark castle and the dank, chilly air hit him, whatever happiness he'd gained from the sunlight of the other-world vanished.

Expecting to go back to his side of the castle, Bell tried to hand his sack of petals to the creature. Instead, the creature gave him both sacks.

"I need to go back for something," the creature said. "Would you take those upstairs to the first room on your right, please?"

Bell held the bags close to his chest and nodded. "Sure."

They had fallen into this routine of talking but not talking. The creature was all manners and grace, saying 'please' and 'thank you' and speaking when necessary. He said 'excuse me' in the hallways, made sure Bell had enough food and drink and that it was all to his liking, but they never went beyond pleasantries, and despite Bell's efforts to get the creature to open up, he was infuriatingly quiet.

But Bell longed for real, messy conversation. The kind that made you look away from the other person as you spilled your guts. The kind you turned over later in your mind, wondering if you'd said too much.

If Bell had been braver, he would have asked the creature about what they saw earlier. He was sure it was a piece of the puzzle regarding the creature's history.

But no one ever accused him of courage, and he obediently started up the stairs with the petals. His sore muscles strained with each step, and he was nearly to the top when the creature called out, "Come straight back down when you're done."

His warning was clear: Don't wander.

As soon as Bell neared the iron door at the top of the stairs, magick tingled inside his fingers, and the door creaked open.

The sweet, cloying smell of flowers filled his nose. Inside, iron racks covered the stone walls, and each rack was jammed full of colorful glass vials. They reminded him of the vials Haven carried around with her. Most were labeled with elegant penmanship he doubted the creature could manage with his thick, gloved hands.

Below, waist-high counters ran the length of the wall. The stone countertops were filled with cauldrons and burners, drying racks, and more vials. Bell ran a finger over the inside of a mortar and pestle tinged yellow from whatever flower was last crushed, and put it to his nose. *Marigold.*

The flowers Bell carried went on the counter beside five more sacks. Then he exited, started to walk down the stairs . . . and paused.

More rooms lined this hallway, but only one door was closed.

Bell had never been curious like Haven. There were rules and procedures for a reason. Who was he to challenge them?

Only, now that he was days from death, he didn't share that same respect for rules. After all, rules were why his magick belonged to the Shade Queen.

Maybe to save his own life and finally gain some answers, he'd have to break a few of those rules. And if doing so finally gave him clarity on the creature's past, then all the better.

Glancing around, Bell slunk on quiet feet to the last room. Once again, the runestone Haven gifted him heated in his pocket, his magick buzzed, and the door unlocked.

Bell's hands were clammy as he slipped inside and shut the door, his heartbeat echoing inside his skull. The room was dark.

Watery moonlight trickled in from a pair of windows on the far wall and painted the middle of the floor silver.

It was a . . . bedroom. A giant poster bed filled one side along with two nightstands and a towering wardrobe. There was a heaviness in the air, how he imagined the inside of an old tomb would smell, and the feeling that this place hadn't been touched in centuries.

Thick, thorny vines had broken through the window panes, and they twined around the massive bed, the deep-red roses that bloomed from the vines the only color in the room. Everything else was faded beneath a layer of dust.

He explored the chamber, his stomach pooling with dread as he saw his footsteps clearly tracked across the centuries' worth of dust on the floor.

But it wasn't enough to dampen his curiosity, and he inspected everything. The knickknacks on the dresser, the tarnished silver morning tray laden with a tortoise-shell brush and a hand mirror engraved with roses.

As carefully as possible, he eased the door to the wardrobe open. His heart nearly stopped as two moths fluttered out, their tiny brown wings flapping wildly.

Releasing a nervous sigh, he switched his attention back to the wardrobe and the beautiful pieces hanging inside. Used to the royal fineries, he recognized the craftsmanship of the dinner jackets and waistcoats in front of him, the exquisite dyes and expert tailoring. Bell ran a finger over the fine fabrics: plush velvets, creamy silks, beautifully tanned leathers, fine-spun wool.

Whoever lived here had good taste, at least.

Goddess Above, I miss my closet at Penryth. It was a silly thought, but the one good thing about being a prince was the luxurious wardrobe.

He strolled to the sitting area on the other end of the room, noting the blue tufted chairs and loveseat painted silver by the watery light. A tall dressing mirror sat in the corner, shattered beyond repair. But Bell was drawn to the painting that took up the entire wall above.

A dark sheet covered it, and he gently tugged the linen down in a whoosh of dust.

Inside the golden frame, a boy on the verge of adulthood was poised on the edge of a deep wooden throne, his blond hair and honey-gold eyes made brighter by the navy-blue jacket he wore.

Bell recognized the prince immediately from the encounter earlier in the garden. Renault. Frowning, he stood on his tiptoes for a better look—

There was an explosion behind him. Bell turned just in time to see the door burst open, splintering into a thousand pieces.

Bell gasped, but before he could flee, the creature was towering over him.

"How dare you come in here!" he roared, his voice reverberating through Bell's ribcage.

Bell held up his hands. "I'm—"

"I allowed you into my life. I fed you, clothed you, and this is how you repay my kindness!"

"Please!" Bell fought the urge to shrink from the creature, and he steeled a breath. "I only—"

"Only what?" The creature bent down, the darkness inside his hood covering his expression. "Wanted to see the fallen prince? Did you laugh when you realized how far I've truly fallen?"

There was rage inside the creature's voice, but it was laced with agony and shame.

Bell swallowed, glancing up at the image of Renault. "I don't . . . I don't follow. Who are you? And who is that?"

But even as he asked the question, something inside him was already putting the pieces in place.

The creature.

Renault.

Ravenna.

"You're . . ." Bell tore his gaze from the painting to the creature hiding behind the cloak, feeling stupid for not realizing. "You're the fallen prince?"

The creature replied with a sharp grunt, followed by a long stretch of ragged breaths.

"You are!" Bell took a step backward. "You murdered your family and brought the Curse on our lands. You . . . you . . ."

"Are a monster?" the creature finished, almost wearily, as if he'd done this before.

Bell's chest heaved. "You sat there and listened to me cry. You made me think you were my friend. I told you about my best friend, and you pretended to care, knowing her death was your fault." Anger slammed through him. "In fact, the only reason I'm here is because of you."

Everything was the creature's fault. Bell's kidnapping. Haven's death. It felt good to remove that burden from himself.

"You killed her," Bell whispered, and for once that accusation was on someone else. "You caused so much death and destruction, so much pain. All because . . . what? You wanted to be king?"

The creature was frozen as if Bell's words had cast a spell over him. Bell wanted to see his expression, to at least know the creature felt remorse for his actions, but shadows covered his face.

How dare he get to hide from what he's done.

In a fit of rage, Bell grabbed the edge of his hood and yanked it back.

And then he screamed.

Half of the fallen prince's face was the beautiful visage from the painting. The perfect, rounded lips, polished skin of pewter, and whiskey-colored eyes that reminded Bell of bronze sparkling beneath the sun.

But the other half—Shadeling Below—the other half was monstrous. Scaled in various browns and greens, his skin had the rough look of a wyvern's. Jagged teeth peeked from a lipless mouth. Above, a red reptilian eye regarded him, no trace of humanity or emotion inside.

The creature stood still as if not moving could somehow make it better. "Would you like to see the rest, prince? My tail, perhaps?" Bitterness soured his voice. "The claws curving from my fingertips?"

Bell tried to suck in a breath, but his heart felt lodged in his throat. Being so close to this . . . this *creature* after sharing so many days with him, it was all just too much to process.

The creature's gaze collapsed to the ground. "I warned you not to come here." He glanced back up, that one savage eye unblinking, and slowly reached out his right arm. "But part of me is still . . . human."

Bell wanted to feel sympathy for the creature. But betraying family was a sin he could never forgive. His own father treated him horribly. His step-mother abused him. His half-brother bullied and tortured him.

Yet, he would never spill their blood or wish them true harm.

"No," Bell breathed, his mind made up. "You stopped being human the day you betrayed your family and our lands to a Noctis monster."

Bell couldn't be here a second longer.

Without thinking, he darted beneath the creature's arm and slipped through the open doorway as his world careened.

The creature yelled his name behind him. But Bell kept going. Past the stairs. He was running, sprinting, his anger and betrayal pushing him deeper into parts of the castle he'd never explored.

He could feel the monster breathing down his back, laughing at him for being so dumb. For not knowing who he was.

Did the creature and the Shade Queen laugh together at him? The dumb little sacrifice? Tears warmed his cheeks and blurred his vision as he tore through the halls. He didn't know where he was going. Only that he had to get out.

One second he was sprinting down the dark halls.

The next, he found himself lunging across the roof, unable to stop running, running, running, until he blinked and found himself inside Spirefall.

Alone.

TWENTY

Bjorn's dark prediction hit Haven in the chest, as real as a physical blow, and she jumped to her feet, knocking her chair back.

"Why would you say that?" she asked. Her throat was knotted, her voice croaky and wild.

Surai flew to her shoulder, landing softly. Haven knew it was an effort to comfort her, but it was too late. She read the truth in the seer's sightless eyes.

"How?" she demanded.

Bjorn's sharp Adam's apple slid up and down his throat as he swallowed. "A seer may not divulge the details of someone's death. It's against the Goddess's Law."

Goddess's Law be damned, she wanted to hiss. Instead, she worked to control her ragged breaths, the erratic beats of her heart. "Can you tell me anything useful?"

"Only that it cannot be stopped. I'm sure now."

"Now?" Haven asked. Archeron looked down at the table, and she sucked in a deep breath as the realization hit. "You knew? Both of you?"

A muscle feathered in Archeron's square jaw, but he refused her gaze.

Rook snarled and muttered a Solissian curse beneath her breath at them both while Surai took to the air and circled their heads, squawking.

Archeron glared down at his plate. "I wanted him to be sure before he told you."

"What about the Curse?" Haven asked.

Bjorn ran the pad of his thumb over the body of his fork. "There are still many possibilities."

"So, I can die, and the Curse can still be broken? Bell can still be freed?"

"It is possible, yes, though not probable."

"As long as it's still an option, I keep fighting." She lifted her chin, feeling strangely hollow inside. "My death has to mean something."

Archeron whipped his head up to look at her, his eyes searching her face, but she looked away. She didn't need the Sun Lord's pity.

"What else did you find, Seer?" Archeron asked, directing his attention to Bjorn as he poured him another drink.

After Bjorn emptied the cup, he set it down, hard, staring into its empty depths as if the bottom of his chalice held all the answers. "Chaos and death. Lots of death."

Rook leaned across the table and took his hand. "Ours or theirs, Bjorn?"

Heartbeats passed as they waited for the seer's answer. Finally, he shook his head. "The only thing I can say for sure is that along with Haven, one of us will die, one will fall in love, one will sacrifice everything, and one will betray the others."

Haven buried a mad laugh as she poured herself a drink from the decanter the Solis drank from. Whatever deep red liquid swirled inside her cup, it must be potent for mortals because Rook opened her mouth to protest before thinking better of it.

Haven was dying, after all. She could do whatever the Netherworld she wanted.

And she wanted to get drunk. To forget the seer's words. To forget death was around the corner.

Swilling the drink, which tasted sweet and tart, she swiped the decanter from the table and headed toward the tents Archeron had invoked earlier, choosing the largest one for herself. No doubt Archeron had meant that as his.

Even better.

Grinning like a fool, she poured herself another drink.

By the time Archeron showed up, Haven was half-drunk—maybe more. And by the way Archeron kept morphing into two gorgeous, swaggering figures, that maybe was a probably.

The empty bottle lay on its side on the bed beside her, where she sat cross-legged on a lovely mound of plush white furs, her map and notebook scattered about.

As the two Archerons prowled beneath the flap of her tent with the stealth and grace of a wild animal, her heart leapt against her ribcage, and any resentment or anger she felt for him—both of him—melted away.

"I love that bed," both Archerons murmured as they strolled to stand near the head. Thankfully, they merged back into one man—Haven wasn't sure she could handle two of the smarmy Sun Lord.

Not in her current state.

Haven forced herself to study the map and not him, pretending she could actually make out the blurred lines beneath her finger. Bottom lip caught in her teeth, she absentmindedly ran a hand over the soft fur around her. "I can see why."

"You knew it was mine." His statement didn't hold a question, only a trace of amusement. "You're trying to punish me."

She did indeed know it was his, and she was indeed trying to punish him.

"For?" she murmured, playing coy.

The feather mattress sank as he joined her on the bed, stretching out his long legs and sighing. "A bed such as this could keep a Solis like me content."

She grinned. "That's all that's required to keep you happy, Sun Lord? A fancy bed?"

The wolfish look he gave her chased away some of her drunkenness as he drawled, "That and a warm body to share the covers with."

"Really? And would any warm body do?" she teased, feeling like some harpy had taken over her body. *What the Netherworld had gotten into her?*

He chuckled, unblinking as he stared at her, suddenly serious. "I have just one in mind . . ."

A wave of embarrassment crashed over. *Would any warm body do?* She stifled a groan. *Yes, idiot, you said that.*

What the Nether-frigging heck had gotten ahold of her? "You said I was punishing you," she blurted, desperate to guide the conversation back to safe ground. "Why would I do that?"

"Keeping Bjorn's vision from you for starters." He plucked the sketch of Surai and Rook playing in the pond and examined it. "This is a good likeness. You enjoy drawing?"

"Yes." She finally lifted her gaze to his, and again, a tiny shock went through her at the sight of Archeron—his tawny skin and striking emerald eyes, the way he looked at her with the intensity of the blazing sun.

And his lips . . . Goddess Above, his soft, curving lips begged to be kissed.

Nethergates! She was definitely full-on-raging-drunk.

She felt a flush crawl up her neck, one that couldn't be blamed on just alcohol. "I would have liked to have been properly trained," she added, clearing the huskiness from her voice, "but King Horace said it was beneath the prince's Royal Companion Guard to learn a common trade. So I learned to kill people instead."

"King Horace is a fool like all mortal kings." His voice was an angry growl, but just as quickly, it became soft and wistful. "In Effendier, artists are revered for the beauty they add to our society. There's even an academy for the arts where pupils who are accepted commit to studying for one-hundred years. It's considered one of the greatest lasting gifts to our culture."

"Tell me, Sun Lord. Is Effendier why you fight to break the Curse?"

Even drunk, Haven caught the tiny tremor that flickered across his face. "Most people have someone they love enough to give their life for," he said.

"But not you?" she asked, acutely aware of the way her breath hitched.

"Loving another being like that isn't in my destiny. For me, that love is reserved for my homeland."

"That sounds . . . lonely."

"You understand nothing, Mortal." Maybe it was the liquor, but his voice didn't sound angry, only disappointed.

"Then help me understand," she said softly.

Frowning, he retrieved his dagger from his waistband and picked his already clean nails. It was a casual gesture, one meant to deflect from the agony that rippled beneath the surface of his indifferent mask.

"Effendier permeates my dreams." There was a vulnerability inside his words that pierced her core. "The waves of its turquoise sea crash in time with my heart; its magick calls to me in a way no woman ever has." He flicked his gaze up to her, his mouth a tight line. "I will either break the Curse and ask that my enslavement to your king be ended, or I will die trying. But I will never go back to Penryth in chains."

"So you've never had someone you loved like that?"

His jaw clenched, and he stared down at his hands before speaking. "I had a brother, once. A soulmate in arms. His name was Remurian."

"What happened to him?"

"Killed." His terse voice kept her from asking more details.

"And Avaline?" Haven asked carefully, her voice only slurring a little. "Do you not love her as much as that?"

"Ah. The other reason you are angry with me."

"No. I'm not angry. Just . . . disappointed."

He raised an eyebrow. "Disappointed?"

"That you're pledged to someone else."

She could swear a muscle in his neck trembled. "Would you have me pledged to you instead, Haven Ashwood?"

"Pledged? Shadeling Below, I'll never get married. Not to anyone."

"Then?"

The flush creeping up her neck was now a fire scorching her face. "I refuse to help you betray Avaline."

He chuckled—the bastard *chuckled*—his head falling back and white teeth flashing. "Avaline and I are betrothed, not enslaved to one another." He leaned forward, an amused sparkle in his eyes. "Solis live very long lives, Haven. Unlike mortal culture, marriage for us means a vow to raise children and support one another, an alliance to strengthen our lines. It's a political marriage—not that I don't have feelings of respect and affection for Avaline—but we're allowed to have other courtships as long as there are no children."

Haven's mouth parted. Her head was spinning, her heart pounding loudly inside her ears. "It isn't just your vow that bothers me. I can't be happy while the Shade Queen has Bell, Archeron. He is . . . he is my Effendier." Her heart was now in her throat, a thousand butterflies swarming her stomach. "Or, at least . . . I thought I couldn't."

Archeron had been looking down at his knife, and his head whipped up, a feral look in his eyes. "Thought? And . . . now?"

Feeling as if every nerve inside her body was on fire, she leaned across her mess of sketches until she was nearly touching Archeron—nearly, but not quite.

A sliver of space stretched between them. Never had such a tiny thing felt so large, so full of promise.

Archeron stiffened even as a smile stirred his lips.

"Haven't you heard?" she breathed. "I'm going to die. And I refuse to let another second go by mired in guilt. I want to live. I want to feel . . . everything."

"Everything?" he asked quietly.

She nodded without breaking his gaze.

An uneven breath burst from the Sun Lord's lips, a vein just below his jaw jumping. He studied her unabashedly, taking in every detail, every scar and freckle and pore.

His gaze wandered lower, catching on the sharp edge of her collarbone before diving below. A mortal man would have stolen glances behind an ashamed grimace, embarrassed for finding her body attractive.

Not Archeron.

He took stock of her with the appraising eye of a painter admiring his subject, a worshipper looking upon a deity. His pupils flared as his languid stare caught on her curves.

"What?" she whispered.

"You are like no mortal I've ever met," he murmured in a throaty growl, his gaze traveling back up her throat to meet her curious eyes. "You confound me. You excite me. You intrigue me."

Then, slowly, so slowly she imagined she was making it up, he reached his hand out. As he brushed his fingertips lightly against her cheek—lazy, sensual caresses that sent burning waves rippling down her body—he studied her face, watching her reaction.

She leaned into his hand. "Kiss me." It was a demand and all she could think about. His lips on hers. The feel of his body pressed into her flesh. And more . . . so much more.

"Kiss me," she repeated, her voice a husky rasp.

"No."

She stiffened and blinked as if falling out of a trance. "What? Why not?"

His amused expression made her want to smack him, but somewhere buried beneath his grin was longing. She could see it in the way his muscles corded and tensed, the way his pupils had enlarged to the size of small grapes, his lips parted and breath ragged.

He exhaled. "You are drunk—"

"I know what I'm asking," she interrupted. "I can still give consent."

A rueful smile tugged one side of his lips as he shook his head, his golden hair falling over his forehead. "Even if that were true, your senses are dulled. And when I take you to bed, Haven, I'll have you feel everything."

Holy Goddess Above.

"I only requested a kiss," she clarified. "Not to be *taken* to bed. Although, I might point out I'm already in a bed, a nice, soft one."

"In my experience, one leads to the other. Besides," he continued, "unlike the clumsy, boorish attempts at coupling from your mortal men, a Solis courtship is a long, exquisite dance."

She took pleasure in the way his voice was thick with need. "Sounds time-consuming."

"Everything in this life worth doing takes time. And as much as I want to kiss you right now and then take you on these luxurious furs . . ." His words trailed away as a growl rumbled deep in his throat, the fur caught beneath his clenched fingers. "Rushing it would mean dulling the pleasure. I promise you, Little Mortal"—his lips curled wickedly at the edges—"the wait will be worth it."

Haven jutted out her chin, using all of her willpower to keep from running her hands over the smooth, tawny flesh of his chest where it peeked out from his tunic. Her fingers itched to trace the fleshrunes mapping his body. To touch him and see his reaction.

In his excited state, it wouldn't take much to change his mind. The thought was intoxicating.

"What if I die before then?" she asked.

His eyes grew solemn. Leaning forward, he trailed his lips over her cheek before finding the sensitive shell of her ear. She froze with the pleasure of that simple act.

"I will try very, very hard," he murmured, "not to let that happen. For selfish reasons, obviously."

"Obviously," she breathed.

Then, he stood, leaving the air where his powerful body had been cold in comparison. Before she could protest, he was strolling toward the exit. Tension corded the muscles of his back, and he walked stiffly as if every step he took away from her was painful.

One side of her lips tugged upward. *Good.*

She knew then, if she called out to him, the last of his willpower would die, and he'd let this sudden . . . whatever this was between them overtake both their senses.

Her blood, sluggish as it was with alcohol, surged at the thought.

Yet part of her understood the excitement of waiting, too.

"Hey, Sun Lord," she called.

His head whipped back, eagerness brightening his eyes.

"That was way longer than five minutes," she said, giving him the thumbs up. "Good job."

His shoulders shook with laughter. "Get some sleep, Little Mortal," he ordered, the roughness of his tone smoothing out to his usual arrogant purr. "I meant what I said about keeping you safe. Any fairy that approaches will have to deal with me."

As soon as the tent flap closed behind him, she released a breath, her head spinning. Her entire body felt hot and achy, and she flopped down on an ivory pillow, snarling at the air.

How the Nethergates was she supposed to sleep now?

TWENTY-ONE

Haven was sure she would dream of Archeron, but as soon as her eyes closed and she fell asleep, she was transported to Bell's meadow beneath the giant oak. The sky was a deep midnight blue, the stars hidden behind a black shroud of clouds.

"Stolas?" Haven called as she sprinted to the tree. She couldn't wait to work on more magick. There was so much left to learn and so little time to practice. "Shade Lord?"

She froze beneath a low, twisted branch, her heart jumping wildly. Her breath blew out in a milky cloud.

Something was wrong.

A darkness probed her dreamscape, she could feel it. Tentacles of evil searching for a way to get in.

Dread tangled around her insides. She shifted uneasily. *Something wrong here. You need to wake up.*

Inhuman laughter echoed over the landscape. "Are you the mortal girl trying to break my Curse?"

The voice was a primordial growl laced with malice and hatred, and Haven froze as a pit of dread opened inside her.

"Did you think you could hide from me?" the voice continued lazily, *cruelly.*

There was no doubt who this was . . .

"Shade Queen," Haven whispered.

The Dark Queen's depravity polluted the meadow, a dark cloud of hopeless despair tainting everything it touched.

How had Haven ever thought she could face such a darkness?

Despite the fear curdling her blood, Haven gathered the few shreds of courage she had left and lifted her chin. "Do I look afraid?"

More laughter rattled off the brittle dreamscape, loud enough Haven thought the world would crack. "Let's see how brave you are now, Mortal Girl, when you open your dull little eyes and see my creatures. They will rip out your throat and feast on your entrails. How does that sound?"

Haven tore from her dreamscape back to reality. As she wrenched up in bed, sweat plastering her soaked hair across her forehead, she came face-to-face with two large, pitch-black eyes.

They belonged to a delicate creature of nearly transparent skin with elongated ears that ended in sharp points and a row of needle-like teeth. Dark wings spread behind it, papery and iridescent like a butterfly.

Haven went for the dagger under her pillow, but the fairy hissed and jumped at her throat—

A whoosh of magick sent twin daggers darting across Haven's periphery, pinning the fairy against the tent wall by her delicate wings. Haven's relief transformed to shame as she watched the fairy struggle. Watched the blade shred the papery-thin material of her dark wings as easily as a butterfly caught on a nail.

Archeron emerged from the shadows, and the fairy began shrieking in fairy-speak, the high-pitched screams oozing rage. Archeron chuckled, and the fairy switched to Solissian.

"Release me, Sun Lord!" the fairy screeched, her muscles squirming beneath her skin as she struggled to pull the daggers free—but the magick that held the daggers in place was too strong. "Release me and you will have riches! Anything—anything you desire."

Archeron ran two fingers over his jaw as he studied the creature. "I desire, Fairy, for you to be quiet."

Surai and Rook burst into the tent, followed by Bjorn. The fairy hissed and gnashed at the air as they surrounded her, and she pulled even harder at the daggers. Haven winced as her wings shredded even more, the ripping sound horrible to her ears.

"What is this?" the fairy cried. "A trick? I've been tricked by the Solis for a mortal?" Her skin began to shimmer, the dark leaves, which fell from her head like hair, changing to an angry red. "Treachery! All the kingdom will know of it! Treachery!"

Rook sighed and placed her dagger at the fairy's pale throat, and the fairy went still, her dark eyes wide. "You would not dare, Sun Queen," the fairy said. "We fairies would haunt you until your end of days. You would not dare!" she repeated.

"Watch me," Rook growled.

All at once, the fairy stopped struggling and went still, a cunning smile exposing her sharp teeth. "What is it you want, beautiful one?"

"You know what we're here for," Bjorn said.

The fairy's head snapped to Bjorn. "A wish, Seer? Oh, but I cannot grant them anymore. My magick is weak as I am weak."

"Save the act, sprite," Bjorn continued. "We need your tears."

"No!" The sprite banged her head back against the tent wall, her tiny neck thrashing, wings fluttering madly as they ripped against the blades. "You know I cannot give you that! Please. The Shade Queen . . . she will hurt me, she will punish me. She will make me suffer in the most horrible ways. I have seen what she can do."

Fear dripped from the sprite's voice, and Haven swallowed, her throat suddenly dirt-dry. Four Solis with daggers failed to intimidate this fairy, but one mention of the Shade Queen and terror consumed her.

Rook pressed her dagger harder against the fairy's trembling throat. "And what do you think we will do to you, Sprite? Make you dance a jig?"

"I cannot help you! You do not understand. The Shade Queen will know. She will know!"

Blade still poised over the fairy's throat, Rook glanced back at them. "What now?"

Haven slipped between Surai and Archeron until she was close enough to see the irradiant markings that covered the fairy's skin. She was beautiful, in an alien sort of way. The kind of whimsical, magick-filled creature she thought lived in books, not real life.

The fairy's eyes were depthless pools of midnight when they fell on Haven.

"Don't be afraid, Fairy," Haven said. "We don't want to hurt you. All we want is to break the Curse and free my people."

She bared her sharp teeth in a sneer. "Liar! Flower thief!"

"I'm telling the truth. We want to help you."

"Help me? Your people cast me into the Netherworld with the Noctis. They fed off my magick and . . . and worse. The Shadeling was there. You cannot imagine the things he did. You cannot imagine . . ." Terror had widened her eyes to the size of teacup saucers, but now something bitter and cunning flashed over them.

"Mortals betrayed me, so why would I help you, mortal girl?"

"Because," Haven began, trying to imbue every word with sincerity, "I'm friends with the Prince of Penryth. I'm going to save him right now. And when the Curse is broken, I promise you, he will allow the fairies to live once more amongst the mortals. You will have great sweeps of land to call your own, not this tiny glen, and best of all, you will not have to pay tribute to the Shade Queen anymore."

Surai touched her arm. "Haven, don't bargain with her. Fairies are wicked, tricky creatures—"

"Do you swear it with magick?" the fairy interrupted, her eyes never leaving Haven. "Bind your promise with magick, and I will allow your friends one chance to make me cry."

"Don't do it," Rook snarled, her knife still held against the sprite's flesh. "We will find another way. I can make her cry a river of tears, trust me."

Haven released a deep breath. She didn't doubt Rook's word, but that would take time, and each second that passed was a second Bell was scared, hungry, perhaps even hurt.

"I bind my promise with magick, Fairy." As soon as the words were spoken, a tiny shiver of magick pulsed through Haven's core almost as if delicate chains wrapped around her insides. "Allow us this chance, and I will intervene with the Prince of Penryth to strike a pact with the fairies. It will be done."

A clever smile brightened the sprite's face. "Very good, very good. My sisters will be pleased by this. Now, which of you will make me cry? A mortal? A Solis? My tears don't come cheap, and . . ." her smile widened with malice. "The Shade Queen is coming."

"Explain!" Archeron snarled, glancing at the others.

"While you feasted, my sisters sent a messenger to alert the

Shade Queen of the mortal girl's presence."

Rook let out a curse, and she and Surai left to stand guard by the entrance. The sound of their blades unsheathing from the other side of the canvas filled Haven's gut with dread.

"Now," the fairy taunted. "Who will try to elicit my tears?"

Haven's hand tightened around the handle of her dagger as she waited for Bjorn to approach the fairy. With his tragic story he seemed the most obvious choice.

But it was Archeron, not the seer, who pressed to the front.

He nodded his head. "I will, Fairy."

"My name is Mossbark," the fairy said, her lower lip pushed out in a pout. "And you are too pretty to make me cry. But perhaps if you let me down . . ."

A knowing smile curved Archeron's lips as he said, "You stay pinned to the wall, Mossbark of the fairies."

Cold anger flickered inside Mossbark's black-pool eyes. "You are unkind, Solis. I will not forget. Now, what is your story?"

Archeron raked a hand through his hair, and Haven found herself leaning forward to listen, curious.

"I am Archeron Halfbane, born to the Sun Sovereign of Effendier, a bastard son from a nameless courtier. I grew up ridiculed by my brothers and pitied by my sisters, forced to prove myself at every turn. When I was seven, two political hostages came to live at our court: Avaline and Remurian Kallor of Lorwynfell. They were also bastards, born to a mortal princess who'd been kidnapped and taken to the Netherworld. When her parents got her back, they were unhappy to discover her pregnant with twins.

"Just like me, they were outcasts, and perhaps for that reason, we became inseparable. They were the only friends I'd ever known. When peace was made between Effendier and their kingdom, and they were allowed to return, I went with them to fight for their kingdom in the name of my mother. Just as in Effendier, it was us against the kingdoms. We traveled the mortal lands and even across the Glittering Sea fighting the Noctis." Archeron gestured toward Bjorn and the two girls outside. "We collected other outcasts as we went, and soon, we were a family. Do you have a family here, Mossbark?"

Mossbark blinked, delicate silver eyelashes flashing. "Yes."

"Then you know what a special thing that is. To love someone enough that you would give your life for them without hesitation. Remurian and I, we were what the Effendier call Soulbrothers, souls who find one another in every life. He was my best friend. The kind of mortal who was kind to everyone, even fairies such as yourself. You would have found him handsome, Mossbark. Goddess knows the entire realm did."

Without thinking, Haven crept even closer, drawn in by the story. Archeron's body was rigid, his voice uneven.

"What happened to him, Solis?" Mossbark asked. She too was leaning forward in rapt attention.

"The mortal King of Penryth begged us to join him in battle against the Noctis during the last days of the final war. I didn't trust him, but Remurian saw peace for his kingdom close at hand, and he agreed. We fought for two days, and on the third day in battle, the Penrythian King betrayed us to the Noctis for a promise of protection from the Shade Queen's army. We managed to fight our way out and escape, but Remurian was taken by King Horace's men to Penryth as a prisoner. By then, the Solis had conceded the war and fled across the sea, and Avaline and Remurian's kingdom had fallen. The rest of us were ordered to leave as well by my mother, the Sovereign of Effendier."

The fairy hardly seemed to feel the daggers she strained against as she said, "What happened then?"

"We decided we would infiltrate Penryth and free Remurian, damn my mother and the consequences. Only, when we stormed the gates of the castle, the King of Penryth had his eldest son run my brother, my *friend*, through with a sword. The mortal prince dismembered him until he was unrecognizable then hung his parts over the ramparts as a warning."

Silence fell, heavy and thick, as Archeron pulled in a deep breath and continued. "So I killed the eldest Prince of Penryth right in front of his father before they captured us."

"As was your right," Mossbark whispered.

"Yes, well, when my mother came, she saw it differently. She was furious at us for jeopardizing the truce with the mortals, and she performed the final betrayal by cursing us all. For their part in battle, Rook and Surai were locked into their shifter forms opposite halves of the day. Bjorn was released to wander the mortal lands, sightless and without a home. And I was bound to the King of Penryth, the coward who betrayed us and murdered my friend, a slave to his every whim and will."

"A mother would never do such a thing to her son," Mossbark insisted.

"Oh, my mother would. She had no qualms handing me over to a depraved, spineless king. So you see, Mossbark, I may be pretty, but my soul has been forever shattered. For what am I without my family and my dignity?"

Mossbark's eyes were wide, glazed. Haven held her breath, her own eyes glassy as a diamond-sized tear formed in the corner of Mossbark's eye and then released.

Still caught in the sadness of Archeron's confession, Haven nearly missed the tear, and she hurried with one of her vials to collect it. The tiny drop shimmered in the faint light as it slid over the rim of her vial and pooled at the bottom.

Once the vial was safely in her pocket, she let herself go back to Archeron's story of betrayal. She had always known the king was capable of cruelty, but turning on his allies in battle? And killing Remurian, a political hostage?

Her hands balled into tight fists. In that moment, if the king were present, she would have run a blade through his throat. *Coward. Murderer.* He didn't deserve the crown on his head or the title that went with it.

Ignoring the fairy, Haven turned to Archeron. "Archeron, I'm . . . I'm sorry."

But Archeron stared beyond her into something she couldn't see, lost to the darkness of his memories.

Before Haven could say anything more, the fairy's head whipped up, and she gazed wide-eyed at the door. "The Shade Queen!"

At the same time, Rook and Surai bounded through the entryway, their swords gleaming in the firelight.

"Gremwyrs!" Rook hissed. "We have to go out the back. There's a tunnel through the mountains we can use . . . if we can make it."

Raising her sword, Surai sliced a hole in the tent with a loud rip, and then she and Rook funneled through. The fairy latched onto Haven's arm with her spindly fingers. "Set me free, Mortal!"

Archeron waited for her, and he shook his head. "No, Haven. She's with them, not us!"

Haven hesitated. True terror pooled in Mossbark's eyes, and she squeezed harder around Haven's arm.

"Please, she will know of my betrayal already, and she will slaughter us all. Please!"

Haven ripped her arm out of the fairy's grasp and fled. When she got to the hole Surai made, she let out a sigh and flipped around, waving her hand.

After a few pathetic tries, her magick sizzled to life, and the daggers popped free from the fairy's wings.

Mossbark fell to the ground in a bony heap, her torn wings collapsed over her back.

For a split second, their eyes met. "Find the Basilisk to help you for the next part of your journey," the sprite said. "And use the bloodbane flowers you stole. They are more powerful than you know."

Then, Mossbark darted beneath the tent and was gone.

Archeron waited for Haven just outside, and they caught up to the others near the mountains. The screams from the fairies haunted the air, the growls and roars of the gremwyrs and whatever shadowlings the Shade Queen had sent after them soon following.

Mossbark was right. The Shade Queen must have already known because her monsters were killing without discretion. Clouds of magick colored the air as the fairies tried to fight back, the cloying perfume of roses filling her nose, but the shadowlings outnumbered them.

Finally, Haven had to turn away from the carnage.

Bjorn led their group to the hidden tunnel in the mountains. As they walked in silence through the darkness, lit only by Haven's magick—a light sphere shelled in dark magick—she wondered if the fairies had known the horror that awaited when they sent their emissary to reveal Haven's presence here.

Surely not.

Her hand tightened on the pommel of her sword as she thought about the kind of demon it took to slaughter those fairies.

And that demon had Bell.

"Not for long, Bell," she promised, willing her words to somehow reach him. To somehow become true. "I'm coming for you. Just hold on a little longer."

TWENTY-TWO

Now that his anger was spent, Bell knew he'd made a terrible mistake. He'd fled one beast to a castle full of monsters.

A cackling shriek came from somewhere nearby, and Bell pressed against the granite wall of the hallway he slunk in, his heart beating through his back and into the stone.

Great idea, Bellamy, he mocked. *One of your finest.*

Just like so many mistakes in his life, he hadn't meant to enter Spirefall. Two Noctis had dropped from the sky as he fled, and in true Bell fashion, he'd panicked. The only place to hide was through a half-fallen wall of the castle.

When he heard the Noctis laughing close by, he burrowed further into the black maze of stone, a stupid rabbit frightened into a trap.

By the time he'd lost the sounds of the Noctis, he couldn't find his way out.

Get out. You must get out.

Desperation was taking hold. Bolting from hallway to hallway, he slammed into walls and tumbled over broken piles of stone, skinning his knees and elbows. The coppery tang of his blood only intensified his terror.

Noctis could smell blood—he'd read that in one of his books. He'd also read about their depravity. How they fed off mortals' fear and made soups from their marrow.

For once, he wished he hadn't opened a book. Ignorance would have been appreciated on the subject of the monsters surrounding him. How did he ever feel sorry for these creatures?

More horrifying sounds filled the cold, empty corridors behind him. Crying. Wings shuffling. Cruel taunts. Bell fled up a flight of obsidian stairs and down another hallway, and another, reeling from flickering shadows and scuttling darkness.

And all the while, he seemed to be watching himself from above. The scared little rabbit. The cowardly prince.

Falling into a chamber, he spun around. As soon as his eyes adjusted to the flickering torchlight and he saw what hung from the ceiling, nausea tugged his stomach. Iron cages were suspended from the high ceiling, at least fifteen of them.

Each cage was filled to bursting with mortals.

Despite his fear, the overwhelming smell of unwashed bodies and waste, he drew closer. Filthy fingers clawed through the latticework of flattened iron bars.

"Please," someone whispered. "Help us."

Bell fell back from the sight as the cages began to rock with agitated people. The air filled with their pleas. On the other side of the room, a door slammed open.

Silence. He pressed close to the nearest cage, hardly breathing. The fingers were gone. The people inside the cages were dead quiet. The pure dread that bloated the air made it hard to breathe.

"Another peep," hissed a cruel male voice, "and I'll bleed you early."

As Bell pressed his face against the cage, terrified to move, he glimpsed the wide blue eyes of a girl peeking back at him. She couldn't be much older than nine or ten. Dirt smudged her gaunt cheeks, and greasy cornflower braids hung in ratty strips over what once must have been a white blouse but was now a stained rag.

Unblinking, she pressed a shaking finger to her lips.

Bell held her frightened gaze until the door on the opposite side of the chamber clicked shut.

Then he raced from that room, blinded by the rage and fear that coursed through him, more potent than the shame he felt at leaving those people.

He should have tried to help them. But how could he? Even if he set them free, they were too weak to run. They would've been punished, maybe worse.

Cowardly prince. Haven would be ashamed of you—if she was still alive.

Guilt coiled his gut, and he stumbled up more winding stairs. If he could only find another broken wall to escape. A door. Anything that would lead him to the outside.

The next level opened into a domed room lit by moonlight streaming through a line of open windows. The silvery light converged on a long glass case shaped like a coffin in the middle of the room.

Bell halted a few feet in. Something was different here. The air heavier, the magick stronger. But it was more than that. He suddenly had the feeling he wasn't alone, as if a presence lurked in the shadows.

And the room was cold as death, he realized, his breath curling out in smoky puffs.

An invisible talon scraped down his spine as something hidden prodded him.

Who comes here? a female voice whispered, the voice so real it took him a moment to realize it was inside his head.

I feel you, mortal boy, the voice purred. *Come closer, please, so I may look upon your face.*

Even though his brain screamed to run, to flee this place and never return, his body moved as if not his own. He took a step. Something crunched beneath his boots.

Bones.

Closer.

How had he not seen them before? Ivory bones scattered across the floor, so thick he couldn't avoid smashing them as he was drawn closer.

Closer, boy.

Until he could run a hand over the pale stone altar upon which the coffin lay.

Don't be afraid, the voice cooed. *Come closer.*

As if each of his bones were pulled along by invisible threads, he leaned over the curving glass to peer inside even as he cringed. Even as he fought to turn and run.

You smell like nectar. Like a fresh, fatted child. Your blood . . . your blood is so ripe.

Frost crackled over the glass. He wiped a swath clear with his hand, drawn to look at the horror he felt lurking below. His heart lashed his sternum like an animal trying to escape her. And somewhere deep down, he knew this only excited her . . .

Are you afraid, sweet, sweet boy?

A woman lay inside the scarlet-lined coffin, her hands crossed over her chest. He cleared more frost, revealing a neck of the palest moonstone and cruel lips of the darkest crimson. Her eyes—Goddess Above, her eyes were filmed with frost.

Yet, even in death, hatred burned beneath the layer of ice. And he could have sworn her lips were sneering.

"Ravenna," he whispered.

His spine went rigid, his muscles locking up as he tried to fight, to force his limbs to carry him away from this monster. But he was trapped in a spell, unable to move on his own.

Will you scream for me, Prince?

He grunted as he tried to rip his arms from the glass.

I'm so hungry! Open my lid, sweet boy. Come inside.

Eyes wide, he watched as his traitorous hand slipped open the clasp to the glass lid.

Good, sweet boy—

With a wild yell, Bell gathered every bit of energy he had and wrenched his body back. He fell on his ass in a pile of bones, scuttling along the floor. One of his feet kicked a skull, and it rolled across the stone tiles, thumping like the beat of his heart.

He jolted to his feet, tripping over more bones as he darted for the doors.

No! Ravenna screamed inside his head. *Come back, boy. I'm starving!*

At some point, the iron doors had shut behind him, and he ripped them open, staggering down the stairs.

He made it halfway through the corridor when two Noctis found him.

Bell froze, his terror locking up his limbs.

At the sight of him, the Noctis went rigid. They sniffed at the air. They were the hideous kind from before, their dark, membranous wings furled against their backs. Talons hung from the bottom of their wings, and wicked smiles curved across their bloodless faces.

They assessed him with hungry eyes.

"What are you doing here, mortal boy?" the hairless one asked, his tongue flicking over his bottom lip. He was gnarled and bent as if he'd been broken and put back together.

The second Noctis hissed at his friend. "The Night Princess can hear us."

Slowly, the gnarled Noctis tore his gaze from Bell to his friend. "Ravenna takes them all and gives us the scraps. But I'm tired of scraps."

The frenzied tone of his voice scraped under Bell's skin, burrowing until it became a vise of fear around his heart.

Finding his courage, he retreated a step—only to remember Ravenna was waiting down the other hall.

"Leave him, Malix," the second Noctis warned. "The Shade Queen—"

There was a whoosh of wings, and Malix lunged at his friend.

For a moment, shock rooted Bell in place as the two Noctis fought . . . over him. Snarls and whines echoed off the granite walls, the scrape of talons over stone like swords clashing.

The Noctis moved so fast they were but streams of dark smoke; a shred of wing flickering here, a flash of fangs there, blood splattering all around.

Blood. The bright red speckling the walls woke Bell from his stupor, and he bolted through the battling creatures and across the hall.

Breathing so loudly he could hear nothing else, he made it all the way down the winding set of stairs to the bottom when a dark shadow flickered above and landed with a loud thud in front of him.

Goddess Above, Bell prayed, lifting his eyes to Malix. *Give me the courage to fight.*

Blood slicked Malix's wings and chest—not his own, apparent by the vicious grin that slowly spread across his face. A spot of blood specked his jaw, and he wiped a crooked finger over the red stain.

"Now, Prince." He slipped his blood-tipped finger into his mouth and shuddered, pleasure sparking in his eyes. "Where were we?"

TWENTY-THREE

They were halfway through the mountain pass when Haven realized something was wrong with her magick. Her hand was out, the sphere lighting their way hovering obediently above it. But the circle of orange and blue fire was changing.

First, it was just a tiny movement. A shift in the ball's shape. The light from the magick seemed to bleed into the darkness and leave a trail of patterns. She blinked, and the light blinked back. She moved her hand, but the magickal orb stopped following.

It was alive, corporeal.

"What are you looking at?" Surai asked, narrowing her eyes at the orb.

Haven grinned, but her mouth felt strange. "My magick is playing tricks on me."

Surai looked from the sphere to her and back. "No, Haven, it's not."

But it was. It was laughing at her. There. A mouth, two mortal eyes. A nose. It was changing, flickering and morphing.

It was teasing her.

"Haven," someone called, but all Haven saw was magick and darkness. Where was she? "Haven?"

The magickal orb had grown—when had that happened? It had teeth now—sharp, gnashing teeth and wings and claws and . . . a wyvern.

"So big," she whispered as the wyvern grew and grew to fill the cavernous space. The massive head reared, nearly taking out a stalactite. A rider sat on its back.

She knew him; she feared him.

"Damius?" she rasped. Pain in her knees. Pain in her shoulder. Pain in her head. When had she fallen?

Warmth spread over her back. Someone was trying to lift her. "Haven? What's happening? Are you hurt?" The voice sounded familiar.

"Something's wrong," the female voice continued. Surai. Haven held onto the name of the speaker but it was floating away, her mind a thousand shards of glass she couldn't put back together.

Hands on her arm. Cool air over her shoulders as someone stripped her cloak and pulled down her tunic, exposing her collarbone.

A male voice said, "There, see those tiny pricks? They're already festering."

Another female voice. "The fairy must have bitten her before she awoke. She's hallucinating."

Haven tried to laugh, but suddenly she was above them in the cavern, floating. Her body lay below. The orb of magick hovered between her body and soul as if unsure where it belonged.

How strange she looked. So small and fragile. Her hair fanned around her, a wavy tapestry of molten gold tinged with blood. The Solis wore worried masks as they stared down at her.

A near imperceptible voice urged her to return to her body. What if she couldn't get back inside that unimpressive pile of flesh and bones down there?

Then again, why would she want to when she felt so light, so *free?* Her body was a prison, she realized. A prison of hunger and pain and sweat.

Why would she ever return?

Archeron was shaking her body, his lips sterner than usual. "Haven, come back!" He turned to Surai. "The magick in a fairy's bite is sometimes used by experienced lightcasters to soulwalk. But it's incredibly dangerous."

Surai's face went white. "She doesn't know how to re-enter her body."

Well that can't be good. But the thought drifted away, much like her spirit, drifting and drifting through the darkness, the scene below growing smaller and smaller until it was a star of light.

She was spinning. Untethered. The urge to remain with her flesh was gone.

So this was what it was like to soulwalk. Haven waved her arms, surprised by the faint outline of her body. She felt light, hollow. As if she could float anywhere in the world . . .

Anywhere? If that were true, where would she go? Hadn't Damius talked of visiting exotic lands across the sea just by imagining them?

Forgetting Surai's warning about coming back to her true body, she concentrated on the one person she wished to see more than anyone in the realm.

Bell.

The second she thought his name, the world around her

changed from darkness and shadows to a broken landscape of onyx mountains, their shattered peaks jagged against the gray, watery sky. Even without a true body, she felt the prickle of dark magick as she traveled through the heavens. It sizzled around her like poison.

A castle appeared, spires like thin daggers impaling the dirty clouds. Before she could study the structure, she was inside. Labyrinthine walls of onyx stone, carved from the mountains, floated past her on either side.

And then she saw him. Bell. He was at the bottom of a narrow stairway, dressed in an out-of-fashion waistcoat and pants, both soiled with dirt. Without the pomade he normally used in his hair, his curls were looser than usual and softer. Dirt smudged his nose, and his cheeks were pink from the sun.

He was okay—

But her cry of excitement died on her lips as she took in the terror on his face. His eyes stretched wide, nostrils flared, body crouched low. That's when she noticed the person blocking his way.

No, not a person. Noctis.

She took in the leathery wings, the talons. And blood . . . the Noctis was covered in it. A smile stretched the monster's face, but it wasn't a nice smile and only served to show off his curved incisors and malice-filled eyes.

Alarm surged through her at the way the Noctis was looking at Bell . . .

He's in trouble.

Touch him, and I'll tear you apart.

Without thinking, she launched herself at the Noctis. If she could take control of his body—if she could soulbind him—she could keep him from hurting Bell. But the second she touched his skin, a spark of dark magick sent her flying back.

Twice more she tried, and twice more she failed.

Remembering how Damius choked her while soulwalking, she reached out to hit the Noctis—but her fist went straight through his throat. She glanced at her arm and froze. It was fainter than before.

Something told her that was bad.

"Ah, finally catching on, Beastie?" purred a voice behind her.

She whipped around. Stolas was posted against a pillar watching her. Despite his casual appearance, his face was livid, his wings flared out on either side. The rings around his irises flickered, twin bonfires of gold.

"He's in trouble," she hissed.

"Not as much trouble as you, I'm afraid." His wings stretched wide as he stalked toward her. His body, she noticed, was not quite opaque, and she could make out the background shimmering behind him. The dark parts of his body—his horns and wings—had the consistency of shadows.

He was soulwalking too.

She glanced back at Bell. "Help him. Please."

"I'm afraid," Stolas said, grabbing her by the arms, "I'm only here to assist you."

She slid her gaze to his hand around her arm. Incorporeal or not, his grip was powerful. He was taking her away whether she wanted to go or not.

Desperate, she kicked and thrashed against the Shade Lord, trying to get to Bell. "I didn't ask for your assistance!"

Growling, he yanked her into his chest, vising his arms around her body.

In their incorporeal forms, his flesh felt different against hers. No longer cold, his dark magick seemed to caress her body, little sparks jumping between them. A tug of need between her dark magick and his formed low in her belly.

"You might not have asked," he snarled, "but I won't let one foolish, hotheaded decision derail everything."

"Why are you always intervening?" she shouted. Any other time, she would have been grateful for his intervention. But panic tore at her from the inside, a writhing and desperate need to help Bell.

"Why are you always trying your best to die?" he shot back.

She tried to kick back against Stolas, but he dodged her blow. "Why do you care?"

"Because I don't want you to perish, you stubborn idiot," he growled, his breath cold against her neck. "And if you stay a moment longer, your soul will evanesce. You're not powerful enough yet to soulwalk this far. Even if we leave now, there's no guarantee your body will accept you."

Twisting her head back to Bell, she said, "Then how do I help him?"

"You can't, I'm afraid." Was there a hint of sadness in his voice? "The frightened prince must help himself."

She could feel her spirit slipping away into nothing. Her arms were no longer visible, her body barely an outline of pulsing light guttering out. The thought of fading away was terrifying.

Nodding in defeat, she slumped into Stolas's arms, leaning against his massive frame for support. Incorporeal or not, tears pricked her eyes. Before he carried her away, she called out to Bell.

"Do something, Bell!" she urged, willing her voice to break the barrier between their realms. To reach him. "Fight back!"

Stolas soulwalked at frightening speeds. She hardly blinked, and they were in the clouds above Spirefall. From her vantage point, she made out the shadowy veins of dark magick streaming from the castle.

In her emotional state, the threads of dark magick looked like the black tentacles of some monster reaching for her and Stolas. She shut her eyes against the sight even as the darkness called to her to return.

Come back, it whispered. *Join us. This is where you belong.*

Tremors wracked her diaphanous form. She was inept. Broken and fading. A total failure.

Bell was so close, and she couldn't help him! She had made a vow, an oath to protect him, no matter the cost.

And she'd failed.

Unable to properly cry, she shuddered in the Lord of the Netherworld's grip. The pain was unbearable. She was vaguely aware of the comfort she found in his body protectively positioned around hers.

Of the way he cradled her . . .

The second Stolas felt her distress, he gripped her fading form even tighter—one arm firmly pressed into her waist, the other wrapped over her chest and shoulder—and brushed his lips over her ear. "He'll be okay, Haven. You'll be okay. Be strong."

He said her name with the reverence of a prayer, and something about his voice, unnaturally gentle, made her believe him.

Before she could respond, they were speeding through the heavens so fast that the tapestry of clouds and stars and sky wove into a beautiful tunnel much like the one her body waited in.

And then, Stolas was gone, and she was back in her body, wedged into a freezing prison of flesh and bones. She lay facing the ceiling. A coarse blanket weighed her down.

Beneath the woolen fabric, her body felt encased in ice, and she fought the instinct to leave the corporeal realm again. The draw of once again being weightless and unencumbered nearly impossible to resist.

"Thank the Goddess you've returned, Little Mortal," Surai soothed, rubbing Haven's arms to warm them up. "Your skin feels packed with snow and ice. Thank the Goddess you returned when you did . . ." She released a worried sigh and then redoubled her efforts at rubbing Haven's poor flesh. "No worries. You should thaw out soon enough."

The rest of her Solis friends peered down at her with relief and, in Archeron's case, a bit of anger. As if he suspected where she'd gone and the rash decisions she'd made.

Only, he was upside down . . .

Goddess Above, her head was in his lap.

His eyes softened to the color of sun-bleached moss as he muttered, "Welcome back."

Haven tried to speak but found her voice was gone. And then slick heat trailed down both her cheeks, and she realized she was crying. Sobbing uncontrollably as her friends watched with concerned faces.

Oily black clouds bloomed across her vision as if she were crying tears of ink, and she released herself to the darkness.

TWENTY-FOUR

Turns out crying makes people treat you differently. Ever since Haven broke down, her friends catered to her. She already felt weak and useless after soulwalking—and guilty for being the cause of them making camp beneath the mountains and wasting another day—but having her friends treat her like she might break was humiliating.

After Haven rejoined her body, she was in and out of consciousness. The few moments between sleep felt feverish and wrong as her soul rebelled against the constraints of her flesh.

And, as if punishing her for leaving, her entire body hurt. Her bones ached, and her skin felt swollen and tight. She burned with heat even as a bone-deep chill she couldn't shake wracked her in violent shivers.

In-between the flashes of darkness, she heard Archeron's stern voice as he commanded the others.

Surai scrounged everyone's packs for blankets to pile on top of Haven. The blankets were scratchy and smelled of horses and dirt, but they helped.

Bjorn somehow conjured kindling and dead leaves to make a marvelous fire. Luckily, there were cracks in the mountains leading above ground or the smoke would have killed them—something Rook pointed out before Archeron silenced her with an order to collect herbs for a healing tea.

Still struggling to get used to the feel of her tight, constraining body, Haven yearned to be outside in the fresh air. In the sporadic moments of lucidity, she concentrated on the shafts of moonlight piercing the cave. Held onto them like a drowning swimmer holding onto a rope.

When she finally came to fully, Archeron was by her side. Already having apologized twice for letting the fairy get close enough to bite her, he now took turns both frowning and fawning over her, adjusting her blankets and glaring at shadows.

Once, Rook made the mistake of approaching too quickly, and Haven thought Archeron would run the Sun Queen through with his sword.

Thank the Goddess he came to his senses and relaxed, and Rook managed to hand Haven the willow bark tea without losing an arm.

But it was simply all too much.

Throwing an arm out from the smothering nest of covers, Haven inched into a seated position, fighting off another round of darkness. The room spun. The shadows swam around her in predatory circles—

She clamped her eyes shut as bile lapped the back of her throat. Shadeling's shadow, she hadn't felt this ill since Bell and she snuck a cask of elderberry wine from the royal cellars.

Deliciously warm arms slipped behind her as Archeron slid her into his lap, draping her back over his chest and her head on his shoulder.

"I can—"

"No," he interrupted. The sensitive flesh around her stomach shivered as his arm curved protectively around her waist. "You can't. You just soulwalked for half an hour. If you're going to sit up, then I'm going to hold you so you don't pass out again and crack open your fragile mortal skull."

He was right; even with her eyes shut, the darkness behind her eyelids churned in dizzying circles.

She groaned. "Can you make the world stop moving, please?"

"Are you going to vomit?" he asked, and she caught the panic in his voice behind the casualness.

"No," she said, hoping it was true. She cringed as her voice clanged inside her skull. "I think there's a rule about vomiting on someone twice."

He chuckled.

"I'm surprised you didn't murder me then," she added. Despite her discomfort, the memory of puking on Archeron after what happened with the djinn made her smile. "You were so angry."

"You have that effect on people," he murmured.

"It's a gift."

Another chuckle. "No matter how angry you make me, I will never hurt you, Haven."

"Does that include my heart?"

He stiffened behind her, and she flicked her eyes open, wishing she could see his face. The fire was down to embers, but the faint light was enough to spark twin flames of agony behind her eyes.

She moaned.

His lips brushed over the curve of her ear. "If you need to purge your stomach, Haven, it's okay. I won't be mad."

Her throat clenched tight with emotion at the big, surly Archeron being so . . . kind. And protective. And just basically decent.

"I think I'll be okay."

She forced her vision to focus on a dark crevice in the distance until the room stopped moving. After a few minutes of steady breathing, she felt well enough to take in their surroundings.

The other Solis were about thirty feet away. Bjorn rested propped in a sitting position with his eyes open and hands relaxed atop his knees. Surai curled in a ball by the smoldering fire.

Some of her guilt ebbed as she realized they were sleeping—perhaps they needed the rest too.

Well, almost everyone.

A flicker in Haven's periphery drew her attention deeper into the tunnels where Rook's feline form chased rodents. She growled and pounced, her tail flicking proudly as she held something in her mouth by its long, scaly tail.

"Must be hard to sleep when you're nocturnal," Haven remarked, chuckling as Rook lunged and something squeaked. "So . . . how much sleep do you Solis require?"

"Not much." She felt him shrug behind her. "We could go on without resting if . . ."

As his words trailed away, another round of guilt hit her square in the chest. "Just a few more minutes," Haven promised, "and then I'll be well enough that we can leave."

"Leave? Are you mad? It's the middle of the night and you're injured . . . and still mortal, in case you forgot."

"I'm fine," she groaned. "And I'm aware of my mortal-ness; you don't have to keep reminding me."

"Apparently I do. You are disconcertingly breakable."

Rolling her eyes, she tried to get up, but he pinned her to him.

Her squirming and bucking made him redouble his efforts until she was basically encased in solid muscle.

"I hate this," she growled.

"Being cared for?"

"Oh, is that what you call this?"

His arms loosened a smidge, but he didn't release her. "I'm only trying to protect you—is that what you hate, Haven? Having someone stronger than you care enough to hold you when you're being irrational?"

She exhaled, the biting response in her head not quite making it to her lips. "I *hate* being useless. Every time you coddle me, I feel like I'm not doing enough. Like I'm dead weight. I can't help that I require six hours of sleep and sustenance to survive."

"Six?" he scoffed. "I saw you sleep nine full hours once."

Anger heated her cheeks. "You mean, when I was dying?"

"And I wouldn't have to coddle you," he added, ignoring her question, "if you weren't so stubborn. The fairy toxin should be out of your system, but soulwalking without the proper runes can be fatal. Your body thought you died, which is why it was so cold when you reentered. You need to rest and eat and remind your body you're still alive."

As much as it infuriated her to admit, he was right. Just the effort to pry herself from his arms had her head twirling again.

"I didn't ask to soulwalk," she said softly.

She was tired of arguing, but it hurt that he was blaming her for something she didn't purposefully do.

"But you could have stayed with your body and found a way back in," Archeron replied. His voice was gentler—he was trying. "Instead you took the sudden power and wielded it without a thought for the consequences. And that . . . scares me."

"I never said I went anywhere."

He released a dark chuckle. "You didn't have to, Haven. I know you." Shifting behind her, he released a long exhale. "Our magick has been around since the beginning of time. It is ancient and powerful and unforgiving, yet you toy with it like a shiny new dagger, a plaything you can control. Still, even with a thousand years of training, you will never learn to fully control it. The most you can hope for is keeping the magick from controlling you."

She hesitated, gauging his mood before saying, "If I had fleshrunes—"

"No. We're not discussing that." His voice held no room for argument.

Admitting defeat—for now—she relaxed against him. "So what, exactly, are we having for breakfast?"

She didn't bother hiding her disdainful tone as she glanced at Rook and the scaly, hairless creature hanging from her teeth. She was playing with the poor thing, tossing it into the air and catching it.

His chest shook against her back with barely suppressed laughter. "Bjorn's mystery stew, of course. Your favorite." A pause. She could tell he wanted to say something but didn't seem to know where to start. "Where did you soulwalk tonight, Haven?"

Her chest tightened as she remembered Bell, the fear transforming his kind face into someone almost unrecognizable.

"After you returned, you sobbed in your sleep," Archeron added, his voice gruff as if the memory bothered him. "You said the prince's name more than once."

"I saw him—Bell." Her body went taut against his as she waited for his disapproval, but he didn't react. "I didn't mean to soulwalk to him—or maybe I did—but I ended up in Spirefall. Bell was in trouble. He was so scared . . ." Her voice cracked, and Archeron pulled her tighter against him. "But I couldn't help him."

"So that is why the girl who never cries was bawling."

"I wasn't crying," she said before adding, "It doesn't count if I'm unconscious."

"Sometimes," he said carefully, "it's okay to cry. Just like sometimes those we love have to learn to fight their own battles. The prince is strong. Not like the king's strength which comes from knowing he has soldiers and allies and power at his disposal. Prince Bellamy's strength comes from within."

"I thought you didn't like him?"

Archeron stroked his thumb over the sharp curve of her hip bone, and she could tell without looking that he was smiling. "Perhaps the mortal race is growing on me."

Her heart thumped sideways in her chest, and she teased, "Why the sudden change of heart, Sun Lord?"

Archeron's laughter sounded more like a purr. Leaning forward, he kissed her jaw gently, purposefully.

Once.

Twice.

Thrice.

Each kiss caused her toes to curl and her breath to catch.

Dragging his lips up the side of her jaw, he nuzzled the shell of her ear, making her squirm. "Dear Little Mortal, do you really not know the answer to that?"

Haven did know—she was the reason. She had changed his mind. And, in a strange way, that was terrifying.

What if his feelings for her dulled? Or if she allowed herself to care for him and then he was hurt? Could she really handle the heartache?

Then there was the matter of Avaline. Caring for a man promised to another would be hard.

She shivered as Archeron's warm breath tickled her neck. Goddess Above, this could be a drug. Being in his arms. Feeling his breath on her skin and his body warm against hers.

Truth was, at least in this moment, she did want this. Him. All of it. The uncertainty along with the pleasure. And if risk and vulnerability were part of having Archeron, even for the brief time she might have left, then she would just have to be brave.

According to Bjorn, she would be dead soon anyway. What did she have to lose?

Feeling half-possessed, she found Archeron's massive hand. It was hovering over her hip, and she slid her fingers over his until they were entwined. He tensed behind her as she guided his hand to her belly.

In a brazen act unlike her, she tried to tug his hand lower, but he resisted.

"What about the others?" he murmured, his voice like sandpaper.

She ground against his body. "What about them?"

"Have I ever mentioned," he began, stroking her stomach, "our excellent hearing?"

"I can be quiet."

Her abs tensed as he drew slow, lazy circles around her navel with the pad of his thumb. Her head fell back onto his shoulder. The circles became wider.

His thumb brushed beneath her waistband and she gasped. Loud.

"Liar." The puffed-up bastard laughed. "You're a mortal, and mortals have no concept of silence."

She could feel his pleasure as she settled further into his chest, scooting her hips back until there was no space between them. One large, capable hand stroked the sensitive inner portion of her left thigh, producing trails of fire that pierced the leather of her pants.

The other began to map out her flesh. Her stomach, her hips.

Slowly—so Nether-frigging slowly—his hand dipped lower.

At the same time, his mouth began exploring the tender spot where her neck met her collarbone. In response, she arched her back, a sigh tumbling from her lips.

Goddess Above and everything holy, this felt amazing. Archeron's body was hard as stone, the feel of his muscles and power surrounding her intoxicating. His heart beat loud and fast against her back, his flesh hot to the touch.

How did she ever hate him?

"Where is this on your courtship timeline?" she whispered. The confident, sultry voice seemed to come from someone else.

Growling, his hand slipped lower down her middle while the one on her thigh traveled up to her jaw. She tried to nip his thumb as it brushed her lips.

Tsking, he caught her chin, holding it hostage while his thumb explored her lower lip. "I was supposed to kiss you."

"Hmm. How's that working for you?"

"I am learning there are other places just as pleasurable as your lips."

"Like where?" she teased. She writhed against him, one arm reaching back to touch his face, the other coaxing his hand lower, lower, lower—

His fingers found the inside of her thigh. She pressed into his hand as he stroked everywhere but *there*, toying with her.

And then his thumb flicked out and found her wetness, and it was his turn to be loud, his growl echoing off the cave walls.

She hardly heard it. She was drunk with desire, every ounce of focus bound to the aching need between her thighs. She was hyperaware of his body against hers, the feel of him wanting her.

Her mind went to earlier—him holding her, protecting her, their bodies sizzling with magick, the sky wrapped around them, soaring; beautiful, feathery wings spread wide . . .

"Stol—" The second the word half-spilled from her lips, she froze in mortification. So did Archeron.

No. No. No! I didn't just almost scream the Lord of the Netherworld's name.

But she had. Pretending did nothing to hide the horrifying reality.

Without a word, Archeron slid his hand back to rest around her waist. The silence stretched out awkwardly.

"What did you say?" he asked, his voice quiet.

She searched his tone for anger as her belly flinched beneath his palms. Her thoughts were a whirlwind of embarrassment and shame.

What just happened? She felt possessed, unhinged. How did her lips say *his* name? Why did he pop into her head like some deranged demon?

Why? Why? *Why?*

Her pulse jumped at her wrist. She brought a hand to her throat, willing air into her lungs. This wasn't happening. It felt like a betrayal of the worst kind.

"I . . ." Words failed her.

It made no sense. She had never thought of Stolas that way. How could she?

"Haven," Archeron said, his voice tight but not unkind. "It's okay if you want to stop."

Stop?

Oh—*oh.*

He thought she'd blurted 'stop.' Not Stolas. Not the name of the most hated Noctis in the realm.

Relief and frustration poured through her. Stopping was the last thing in the world she wanted to do, but it was better than admitting she'd literally almost said the name of his enemy during an incredibly intimate moment.

Had the Shade Lord cast some sort of spell on her? Goddess knew he had no love for Archeron, and she could see Stolas using magick to make her say his name simply because he was bored.

If that were true, she would murder him. *Murder him.* With her own bare hands.

Taking her silence for agreement, Archeron murmured, "Sleep, Little Mortal."

His voice was gentle, lulling. No animosity or anger at her supposed cold feet.

Shadeling's shadow, when had he become so good?

She shook her head. She wasn't tired—or she didn't feel tired. Not until he began stroking her softly, affectionately. Strong fingers caressing her arms, her back—movements meant to ease her into the dream world.

"I'm not a . . . baby you can just rock . . . to sleep," she muttered through a traitorous yawn.

"Aren't you?" he teased. "Mortals seem to fall asleep anywhere. Close your eyes and try."

Before she knew it, she tumbled into a dreamless rest without nightmares or disturbances. And when she awoke countless hours later to the fire burned down to dim embers, she was disappointed.

Stolas hadn't appeared.

TWENTY-FIVE

She awoke at dusk. Instead of the silver trickle of moonlight, dirty gray sunlight lit the cave. Archeron was already up with the others, packing their camp and preparing for the day.

Just watching him sent a pang of guilt into her belly. The night before seemed like a dream—a lovely dream, right up until she nearly called Stolas's name.

Thank the Goddess, Archeron and the others left to scout the cave exit, giving Haven time to gather her thoughts.

After a few languid stretches, she joined Surai on a boulder near the fire. Surai handed her a rodent-sized skewer of meat with a burnt tail sticking straight out. Haven nearly gagged as the tail broke off in her lap.

"I don't think I can," Haven said, holding the creature as far out from her face as possible.

Surai cut her lavender eyes at Haven. "Suddenly you're picky?"

"It has a . . . tail."

"Most things we eat do. And ears. Eyes. A nose." Surai grinned. "The tail is actually quite delicious."

Haven was unconvinced as she turned the skewer over in her hands.

"But if you do not eat it," Surai pointed out, not unkindly, "will you not be hungry later?"

Ah, the pitfalls of being a mortal. From what Haven understood from her time with the Solis, food was needed for sustenance—but not at quite the same desperate rate as mortals. They could easily go a few days without eating much besides a few blades of grass and a couple of berries.

Squeezing her eyes shut, Haven forced herself to put down a few bites. A mistake. The greasy rodent sat heavy in her stomach, and soon her belly churned.

Or perhaps it was the memory of last night.

"Surai," Haven said, tossing the rest of her skewer on the ground. "Can I get your advice?"

Surai lifted a curious eyebrow. "Of course."

"After my soulwalking adventure last night, while you and Bjorn slept, Archeron and I . . . were intimate."

Surai's other eyebrow joined the first, a little smile curving her mouth.

"And it was amazing." A blush warmed her skin, and she rubbed her cheeks.

Surai groaned. "Do not tell Archeron that, or his head will grow even bigger."

Haven chuckled, settling closer on the rock to Surai. "Everything was going well, when I might have . . . called out a name. And not Archeron's."

Surprise widened Surai's eyes as she exclaimed, "Might have? You either did or you didn't. And considering I did not awaken last night to Archeron trashing the place, you either did not, or he did not hear you."

Haven ground her knuckle into her thigh. "I managed to stop halfway through, and he thought I said something else."

Surai let out a relieved sigh. "Thank the Goddess for that small miracle. Archeron can be very understanding with those he loves. But in the middle of a new courtship, a Solis male can be very territorial."

"I feel like the worst mortal in the realm." Haven kicked sand into the fire. "The thing is, I don't know why I said the other name. I don't like this other male. In fact, I can't stand him."

Surai scoffed, not even bothering to hide her skepticism. "I don't know how things work in the mortal realm, but you don't call out another male's name unless you feel something for him." A wicked grin spread across her face. "You don't need to like someone to want to sleep with them."

The statement felt like a slap in the face. If Surai knew the male Haven spoke about was the Lord of the Netherworld . . .

"I don't," Haven insisted. "That's why it's weird."

Surai's lips puckered as she studied Haven for a breath, then she tossed her skewer—picked clean—into the fire. "Do you know, the Solis believe there are two soulmates for everyone? One to teach you how to be strong. And one to teach you how to love. Most of us only find one soulmate . . . some of us never find any. But finding both . . ."

"That's not what this is," Haven said, shaking her head for emphasis. "And I promise, if you knew who he was, you wouldn't even mention that possibility."

Surai chuckled. "Haven, I hated Rook when I first met her. Thought she was a stuck-up princess with entitlement issues and a bad attitude. We could hardly stand to be in the same room.

I said as much to Archeron, and he laughed in my face. He bet we'd be together in a week."

"And?" Haven said as she stood and stretched her legs.

"And I lost twenty runestones to him. An entire year's soldier's wages. Want to guess what our engagement present was?"

"Twenty runestones?"

"The exact same ones. Plus, a fancy sword I hate—but don't tell Archeron." Surai joined Haven by the fire, warming her hands. "Love doesn't follow our rules."

When Archeron appeared, Haven left the fire to join him. He tossed Haven her pack and gave her a smile that didn't quite reach his eyes. Before she could say anything, he turned and prowled from the cave.

Perhaps he wasn't as fine with her stopping last night as he had put on.

She glanced back at Surai, who was watching the interaction with a grin and her usual sharp curiosity. Haven answered her smile with a tight frown, relieved she didn't have to continue their conversation.

As much as she appreciated Surai's advice, there was no way in the Netherworld it applied to her and Stolas. More like she'd still been groggy and hallucinating from the fairy's toxin and soulwalking, and she accidentally called his name.

She shook her head as she followed the others, pushing the thought away. There was no point whatsoever in worrying over it any longer because it would never happen again.

Ever.

TWENTY-SIX

Outside the cave, the sky was misty and flat and dead. Haven tightened her cloak against the light drizzle and then shoved another branch out of the way, muttering curses beneath her breath.

Halfway through the morning, the rain gave way to bitter cold. But it wasn't a normal chill. It had a presence to it, seeping deep down into her flesh and marrow, invading her slowly.

In a word, the chill felt malignant. And every step she traveled closer to the source of dark magick, the louder the sinister voice inside her head grew.

That's it, the voice whispered. *Do you feel me inside you? Stirring through the hollow of your lovely mortal bones. Growing with power.*

Wiping back the damp, half-frozen hair from her eyes, she shoved the voice from her thoughts—obviously a symptom of her fatigue—and concentrated on her surroundings.

This land wasn't like the lush forests they had hacked through or even the desert Bane. It was sparse, inanimate. Devoid of greenery or life. Dead grass and spindly black trees scaled the terrain, broken with granite mountains that scraped the corpse-gray sky.

Once they were far from the shelter of the mountain face, a constant wind howled through the broken land as if the souls of all who perished here were warning them away.

She could almost see the dark tentacles of magick from Spirefall—wicked threads of ancient power slithering through the rocks, the black streams and silent forests, veins of evil poisoning the land.

Her companions felt the same.

Their worried gazes flitted to the black mist swirling around the Shadow Lands to the north. Surai walked at Bjorn's elbow, ready to guide him over the steep rocks.

Rook prowled along the slope beside her mate. A golden flash flickering between boulders, the magnificent cat snarled at every shadow, her long, sleek tail whipping back and forth in agitation.

All at once, Rook froze. Her hackles raised as she scanned the horizon.

The landscape ahead was pocked with fragmented rocks and steep cliffs, the hard, grass-swept ground riddled with bones. An army of bones, broken and scattered over miles.

Some still wore the armor with the banner from whatever kingdom they'd hailed, and Haven found herself cataloguing the ones she recognized until the act depressed her.

If entire armies had made it this far only to perish, how would they succeed?

As soon as the thought materialized, she buried it with all of the other doubts. Such talk wouldn't win back Bell.

Surai took Bjorn's hand, guiding him around a sharp boulder.

"How much farther, Bjorn?"

Frowning, he said, "It should be here, hidden by the mountains."

"And the Basilisk?" Haven asked, catching up with them.

His eyebrows gathered. "Are you sure that's what the fairy said?"

"Yes. Positive. But only the Goddess knows if we can trust her."

"Oh, we certainly can't," Archeron added, joining them.

He had a blade of grass between his teeth and his tunic unbuttoned so that his polished chest showed, the muscles below practically rippling. Her gaze was drawn to the lips around the grass, soft and bowed at the top.

What would it have felt like to kiss him last night?

She gasped as she remembered his body, his power, the way it felt pressed against those hard muscles . . .

After that, his cold demeanor today felt like a knife to the abdomen.

"Maybe you shouldn't be so skeptical, Sun Lord," Haven replied, wiping sweat from her brow despite the cold. "Maybe you should trust people every once in a while."

He flashed her a sanguine smile that sent heat barreling into her toes. "Testy. Methinks you need more sleep, Mortal. And just so you know, I would have kissed you last night—if you hadn't gotten cold feet."

"You read my thoughts?" she hissed.

"Do my muscles really . . . ripple?" His voice was mocking and hard. Why was he being such a *droob?*

She growled and reached for the hilt of her sword. The others casually scattered, pretending they weren't eavesdropping as they traveled ahead.

"Whoa, don't be angry," he said, lifting his hands in pretend fear. Then, he did that trick where he was suddenly closer without seeming to move. He leaned in, his golden hair slipping over one shoulder, and pinned her against the boulder. "Perhaps I should kiss you right here."

His arrogance grated on her. "What is your deal?"

"Where would you like me to kiss you, Haven?"

"Maybe I don't want to kiss you anymore," she snarled, his flippant attitude after last night's sweetness making her want to stab him.

An emotion close to pain flickered over Archeron's face.

And then, it hit her. He was being a total Nether-frigging *drooh* because he wanted her to admit she didn't want to be with him. Because what he assumed was her sudden rejection of him last night had affected him more than she thought possible.

"Then what is it that you *do* want, Haven? You changed your mind last night; now you say you don't want to kiss me . . ." He dragged a hand through his long hair, darkened by the drizzle to the color of wheat. "Perhaps hearing what I told Mossbark scared you. Perhaps you didn't quite know how broken I am, and now . . . I will not force you into something you do not want."

"Not fair," she said. "You don't get to goad me into being a jerk to validate your suspicions. That's not how this works."

"Then how does this work?"

"Just ask me."

Releasing her arms, he braced a hand on either side of her head. His voice was softer, gentler as he said, "What do you want, Haven Ashwood?"

A vulnerable half-smile tugged at his lips, and a tentative, fragile hope flickered inside his emerald green eyes.

"You know what I want." The anger was gone from her voice.

"Haven," he said carefully, his breath caressing her lips. "You have every right to stop at any point when we are together." His gaze fell to her lips. "But I do need to know this is what you want. That *I* am what you want."

Never in her life would she have imagined someone like Archeron would feel uncertainty when it came to love. The revelation took some of her assumptions about him and shattered them.

She reached up and took hold of his chin, palming the light golden stubble along his flesh, relishing the scratchiness beneath her fingers. "I told you already."

"No, you didn't say it." He closed the few inches left between them, his lips brushing hers. "I need you to say it."

The others were watching them while pretending not to, and Haven shifted beneath his weight. His magick, his flesh—both called to her.

"Do you, Haven Ashwood, want to be with me?"

"Yes." Her voice shook as she made her declaration. "I do. Of course I do. I want every part of you."

"Every part?" His pupils flared, and he dropped his hands to cup her rear.

She nodded, her throat tight. "All of them. Even the undesirable parts."

He gave her a wicked grin. "I've been told *all* my parts are desirable."

Well, it didn't take long to revert back to his confident self. His arrogance caused her teeth to grind. "And, when I *don't* want to kill you, which isn't all that often, I catch myself thinking about you."

His eyebrows lifted with interest. "What type of thoughts, exactly?"

She grinned, which was odd since she felt close to passing out. Her head spun; her heart beat unevenly.

"What you'd taste like," she breathed. *What was she saying?* "What our flesh would feel like pressed together without a stitch of clothing between us."

She felt a shudder of both surprise and desire move through him.

But she wasn't done shocking him as she whispered, "What you'd feel like inside me."

His intense stare was almost predatory. Surai yelled a crass insult, something about screwing later, but Archeron didn't seem to hear his friend.

"And . . ." he rasped. "How are you feeling right now?"

She laughed. "Leaning toward murderous."

Archeron ran the pad of his thumb over his bottom lip as if assessing the fine merits of his mouth, the peacock. "A . . . shame."

A growl broke the spell between them. Haven followed the sound to the large cat stalking across the knoll their way. Rook let out another impatient growl and butted her head into Archeron's thigh, hard.

"Ow," he said, rubbing the spot for emphasis as Rook cast her feline stare at Haven.

Even in animal form, her face was regal. A pattern of black spots formed a mask around her eyes, fringed with fine black eyelashes and lined with a thick sweep of kohl.

Without thinking, Haven reached out to stroke the black tuft ridging a perfectly triangular ear. Rook hissed in response, baring a mouth full of fangs.

"Someone's in a mood," Archeron remarked.

Her amber eyes were the only part of her now that resembled her Solis body. They slid from Archeron to Haven, glittering with an unmistakable order: *Enough chit-chat, now move your asses.*

She nipped at Archeron's hand to drive the point home and

then bounded off to the group, who were laughing hysterically.

Surai caught Haven's eye and made a vulgar gesture.

Embarrassed, Haven nudged Archeron away as she moved to join them, annoyed at how she barely made him budge. She could feel his gaze on her back as she did.

How was it possible to want to both strangle and kiss someone?

He chuckled behind her. *Stop soulreading my thoughts,* she growled back at him before remembering the trick *someone* had taught her for that.

Make me.

Grinning, she accepted the challenge. The second she felt him lazily stroke her mind with his, she thought the word *foetor.*

A few seconds passed . . .

When she turned around, his face was the color of old bone, and he looked moments from puking, his hand balled into a fist and pressed into his stomach.

"Feeling okay, Sun Lord?" she teased, walking backward. Stolas's recommendation to keep her distance was heavy in her mind.

With a grimace, he waved her off. A moment later, he slapped a hand over his pretty little mouth.

"Where did you learn that dirty trick?" he groaned.

She cast a smug look back. "Wouldn't you like to know?"

Thanks to Stolas, it would probably be awhile before he tried to soulread her again.

TWENTY-SEVEN

"There," Bjorn called, pointing toward a gully. "The only Basilisk I know of would be around that stream. The selkies let him have it."

The slash of pine and redwoods were the only green for miles around. A stream sparkled between flashes of leaves.

As soon as they neared the water, Haven felt the shift from dark magick to light, the air warming and becoming sticky. She breathed in the rich scent of life—earth and trees and water—as birdsong and the sluggish river's low *burble* filled the air.

"Selkie territory," Bjorn explained. "Similar to the fairies, they also use light magick and are protected from the Shade Queen by the same bargain."

"They deliver mortals to her?" Haven asked, shivering at the thought.

A dark smile lit his face. "The ones they don't eat, yes."

"Why? What does the Shade Queen want with mortals?"

Surai looked into the forest beyond, lips pulled into a grim line.

Bjorn glanced at her with eyes that seemed to pierce her soul. "The Noctis feed off your magick until you're a shell of flesh and bone, and then Morgryth binds you to her will. Every mortal who entered these lands and did not die is hers to do with as she pleases."

Haven felt the blood drain from her face, and she studied the darkness churning the sky to the north. "But why?"

Surai released a ragged breath, her dark braid slipping over her shoulder. "We think she's building an army."

"But then." Haven shuddered. "All those mortals who marched into the Ruinlands . . ."

"Like an arachnid," Bjorn whispered as if Morgryth could hear them, "she drew the mortal armies to her web with the promise of a wish to whoever breaks the Curse, knowing it was near impossible to do. I've seen the legions of undead mortals she keeps beneath Spirefall, have heard their screams of torment."

"Who daresss crosss here?" a male voice hissed from somewhere high up in the trees.

Metal scraped as the Solis drew their swords, and Haven retrieved her bow and nocked an arrow, pointing it at the treetops.

"Show yourself, Basilisk," Archeron shouted.

"Sss." The hissing seemed to come from everywhere, and Haven swung her bow in a circle, searching the branches.

A pop of orange caught her eye, and she trained the tip of her arrow over the bright shape as the basilisk slithered down the trunk and onto a lower branch.

Haven's mouth parted as she took in the creature. Except for his yellow eyes and black, forked tongue, his top half was the image of a man. But the similarities ended at his waist, gleaming orange and brown scales forming a thick serpentine body twice as long as the torso that ended in a sharp snake-like tip.

Haven stepped forward, fighting to hide her revulsion as the basilisk dropped low and flicked its long tongue over her face.

"*Sss*illy mortal," the Basilisk hissed, "you *sss*hould not be here."

The basilisk's slashed pupils focused above her head, and she felt Archeron's body draw up behind her.

A serpentine smile flashed the basilisk's finger-length fangs. "And a *Sss*un Lord too. How *sss*erendipitous."

"Enough talk," Archeron snarled. "We were told to find you."

"By the fairy, Mossbark," Haven added.

The basilisk's tail whipped side to side as he studied them. "Mo*sss*bark? How i*sss sss*he?"

Haven dropped her bow an inch. "Probably dead."

"Ssshame for you," the basilisk said as he turned and began to slither away. "Her death endsss the favor I owe her."

"Wait!" Haven put up a hand. "Please. We are here to break the Curse, and—"

The basilisk flipped back around. "I know why you're here, mortal girl. Every mortal to ever crossss these landsss wantsss the sssame thing. They sssee richesss insssstead of death—that is their missstake."

"Then help us. Or do you want to live under the selkie's rule, with only this tiny little stream?"

"Thisss tiny little ssstream isss more than the mortalsss gave me."

"Yes, and that will change. I can give you the same promise I made the fairy. Help us, and the mortal Prince of Penryth will guarantee you land."

"*Sss*." The basilisk's tongue flicked the air as if he could taste the truth of her statement. "And who are you to make sssuch promisssesss, girl?"

Haven stripped back her hood, for once unembarrassed by her odd colored hair. "I am Prince Bellamy of Penryth's Royal Guard and friend, and I speak for him."

"Even if what you sssay isss true," the basilisk said, "why would I go againssst the Ssshade Queen?"

"You have light magick, right? What do you think will happen when the Shade Queen runs out of mortals to drain of power, and all the Solis are across the sea?"

Archeron pressed closer as the basilisk leaned down to meet her gaze, his head tilted to the side. "When the sssun touchesss the horizon at dusssk, the Ssselkies go into a docile trance. That isss your bessst time to have the pretty Sssun Lord here"—he nodded to Archeron—"dissstract them while you take a ssscale. Once the sun goes down, the trance is broken, and they will kill him and you."

"Thank . . ."

But the basilisk was already slithering away into the trees. Before she could blink, he was gone, leaving only the rustling of leaves to mark his ever being there in the first place.

Haven turned to Archeron and grinned. "Time to charm some bloodthirsty selkies, Sun Lord. Let's see if they find all your parts as desirable as you claim."

TWENTY-EIGHT

The selkies' cove was a jade pool nestled between three sheer cliffs and the forest, half of the depthless water shaded by overhanging oaks and elms. They waited behind the cover of trees, occasionally hacking at the thorny vines that tugged at their clothes and flesh.

"This is a horrible idea," Archeron added, not for the first time.

"I think it's a wonderful idea," Rook said, clapping Archeron on the shoulder. She had changed back to her human form not long ago. "We finally found a use for your beautiful face."

Archeron grumbled beneath his breath, staring sulkily at the still waters. "I'm sure the selkies will find it delicious."

"Scared of a few fish, Sun Lord?" Rook teased.

Haven bit down a laugh as Archeron glowered. "Fish don't scrape a man's flesh from the bone with their teeth."

"True. But it's Haven, not you, entering the water."

They had all decided earlier that Haven's dark magick would

be less noticeable to the Shade Queen if she had to use it in the water. Hopefully, she would slip in and out unnoticed.

Still, dread curdled in her gut as she glanced over the rippling surface of the water. A lone selkie sunned itself across the reservoir, a squirming eel wrapped around her webbed fingers as it tried to escape. The fading light caught in the selkie's orange and pink scales and vibrant fins.

As the selkie opened her mouth—revealing rows full of jagged teeth—and bit off the squirming eel's head, Haven felt the first stirrings of true panic.

Bjorn leaned against a young elm, and Haven touched his shoulder. "Is this, you know?"

Bjorn arched an eyebrow. "Where you die?"

She dug the toe of her boot into the mossy ground. "Yes."

"I cannot—"

"I know, I know." She stole a ragged breath, her mouth suddenly dry. "It's just so . . . deep."

"Fathomless, actually," Bjorn corrected. "It's said beneath these eerie waters are passages that lead to every body of water in the realm."

"At least say they'll drown me first before eating me."

Bjorn's lips twisted into a dark smile. "Will that make this any easier?"

She flicked up her eyebrows. "Just . . . lie to me or something."

"If you are lucky, the water will take you first."

"Wonderful. You're a true friend." She glanced down at the rune Bjorn had carved into the flesh of her arm. "You're sure this lets me breathe under water?"

Bjorn nodded. "Yes. But your dark magick is healing the mark faster than I predicted. We must hurry."

He was right. Already, the edges of the rune were scarring

over and closing. If they weren't running out of time, she would have been fascinated by her mending flesh and the questions it brought.

Like, did that mean wounds made by dark magick would also heal?

But none of that mattered now—especially if this were her last few minutes alive.

Way to be optimistic, Ashwood.

Her focus skipped to the patches of sky between the trees. Surai was up there somewhere. The second the sun began to set, she would alert them.

From there, they would have maybe five minutes.

She removed her boots and tunic, and they began to pick their way closer to the murky water in preparation. The thin undershirt she wore wasn't enough to brace against the light chill in the air, and gooseflesh cropped over her exposed flesh.

Not even ten feet from the shore, a hand ran down her arm and clasped her elbow. The gesture was intimate enough that she knew it was Archeron before she turned.

The intense look on his face froze the breath in her chest.

"I can still go in your place," he said, his voice a low rumble.

"But I'm not as pretty as you," she teased, forcing the nerves from her voice. "I could strip naked, and the selkies wouldn't even blink."

He opened his mouth to say something naughty—considering the sparkle in his eyes and the way he slid his gaze over her skimpy top—then seemed to think better of it. "Rook can go. She's a strong swimmer."

Haven shook her head. "If something happened to her . . . I can't. Surai is my friend and Rook her mate."

"And you are my . . ." He raked a hand through his golden

hair, glaring at her as if it was her fault he couldn't find the word.

Truth was, there wasn't a term for what they were. They weren't betrothed. They weren't even lovers . . . yet.

"I thought we agreed using light magick would call too much attention from the Shade Queen?" she reminded him gently. "Last I checked, I'm the only one with dark magick. Besides, I'm already going to die, right? What does it matter if it's now or in Spirefall?"

A frown twitched his lips as he held out a small piece of driftwood. "Put this in your pocket."

Confused, she eyed the faded wood with distrust. "Why?"

"If something goes wrong in the water and you need help, release the wood, and it will float to the surface."

"And, what?" She turned to leave. "You'll jump in to save me?"

Using gentle pressure on her elbow, he swung her to face him. "I said I wouldn't let you die, Haven. Did you think I was joking?"

"And if I survive this task?" she asked in a breathless voice. "Will you kiss me then?"

A feline smile captured his lips. "Yes, Little Mortal. I've already promised as much . . . although, I didn't specify as to where."

Her toes curled into her boots. *Goddess help me.*

Wings fluttering through the leaves called her attention to the treetops. Before she could respond to the cheeky Sun Lord, Surai landed on the nearest branch as dappled light slipped through the canopy of trees, highlighting the brilliant indigo inside her dark feathers.

The signal.

Without a word, Archeron pushed the wood into her open hand and glided across the flat gray rock formation leading to the water.

He strolled casually with his hands in his pockets, limbs loose as if he had no idea what lurked in the water below, even as dark heads began to bob to the surface of the water to watch him. The selkies drew closer as he sat on the edge of the rocks, stretching out the length of his impressive torso.

"Show off," Haven murmured, watching as slowly, deliberately, he tugged his tunic over his head, revealing chiseled muscles and a lithe waist.

The last meager bit of tangerine sunlight shone inside the silver runemarks that wound over his smooth flesh as he lifted his hands behind his head. Cutting his eyes to her, he winked, and she tore her gaze away.

Pompous pretty boy. I hope they eat him.

More sleek heads appeared, drawing closer. The water around him thronged with selkies, and she readied her mind for what was to come.

It was time.

Her heart was in her throat as she skirted around the edge of the trees and slipped into the lukewarm water, a stagnant stench rising to meet her.

The scale of a selkie burnished gold, she repeated, reminding herself what she was doing.

But the words failed to calm her nerves.

For a moment, she fought going under. But there was no time to be afraid, so she forced herself to release all of the air in her lungs and sink.

Sound became muffled. The water was murky, but she could see four or five feet ahead. Below, the water seemed to go on forever, and she buried the panic that clawed at her chest as she sank deeper still. Down, down into those dirty depths, into an unwelcoming place of water and death.

Despite the tingling rune on her arm, instinct made her hold her breath until her lungs burned and she gulped deep lungfuls of water.

She expected to cough . . . but the rune worked.

Her body relaxed as the oxygen reached her bloodstream, and after a few failed gags, she was breathing water as if it were air. Movement drew her eyes to the rocks where Archeron was putting on his show. She swam toward the chaos of thrashing selkies, looking for the bright colors of their tails.

That's right. Watch the swollen-headed peacock.

The plan was simple. Pluck a gold scale from a selkie and get the Netherworld out of the water before the sun fully set and the selkies noticed her.

Silver and cobalt flashed to her right.

She froze in the water below, mesmerized by the beautiful metallic colors of the selkie tail, the translucent coral and silver fin undulating in the water like threads of the finest silk.

More selkie bodies flashed over Haven's head, a tapestry of colors drawn to Archeron, weaving the most beautiful canvas of death.

Haven could almost feel their excitement over their gorgeous prize. *Been there,* she thought, remembering last night.

If beauty could be used as a weapon, Archeron's was like the dagger she stole—and lost—from Stolas. The blade of which wasn't felt until after one lay dying from its bite.

The water churned with selkies clawing and fighting one another, drawing her attention back to the mass of creatures as each one struggled for the best view of Archeron.

He must be putting on quite the show.

Haven was terrified the creatures could hear the frantic pounding of her heart as she swam closer. Her gaze flitted over the metallic flesh, desperately searching for a golden scale amidst every color but gold, it seemed.

You're running out of time, Ashwood.

If only the selkies would stop moving long enough for her to find the right color. Their quick, darting movements reminded Haven of the fat fish in the ponds back at Penryth, the way they became frenzied by a few crumbs dropped into the water.

She kicked and clawed her way closer still, wishing she'd swam more at Penryth as her arms began to tire.

And then, in the midst of crimson and yellow and azure, a pop of gold flashed so fast she thought she made it up.

Slick, meaty tails beat against her shoulders and cheeks as she squirmed between them, praying to the Goddess the creatures were too captivated by the pretty Sun Lord to look beneath the water's surface. Webbed claws scraped down her side.

Haven swallowed down a cry as a ribbon of her blood spread in the water.

Kicking free from the chaos, she spied the selkie with the golden scales a little way off from the group. The few bits of gold on her tail contrasted against the teal and silver scales, and Haven slowly drew closer.

That's when she noticed the shafts of sunlight piercing the water were gone, the pool darkening by the second. She needed to grab the scale and get out of the water.

Four feet separated her from the selkie with the golden scale, and she gave one hard kick to close the distance, reaching for a smooth oval of gold just as the water went almost completely dark.

Holding her breath, she pinched the scale and pulled. It released easily, and after a quick glance to ensure it was the right one, she stuffed the tiny disc into her pocket and turned, kicking furiously away.

She swam through the murky water, her heart a wild drumbeat, heading for the direction she came from. Behind her, the water churned as the selkies grew savage again.

Soon, the darkness filled with the sounds of the creatures fighting.

Was she close? A wave of panic crashed over her as she realized she wasn't sure which way was up and which was down. What if she was swimming deeper into the abyss?

Without a second thought, she drew an orb of light magick and released it, willing it to float. As it traced a bright path straight up to the surface, relief surged over her. She was going in the right direction.

The light was still bright enough to illuminate five feet all around her, and a sudden shadow below caught her eye. She glanced down—

All-black eyes gleamed at her above razor-sharp rows of teeth. Then the selkie grabbed her leg and yanked her down.

Down, down, down.

Haven kicked and punched the slippery creature, but the selkie didn't budge except to wrap tighter around her thigh. A flash, and another selkie had her other leg and was dragging her deeper.

Sharp claws came from everywhere. Fingers wrapped around her arms and hair.

Then Haven's rune stopped tingling and the next breath she took burned like liquid fire.

She was going to drown.

TWENTY-NINE

Haven always assumed drowning would be painless, but she was wrong. Burning glass shoved into her lungs and chest, searing and heavy as she sank down into the selkies' cove. Panic wound round her ribs and lodged beneath her sternum, heavy and suffocating and so real it could be a living thing.

In shock, her first thought was that Bjorn should have warned her, damn his stupid seer laws. Then darkness and desperation clawed at her mind, and she understood she was dying.

Fight back!

Again, she hit the selkie on her leg.

Again, the creature wrapped tighter.

Two more slithering females locked onto her arms. She couldn't move. Couldn't see.

Use magick.

As soon as the thought came, her hand, pinned at her side, became warm with a spark of magic, illuminating the bizarre creatures trying to kill her.

She waited until the power raged up her arm and then released it. The selkies shrieked as her magick sent them sprawling back, stunned. Two kicks. That's all she got before four more selkies captured her once again.

Haven pulsed another flash of power, sending the new selkies flying into the depths, but more took their place. This time, countless bodies wrapped around her. Slick, meaty flesh pummeling her as they shoved her deeper to her death.

Her ears popped.

Her lungs screamed.

She had the energy for one last wave of magick. This time, as the selkies released her, she reached for the dagger in her waistband. Blind. She couldn't see, couldn't feel anything.

She struggled with the dagger . . . and then it slipped from her fingers into the depths.

Anger roared in her chest even as the slippery beasts surged once again to drag her to her end.

Goddess Above, not like this.

All at once, there was a radiant explosion of light. The selkies screeched, clawing with their webbed hands to get away from the figure cutting through the water toward them.

Archeron. Magick seemed to come from everywhere as he flung wave after wave of selkie back to get to her.

Weak and fighting to stay conscious, Haven threw out a hand and somehow caught Archeron's wrist. He drew her into his chest, smooth and slick, and she wrapped both arms around his neck.

The heat from the magick he sent searing through the water warmed her skin.

Then they were on the shore, and she was falling to her knees and vomiting what felt like the entire lake.

She felt his hand, warm and wet and heavy on her back as she expelled the stagnant water from her lungs. It seemed never ending. Each wracking purge twisted her body, making her shake.

Rook ran to them and covered Haven with a thin blanket, and Haven's body shuddered with convulsion after convulsion until she was dry heaving air.

Then, she flopped onto her side in the mossy earth and just breathed.

Her world spun, her body begging to slip away for a bit . . .

No. Stay awake.

Archeron leaned down, his wet hair raining droplets over her cheek, and lifted her into his arms. Grunting, he nudged the blanket higher with his chin.

"Put me down!" she snarled.

He looked straight ahead as he carried her to the forest, ignoring her plea. His jaw was taut with anger.

"Down!"

He flicked his livid gaze over her. "All you had to do was send the wood to the surface, but you're too stubborn. You would rather die than ask for help."

Anger surged through her. That wasn't true. Her arms were trapped, and releasing the wood had been impossible. But that wasn't the point.

"I shouldn't *have* to," she said. "I have the same powers you do, maybe more. But I can't use them without draining all my energy!"

His body stiffened against her, then he halted and dumped her to her feet. "That's what you're mad about?"

"Yes!"

Bjorn and Rook had followed them into the forest. They shared a look and turned to leave.

Haven planted her hands on her hips. "Stay!"

Archeron gave them an incredulous stare. "She is—is mad because . . ." He scowled at her. "Well, you tell them."

"I know why she's frustrated," Rook said, regarding Haven with a cautious expression. "Surai mentioned your interest in fleshrunes to me."

Haven picked at the fringe of her blanket. If Surai mentioned it to her, then it was an even bigger deal than she made it seem. And the way Rook spoke now, she didn't approve either. But, of course they wouldn't know what it was like to have all this power inside, yet not know how to use it.

Rook stepped forward. "What are you asking?"

"What I'm asking is for the same privilege as you. I need runemarks . . . or some other way to harness my magick." She wrapped the blanket tighter around herself. "If I had runemarks, I wouldn't have almost drowned because my magick wouldn't have run out."

Silence fell over the forest as the Solis stared at her. "But you didn't drown, Haven," Archeron said in a low voice. "I wouldn't have let you."

"That's not enough!" Her jaw clenched. Why couldn't he see it wasn't the same? "While I appreciate your help, I don't want to *have* to depend on you, Sun Lord. Or any of you."

Rook looked away while Archeron shook his head, and Bjorn said, "Fleshrunes on a mortal is against both mortal and Solis law, Haven."

She jutted out her chin. "I know that."

"Then why continue pursuing something that can never happen?" Rook asked, truly curious.

Haven shrugged, hard. "Have you never wanted something

everyone said was impossible?"

Surai was perched on a branch above, and Rook couldn't hide the fleeting glance she sent her.

"If you had followed the rules," Haven continued, "you would never know what true love feels like." She turned to Bjorn and then Archeron. Giving each a pointed look. "Both of you, I'm sure, have broken rules before when it suited you. How is this any different?"

"Careful, Haven," Archeron said, his soft tone doing nothing to hide his coldness. "This isn't some mortal game. If we allow you to be fleshruned, you will be marked for an eternity as an abomination. There will be no place where you can hide and no magick strong enough to prevent the entire realm—Solis, Noctis, and mortal—from hunting you down and ending your life."

"That is my choice to make," she whispered.

"Actually," he growled, pivoting to leave, "it's not."

"And according to Bjorn, I'm going to die anyway, so it doesn't matter."

Archeron's back was turned, and he stiffened before stalking away.

Rook walked over and placed her arms around Haven. "It has been a long evening, and the Shade Queen will have noticed the surge in light magick. Let's find a place for the night."

Haven nodded but only because she now realized she could never talk them into giving her runemarks.

Still, as they made their way back into the woods, countless selkie heads bobbing in the water to watch them pass, Haven vowed to find a way to channel her magick—whether the Solis liked it or not.

If she was going to die, she would take as many of the Shade Queen's army with her as possible.

THIRTY

Bell knew screaming was pointless—yet the noise rushed out of him anyway. A ragged wail of terror that echoed off the granite walls of the empty hallway and only seemed to arouse the Noctis in front of him more. Feral excitement flashed inside Malix's oily black eyes, a predatory grin cutting across his pale face.

The Noctis held out a hand. "Come, Prince. If I have to chase you, it will be much worse."

Already, Bell could feel paralyzing terror seeping into his limbs, making him helpless. His gut clenched, hot bile searing his throat. Just like always, he was too afraid to fight. He inched a foot forward.

"Yes," Malix purred, his chest heaving and mouth parting, jagged teeth peeking out. "Yes, that's right. Come here."

Another step. Bell's heart was in his throat. His body shaking.

And then, he felt . . . something change. A presence filled the space. He knew it somehow. *Haven?* Any other time, he would have questioned his sanity, but now it made sense. Even dead, she protected him. He expected nothing less.

"Haven?" he choked out.

Malix canted his head sideways in confusion.

And then, impossibly, his best friend spoke. *Fight back, Bell,* she urged, her voice as real as if she were still alive and right beside him. *Fight back.*

Adrenaline flooded his veins.

Fight back!

He took two more steps forward. Malix was grinning as he reached for him.

Bell slammed his fist into the creature's nose, his knuckles cracking against flesh and bone. Hot blood spurted across Bell's face. For a stupid second, Bell stared in shock at Malix, unable to believe what he'd done.

Then he bolted. A cry escaped his lips as the talons along the bottom of the creature's wing scraped Bell's cheek.

Malix roared with rage behind him, but Bell lunged down the hall, running faster than he ever thought he could. Newfound courage spurred him on.

Goddess Above, that felt good.

He careened around a corner. The Noctis thundered behind him. Another corridor opened and Bell cut left, slamming into stone.

He hardly felt the pain in his shoulder. Hardly felt the gashes in his cheek spurting blood onto the floor with every thundering beat of his heart.

A dead end. *Crap.*

Bell whipped around to run, but it was too late. Malix's talons scraped the floor as he stalked toward him, his wings spread wide and casting deep shadows over Bell.

Rage—the monster's black eyes glittered with rage and hatred, his lips twisted into a jagged sneer.

Bell was trapped . . . without a weapon. Without chance of escape. Where was his magick? He lifted his hands as if somehow his desperation could will his powers into existence.

But there was nothing in his palms except dirt and sweat.

"Trouble with your magick?" Malix purred. He snapped his wings closed and stalked closer. "Don't you worry, Prince. I'll take your magick and put it to good use. Perhaps . . ." A blink, and Malix was inches from Bell's face. "Perhaps I'll use your magick to keep you alive while I rip open your ribcage and feast on your heart. How does that sound?"

Bell swung at the Noctis's face, but this time, Malix was ready, and he caught Bell's arm and twisted. Fire shot through Bell's shoulder.

He groaned, trying to jerk away.

With a high-pitched laugh, Malix whispered into Bell's ear, "Told you not to run, Prince."

Then he lifted Bell by the neck and slammed him into the wall. Darkness flashed, followed by shooting pains everywhere. Bell came to on the floor with the Noctis monster hovering over him.

The tang of blood was sharp in his mouth. The tang of fear was sharper . . .

Lifting on his elbows, Bell began dragging himself backward to the open hallway. Maybe someone would see him. Maybe—

Malix's talons dug into Bell's ankles, yanking him back into the darkness. Bell screamed, kicking at the monster's hideous face. His movements wrenched the talons out of his flesh, and he screamed again, using the pain to fuel his anger, his will to fight.

He tried to stand.

A crack to his head sent him sprawling onto his back again.

More darkness. When he opened his eyes, Malix was spread over him, his wings curled around them to hide what was about to happen.

Hot, rotten breath slammed into Bell's face as Malix flashed his fangs and said, "I would love to play more, Prince, but others might want a taste. And I don't like sharing, so . . ."

Bell's heart wobbled inside his chest. He couldn't breathe. Malix had both of Bell's arms pinned above his head with one hand. The other drew a long, curved gray talon.

That talon tapped along Bell's sternum. Once. Twice.

"Did you know," Malix breathed, his voice raspy and quick with excitement, "our talons can shred bone?"

Bell squirmed as the talon pierced his flesh and dug into his ribcage—

A roar shattered the air. Bell's hands sprung free as Malix released him. Green flashed through the shadows, and Malix was flung into the wall. The Noctis bared his fangs and tried to stand, but whoever threw Malix followed him, pouncing before the Noctis could recover.

Bell blinked in shock at the green cloak, the hunched back.

The creature.

Snarls and shrieks of pain came from the writhing males as they fought, and Bell had to turn away. Should he stay? Run? No, he should fight. Help the creature.

But two steps sent him careening onto his side, his head spinning. Gasping, he pressed against the wall and waited until, at last, the creature pulled a dagger from somewhere and plunged it into the Noctis's chest.

Flames of gold and silver lit the shadows, and the Noctis turned to a mound of ash on the floor.

Just like that, the fight was over.

The creature stumbled to his feet. For a second, he stared down at the ash on the floor, panting, his hunched shoulders heaving with every ragged breath. He looked to be in worse shape than Bell, if that was possible. Then, as if remembering the prince, he turned, slowly bent down, and lifted him over his shoulder.

Bell cried out at the shooting pain in his shoulder and head.

"I'm sorry," the creature panted as they slipped down the hall. "The pain cannot be helped. I will heal you when we get back to my side of the castle."

Bell was in and out of consciousness. He blinked, and the obsidian walls of Spirefall were replaced by stars and an almost-full moon. Another blink, another ragged breath, and they were inside the creature's house, the fires raging.

Bell finally allowed his eyes to close. He felt the softness of the couch. The creature's gloved fingers were suddenly gentle as they prodded his bruised and broken body for injuries.

Then fire raged along his bones, his flesh.

But the burning was far away, the kiss of the sun on a winter's day. He only groaned when the flames entered his head . . . but even that seemed so distant.

Someone else's life. Someone else's pain.

"Sleep." The words trickled from another realm as he obeyed.

THIRTY-ONE

They made camp on a large bluff overlooking a wide, half-frozen river of glittering black, shadowed by the jagged cluster of mountains separating the Ruinlands from the Shadow Kingdom. Haven gathered her poor cloak around her body for protection against the biting wind and gazed at her companions huddled around a fire, coveting their warmth.

Her own dark magick fire, a beautiful flame of ice-blue laced with black, had burned out long ago, her body too drained to sustain it.

Which only fueled her resolve to obtain fleshrunes.

The others watched her from their warm position with amused, slightly concerned expressions. They probably assumed she would have to join them eventually or face freezing to death—which was true.

Surai landed on her shoulder for a spell, her concerned squawks loud in Haven's ears, until the cold proved too much for the bird.

Haven knew she was being ridiculous, but she didn't care. They were wasting time. Time that Bell didn't have. She felt certain the answer to everything hid beneath her fingertips, in her magick, and yet she couldn't harness it. Not properly.

Maybe if she had twenty years to practice . . .

Yet she wasn't even guaranteed a day. An hour. Her life was running out, and the Solis couldn't look past stupid rules and tradition to use the last hours of her time here to be useful.

Make me a weapon, she thought, scowling at Archeron, warm and cozy by the fire. *See how useful I am then.*

As if her demand traveled across the frigid air and into the Sun Lord's pretty head, Archeron glanced her way. They had all taken the opportunity to invoke warmer clothes in the protected selkies' cove, and he was buried beneath a black ermine-lined cloak, honey-gold eyebrows lowered in a glower.

When he noticed her looking, an amused grin brightened his face, and he stood before gliding over with his usual stealth. Steam curled from the bowl of Bjorn's stew held between his hands.

He offered her the bowl. She glared at it.

"Goddess Above, Haven," Archeron purred, "are you going to refuse food?" Beneath his imperious tone ran an undercurrent of concern.

Her gaze slid greedily back to the bowl. Runemarks glowed orange along the inside lip, reflecting off a thick, lumpy stew. "What's in it?"

He chuckled. "Do you really want to know?"

She shook her head and accepted the offering. A sigh fled her throat as the heat worked into her frozen fingers. When he refused to leave, she shoved a searing bite into her mouth and then flicked up her eyebrows at him. "What?"

He tsked softly. "You ungrateful thing."

Strange chunks of something swirled around her mouth, and she quickly swallowed without chewing before forcing out a, "Thank you."

His throat bobbed. Shrugging off his fur-lined cloak, he slipped it over her shoulders. She shivered as the warmth from his body leeched into hers.

"Thank you," she muttered, again. This time with more feeling.

"Your manners need some work."

"And your arrogance needs its . . . its own castle!"

A moment of silence passed, and then half his lips curled up. "I think that was supposed to be an insult, but I'm not sure."

She glared at the chunks of meat in her bowl so he wouldn't see her eyes crinkling. "It was."

"Then I'm deeply offended," he teased, sitting next to her on the rock. "Although its own kingdom is probably truer." He waited for a moment, rubbing his hands together before continuing. "What you ask is impossible, Haven. I know you must be frustrated—"

"No. You don't know. You were born with runemarks to guide your magick. All you have to do is think, and it's done."

He snorted. "That's what you believe? Yes, I was born with the fleshrunes of my ancestors, but I still had to learn how to temper my magick. The runemarks on my flesh may give me the specific power of creating a leaf from a grain of sand, but I had to practice to ensure that leaf didn't become a forest."

Haven bit down several childish remarks. The idea of a young Archeron growing frustrated by too much power didn't exactly inspire pity . . . but he was obviously *trying* to make amends.

She set her bowl down, glancing over at the others who were pretending not to watch them. "There must be a way to add runemarks to my body. And if you're worried about offending the Goddess, I'll be dead soon anyway, so I can personally tell her it's not your fault."

A growl rumbled in his chest. "That's what you imagine? That I'm worrying about upsetting the Goddess? If I thought it would make you safer, I would break every damn law of hers without apology."

"Then why are you against this?"

"Because once you become runemarked, my kind will hunt you to your death. Shadeling's shadow! I might be ordered to find you and hang you from the ivory palace gates of Effendier, your flesh stripped off and burned. Is that what you want?"

"I want to break the Curse. I want my best friend to—" Her voice broke, and she cleared the emotion from her throat. "I want Bell to live past eighteen and have ten beautiful children just as kind and smart as he is. I want a mortal kingdom that doesn't cower beneath the shadow of the Shade Queen."

He must have thought she was done speaking because he opened his mouth—

She held up a hand to silence him. "And I want to die doing something amazing with the power I've been gifted. Something *worthy*. As stupid as it sounds, I want to make our kingdom—our realm—a better place."

He stiffened. "How many times must I tell you I will not let you die?"

Biting her lip, she reached for his hand. Her heart fluttered sideways as she slipped her fingers over the smooth skin on the back of his knuckles. "And I believe you will try. But I'm not afraid of death, Archeron. I'm afraid of letting the only person who's ever cared about me die for my magick. And I'm terrified. Terrified of letting him down. Please, help me."

Silence fell over them, hewn only by the low groan of wind. Slowly, his fingers curled around hers. "I will think about it."

That was as much as she would get from the surly Sun Lord.

Grinning at the small victory, she flicked a glance at their entwined hands. "Did I disrupt your Solis courting etiquette?"

A feral look flashed across his face. "You disrupt everything, Little Mortal."

Suddenly, her hand inside his felt hot and heavy, and a hollow feeling swelled inside her chest until she could hardly breathe.

Averting her gaze from Archeron, she focused on the group around the fire. "We should form a plan for tomorrow."

For a breath, his fingers tightened around hers. But then, he pulled his hand away, and they joined the others.

Still, the crackling heat from the fire was nothing compared to the desire stirring within her veins.

There had been boys and almost-men before—a trainer at the academy, a passing soldier from the next kingdom—but none that meant anything to her.

That was the point.

Maybe it was knowing her death was imminent, but now she wanted something more. Not the groping hands of a boy whose face and name she couldn't recall; or the wine-soaked breath of a drunken trainer she could best with her blade.

More.

Perfect time to decide that, she scolded herself as Rook laid out the plan for the last task. She sat on a log. Her back straight and shoulders high despite the weariness lining her face. A backdrop of stars outlined her statuesque figure, and Haven decided she had never seen someone look more like a queen than the Morgani Princess.

Surai—newly transformed into her Solis form—was nestled into her mate's shoulder, her dark hair loose and contrasted against Rook's pale braids.

Surai's hand rested on Rook's leg, the pinky of her delicate-boned left hand pressed against Rook's much larger, more capable one. A small, intimate gesture meant for only them.

What would it be like to love someone that much? To share inside jokes and secret gestures?

A pang of disappointment hit her. If Bjorn's words were true, she would never know.

Rook crossed her legs at the ankle, showing off her knee-high calfskin boots. Each sported a gold buckle adorned with diamonds. "Bjorn and I have discussed our next move while you two were"—Rook's teeth flashed in a grin—"*talking*, and the only way to retrieve the last item on the Curseprice, a sliver of the Shade Queen's horn, is to invade Spirefall."

"You speak madness," Archeron said, his quiet voice prickling Haven's skin as she felt the blood drain from her face and pool, cold and curdled, in her gut.

Madness, indeed.

Haven tugged Archeron's cloak tighter around her body despite the hot kiss of fire dancing close to her skin. "Can we not lure her out somehow?"

Rook glanced behind Haven at the inky clouds blotting out the sky over the Shadow Kingdom. "According to Bjorn, the Dark Queen never leaves the castle."

Bjorn nodded. "Morgryth doesn't have to. Her ravens allow her to see everything from Spirefall, and her gremwyrs act at her behest. She has remained protected in her lair since the Curse was cast."

"Clever," Haven muttered. "How can anyone break the Curse when the final item is locked away inside an impenetrable fortress?"

"Exactly." Rook paced around the fire with her head held high, looking every bit the princess as the flames cast an orange glow against her moon-pale cloak and high cheekbones. "Except, it's not quite as impenetrable as she thinks."

"What do you mean?"

"The Dark Queen has a weakness. She keeps the mortal prince who murdered her daughter in the castle, forcing him to care for every mortal child brought to Spirefall as a sacrifice. Only she would be so cruel."

Archeron put a broad hand on Rook's shoulder to stop her pacing. "And how does that help us?"

Rook gave a fierce grin. "I met this mortal prince once. A vain, selfish prick, like you, Archeron." She winked at the Sun Lord. "But I imagine he would do anything to stop his wicked torture. Like breaking a ward or two."

Archeron let out a warm laugh and wrapped Rook in a bear hug. "Morgani Princess, I could kiss you right now."

And, true to his words, he did. A dramatic kiss on her cheek that had the princess squirming wildly.

"Enough," she growled as she ducked beneath his arms, wiping her cheek. "Those lips have touched every Sun Queen across the Glittering Sea."

Archeron flicked a worried look at Haven before focusing back on Rook. "You speak of nearly five centuries past when I was a young, ignorant soldier. Do not make me dredge up your lengthy history—"

Rook silenced Archeron with an elbow to the ribs. "Focus on the plan, pretty boy."

"What am I missing?" Haven asked before clarifying, "Not about Archeron's wandering lips—I knew he was a manwhore the moment I met him." Rook snort-laughed, and Archeron glared at her. "About the mortal prince. How do we reach him?"

"It is called dreamjoining, Mortal," Bjorn said.

Archeron released Rook and turned to Haven. "Because she has met him, she can contact him in a dream."

"Doesn't she need a lock of his hair?" The question came out before Haven had time to think about the implications, and she added, "I read that somewhere."

"Dreamweaving," Bjorn said, tilting his head in her direction, "is entirely different. To gift your dreams to another for life is an intimate act, and very few are powerful enough to grant such a thing. Fewer still are comfortable with the consequences."

Haven's heart skipped a beat. *Life?*

Several more questions came to mind along with a few curse words for Stolas, but she put them away for later. Asking now would seem suspicious, and Bjorn was already glancing sideways at her with those knowing eyes that saw nothing and everything.

Instead, she said, "How can Rook dreamjoin when there's dark magick in this realm?"

Rook shook her head. "The darkness cannot access my magick in my dreams." She beamed at Archeron. "And if I can talk the fallen prince into breaking one of the wards on the doors to Spirefall . . ."

"We have a way in," Archeron finished. She hadn't heard his voice ever sound so hopeful.

"So we are agreed then?" Rook asked, glancing around. "If the fallen prince can break one of the wards on the doors, we go inside?"

For a few seconds, the only sound was the crackling of the fire and the howling wind.

"Agreed," Bjorn said.

Surai took Rook's hand as she nodded.

No one mentioned the obvious. That the mission was most likely a death sentence. Even if the fallen prince broke the ward and they made it inside Spirefall and past the guards, even if they somehow managed to get close to the Shade Queen . . . they still had to carve off a sliver of her horn, all without magick.

Well, except for Haven's near-useless powers.

She didn't hesitate. "Agreed."

Archeron locked eyes with her, something dark and fierce passing between them. Her throat clenched with emotion as she read his face, his meaning.

They were in this together. They would rise together and fall together and, if the fates desired it, die together.

"Agreed," Archeron said.

THIRTY-TWO

As the near-full moon peeked over the top of the mountains, and a light dusting of snow began, they decided it was time to rest. Once again, Haven felt the shame of her mortal-ness fall over her. Sleep had never felt more like a prison than now.

She nudged a stone near the fire with the toe of her boot, wondering if there was a rune for going sleepless. But then she saw the way Surai and Rook held onto each other and understood tonight wasn't just about sleeping.

It was also a chance to say their goodbyes—just in case.

"We can rest tonight and leave early in the morning," Rook said as she packed up two woolen blankets dyed pine-green. "If we're lucky, we can make it to Spirefall by nightfall and attack while both Surai and I are in our true forms."

Archeron stepped forward. "I can act as watch tonight while—"

"No." Rook tossed a knowing look at Haven before sliding her gaze back to Archeron. "You have other things to do tonight. I can do it."

"Princess, I will stand watch," Bjorn offered. "I am the only one without . . . a partner." Rook motioned to wave him off, but he insisted. "You need to try to dreamjoin with the fallen prince."

Rook sighed, her lips twisting into a frown. "Are you sure? After your last vision, you've seemed . . . drained. We all understand if being nearer to Spirefall has brought back painful memories."

It was true. Something was different about Bjorn from the beginning of the journey. As if he'd lost his spark, grown dimmer, somehow.

Bjorn flashed a weary smile. "I'm only tired of sleeping on the ground and being surrounded by dark magick; that is all." He made a show of filling his cup with some drink heating over the fire. "Go. I couldn't rest if I wanted to."

Rook leaned her tall body over and kissed Bjorn's forehead. She squeezed his shoulder, her eyes tight with concern. "If you change your mind, Seer, come find me."

It was hard leaving the warmth of the fire. Haven was thankful for her two cloaks as bits of snow blew off the mountains and into her face.

Rook caught up beside her, and Haven slowed to walk with her toward the few recesses cut into the mountainside they would use for shelter. Snowflakes frosted the princess's hair and caught in her blonde eyelashes.

"About what you said earlier," Rook began. "The runemarks. I'm sorry, Haven. Having the power that you do, both light and dark, and not knowing what to do with it or how to guide it, that would be hard."

Haven gave a solemn nod, choking down her frustration. It probably wasn't everyday a Morgani Princess apologized.

"You must know the reason we hesitate is because you've

become a part of our family, and we cannot lose another. Putting fleshrunes onto your body would be a death sentence for you."

"Archeron told me."

They were at the first shelter, a low-hanging alcove big enough for two people to stretch out. Rook glanced over her shoulder at Archeron and Bjorn. "Before we lost Remurian, Archeron would have done it for you despite the risk. He could never say no to those he loved. But once someone you care about dies, death's specter is always there, reminding you anyone can be taken away. It changes you."

Haven ran her hand over the slate-gray overhang, tracing silver veins that ran through the rock with her finger. "He told me he would think about it."

"He may have said that, and perhaps he will. But he will not risk losing you, too, and his answer will be no. I just hope you can understand why."

Haven released a cloudy breath. "We'll see."

She refused to think Archeron would say no, especially after she explained to him why she wanted the runemarks. In the morning she would try again.

"Archeron says you are doing all of this to save a mortal prince?" Rook asked.

"I made an oath to protect him." Haven released a breath, watching it frost over into a milky plume.

"Still," Rook said. "Very few people would put themselves at risk the way you have, even for an oath."

"Do you mean very few mortals?"

"No." She tugged on the end of one of her braids. "We Solis aren't as honorable as we think. Everyone—mortal or otherwise—feels fear."

"Even you?" Haven teased, thinking she would say 'no.'

"All the time, Haven." Rook ran two fingers down her neck. "Do you know Morgani royals are told how they will die?"

"So you know then . . . how it ends?"

She nodded, her amber eyes darkened to tarnished gold as a finality came over her. "We're told how we die from birth so that death cannot hold us in its thrall."

"If you know when you will die, can you not prevent it?"

For a moment, her eyes unfocused, and she seemed lost in her thoughts.

Then the Morgani Princess smiled, the wistful grin making her look radiant. "My death is honorable and good. I do not fear it, Haven. Only the sadness that will come afterwards for those I leave behind. And the guilt they may feel . . ."

There was something implied in her words that Haven couldn't quite unravel, and she shifted on her feet.

Rook laughed, any residual seriousness fading beneath that lyrical sound. "Sorry for the change in mood, Mortal. Back to your prince. You must love him very much."

"He was my first true friend," Haven admitted though the statement didn't do justice to what she felt for Bell.

"But not your only friend." Rook slipped her fingers over Haven's arm. "Surely you see that now?"

A shiver of happiness went through her. "I do."

"Surai doesn't have many friends either," Rook continued. "And our isolation here has been hard on her, not that she would admit as much. You've made her smile again in ways I couldn't, and I know you'll be here for her always. So thank you."

Too dumbfounded to say anything, Haven only nodded, again feeling there was something she was missing. Then she realized Rook was still in her Solis form. "Why have you not changed yet?"

Rook twisted at something around her finger—an onyx ring. A fiery blue rune pulsed from the flat center. Something about the rune felt wrong to Haven. Dark.

"There are ways around our curse. This ring allows me to stay in my true form, but at a great cost. I've never used it before . . . but the dark price is worth a full night with Surai." An emotion Haven couldn't quite read flashed across Rook's face, and then she nodded her head at something behind Haven. "Now, tell that pretty one over there not to keep you up too late. As a mortal, you need some sleep."

Haven knew Archeron was behind her without looking, yet she couldn't help but glance back. As if expecting her to turn around, a feline grin stretched across his jaw, his eyes flashing.

She quickly faced Rook again with her own sheepish grin. "Goodnight, Princess."

Rook rolled her eyes and laughed as she bent forward and brushed her lips over Haven's cheek. "I'm not a princess anymore. Just as you are not truly a mortal. You're one of us. And you"—her gaze flicked upward again to Archeron—"my pretty friend, need to let her rest."

Archeron laughed. A warm, sensuous song she could drown in. "As you command, Princess."

Rook snarled playfully at him. But her gaze lingered, her eyes wistful and sad in a way that Haven didn't understand.

Then, with one last threat of disembowelment if Archeron didn't let Haven sleep, Rook retreated to her shelter.

Just like that, they were alone.

Shakily, Haven turned to watch the Sun Lord spread a dark fur skin over the floor of their alcove. Without his cloak, only a thin tunic and pants separated his body from the cold, but he didn't seem to mind the piercing wind as he folded up another blanket for their pillow.

Then he grasped the bottom of his tunic and slipped it over his head.

Goddess save her.

Her mouth parted as she took in the tawny flesh of his upper body, smooth and firm, covered in runemarks the color of the stars. The silvery swirls and lines seemed to dance with his every movement . . . a choreography of muscle and flesh she couldn't quite look away from.

"Your turn, Mortal," he said, his voice low and burning with intention.

"What?"

He spread out on the fur to watch her, laughing even as his eyes burned with power—a fiery green spark that somehow managed to break through the dark magick barrier and danced around his irises.

"We have no fire," he said matter-of-factly. "So skin-to-skin will keep us warm. Unless . . . you want me to build us one? I will if you desire it so."

A pleased look overcame him as she shook her head.

She swallowed, his gaze marking her every move as she stripped off both cloaks and tossed them onto their bed.

He waited with a hungry look as she paused, her hands tangled at the bottom of her tunic. All she had below was a flimsy undershirt and her pants. But the promise of his warmth prompted her to continue, and her tunic fell to the ground with a quiet whoosh.

The freezing air raked over her skin, and she jumped into the shelter beside him, her heart pounding in her ears. He slid the heavy fabric over them both, the cloaks soft on her naked arms.

For a moment, she lay there facing outward, her heavy breathing the only sound. His body lay warm and massive at her back.

A tiny gasp escaped her lips as he slid one arm over her stomach, the other under her neck to cradle her head. Then he pulled her into his hard body. Heat rolled over her, filling her like a wave of fire. Hot breath spilled into her neck.

On instinct, she tried to push her rear into him, but he pulled away, his arms tightening around her. "One thing at a time, Haven."

"I thought you were going to kiss me?" Her voice was a breathy rasp.

His heart hammered against her left shoulder blade as she waited for his response. "Do you want me to kiss you?"

She wriggled inside his tight arms to face him, inhaling his scent of leather and some exotic flower she couldn't name. His chest pressed against hers through her thin undershirt, and she slid her bare foot over his waist, locking it behind his back.

"Odin's teeth, Mortal," he groaned. "Your feet are made of ice."

She dug her toes into his flank. "Shut up, and kiss me."

He released an uneven breath. "And where would the mortal like me to kiss?"

"I don't know. Where did you kiss all the countless Sun Queens Rook mentioned?"

He frowned. "I was young, Haven, a reckless, selfish warrior—"

She slid two fingers over his lips to silence him. "I don't care about that, Archeron. We both have pasts we'd rather not relive."

The skin around his forehead and mouth softened as he visibly relaxed. "Back to the question, then. Where?"

She shivered, imagining his lips over her flesh, all the intimate places she hid from the world . . .

"The back of my knees."

His head canted to the side. "Your . . . knees?"

She shrugged. "You said anywhere. Besides. I imagine you didn't kiss half the Sun Queens in the realm *there*."

"No."

"Good. Then I'll be the first."

Even in the low light of the stars and dying fire behind her, she could see the feral expression that flickered across his face. "Before I do, you must tell me something personal. Something private."

Her eyebrows pressed together. "Not fair."

"I want to know you, Haven. Not just your flesh but your soul."

For a second, fear made her almost say no. After all, it was easier to expose a piece of her skin than a piece of herself. But she nodded, swallowing as she thought of what to say.

And then, she had it. The one piece of her story that had shaped her into who she was. Speaking it aloud was something she'd never done, not even for Bell—and she fortified herself with a lungful of air before beginning.

THIRTY-THREE

"You already know what the Devourer did to me from the memory I sent you," Haven began. She tried to cleave the emotion from her voice, but the words shivered in her throat and tumbled out soft and haunted.

Archeron's body went rigid at her tone, anger flickering across the depths of his eyes and nostrils flaring.

"I should have ripped his head from his body in the Devourers' camp," he snarled.

Damius. His face flashed across her mental landscape. The dark, corrosive hatred and possessiveness he felt for her.

A trickle of dread nestled between her shoulder blades, her chest tightening, but she steeled herself to continue. "It wouldn't have made a difference, Archeron. Dead or alive, he'll always live inside my nightmares."

"Not if I can help it." Archeron rested one massive hand on her hip and nodded for her to continue.

"After I escaped," she began, forcing her voice louder to mimic strength. "I wandered the Ruinlands for Goddess knows how long, barely surviving. But my body was just going through the motions. Inside . . . inside I was already dead. Damius had broken me, and even though I'd escaped, he was still right there, my never-ending nightmare."

Her voice cracked. It had been years since she teared up at the memory, but something about speaking the words gave the nightmare new life.

Other than the pressure of his fingers on her waist, Archeron was silent. He was giving her time to collect herself. To find her strength.

She pulled two calming breaths into her lungs and continued. "Then one day, I was scrounging for berries in the woods, and I found some white snakeroot. Without thinking, I boiled the leaves with some water from the stream and then waited until nightfall to drink the poison and end my life."

She paused as Archeron's arms tightened around her, the muscles of his jaw trembling.

"Go on," he insisted, his voice unreadable.

"I can still feel the bitter, poisonous steam burning my lips as I prepared to drink the tincture, the way my mouth tingled and my eyes stung. Right when I lifted the cup, a star streaked across the sky. Suddenly, despite having no memories of my home or life before, I recalled my mother's voice clear as anything, reciting the story of the Goddess, Freya. How Odin and the Noctis had imprisoned her in the Netherworld after the War of Gods, and rather than live in darkness for eternity, she was reborn.

"First, she set her heart into the sky to rise and fall each day and bring us light. Then she scattered her magick across the heavens, so in the darkness, we would remember her love for us. And every time someone sees a star fall, Freya is reminding them of that love."

She paused, choking back the emotion that knotted her throat. Even now, she could hear her mother's beautiful voice telling the story.

"I knew then," she added, "that the Goddess had a plan for me. So I put the poison down, cut my hair with the dull blade of my dagger, and was reborn just as she was."

Archeron's ragged breath was hot on her face as he ran a thumb over her cheeks, wiping away invisible tears.

Then he lifted onto his elbows and slid his heavy cloak over their heads. Her breath hitched as she felt him slide down her body. His fingernail flicked beneath her waistband, unbuttoning her pants, and the flesh of her belly shivered. She lifted her butt so he could slip them off her, feeling the cool air prickling her naked legs.

For a few erratic beats of her heart, there was nothing but darkness and anticipation. And then his broad hands slipped under her ankle, and he lifted her leg a few inches.

His lips gently pressed into the delicate spot below her knee, and she gasped at the feeling. Both tender and wild.

She tried to wiggle her leg, but he held it firm as his lips traveled up the inside of her thigh. Somehow finding the most delicate parts of her body. Waves of heat crashed over her, and she lost herself to the feel of his lips on her flesh. Nothing was off limits, not even her feet, worn from days of travel.

She began to arch her back, and his hand pressed into her stomach, the other cupped beneath her rear as he pulled her toward him. His lips found her stomach and she cried out, trying to buck, but he held her in place.

Fire consumed her skin, her bones, her marrow, until her magick skittered along her veins and she had to fight releasing it.

Goddess save her, his lips weren't enough. She wanted it all. Everything.

Battle was in her future, and the cold sleep of death was coming soon.

But amidst the carnage and uncertainty that awaited, she needed to feel the exquisite truth of two souls colliding in the most intimate way they could.

She needed Archeron inside her.

"Please," she begged.

She felt him pause just over the hollow between her two breasts. Then he dragged his mouth over her neck, scraping his teeth lightly over her collarbone.

"This part of you is my favorite," he breathed. He ran two fingers over her throat, and she blinked as he pulled back the blanket, letting in the moonlight. "You have no idea how many times I've watched the curve of your neck move as you laughed or made some scathing remark toward me."

She opened her mouth to apologize, but he pressed his fingers into her lips. "Which I'm sure I deserved. Mostly." Lifting the blanket, he raked his gaze over her body then released a deep, aggrieved sigh. "You must sleep now, Haven. Rook will disembowel me if I don't present you tomorrow rested."

"You can't be serious?" How was she supposed to sleep now?

"I am."

"What if I don't want to sleep?"

"Then do it for me, Little Mortal, with the promise to live so we can continue after the Curse is broken."

"But Bjorn—"

"Bjorn is wrong," Archeron snarled. His pupils flared as he held her stare. "Say it. Say you will live."

"Has he ever been wrong before?" Her voice was a whisper. She wanted to believe Archeron, that there was a chance Bjorn could be mistaken. That there was a tiny sliver of possibility she might not die.

She wanted it now more than ever.

The vein in the middle of Archeron's forehead pulsed angrily as his lips curled back. "Since when do you let someone tell you your fate?" He settled on his elbow. "I am only sure of one thing—death will come for you tomorrow as it will us all. But only you can decide if it takes you. Now say it."

She lifted her chin. "I will live."

Speaking the words was its own sort of magick, and for the first time, she imagined a world with the Curse broken . . . and what might come afterward.

Only, that brought more questions.

"If we succeed," she said. "Will you go back to Effendier?"

"Yes, if my mother will allow my return. But I'll be free of my enslavement to King Horace."

"How does he control you?" she asked, shivering as she recalled when the king ordered him to obey, the way Archeron's cheeks slackened and eyes glazed over.

A shadow passed over Archeron's face, and he ran a finger over his chest—just above his heart. "A ring. He wears it always on his right hand."

"It forces you to do his bidding?"

"The gemstone imprisons a shard of my soul." A muscle jumped in his jaw, and he shook his head before pulling her to him. "We should not speak on such dark matters. Not tonight."

Thankful for the change of subject, she settled back into his body. "Once we break the Curse, the wish can be anything?"

"According to the myths." His voice had taken on a slow, syrupy sleepiness. "When broken, the power of the Curse is transferred into granting one single request."

"Only one?" She thought there were more.

"Only one," he confirmed. "The mortal kings needed a way to entice their armies into the Ruinlands, so they started the myth of multiple wishes, but I've read the ancient tablets myself, and the Goddess's law states one wish granted for a broken curse, nothing more."

"And the others are okay with you taking the one wish?"

"Of course," he said. "I am their leader and the eldest Solis. It is mine by right."

She snorted at his arrogance.

"Do you find something offensive?"

"What if *I* desire the wish?"

He brushed a thumb over her stomach, making her catch her breath. "With the Curse severed, your prince goes free. What more do you desire? Tell me, and I will do everything in my power to make it happen."

A fleeting image of her parents—the faceless forms she'd created for them years ago—flashed in her mind. If she could have anything in this world, it would be to find them.

And yet, after years of building them up to be perfect in every way, a part of her was terrified of the prospect. "It's . . . nothing. What about the others, though?"

"When my enslavement to the king is broken, I will ask my mother to end Rook and Surai's curse and give Bjorn a place at court."

"Will she listen?" Haven asked, trying to imagine the Effendier Sovereign. There was a portrait in a book from centuries ago of her on a throne surrounded by fierce Sun Queens. All she could picture now was a stern Sun Sovereign, even more regal and beautiful than Archeron, with eyes of jade and severe, unsmiling lips.

"If we break the Curse, it will look bad for her to refuse. Besides, it was me she wanted punished more than anyone."

"How can a mother be so cruel?"

A dark laugh slipped from his lips. "I am the accidental son of one of her countless male concubines. If not for the remarkable powers I displayed early on, I would have been ferried from court along with the other bastards my mother has conceived, to disappear in some ignoble kingdom. But I can never escape my lineage, and I must prove myself a thousand times over."

"Even to your own mother?" Haven said.

"Especially to *her*." The last word came out sharp and cold. "Once King Boteler no longer owns me, my honor will be intact, and she will be forced to welcome me back. My lineage may be questionable, but my magick is more powerful than any true son or daughter of the Sovereign. She may despise me—but she cannot deny me a place at court."

Haven ran a finger down the corded muscles of his forearm tight around her belly. "Then I pray to the Goddess you'll be free soon."

"Free—the word has never sounded so beautiful. Now sleep, my Little Mortal."

Haven sighed as he tucked the blanket around them, disappointment filling her chest. Her body ached for more of him, more exploration, more something . . . but she settled for his arms encircling her waist instead.

His chin nestled into her neck, and he drew her body flush against his. "If the stars are the reason you're here now with me, Haven Ashwood, then I will thank them every night for the rest of my immortal life."

She laughed, sinking into his warmth. Now she understood why her people called them Sun Lords. He was a flame encased in flesh and bone. A fire that warmed the deepest part of her.

"A lifetime of gratitude?" she teased. "I didn't know you were capable, Archeron Halfbane. So does that mean I'm no longer a chinga?"

He kissed her neck, a soft, gentle kiss that reverberated through her body. "Oh, you're that more than ever. An incessant creature that's wormed your way into my heart, for better or worse."

"Romantic," she murmured.

As she felt herself slipping into her dreams, lulled by his warmth and protection, she said a prayer to the Goddess to save her once again.

Please, Goddess of all things good and true, if it is my destiny to live, I beg you to help me.

Damn the seer's visions.

She refused to die. Not when she had so much to live for.

THIRTY-FOUR

Stolas was waiting for Haven beneath the great elm of her dreamscape, leaning against the tree with one arm behind his back. The other tugged on a lock of silver-white hair that had fallen over his forehead. A waistcoat of satin, black as the wings tucked behind his back, tapered neatly around his waist, reflecting the moonlight running along the silver embroidery.

She hurried across the swaying grass to meet him, glancing over the landscape for signs of whatever had been there last time. But other than the bright flicker of stars and whisper of wind, it was quiet. No dark entity in sight.

As she neared, Stolas's lips curved into a grin, and he lifted from the tree and glided around her, his wry gaze sliding down her body the way hers had the horizon.

That's when she realized she wore the last thing she had on—her undershirt and underwear—nothing else. Clenching her fists, she quickly added pants to her dream outfit.

"Don't bother," he said. "I saw everything earlier."

Her gut clenched, and she forced her arms down to keep from raking her nails down his cheek. "You spied on me?"

"I always spy on you." He shrugged. "Although, I prefer to say 'watch to see if you have gotten yourself killed yet.'"

"Funny."

"Hilarious, bordering on horrifying. You forget, Beastie. I've seen your toes, and I will never purge the image of Archeron kissing them."

"How about making me call out your name when I'm with him?"

A flicker of confusion rippled across his face. "I assure you I would never stoop so low." He ran a thumb over his jaw. "Did you really say my name? I imagine he didn't react well . . . he didn't hurt you, did he?"

"He would never—just, never mind, forget it." She glowered at him, but her expression softened despite her annoyance. "You're okay? I thought . . . when you didn't show up . . ."

A muscle jumped in his pale neck. "I had to be sure the Dark Queen was not monitoring me. She hasn't said a word, but I can feel a shift in her attention. Which is why we need to keep this brief and—"

"What about practicing my magick?" Haven asked. Now that she was hours away from invading the Shade Queen's castle, the little bit of magick she'd learned in her dreams seemed alarmingly inadequate.

He pinned her with an impatient glare. "Beastie, your tricks will have to wait. We must keep our encounter brief."

She released a frustrated breath, but she didn't argue. He was right. Especially after what happened last time. "Then why are you here?"

"I need to know your plan for tomorrow. Tell me you have a better strategy than the ridiculous scheme I overheard."

She crossed her arms over her chest. "What's wrong with it?"

He snorted. "Shadeling Below, how have you and your bumbling Solis made it this far?" He scraped a hand through his silver-white hair as his wings flexed behind him. "The Morgani Princess won't dreamjoin with the fallen prince. Do you really think Morgryth hasn't already warded his dreams from such things?"

Haven gouged her toe into the grassy earth. "Then what do you suggest?"

"Find another way."

"There isn't another way!" She tugged at the hem of her undershirt. "The castle is warded. Only someone from the inside . . ."

He raised a sharp eyebrow as she stared at him.

"Someone from the inside," she repeated, her heart racing. "Morgryth will be watching you too closely now for you to do it, but what would she care if you found time to torment the fallen prince? And maybe while you do, you slip him the message."

"No." His voice was barbed with finality. "You do not understand what you ask of me."

"But it's okay for me to nearly drown? To almost bleed to death from a vorgrath's claws?" She marched until they were nearly nose-to-nose. "Coward."

Fury made the yellow rings inside his eyes erupt, and he bared his fangs in a hiss. "You know nothing. I've lived beneath Morgryth's insidious reign for longer than you've been alive with only my wits to keep from being broken. I know what she's capable of, Beastie, because I've endured it. She snapped every bone inside my body and let her gremwyrs drain my blood until my veins were dried-up husks the first time I refused to marry her daughter. Still, I refused her seven more times, and each time became worse than the last. If I visit the fallen prince, she will rip off my wings feather-by-feather and bone-by-bone."

Haven glared back at him, refusing to cower from his bared fangs. "Then she's already broken you."

His cheek trembled as if she'd struck him. Raw, searing pain flared inside his eyes, and suddenly he was the kidnapped, tortured boy who watched Morgryth slaughter his family. The lost prince imprisoned in the Netherworld, grieving and alone.

Then the mortal-like emotions morphed into his usual indifference. The yellow fire circling his irises faded, his incisors retracting.

A deep sigh parted his lips. "You ask too much."

"No more than you ask of me." She hesitated as the danger of her request sank in. Stolas was a monster—but he had once been a simple prince before the Shade Queen molded him with her unfathomable cruelness into the wicked Lord of the Netherworld.

Asking him to risk the Dark Queen's wrath again felt wrong . . .

There's no other way.

"You know I'm right," she added softly. "Which is why you'll do it."

His pale throat bobbed. "Yes."

"For whomever owns that silver brush?"

He blinked, and something dark and haunted flashed beneath his callous porcelain mask. "Yes."

Relief eased the tension from her shoulders. She retreated a step, trailing her hands over the tall grass. "We strike tomorrow night when the moon is high. Do you—"

Stolas's head whipped up and he snarled. "They're here! Wake up!"

As if shoved by an unseen force, she lurched awake, sweaty and hot despite the frigid air. She leapt to her feet—and nearly brained herself on the ledge above.

Dragging her palm across her face, she worked to rid the last dredges of sleep from her senses.

The night was still. The only sound the wind shrieking through the bluffs and her own panting breaths.

Heart in her throat, she scoured the camp for anything unusual as her breathing began to even out. A light smattering of snow swirled in the wind. The night felt flat, dead.

She honed in on the cold prickle of dark magick buzzing the stale air. It churned through her marrow like fire ants, imparting a restless feeling.

Something nagged at her. What was wrong?

Silence.

Her breath curled out in clouds.

The fire was long-extinguished.

Where was Bjorn?

"Haven."

The whisper drew her focus to Archeron as he slid noiselessly to the ground, his eyes never leaving the sky. His golden hair pooled over one shoulder, his hastily buttoned tunic open at the chest to reveal the pulse of light from his glowing fleshrunes.

They glowed brighter than normal, the iridescent light spilling from the elegant lines nearly as vibrant as the moonlight above.

Orangish-gold runelight glimmered inside the steel of his longsword as well.

He flicked a quick glance her way, the intensity in his eyes prompting her to slide on her pants and retrieve her weapons without a sound.

The dark magick was now a whirlwind beneath her ribcage. A

sense of primal dread clung to her like stench to a rotten corpse. She buried the panic tightening her chest and focused on reaching the others.

She made it two feet from the cave when the first gremwyr struck.

THIRTY-FIVE

With a dark flash, the gremwyr came screeching through the air toward her, curved talons aimed straight at her face. The beast's decaying odor stung her eyes and seared the back of her throat.

Fighting the urge to dry heave, she unloaded her arrow into its belly and drew another before it could even hit the ground.

A second gremwyr appeared, wings churning the sky as it dropped something . . .

She gasped as a wet thud sounded by her feet.

On the rocks a few yards away, orange scales flashed, all that was left of the basilisk.

As she took in its broken, tortured body—the price for betraying the Shade Queen—horror filled her mind. Most of his torso was gone, his tail sliced and shredded, but she recognized the beautiful diamond pattern that had been so out of place in that wood earlier—the scales the color of the setting sun.

That was what she was asking the Shade Lord to risk: the wrath of a monster.

Tearing her gaze from the wretched, bloody sight, she steeled herself for what was coming. This time, the Shade Lord wouldn't be able to intervene and stop the onslaught.

The Shade Queen was sending a message.

Metal hissed behind her as Surai and Rook readied themselves. Archeron joined them right before they stepped out onto the ledge where the fire smoldered.

"Gremwyrs," Haven breathed, scanning the sky.

And then, as if the name alone conjured them, the great winged beasts swarmed above, a countless horde of monsters obliterating the stars. They seemed to come from every direction, their snarls and growls rattling her bones as they landed around them on the mountain.

Each heavy thud, each scrape of talons over stone, filled her with a deep, ominous doom.

Haven spotted Bjorn sitting still by the dead fire. He was caught in a vision.

"Bjorn!" she screamed, but he barely stirred.

Rook reached him just as a gremwyr dropped down by the fire. She ran the creature through with her sword then shook Bjorn by the shoulders. He startled awake, his bald head whipping around as more gremwyrs landed, the wind carrying whiffs of their putrid stench.

Rook dragged Bjorn across the ledge to join them, and they formed a loose circle facing outward—Haven with her bow, Surai swirling her katanas, and Archeron with his runed longsword. Rook's whip uncoiled over the ground, and Bjorn's axe twirled inside his hand.

For a fleeting moment, Haven locked eyes with Archeron,

watching as his gaze repeated his plea for her to live.

The shared emotion renewed her determination.

I will not die tonight.

Lifting her bow to the sky, she yelled just as the gremwyrs rained down upon them. They hit the ground so hard it trembled. A second later, the air erupted with the sounds of battle. The bloodcurdling symphony of steel against flesh and bone, of arrows twanging, whips cracking, and the screams of dying shadowlings.

A gremwyr shot from the sky into Haven's shoulder with a force strong enough to knock the bow from her hands and send her sprawling. Pain ricocheted through her chest, but she managed to catch herself before she rolled off the cliff.

A shadow fell over her—

She turned just as the gremwyr reached her, its fanged mouth spread wide and inches from her face. It was so close she could feel the creature's foul breath on her cheek, see the threads of saliva between each razor-edged tooth.

Throwing up her hand, she shot a bolt of light magick wrapped in dark magick straight down the monster's throat.

The gremwyr shrieked, the magick consuming it from the inside out. An orange glow seeped from cracks in its leathery flesh, pulsing like a firefly. Before she could maneuver out of the way, the creature burst into ash that rained over her face and into her mouth.

Spitting, she scoured the rocks for her bow just as another gremwyr appeared. Black talons slashed at her throat.

She rolled back and over and came up on her knees, and the claws barely missed her flesh. The end of her bow stuck out a few feet away, resting between two rocks.

She lunged for it. When the gremwyr saw the weapon in her hands, it lifted its wings to fly away—but she had her arrow nocked and barreling toward its own throat before it could escape.

She killed four more creatures before she could make her way back to the others, leaping over the bloodied mound of gremwyr carcasses encircling them and landing next to Archeron. He tossed her another quiver full of arrows.

When she ran out of those, she began invoking them.

They were fighting like Solis warriors, but the onslaught kept coming. Soon they would be buried in gremwyr bodies. Already, the wall of dead was to her waist—and growing. The air ripe with the stench of blood and guts.

And still the sky churned black with gremwyrs. An endless wave of monsters meant to end them.

"We won't last much longer," Haven shouted as another arrow found its mark. The corpse of the gremwyr she killed rolled into their circle, and Archeron kicked it back and glanced at her.

"The mountain passes?" he growled.

When they chose this place, they made sure there were two paths for escape. And if they had been warned ahead of time, they could have used them.

But now . . . now both passes swarmed with the dark, winged bodies of the beasts, and Haven shook her head, her brain whirring to find a solution. If they couldn't go back down the mountain, the only other way was the cliff.

Haven grabbed Archeron's shoulder. "The river below!"

Understanding flickered across his face as he sank his sword into the leathery chest of a gremwyr, steel scraping loudly through muscles and bone. The gremwyr shrieked before collapsing onto a pile of its brethren.

Grunting, Archeron forced the body off his blade with his boot. "That could work. Rook? Surai? Feel like jumping off a cliff?"

Rook glanced over her shoulder at Archeron, a lazy grin on her face.

Her cloak was ripped in two, her athletic arms dripping with black blood. At some point, she'd lost her whip, and she swung her sword through the air so fast it was nothing more than a blur of steel. "Afraid of a few gremwyrs, Archeron?"

Archeron's eyes flashed as he lunged, ramming his blade into a gremwyr a split second before it could take off her head.

"No, Princess!" he replied. "You?"

"What do you think, Seer?" Haven shouted, turning her attention to Bjorn. "Did your vision give you any insight into escaping?"

He paused from hacking at the wall of creatures clawing toward them with his bloodied axes and met her gaze. His haunted expression sent an inexplicable wave of dread pooling at the base of her spine.

"Bjorn!" Archeron called.

Bjorn canted his head to the side at his friend's voice, and the dark shadow left his face.

"The cliff is the only way," he answered, his voice unusually clipped.

As Haven slid her gaze to the ledge, a shock of panic took hold. The path leading to the edge of the cliff was riddled with dead gremwyrs.

The moment their circle broke, they would be picked off.

She twisted to appraise the sheer face of the mountain. Moonlight shimmered over the unbroken crust of snow blanketing the peak. So much snow . . .

Haven didn't have time to think about the consequences as she shouted, "You go while I form a shield around us. As soon as everyone's over, I'll cause an avalanche from above to bury them."

Archeron snapped his gaze to her, his face livid. "No! We go together or not at all."

They didn't have time to argue or for her to say the things she wanted to say.

So she simply said, "Trust me, Sun Lord."

He held her gaze for a second longer—a second that felt like an eternity. *You made a promise to live*, his expression implied.

Then he nodded. "Let's go!"

She'd practiced the shield twice with Stolas, and in both instances, it was a struggle. But this time it felt almost too easy to summon the iridescent, half-invisible shield around them, layered in both dark magick and light with veins of blue and gold weaved together tightly.

As her friends pushed their way to the ledge, she propelled the shield outward with her mind. It felt similar to lifting something heavy, and she could feel her control slipping the way a muscle might tremble before giving out—but she pressed on. Determined to save them.

Right as Surai jumped over the edge, Haven's power flickered. A gremwyr broke through the barrier. Haven cried out in time to alert Archeron, and he delivered a killing blow to its neck as she closed up the breach.

He found her gaze. One word from her, and he'd come back. Instead, she nodded, urging him onward as she worked to hide her slipping power.

Goddess save her, the energy was draining from her as fast as she could summon it, her body weakening by the second. Tendrils of magick bled from the shield and into the sky, her rough skills unable to conserve it.

It felt, in a way, like bleeding out. Only it was her magick and not her blood being drained.

Bjorn leapt next.

Haven gritted her teeth as she struggled to retain her power. Countless gremwyrs bounced off the shield, screeching and clawing at the invisible wall. If the barrier failed, they would be buried in the creatures.

She could hardly hold her sword, but she forced it up high to hide her fading energy from Archeron.

More gremwyrs broke through, swooping down over her friends.

"Go!" she screamed. "*Go!*"

But Archeron was turned around, his sword glinting as he began to carve his way through the creatures back to her. They were everywhere. Their loathing for him palpable.

They snarled and hissed his name, "Solis bastard," their hate-filled, otherworldly voices evoking blind terror.

No! A nightmarish image of the gremwyrs tearing into his flesh popped into her mind. They were going to rip him to shreds.

Archeron cut down two of the beasts, and they locked eyes.

"I'm sorry," she mouthed.

Lifting her hand, she gave up on the shield and used her energy to summon a gust of wind powerful enough to knock him backward. The cloak he used to cover them earlier spread in the wind as he fell over the ledge.

With her shield gone, the creatures converged all at once, their snarls so frenzied they seemed to ricochet inside her skull.

She managed to lift her sword, managed to fight them off for a few seconds, a few heartbeats, a breath. And then her knees buckled, and she stumbled sideways, the sword sparking as the blade dragged across the stone.

Red, hungry eyes flashed. Haven spun and the gremwyr's talons skimmed her shoulder, causing blinding pain.

She blinked, and the creature's wicked claws were arcing

toward her face—

Rook slammed her blade through the gremwyr's spine, and it fell at her feet. "Get up, Haven!"

Her friend's voice roused her to stand, her body surging with hope as they somehow managed to clear a path to the ledge. The Morgani Princess was everywhere, dancing in circles of death, wielding her blade like it was a part of her, and *grinning.*

In that moment, the princess was the most beautiful thing Haven had ever seen. A miasma of steel and death and destruction.

Haven stopped when the icy river came into view. "The avalanche!"

"Hurry!" Rook yelled, slicing her blade through the membrane and tendons of a gremwyr's wing. The creature screeched over the cliff and went silent.

If Haven didn't bring the snow down on the creatures, they would keep coming.

Saying a quick prayer, she focused on the snowy peak. Drawing every last bit of power left in her veins, willing it into a tornado of wind that pummeled the giant slab of snow into a weapon.

A crack split the air. The mountain began to rumble as the snowy peak shifted and groaned.

Utterly drained, Haven heaved a bone-weary sigh. "We did it."

Rook opened her mouth, and then her gaze flicked to something behind Haven—

By the time Haven turned, it was too late to jump out of the way. The gremwyr was already upon them. She flinched, lifting her hands in a knee-jerk reaction to use the magick that wasn't there, when Rook shoved Haven out of the way.

The Morgani Princess took the full force of the demon's talons.

Haven heard herself scream as she was flung sideways. She tried to grab hold of something, but her fingers scrabbled uselessly against smooth rock.

She slid over the side of the cliff as if in a dream.

For a split second, she saw Rook, a gruesome wound gushing blood from her chest. Somehow, she was still swinging her sword as the gremwyr's claws sank deep into her back. Still fighting with that warrior grace even though she had to know what came next.

The monster spread its wings and heaved into the air. Rook's sword flashed. She screamed—but it was a cry of rage, not fear.

Even as the gremwyr arced higher into the stars, the princess continued fighting. She might have had a chance, if not for the rest of the monsters. Sensing blood, they converged over the Morgani Princess, ripping and shredding like demons from the Netherworld.

Right before Rook disappeared beneath the leathery cloud of talons and teeth, and Haven began her free-fall to the river below, their eyes met. Something traveled between them.

A cry to arms—and a *goodbye.*

And then Haven screamed and screamed all the way to the icy water as her dying friend billowed across the sky.

A falling star; a true Morgani Princess.

THIRTY-SIX

Bell woke from a dreamless sleep. For a breath, before he saw the fireplace burning with the golden magickal fire or the slouched form of the creature in the chair across from the couch, he thought he was in Penryth.

The truth crashed over him in a wave of despair. The Noctis. The fight. His injuries.

The pain—Goddess Above, the pain.

Except, as he stretched out on the couch, he realized the agony from earlier had faded to a dull throb in his shoulder. His neck ached, but that was probably from sleeping on the hard sofa—although someone had been thoughtful enough to place a pillow beneath his head and cover him with a blanket.

Not a blanket. A pine-green cloak frayed at the ends. Bell sat up and noticed a long gash across the velvet, dried blood staining the edges.

Had the creature been hurt?

The thought formed a lump in his throat. Throwing off the cloak, Bell slipped from the couch to check on him. He was slumped on his back with his eyes closed, his huge body spilling out of the chair.

It was strange seeing the creature without his hooded cloak, and Bell tried not to cringe from the green and amber scales cascading down the right side of his face and neck, polished and bright as gemstones.

But it was the other half that drew him in. The boy-prince inside the monster, sandy flesh pale against the colorful scales. His sun-drenched mortal hair had fallen over the inhuman half of his scalp, covering the ruined side of his face.

A cruel fate—to have both the beauty of his youth and the horror of his Curse side by side. It felt like looking at a raw emerald trapped inside its host rock.

The creature's eyes flicked open, and he blinked wearily at Bell. "Are you not . . . afraid?"

Bell shifted on his feet. "No, at least, not like before."

"Your fear has turned to a morbid curiosity. Perhaps you are wondering how a prince as handsome as I became this wretched creature."

The bitterness in his voice couldn't hide the anguish hewn into every word. As he repositioned himself in the chair, a groan slipped out, and his gloved fingers fluttered over his chest.

"You're hurt?"

"The Noctis scratched me with the poisoned talons along his wings."

Forgetting about the scales, Bell began to unbutton the creature's navy-blue shirt.

The creature's arm shot out and grabbed Bell's wrist. For a heartbeat, he just looked at Bell, his chest heaving. Then, his head fell back, and he released a ragged sigh.

Bell swallowed as he continued unbuttoning. When the last button slipped free, he parted the shirt, barely holding back his gasp. A nasty gash furrowed across the mortal side of his chest, leaving black veins sprouting from the festering wound like angry vipers. "That's more than a scratch!"

The creature's throat bobbed. "I've received worse. It will heal . . . in time."

"Why not use the magick that healed me?"

The creature closed his eyes as if just keeping them open was a chore. "I used all of it on your wounds."

"But surely we can do something?"

"Yes. Let me rest."

But Bell was already crossing the living room floor in search of supplies. It took a few minutes, but he found a silver pitcher of water on the dining room table, and he used a paring knife from a drawer to cut strips from the curtains to use as rags.

He could tell the creature wasn't sleeping when he returned by the too-quick rise of his chest. Still, Bell was quiet as he soaked the first rag in water and washed the dried crust of blood from his skin.

The youthful flesh shivered beneath Bell's touch, and he couldn't help but think about Renault, the prince whose skin he was cleaning. Who, according to legend, had once thrown lavish, week-long parties the entire realm still talked about.

How could this creature, this ruined young man, be anything like that prince?

Finally, when the water in the pitcher was dark with blood, and dry, blue strips wrapped around the creature's wounds, Bell stood to leave. He rolled his neck.

"Stay." The creature opened his eyes, one golden and beautiful, the other reptilian. "Please."

Bell hesitated. There was still so much about this prince he didn't understand, didn't trust. Yet, he'd saved Bell, using the last of his magick to heal Bell's injuries rather than his own. That didn't sound like the fallen prince he'd read about. One who could orchestrate his family's murder.

"Shall I bring us some food?" Bell offered.

Still watching him, the creature nodded slowly, and Bell once again entered the dining room. The table was set for dinner.

He hesitated briefly before grabbing a tray of spiced lamb and potatoes along with the silverware and napkins.

The creature was sitting up in the chair, his eyes brighter than before. His shirt was still unbuttoned, and after fumbling with the buttons with his gloved left hand, he let out a snarl. "Can you help me?"

Bell set the food on the coffee table and then dropped to his knees. The creature huffed an uneven breath as Bell began to button his tunic.

"I was left-handed. Before." He held his gloved hand up, and for the first time, Bell noticed how much bigger it was than his right. How crooked the fingers were. "It's hard to button a shirt with claws. Usually, I use magick."

After Bell finished, he dragged the wooden coffee table between the two chairs. The creature took the soup spoon, Bell the fork.

"Shall I . . ." The creature cleared his throat. "Shall I put on my cloak?"

"No. I mean, not unless you want to."

As they ate, Bell noticed the creature kept flicking quick glances over him as if worried that, at some point, Bell would decide he couldn't eat next to such a monster.

"Did any of the other sacrifices ever see you without your

cloak?" Bell asked.

"In the beginning, I didn't look like this. And when the scales started to grow, I—no, I never dared."

Bell chewed his lip, hesitating before his next question. "Why are you changing?"

The creature set his spoon down on the platter with a clang. "The dark magick eats at me. Slowly changing my insides. My flesh." He swung his arm in a half-circle over the room. "Here, my magick mostly protects me. But when I leave the protection of my side of the castle, I'm affected."

Bell swallowed, thinking how the creature left to save him. "Why does the Shade Queen let you retain your magick?"

A dark shadow flickered over his face. "Because it keeps me human longer. Once I succumb to this beastly form, I will no longer possess the humanity to feel as I do now. All my torment, all my grief and agony will slip away."

Bell's gaze collapsed to the picked over tray.

"Go ahead. Ask me if the rumors are true. The others did until I learned to hide my identity along with my monstrous face."

"Are they?"

"Yes. And no." It was the creature's turn to drop his stare, and his ruined hand clawed into the rolled arm of his chair without him seeming to notice. "I was the third born son and a disappointment to my father from the start. I cared more about clothes and balls than politics, preferred polished boots to swords. But I never hated him enough to want his death."

Behind him, the fire crackled and grew as if his emotions were tied to his magick.

"When I turned eighteen," he continued, his voice barely more than a whisper, "my father set my engagement to a thrice widowed mortal queen renowned for her cruelty and ugliness. It was a punishment that would have taken me far from my beloved kingdom . . . and my lover."

Bell was on the edge of his chair. "The beautiful woman I saw in the other-world?"

A wry smile carved the creature's jaw. "No. Her brother."

Oh—*Oh*.

Canting his head to the side, Bell studied the creature in a new light. Never before had he met someone like himself. He'd heard rumors of male courtiers who preferred the company of other men, of course.

But meeting someone like him, in person, was different.

"But it was his sister, Ephinia," the creature continued, oblivious to Bell's newfound curiosity, "who suggested we summon a Noctis from the Netherworld to work a spell with dark magick. All three of us had powerful magick, although we didn't know at the time how powerful, and one moonlit night, we summoned Ravenna."

"Did you know she was the Shade Queen's daughter?" Bell interrupted.

Reddish-blond hair slipped over his face as he shook his head. "No. She was so kind at first, playing off my desperation, my vanity. The spell was only supposed to change their minds. It was—she said they would sleep, but only for a while. They would not suffer."

His voice broke. His fingers squeezed the arms of his chair so hard the wood beneath groaned before he continued. "After the spell was cast, and my father, mother, and brothers died, her demands grew. If I agreed to them, she promised to use her magick to hide the murders from my people. By then, I knew she was wicked, but I was trapped. Bound by our secret, our bargain."

Bell released a jagged breath. "What did she want?"

"To rule beside me as queen. I knew nothing of her husband in the Netherworld or who she was. She said my lover and his sister wouldn't be hurt, but I knew it was a lie. She wanted claim to my mortal kingdom. So on our wedding night, I stabbed her with a poisoned dagger that rendered her powerless, and then I cut out her heart."

Bell sagged into his chair, the room suddenly heavy with shadows. "You still didn't know . . ."

The creature glanced at Bell as if he'd forgotten he was there, his eyes haunted with remorse. "I didn't understand the ancient, evil magick of the Noctis, nor the repercussions of breaking an agreement bound with it. But as soon as I pulled out her black heart and the entire earth shook, I knew there was darkness to follow."

"The Curse," Bell added softly.

Blinking down at his hands, the creature eased his grip on the rolled arms of his chair; the dusty blue fabric beneath was shredded. "When the Shade Queen arrived with her army of shadowlings and Noctis, I tried to hide my friends. But she found them anyway and did horrible, monstrous things to them. I haven't seen either Ephinia or Bjorn in over three centuries."

"And the portal?"

"I was confined to the only part of the castle the Curse hadn't touched. At first, the solitude was unbearable, and I selfishly looked forward to the mortal sacrifices that came. The Shade Queen made me take care of them. Made me care for them. And then, every full moon, I was forced to watch as Ravenna came back to life and feasted on their magick, flesh, and blood to survive. Over the centuries, the nobles with magick began to diminish, so I had time to practice my magick, to hone it. It was then that I discovered what I could do."

"You can go back in time?"

It almost seemed silly to suggest, impossible, yet the creature nodded. "In a way, yes. I cannot alter it, but I can interact in certain ways. At first, I created the portal so I could relive my days before the Curse. But then, I remembered something. The blade I used on Ravenna had been poisoned by Ephinia with some rare type of flower that grew in our gardens. I knew if I could find it again and increase its potency, I could perhaps use the poison to kill the Shade Queen."

Bell ran a hand through his hair. "That's what we've been doing?"

"Yes. I've tried every bloom that grows in that garden, killing a shadowling or a Noctis a couple times a year and hiding the evidence so the queen would not get suspicious. But I never had any success finding a poison strong enough to outright kill them . . . until today."

An image of Malix catching fire and turning to ash flashed across Bell's mind. "Which flower was it?"

"Not a flower—a thorn. I hadn't been inside that chamber for over a century until I found you there. After you fled, I tore the room apart, and one of the rose thorns drew blood. So I ground it up, covered my blade with it, and went to find you."

"The poison was here in the castle all along?"

A rare smile flickered across the mortal part of his lips. "Light magick must have been clinging to the outside of the castle all these years. Waiting for me to find it. And if it wasn't for you, I would have never entered my old bedroom again."

Bell felt a flush creeping up his neck, and he cleared his throat.

One second the creature was relaxed in the chair.

The next, his body went rigid, and he leapt from his seat just as a dark shadow entered through the open corner and slid across the room.

Massive, feathered wings. A cruel, angry beauty. Bell recognized the Shade Lord who brought him here what felt like years ago, and he stood too.

"Wait—it's not time," Bell cried. "I have another day until the moon is full."

The Shade Lord sauntered toward the fire, casually, as if he had come for tea. "I'm not here for that. Yet."

"Then why are you here, Noctis?" The creature's voice was a dark rumble laced with fury belonging to the beastly side of him.

Cutting a lazy glance at the creature, the Shade Lord said, "I'm here to talk about a door."

"A door?" Bell crossed his arms. Whatever games the Shade Lord wanted to play, he wouldn't give him the pleasure.

The Shade Lord squared to face Bell, and beneath his bored expression shivered something more. Something important.

"A door, Prince of Penryth. The thing you use to enter and exit places."

The creature snarled as the Shade Lord suddenly prowled toward Bell. When Bell could almost touch the Shade Lord's gorgeous feathers, he stopped.

"You have a friend who would like very much to open one and visit you," the Shade Lord said. "A stubborn mortal girl with rose-gold hair, hideous feet, and very powerful magick."

The name clanged through his heart before it ever left his lips. "Haven?"

"Yes," the Shade Lord purred, a serpentine grin spreading across his face. "Her."

"But she doesn't have magick. Besides, she's . . . she's . . ." Even after all this time, he still couldn't say the words. *Dead. She's dead.* And now the Shade Lord was playing a cruel trick on him.

"I assure you she has not passed into my dominion," the Shade Lord answered. "Although, not for lack of trying. Your friend has the lives of a wyvern."

Bell swallowed down a laugh as hope surged inside him. "So it's true, then? She didn't die?"

The Shade Lord shook his head, his white hair falling over one silver eye. "She is very much alive and intent on rescuing you, no matter the cost. Now, about that door."

THIRTY-SEVEN

They found Rook just after dawn.

Archeron led the search party, walking thirty feet ahead of Haven and the others. He hadn't spoken a word since learning of Rook's fate.

None of them had.

A heavy, strangling silence had fallen over the land, as if even the cursed rocks and withered trees mourned the Morgani Princess. The wind refused to blow. The snow refused to fall. The veiled sun refused its warm caress.

Archeron topped a grassy knoll, and his back stiffened. He froze, still as the grass and the breeze. After a few agonizing moments, he cast Haven a cautious look to keep Surai away as he went to investigate whatever it was he'd spotted.

Even as he kneeled beside something in the grass, even as the life seemed to bleed out of him—Haven still held onto hope that Rook was alive.

That she might have somehow broken free, perhaps fallen into the river.

Maybe she was hurt and waiting for them . . . but she was alive. She had to be alive. How could she not be? The princess was so full of life and love and courage.

People like her didn't die. Not like this.

That hope vanished the moment Archeron stood. He looked away, but not before she caught the absolute grief lining his face. His mouth downturned, and one hand hovered over his throat as if trying to force the air into his body.

Steeling his shoulders, he faced them and gave a quick, jerky nod.

One single gesture that dashed Haven's hopes completely. Her stomach clenched, nausea rolling over her like a wave.

Not Rook. She can't be . . . gone.

They approached slowly. As soon as Rook came into view, Haven had to swallow down a horrified gasp. The Morgani Princess must have been dropped from high up because she was broken and crumpled, lying face down at the foot of the mountain near a cluster of rocks.

Blood darkened her flaxen hair to the point she was nearly unrecognizable. The shreds of her once snow-white cloak still clinging to her were stained completely red, her beloved knee-high boots torn and muddied.

Goddess, no.

Archeron's body trembled with barely repressed grief as he leaned down and replaced her sullied cloak with his dark one. He didn't speak a word as he began working to clean the mud and grime from Rook's body.

In turn, Haven tried to keep Surai away. To hide her from seeing the worst until Archeron was finished.

At first, it was easy. Surai seemed in a trance. Eyes glazed and fixed, breath shallow. She hardly looked at Rook, hardly seemed to understand what was happening.

When she did move, her distant gaze flitted to the sky as if her mate was still up there—as if Rook's broken body was just a ruse meant to trick her.

But then, a lock of Rook's blonde hair caught in the breeze—the only section of her hair not stained red—and Surai's focus slid to her mate. A shudder rippled through Surai's slight body. She blinked.

"Her beautiful hair," Surai whispered. "She hates when it's dirty."

Haven's throat clenched as she shared a painful look with Archeron.

Surai said Rook's name, softly—a question.

Then the Solis warrior shrieked, a sound Haven felt inside her chest, and lunged toward Rook.

Haven tried to hold her, but she fought like a wild animal, clawing and hitting until she broke free and stumbled to her knees beside Rook.

As Surai cradled her mate's head in her lap and wails spilled from her lips, Haven was sure her chest would split open from the inside—each ragged, piercing scream a reminder that she had failed.

She was to blame.

If only she could have held her shield a few minutes longer. If only she hadn't been so exhausted. If only Rook had left Haven to die instead of coming back for her.

I'm to blame. My failings and inability to control my power killed her.

No one said as much. Not when she first told them, minutes after she hit the water and Archeron dragged her from the frigid waters a hundred yards down the river. Not as they fought off the last remaining gremwyrs that hadn't perished in the avalanche that cost Rook her life. And not as they sat silently in front of the fire that warmed the ice from their flesh enough so they could start their search for her.

Before she hit the cold water, Haven knew they would never find Rook alive, but she let the others believe there might be a chance. She was too weak to tell them the truth. Too weak, even, to admit that truth to herself.

Another reason to despise herself.

And now, in the light of day, she felt exposed. Her sins nailed to her skin for everyone to see.

I killed her.

Surai's cries had turned to something else—a keening. Somehow conjuring the courage to join her friend, Haven slipped her arm around the grieving girl's shoulders.

Surai gasped. "She's gone?"

Haven nodded, wishing she could carve out her friend's agony and take it as her own. She could see Surai trying to fit this new reality into her mind. Trying to accept the unacceptable.

"She cannot be gone," Surai said. "Not like this. Not here, in this horrible land."

Then she buried her face in Haven's chest and sobbed.

Only Bjorn seemed unable to grieve. He stood in the distance, watching them tend to Rook with those sightless eyes that saw everything. His face unreadable.

Did he see her fate beforehand?

Haven knew the Seer and princess had been close, but Haven still thought his absence cowardly.

Archeron loved Rook just as much. Yet he was the one who cleaned the blood from Rook's face and body, his half-frozen fingers meticulously kneading snow into her hair and over her skin.

With tears in her eyes, Haven watched the Sun Lord fix Rook's hair, his thick fingers trying to redo her braids and mend the gashes in her clothes while Surai plucked out twigs and other debris. He collected Rook's jewelry, including the ring that allowed her to stay in her true form.

Haven understood now that Rook must have known it was her last night with Surai. Whatever price the ring required—Rook would never have to pay it.

They worked on her in silence, every caress, every brush of fingers over her cheeks or hair or clothes a gesture of love. A part of Haven wondered when her time came if they would do the same.

She certainly didn't feel worthy of such love—especially now.

When finished, Archeron ran a thumb over each of Rook's dusky lids, closing her amber eyes forever.

Now clean and clothed the way a Morgani Princess should be, Archeron lifted her up against his chest, her arms hanging loosely and fine boots glittering beneath the morning sun, and they trekked up the mountain without a word.

When the air was thin, and snow covered the rocks, they found a small shelf of stone to lay her on.

Surai was given time alone with Rook while they waited by the snowy pass. Haven was terrified to face Bjorn and Archeron; terrified they would blame her for not holding the shield.

But the second they were away from Surai, Archeron pulled her into his warm chest, slipping his arms around her neck.

"Are you okay?" he breathed.

She shook her head as her mind replayed Rook's last few seconds alive, still fighting as blood gurgled from her chest.

That should have been her, not Rook. Haven was supposed to die.

Her prayer flashed in her mind, a spear of guilt. Could the Goddess have taken Rook instead? Because Haven asked to live?

She shuddered against his chest. "I could have saved her, Archeron."

"Stop." Bracing his hands on either side of her cheeks, he tilted her face up to look at him. "Rook knew the risks coming here."

Haven barely heard him. "But if my shield had been stronger—"

"No. You are looking at this all wrong. If not for your courage and the strength of your shield, we would have all perished. Do you understand? You saved us, Haven, and you nearly died in the process."

He ran the pads of his thumbs over her cheeks, wiping away the moisture. When had she cried?

"Sometimes bad things happen, Haven," he continued. "Sometimes people we love die. For that reason, loving those who are still here is the most important thing you can do to honor them. You've taught me that." Leaning down, his lips brushed hers, the salty taste of tears stinging her mouth. "Bell is still alive. He's waiting for you. But you cannot save him if you continue down this dark path."

She leaned into him, thankful for his warmth, his steady presence. Her throat ached with tears, but her cheeks were dry, her heart filled with renewed purpose. "Are we just going to leave Rook here?"

A muscle ticked in his jaw as he slid his gaze to the princess. "She will be preserved on the mountain until we return. If she's buried here"—his voice broke, and he cleared his throat—"if she's buried in the Ruinlands, her soul will be trapped, enslaved to Morgryth."

A haunting voice shivered across the air as Surai began a song in Solissian.

"Lay down, my darling, and rest your weary head. Your battle is over, your journey is at an end. Your Golden Shores are calling; your ancestors are near. Go now, Princess, claim your forever throne, and then wait for me until I'm called home."

There were no more tears to shed as they left the Morgani Princess alone on that mountain.

With every step, Haven's pain formed into a growing pit of fury that raged inside her chest. Archeron's words had done the opposite of what he'd intended.

She hadn't cleaved the guilt from her heart; she'd kept it, used it, *transformed* it, stoking that gut-wrenching emotion into a single fiery purpose: revenge.

She wanted revenge. Wanted to spill enough blood to wash away the guilt pounding at her in unrelenting waves.

Her mind relived the moment the gremwyrs killed Rook over and over and over. Each time, the anger surged, smoldering in her marrow, boiling her blood until her magick rolled off her in hot bursts that distorted the air.

The Shade Queen took Bell. She killed thousands of mortals. Desiccated Haven's lands. And the bitch murdered the finest warrior in the realm.

A warrior who should've been married to her lover, not ripped apart by monsters and dropped like trash.

For the first time since all of this started, Haven understood how much Morgryth had taken from her. From everyone she loved and cared about. And if she didn't do something about it, the Dark Queen would destroy the mortal world as they knew it.

Haven's hands were bunched into fists at her side, and they burned with magick. Wild, angry magick. Magick that could've prevented Rook's death. Magick that could make the Dark Queen pay.

"I couldn't save her," Haven choked out. They were at the bottom of the mountain, and the others turned to her. When she saw Archeron's pained expression, the agony twisting his face into an unrecognizable mask, she said a silent vow to the Goddess.

Someday, I swear it; I will rip out the Shade Queen's black heart.

Archeron reached out for her. "You did all you could."

"Did I?" Instead of accepting Archeron's offer of comfort, Haven held up her hands, staring dully at the sapphire and gold flames of magick licking over her flesh. "My magick failed me. I failed."

Surai shook her head. "There is no greater honor in the Morgani culture than to die for your sister."

"But if I'd had fleshrunes, she wouldn't have died at all!"

"No." Tears fell freely down Surai's cheeks. "We all fought as hard as we could, Haven, and her death is no one's fault but the Shade Queen's. Rook is—was a warrior, and she died a warrior's death."

Haven turned to face Bjorn, whose sightless gaze was fixed on the spot where they had left Rook. "You knew, didn't you?"

Bjorn flinched as if she'd hit him. "I loved her, but even I could not prevent her death. She knew her fate, and she accepted it."

"Fate?" Haven scoffed, anger poisoning the word. "The Shade Queen's malice isn't fate. My death isn't fated. We make our own fate." She thrust out her hands, their ineptness never more apparent than now. "I have endless, powerful magick that could finally give us a chance against Morgryth, but I can't access it unless you help me. Give me runemarks. Make me into a weapon to destroy Morgryth."

Archeron shook his head slowly, his shoulders slumped. "I will not sentence you to death, Haven. I refuse to lose you as well."

"But that's exactly what you're doing if you send me to Spirefall without fleshrunes. You're sentencing all of us to death."

"Even if, by some momentary bout of insanity, I allowed this . . . this place is crawling with dark magick, and the ceremony would not work."

"Actually, there is a way," Bjorn said, ignoring Archeron's snarl of protest. Those sightless eyes the color of the snow around them studied her. "But we would need all three of our powers to perform the rite. It is dangerous, and I don't know if mortal flesh will take the magick, but if she survives, she will be runemarked."

"Out of the question," Archeron snapped.

Haven's heart hurt for Archeron as she said, "But it's not your choice, Sun Lord. It's mine."

She hated causing him pain, especially after everything they'd suffered.

But her need to crush Morgryth was all-consuming.

"You're right," he countered. "You and the others may choose to damn you to a life of being hunted." Beneath his anger ran an undercurrent of sadness. "But I refuse to be a part of it."

"Even if my damning meant saving the lives of countless innocents?" she asked softly.

"Even if it meant saving the whole damned world," he responded just as softly. "I will not sacrifice you for them, for anyone."

She looked to Surai, her expression pleading and ferocious. "Will you help me?"

Surai's lavender eyes were rimmed red from crying but also clear. She slipped a gloved hand over the golden hilt of her katana. "I will help you however I can. Just promise me, when we enter Spirefall, you will kill as many of the Noctis as you can, *Soror*."

Soror—the Solis word for sister. Haven blinked back the tears that burned her throat. "That's a promise I can easily make. I'll kill them all, every single black-winged monster until my heart stops in my chest."

Archeron snarled and prowled a few feet, as if to leave, then whipped around and stalked back to her. "Please, Haven. We will find another way. Don't do this."

Archeron's pleas penetrated deep into her heart. The last thing she wanted was to hurt him, and for a breath, she considered giving up on the idea.

But, no matter how hard she tried to bury her anger, it surged to fill her. A growing flame of rage.

She needed revenge, needed to see the Shade Queen's face twisted with the same fear and agony they all felt. "I'm sorry, but you can't sway me, Archeron. It's already decided."

He blinked, searching her face as his chest heaved, his fists clenching and unclenching at his sides. "Haven, you have no idea what unleashing both light and dark magick will do. It could kill you or worse. You could change, become a monster."

"Then put me out of my misery after we break the Curse."

She hadn't meant to sound so harsh or uncaring, not after everything that had happened and so close to Rook's death, but it came out anyway.

Archeron stared at her with uncomprehending eyes, as if she were suddenly a stranger. "How could you even suggest such a thing?"

The hurt in his voice cut deep, but he stormed off before she could make it right.

Surai came forward and put her slim hand on Haven's wrist. "He will get over it."

"I don't think he will," Haven answered, watching him disappear into the dense wood beyond the river. A part of her ached at the thought of losing him, but breaking the Curse, saving Bell, and making the Shade Queen pay for Rook's death—she would do whatever it took to make those things happen.

And if becoming a weapon of magick was the only way, so be it.

Releasing a deep sigh, she turned to Bjorn. "Seer, what do we have to do?"

Bjorn reached into the inside pocket of his cloak and pulled out a small green purse. Her runepurse. It seemed like years had passed since she'd climbed that giant ash tree and retrieved Bell's stone, the one that had started this whole thing.

His lips curled in an almost-smile. "Damius might be missing this. Now, we need to find shelter and make a fire hot enough to melt these runestones."

Suddenly, it all became real, what she was about to do, and her throat felt papery-dry as she struggled to swallow. She imagined Bjorn drawing runemarks over her flesh.

But this, this was something else. "Those aren't runemarks, Seer. Those are powerrunes."

An impressed look flickered over Bjorn's face as he raised an eyebrow. "Very good. Whomever chose these stones had an expert eye. Some of these powerrunes are so rare, so powerful, I've never laid eyes upon them, nor do I know what, exactly, they do."

There was a warning there. She shifted on her feet, nausea churning her stomach.

"Second thoughts?" Bjorn asked carefully.

"No. I just . . ." Her focus drifted to the trees. What if Archeron was right? What if it killed her, or worse?

What if she became a monster?

Forcing out her fears with a sigh, she dragged her gaze back to the seer and his bag of stones. "I'm ready. Just promise me, if I become something . . . evil, you'll kill me so Archeron doesn't have to."

Surai gasped, but the Seer hardly blinked as he nodded. "Now," he began. "Pray to the Goddess that Archeron comes back to help us."

A massive fire blazed inside the cave Bjorn chose for the ceremony, and black smoke drifted up through the cracks in the granite ceiling. Haven focused on the blue patch of sky peeking through as Bjorn circled the fire, chanting in a tongue she didn't recognize. The burning runestones perfumed the smoky air with a metallic, crushed rose smell that churned her stomach.

Except for her undershirt and underwear, her clothes had been stripped away, and sweat beaded along her naked skin, pooling between her breasts. Already, hours had passed inside this heat-drenched cave, hours of chanting and waiting.

Haven turned on her side to face Surai, who sat cross-legged beside her. "He won't come."

Surai blinked, surfacing from the trance of grief that had claimed her the last few hours. "Then we do it without him."

"No," Bjorn called. "We need his power to harness the stones. Even with three of us, it may not take. There is simply too much dark magick here."

Surai shook her head, her messy braid snaking over her shoulder. "Tonight is the full moon. We must do it now."

Haven lifted onto her elbows. "Do it, Seer. I'll take the consequences."

And she would. Whatever they were. For Bell. For revenge.

Bjorn's head canted toward her. For a moment, she swore he could see her clearly from his moon-white eyes. His throat bobbed. Then he shuffled around the fire once more, and she turned her attention back to Surai.

"If something happens," Haven said, "tell Archeron he's a pretty bastard. And . . . that I'm sorry."

Surai opened her mouth, and then her gaze drifted past Haven. "Tell him yourself."

Haven's heart slammed against her ribs as she turned to see Archeron prowling through the cave entrance toward her. He held her stare as he crossed the floor and knelt at her side.

She let out a relieved sigh. "You came."

His hand was cold from being outside as he took hers. Heartbeats passed, and he seemed to struggle for words. "I don't agree with this, Haven, but I will fight alongside you to the end, whenever that may be. You have my sword . . . and my heart. No matter what."

"Took you long enough," Surai snarled.

Archeron cut his eyes at her. "If she dies, I'm blaming all of you."

He didn't mention the alternative—if she became something malevolent. Something just as bad as the Shade Queen. Magick was a dark, duplicitous master, and she could very well wake up an entirely different person.

Before she could respond, Bjorn came forward, and the serious mood turned even darker. Haven's heart threatened to beat out of her chest as Bjorn leaned over her. Steam curled from the worn chalice in his hands.

Once, jewels must have rimmed the cup, but now the only evidence of that were the faint oval and diamond outlines against the tarnished gold.

He settled on the cloak to her left, the contents of the goblet illuminating his solemn face. Silence. All eyes were riveted to the chalice with the melted runestones inside.

All of that magick condensed . . .

Haven lifted to a sitting position and wrapped her arms around her knees as she peeked over the golden rim—and gasped.

In their solid form, the runestones had been polished rocks and gemstones. Pretty, but not amazing.

Yet, melted . . . melted they were a swirling mass of colors and light, shimmering and metallic and alluring, the most magnificent thing Haven had ever laid eyes on.

And the limitless power she felt bubbling over the rim . . . it called to her, whispering in a wordless language. With that, all of her fears and doubts evanesced.

"I'm ready." Her voice was an impatient rasp.

"You will have to drink this," Bjorn said.

She gave a quick nod, and they began to chant, their voices joining together and echoing off the cavern walls until it became one long string of sounds, a song spilling into her veins and stirring along her bones.

She felt light and heavy, hollow and full. Her heartbeat slowed, her breath aligning with some ancient rhythm that beat within everything.

She took the cup, barely aware of the hot metal searing her palm. The magick inside the goblet seemed to surge as she lifted it to her lips, the diaphanous light blinding her.

For a heartbeat, she hesitated.

The mortal girl from Penryth knew she would cease to exist once the magick filled her body; but the girl from across the Glittering Sea was ready to emerge and accept her powers. Ready to avenge Rook and save her friend, whatever the cost.

So she tilted back her head and claimed her destiny.

THIRTY-EIGHT

Bell's mind whirled with questions as he followed the fallen prince, Renault—he was still getting used to his real name—deeper into Spirefall, sticking close to the orange torchlight flickering over the damp stone walls as bats dove around his head.

How could Haven be alive?

He saw her plunge into the fiery chasm. Saw the wyvern shadowing her. Unless the crazy story the Shade Lord told him was true: He saved her, and now she was coming with a band of Solis to break the Curse and set him free.

If it was anyone but Haven, he would have believed it was impossible.

"Hurry," Renault ordered. "The Noctis said the door would be here."

Bell scrambled after the fallen prince, his boots slipping along the worn stairs as he fought down a surge of fear. This place felt evil right down to the slick onyx stone, illuminated by wafts of bluish magick hewn into the material.

Occasionally, if the faded light from the cracks above hit just right, runestones flashed across the walls.

He didn't have much knowledge of runes, but he could feel the evil inside the stone. This place was a fortress of dark magick, meant to keep mortals like him imprisoned forever.

And they weren't alone.

Huge black beetles and moon-white scorpions slithered around his feet; too-large rats squeaked from corners. Near the bottom of the spiraling stairs, a black, hooded viper as thick as his arm hissed at them before lazily slithering into the darkness.

They paused to gather their bearings, and Bell shook off two apple-sized spiders crawling along his neck.

His voice was embarrassingly high as he said, "So you believe him?"

"Do we have a choice?" Renault's frosty breath curled in the air, and he waved his torch to the right, illuminating another set of stairs. "This is the only chance you have."

Bell tried to force down the rising hope in his chest. He couldn't afford to believe. Not yet.

Still, with each step he took down the winding stairs, cold, damp, and swollen with shadows and night-creatures, he let himself hope a little more. Even as they passed nightmarish rooms full of mortal prisoners in cages, similar to the ones he encountered last time, their wails echoing off the runed walls.

If Haven really did come for him, maybe they could try to free them too.

"There," Renault whispered.

Bell followed the large orb of firelight to the door. Strange runes and symbols were carved into the iron door's surface, and they flared bright blue as the two approached.

"This has to be it," Renault rasped. He handed Bell the torch, sending a wave of soft heat over his cheeks, then began whispering spells as he drew runes in the air with his mortal hand.

Bell leaned against the cold obsidian wall on the right, trying not to think about the freedom that lay on the other side.

According to the Shade Lord helping them, the wards on this door, which kept people in, were stronger than the ones keeping forces out. But even if they could break those wards and escape, the Shade Queen would track him easily.

No, letting Haven in was his only chance—if she truly were alive. But did she know what nightmares awaited her inside?

Not like a little death would stop her. When it came to saving her friends—or him, more specifically—she would die a thousand times over.

He'd never admitted as much, but her inhuman loyalty often made him feel less than worthy. Sometimes, he wished her loyalty would falter. Just once—so he could stop having to live up to her idea of him. The best possible him.

Most days, he was barely a shadow of that ideal—not that she noticed. She loved him unconditionally, unwaveringly, and unsparingly. And sometimes . . . sometimes being the person who deserved such love was exhausting.

He lay his head against the wall, pressing a fist into his sternum. He should ask Renault to stop.

Once Haven entered, her chances of leaving were nonexistent. Images of the Shade Queen torturing her filled his mind, and he muffled the cry that followed.

Perhaps he was a coward. Or, perhaps he just needed to see his friend again, to make sure she was still alive. But he watched Renault as he drew his runes and said his spells, watched the bright swirls on the door slowly ebb to dying shadows, and he said nothing to stop him.

All at once, it was done.

Renault turned to Bell with a rare smile. "The wards are broken."

Bell ran a hand over the freezing iron door. "You're sure?"

"Yes. I felt them shatter."

Before they left Renault's side of the castle, the Shade Lord had performed his own spell to protect Renault's light magick from the dark magick here, at least long enough for him to break the wards.

"We need to go, Bellamy."

It was the first time Renault said Bell's name, and for some stupid reason, he felt heat rise in his cheeks. "Thank you for doing this. I know if they catch you helping me, you'll be punished."

Renault's throat bobbed, and he slowly turned to look at Bell. "I should have done this years ago. Thank you . . . for reminding me that there is still some good in this world. And that I can still be part of that goodness, even after all my sins."

"Of course you can," Bell said. "Whatever you've done, however you've failed yourself and others, it's never too late to do the right thing. And everyone deserves to be forgiven for their failings. Goddess knows mine are countless."

"Yours?" Renault scoffed. "What failings could you possess, Prince? You are the kindest man I have ever had the misfortune of holding prisoner."

Kind? Bell stared at Renault, shocked at his sincerity.

In Bell's world, kindness was a sin and cruelty the answer. He'd decided long ago he would never measure up the way Renk did.

But now, to have someone see his kindness as something worthy . . .

A bubble of warmth grew inside his chest, filling him with a strange sort of hollow euphoria.

On impulse, Bell reached out and took Renault's clawed hand. He went absolutely still as Bell removed the glove, taking care with each crooked finger. Torchlight flickered off dark green scales. Curved gray claws hung limply from his fingertips, half-retracted.

"Soon," Renault said, "I will be just like the creatures hiding in the shadows around us. A monster beholden to Morgryth. Will you still look at me so tenderly then, kind Prince?"

Bell almost laughed as he realized how unworthy they both felt when it came to love. He ran a finger over Renault's beastly hand, eliciting a ragged sigh from Renault.

"I don't think you're a monster," Bell said. "And I think you deserve love."

Renault's eyes glimmered.

Gathering a lungful of courage, Bell lifted his hand and ran it down the scales over the ruined side of Renault's face, marveling at their smoothness, the way the light changed their color.

Now that he was used to the scales, they weren't so hideous. In fact, he hardly noticed them at all as he stood on his tiptoes and brushed his lips over Renault's.

Renault stiffened. "Prince Bellamy, I—"

Suddenly, he went rigid, his reptilian eye constricting and claws thrusting out his fingertips. He whipped around to face the stairway. That's when Bell caught a glance of midnight wings and savage eyes.

Magewick.

"I see you found the one door to the ground," Magewick purred in that cruel voice.

He glided down the stairs with preternatural stealth, not making a sound. Behind him, gremwyrs crawled along the walls, scattering the bats along the ceiling.

"Don't look so surprised," Magewick continued. "Do you really think you're the first to try to escape?"

Relief found a place next to the fear in Bell's heart. Magewick didn't know the true reason they were here. "If you knew it wouldn't open," Bell said, "why come all the way down here?"

"Could it really be that you forgot? The moon is swollen and full." Magewick grabbed Bell by the neck, and his heart stopped. "Time to feed our ravenous princess."

"No!" Renault lunged for Magewick, but the gremwyrs descended over him, clawing and biting at his flesh. Bell tried to fight, but Magewick hit him on the left cheek, stunning him.

Darkness. Bell fought unconsciousness as they violently dragged him up the stairs . . . so fast. Twisting in the Noctis's grasp, he managed to turn back and catch sight of Renault.

The last image Bell saw before the Noctis dragged him up the stairwell and out of sight was the fallen prince disappearing beneath a swarm of *true* monsters.

THIRTY-NINE

Haven awoke from a darkness she couldn't remember, her skin feverish and covered with sweat. The fire inside the cave had dimmed, the air cool against her skin.

The first thing she saw was Archeron's concerned face.

The second, the silver runes that snaked across the flesh of her arms.

They were beautiful—the most beautiful thing she had ever seen. Tears pricked her eyes as she beheld the markings and what they meant.

Power. *Revenge.*

She tried to stand, but Archeron slipped an arm around her back before she could make it two inches, steadying her as he helped her sit up.

"Haven?" His voice was a breath of cool water against her hot skin, but his eyes were tight. "Haven?"

"Please, Girl," Surai breathed. "Say something."

"How long was I out?" she rasped, her throat aching and dry.

"Too long," Archeron said. "We thought . . ."

"We thought you died," Surai finished carefully, glancing at Archeron.

His body went rigid. All at once, he stood, fists bunched at his sides, and stalked from the cave.

Surai touched her searing skin. "Give him time. Twice, your body didn't have a heartbeat. He was so distraught, I thought he was going to chase you down to the Netherworld and drag you back."

"Now that I would have liked to see," Haven murmured, imagining Stolas and Archeron together.

"Do you feel any different?"

"Hot. I feel hot but also cold." Once again, Haven let her gaze travel the shimmering marks running along her flesh. They were everywhere, a latticework of iridescent bands marking every inch of her body.

As she traced a finger down one arm, she realized the mercurial warmth came from the runes themselves.

"I don't feel . . . changed, though." Haven's voice trembled. "Not in *that* way."

She didn't have to spell out what she meant. Both girls remembered Archeron's fear that she would somehow become twisted into something dark.

"A monster wouldn't know it's a monster," Surai pointed out before realizing what she was saying and clapping a hand over her mouth. "You know what I mean. Besides, the fleshrunes won't take full effect until months from now—so any lasting changes may not happen until much later."

"Comforting." Surai's statement should have worried her more, but she was too entranced with her fleshrunes to pay it much thought.

"What are you looking at?" Surai's words came out slowly, as if Haven was a delicate vase that would shatter if handled too roughly.

Haven uncoiled to a stand, ignoring Surai's offer of help. The icy-heat permeating her body had become a whisper of fire and ice, flame and power and promise.

She turned to Surai, waving her arm in front of her face. "Can you not see the runemarks?"

Surai shook her head. "You can?"

"Yes, I wish you could too." Haven shoved into her clothes, reveling in the powerful energy she felt flowing through every part of her. It seemed a shame to cover the marks, and she kept holding up her hands to marvel at the delicate lines that curled and spiraled down to her fingertips. "They're magnificent."

"But do they work?"

Haven grinned as she buckled her baldric of daggers across her chest. "Only one way to find out."

A grin cracked Surai's face, and she flung her arms around Haven. "There's our feisty mortal. Now I know you're okay."

"I am, truly," Haven said, slipping her arm under Surai's braid and around her slender back. She pressed her cheek into Surai's. "Are you?"

Surai released a ragged breath, pulling away to look at her. "My mind knows she's gone, Haven, but it will take time for my soul to believe it. I catch myself looking for her, listening for her voice as if she's just out of sight. All my clothes still bear her fur . . ." She swiped at the tears wetting her eyelashes. "I'll grieve for her later. Now, I draw comfort from the Netherfire we're about to rain down on Spirefall and the Shade Queen."

"Wait." Haven studied Surai's face. "Why are you still in your true form?"

Surai touched the round apple of her cheek. “I don’t know. I think when Rook died, our curse was broken. But it feels wrong, somehow. This was supposed to happen for both of us, together. Otherwise, what do I care if I’m a raven or Solis?”

The Sun Queen’s voice was hollow, and Haven knew she would stay a bird forever if it meant getting Rook back.

“Rook would want you to enjoy your true form,” Haven urged softly.

“You have no idea.” A weak smile found Surai’s lips. “I can only imagine the curses she would yell at me if she knew I was grieving this hard. She told me when we first met that she would die young . . . but we both thought we still had time. She had visions of her death, but not the context. I think she realized last night because she kept talking to me about carrying on and being strong.” Her voice broke, and she cleared her throat. “If I had known those were my last moments with her . . .”

Haven pulled Surai into a fierce embrace. “Turn your grief to rage. Together, we’ll make the Shade Queen regret taking Rook from us.”

The girls pressed their foreheads together. Then Haven slipped away to gather her weapons, the runes along her flesh pulsing as if anxious to prove themselves.

“I’ll check on Archeron,” Surai called over her shoulder as she left. “But you really should talk to him soon.”

Once Haven had her sword strapped to her back, along with her bow and quiver, she finally felt ready. As she made to leave, Bjorn found her. He was the only one who hadn’t seemed worried after the transformation, and she studied him for a moment.

Dark shadows shifted around him, faint enough they could be smoke from the fire. Everything about him seemed different now. His energy. His movements. But she knew he’d been close to Rook. Perhaps he was taking her death harder than he let on.

Or, perhaps being so close to the place where he was tortured and made sightless was weighing on him.

He held out his hand and uncurled his fingers. Red flashed from his palm. "Take this. It will protect you."

It was a ruby inside an elaborate iron cage of runes hanging from a delicate chain.

As she slipped it over her head, the gem hanging heavy and cold against her breastbone, she felt a pulse of dread. "Thank you."

Bjorn bowed his head, and he stayed that way until she went to speak with Archeron. She found him standing near a cluster of rocks with Surai, readying weapons. Fresh snow had fallen while she was out, and she shielded her eyes from the glare of white as she made her way over to Archeron.

Surai saw her first, and she slipped away without a word.

Haven was prepared for a host of emotions when she dealt with Archeron, but all she felt as she approached him was pride.

The Sun Lord looked ready to do battle. His honey-gold hair was pulled back with a leather band and draped over a fine-tailored leather breastplate engraved with runes, the edges of each piece gilded. Two long swords poked from between his shoulder blades, a short sword ready at his hip.

His throwing knives would be hidden inside his cloak, she knew, along with an assortment of daggers in his boots and other places.

His spine straightened as she touched his arm, corded with muscles.

"Do you always dress so fancy for battle?" she asked.

Despite his gathered brows, half his lips twitched in a smile. "I left my gold suit of armor at home."

"A shame."

The muscles in his jaw trembled as his eyes turned solemn. "Did the spell work?"

She held up her arm, admiring the silver runes, the way they gleamed in the light. "You can't see them? My runes?"

He shook his head, slowly, his troubled gaze traveling her flesh. "They must be hidden. Good. That will keep you safe—for a while."

Her fingers slid down to his elbow, and the muscles below his flesh tensed beneath her fingertips. "Archeron, I'm sorry if the transformation scared you."

"Scared?" He snorted, lifting a dubious eyebrow as he prepared to make some sarcastic response—then stopped. His arrogant expression melted away, his jaw tightening. "When I felt your flesh turn to fire and your heart stop beneath my palm . . ." He looked away until he schooled the horrified emotion on his face into one of cold fury. "I never want to feel that pain again."

"I'm sorry I hurt you," she said, hoping he heard the sincerity in her voice. "I don't know what will happen in a few hours. But I do know that I want you by my side. As a partner. An equal." She slipped her hand inside his, her soft palm meeting the skin calloused from centuries spent holding a sword. "Will you fight alongside me, Archeron Halfbane?"

A slow grin spread across his jaw. "With pleasure, Haven Ashwood. And I can think of a few things we could do afterward."

Her runemarks tingled and burned to match her insides. She knew he wasn't just being coy; he was trying to give her hope, the promise of a life after. Of making it out of Spirefall alive.

"More kissing?"

"Oh," he breathed, drawing close to brush his lips over the shell of her ear. "I think we're way past that now."

Indeed.

As soon as they crossed the mountains into the Shadow Kingdom, the dark shadow of night fell. Haven stared at the jagged castle of spires and mist silhouetted against the blue-black sky, claws of dread scraping down her insides.

Shadowlings circled above, dark specks cast against a swollen too-big moon. Below, ravens gathered over the rocks and boulders littering the landscape. Occasionally, a sound would startle them, and they'd take flight, spilling into the sky like ink dropped into water.

Bjorn took on the dark task of felling the birds until Haven grew used to the thud of the Shade Queen's spies raining over the dead landscape.

Dark magick seethed from this barren wasteland of granite. There were no forests, no trees, no signs of life beyond scuttling insects and terrible night creatures.

Only mountains and snow and ice and . . . fear.

She shivered as the wind howled through the valleys like the angry cries of an ice wyvern.

Haven hadn't had a chance to test her runemarks, and Archeron and Surai dispatched the few shadowlings they encountered before Haven could lift a finger. By the time they reached the onyx cliffs at the base of Spirefall, she was trembling with cold, despite the fiery runes warming her flesh.

From directly below the castle, the wall of mist veiled everything but the uppermost peak. But she could feel the dark magick inside scuttling along her skin. Filling her with a cold emptiness.

The darkness traced over her new runes as if taunting her, the feeling akin to having an icepick dragged over her flesh.

There was an ancient magick here that even she didn't understand. A distant, cruel sentience that warned what would happen to her soul if she let the dark magick overcome her.

As they gathered together, no one mentioned that they didn't actually know if Rook had time to reach the fallen prince before the attack. And Haven didn't feel like bringing up the Shade Lord's help. That would open up another round of questions she wasn't ready to answer, along with the most important question—why would they trust him?

For that, she still didn't have an answer.

"Here." Bjorn pressed a hand into the craggy cliff, and the faint red outline of a tall door appeared.

"Wait." Archeron was the last to follow, and he turned around to watch something in the distance.

"What is it?" Haven asked.

His body was rigid, alert as he studied the valley behind them, steeped in shadow. "Maybe nothing. I thought for a moment we were being followed." He cracked his neck. "Whatever it is, they won't want to follow where we're going."

A strange look flashed across Bjorn's face, and he canted his head in her direction. "Last chance to turn back."

The rock was rough against Haven's palm as she placed it next to Bjorn's. "You can flee if you want, Seer. But I'm going to get my friend."

He gave her a tight smile. "That is your decision, then?"

"It is." The door opened beneath her fingers to a pitch-black space. Haven summoned a flame of magick, light wrapped in dark, the act as easy as breathing. With her other hand, she drew her sword, enjoying the hiss of steel that rang loud against the quiet.

A crude stairwell had been carved into the obsidian, and they snuck up the winding steps on quiet feet. Insects and other creatures scuttled in the shadows.

As they drew higher, a sour stench filled the air. It didn't take long to find the source: hanging cages filled rooms on every floor, crammed with mortals. Some still wore their armor—not much more than corroded flaps of metal now, the insignias of the kingdoms they came from unrecognizable.

Most, though, were lucky to possess clothes at all.

Haven forced down the bile creeping up her throat. The smells and sounds were like something from a nightmare.

How many of these people were once soldiers? How many came here like she did, to break the Curse, and never returned?

It took all of her willpower to ignore their cries, their whimpers and pleas for death.

This was the fate of her world if she didn't break the Curse. Her people tortured and enslaved, used for food and entertainment and worse.

Nausea churned her stomach. Nausea, and rage.

Part of her begged to stop and help them, but there was nothing she could do other than continue climbing the eternal flight of stairs, spiraling up, up, up—

Haven heard the steps a second before the Noctis appeared around the curve. She was ready with her magick. As she flung the sphere of flames at the creature, it tried to duck—but her magick swerved. She watched it lick over his wings and ivory skin with a strange fascination.

The creature hardly had time to scream before he became sparks and ash.

All in all, the kill was effortless. Easy.

More came. Each one met her fiery wrath.

She was remorseless, sending flame after flame until bits of ash clung to her skin and mouth. They died quietly, without a sound, which made it all the more enjoyable to see the surprise on each monster's face as she wiped it from existence.

The others didn't even get a chance to wet their weapons.

You like this, a dark voice whispered. *This is what you were made for. Your destiny.*

Archeron grabbed her arm. "You need to slow down, Haven."

"No," she hissed. "Not until they're all dead."

A part of her knew he was right. Her emotions were all over the place, her chest aching with rage. Hatred seeped from her like a poison . . .

But the cages flashed across her mind. She saw the skeletal figures clawing at the bars. Heard their anguished screams as if she were still there in that room. She pictured Bell's feet kicking as he was stripped from the temple. Rook's brave face as she fought against soulless creatures and died right in front of her eyes.

So she embraced her rage, twining that glittering fury into her magick, letting it set fire to her insides. If she was going to the Netherworld, she would take half this rotten castle with her.

Haven took the stairs two at a time. Bjorn said the Shade Queen would be on the highest floors of the castle, but they had no idea how far up they were. Sometimes, they had to cross through rooms before finding the next stairwell, and they encountered gremwyrs and other shadowlings.

Haven forced herself to finally let the others dispatch those. She could have used her magick, but they needed to wet their steel and loosen their muscles before the real battle began.

Any nervous energy she felt faded with each release of power from her veins, the feeling strange yet pleasant, a building pressure and then climax, like a sneeze. Another floor. Two Noctis dropped from the ceiling, their wings spread wide and talons glittering.

This time, she tore the wings from their bodies while they were still midair, the delicate, membranous flesh shredding and their hollow bones snapping.

Then she drowned them in their own blood

She felt the others' worried looks as they sprinted up more stairs, this time wide enough for all four of them to climb shoulder-to-shoulder.

Archeron flicked his gaze to her, his steel already black with blood, but she ignored him.

Sprinting—she was sprinting now. Her magick calling for more to kill. *Make them pay,* it whispered. *Show them what you are. Tear out their insides. Destroy them.*

How dare they take Bell.

She flicked her hand and an entire wall crumbled onto a group of Noctis soldiers, crushing them.

How dare they try to hurt me.

She flung spears of flame into the three gremwyrs that came darting down from the rafters. They fell dead at her feet.

How dare they kill Rook and drop her from the sky like trash.

How. Dare. They.

More died. Countless. She was a whirlwind of death, a harbinger of wrath and ruin. Her friends fought beside her, their weapons flashing against the shadows, but she hardly noticed them.

Hardly noticed the dark magick raging from her fingers, absent of any light.

Kill.

Kill.

Kill.

Hardly noticed as the flames grew smaller, dimmer.

Wide onyx doors carved with all manner of creatures appeared, and Haven flung them open, ready to charge—and froze.

A giant cavern lay ahead with creatures squirming inside the catacombs lining the walls. The high ceiling churned with gremwyrs, and unnatural shrieks reverberated off the walls. A natural dais of stone waited at the bottom of the stairs, carved into the obsidian.

And tied to an altar beside the Shade Queen and a retinue of Shade Lords, his arms and legs spread across the dark stone, was Bell.

FORTY

Whatever dark trance had hold of Haven dissipated as she took in her friend.

"Bell!" Haven's scream sliced the air, and Bell's head whipped to the side. Their eyes met. Something passed between them—a pulse of hope and love. "Bell!"

Fear gripped Haven's heart. She needed to get to Bell. Before she could run, Surai grabbed her arm. "Wait, Haven! It could be a trap."

"They're going to kill him!" she hissed.

A dark understanding flickered inside Surai's lavender eyes, and she gave a grave nod. "Go get him. And Haven . . ." Her gaze drifted to the Shade Queen. "Kill the bitch."

A whoosh drew Haven's focus upward. Noctis and gremwyrs were dropping from the ceiling.

She lunged, releasing a blast of magick that rippled across the wall of creatures. They thudded to the ground, burning to ash at her feet as she leapt over them.

The ones her magick didn't kill were met by the Solis.

Archeron had both swords out, and they cut through gremwyr after gremwyr in a blur of silver and red. Surai was by his side, carving a path through the shadowlings that blocked her way. Bjorn's axes flickered like jewels.

Two Noctis males came forward, wings spread in aggression. Dark magick flared from their hands. But she remembered Stolas's lesson on defensive maneuvers, and she threw up an orb of mixed magick, distracting their flames as she tossed her own.

They screamed as they died, shriveling to ash.

The sound of her name being screamed snapped her attention to the dais. A female Noctis was hovering over Bell, her skeletal wings curved around him as if she was claiming him. The sharp knobs of her spine protruded from her back, a tattered black gown dressed with rubies clinging to her emaciated form.

Ravenna.

Suddenly, Haven was beside them, and she grabbed the Shade Queen's daughter by her pale throat and flung her back. It was only when Ravenna slammed into the wall and screeched with rage that Haven knew she had soulwalked from her body like Damius had done.

One glance at her still, lifeless body standing amid the chaos confirmed it. Archeron and the others realized what she had done, and they formed a protective circle around her.

Lifting a hand, she saw air where her arm should be.

Ravenna snapped to her feet, her dead, filmy eyes darting around as she searched for whoever threw her back. Her gaze skipped right over Haven. All at once, her ghoulish wings snapped open, and she took a step back toward Bell.

"Not a Nether-frigging chance!" Haven snarled. Then she had

her by the throat again, her fingers sinking deep into emaciated flesh and bone, and was somehow lifting her into the air, propelled by fury and magick.

Ravenna screamed and kicked, her wings flapping wildly as they tried to harness the air. Her cloudy-corpse eyes bulged with fear, the sight filling Haven with sick pleasure.

"Leave him alone, bitch," Haven growled into her ear. Then she threw the Shade Queen's undead daughter to the ground with a sick crack.

If she kept soulwalking, her body would be unprotected, so she snapped back to herself, the sensation like forcing a swollen foot into an old, dried out leather boot a size too small.

Her head spun. After a few steadying breaths, the dizziness passed.

Archeron threw her a stern glance. "Don't do that again."

She nodded and together, they fought their way to the dais stairs.

The Shade Queen stood in the center, four massive Noctis soldiers dressed in onyx armor surrounding her. Her gaze was on Haven, her head tilted to the side and teeth bared in a bored smile. Her skeletal wings hung loose behind her.

Something was wrong. Why wasn't she more concerned?

Haven flung a wave of magick at her, but the soldiers must have had some sort of shield over the queen because the blue and gold flames just rolled around her.

The Shade Queen picked at something on her shoulder armor.

Haven tried again, but this time the flame of magick that streamed from her fingers was barely strong enough to reach the queen. The next time she tried, it was a trickle.

Her runes. They were cold. Dark. Barren.

A jolt of panic surged through her chest. What was happening?

She pivoted to clear a path toward Bell just as a Noctis soldier swung a jagged sword at her neck.

She flung magick at him. Nothing happened. The blade clipped her hair as she ducked, and she had to finish him with her steel.

"Why aren't you using magick?" Surai hissed as they pressed their backs together and fought their way up the stairs.

"It doesn't work!" Haven breathed between pants. She sheathed her sword and drew her bow in preparation for the incoming onslaught. "Something's wrong!"

Archeron joined them. His face was haggard, his armor slick with dark blood. Still, he fought.

They all did.

Even as the monsters kept coming, faster than they could kill them. Even as the arrows Haven released at the Shade Queen shattered one after the other against her shield.

Even after her quiver ran empty and she switched back to her sword, her muscles screaming as she swung, chopped, and stabbed.

And then a scream pierced the din of bloodshed, and Haven turned to see a Noctis with massive black wings standing over Bell, a dagger carved from obsidian poised over his chest, right above his heart.

She stopped breathing. In the span of half-a-second, she saw Bell's short life pulse behind her eyes. His soft, boyish smile; the way he twirled his hair while reading; his unfettered laugh.

All of it was about to be snuffed out.

A guttural scream tore from her throat.

As if on some signal Haven couldn't hear, the battle halted, the creatures retreating to the air. Their wings created a wind that blew back her hair as they ascended.

The queen slithered over to Bell, slowly, so slowly, her deep crimson cape sliding over the stone even as her eerie gaze never left Haven's. She walked with a strange, otherworldly gait like a serpent gliding over the surface of a lake.

All of the creatures and the Noctis bowed except for the one holding the wicked blade over Bell's heart.

The only thing more terrifying than the sudden quiet was the queen herself. In person, she was hideous, a demoness from the deepest chasms of the Netherworld.

Watching her walk, the way her ancient body moved without seeming to beneath that black armor, the inhuman way her head ticked to the side, all of it made Haven instinctively want to flee.

When the queen neared the Noctis with the dagger, he bowed low and stepped back, removing the blade from above Bell's chest.

A whoosh of air escaped Haven's lips, relief pumping through her veins.

The queen's lips twisted in a serpentine grin. "That was quite an impressive display, girl."

Haven gritted her teeth to keep from hurling insults at the queen.

Bell squirmed beneath his ropy binds as the Shade Queen dragged a talon down his middle.

As the sound of his shirt ripping found her, Haven growled, her hand tight on her sword handle.

"I wonder, what does he mean to you, this weak, powerless boy?"

For the first time since Haven climbed the dais, she let herself meet Bell's wide-eyed gaze. His blue eyes blinked at her, and her heart plummeted as he tried to smile through his fear.

He was nine again, terrified of his father, shrinking beneath his shadow as they walked the slave markets. Yet, he still found the courage to smile at her as they passed. To tug on his father's emerald-bejeweled sleeve, twice, to make him stop.

To save her.

Oh, Bell. Her lips parted, and she almost whispered it was going to be okay. *Almost.*

But that would be the worst kind of lie.

"Why do you ask?" Archeron's voice rang strong, his spine straight and shoulders back, making it clear he was willing to fight to the death. For her.

Ignoring his question, the Shade Queen looked beyond Haven. "Bjorn. I think you have something for me."

Before she could turn to look at her friend, Bjorn grabbed the ruby amulet he had given her, the chain strafing her skin as he ripped it off her neck. The loud snap of the chain severing split the air.

Archeron snarled, his sword hissing from its sheath, but at the same moment, a familiar figure appeared.

At the sight of Stolas, adorned in his Netherworld regalia—glittering midnight armor and the sinister cloak made from his mother's feathers—Haven went still. He hardly glanced her way as he threw up his hand, freezing Archeron in place.

Haven touched her chest; the spot where the ruby had hung just above her sternum was ice cold . . . and achingly empty. A deep sense of loss, of something stolen and missing, pitted inside her gut.

Her magick. It was gone. Taken from her.

Bjorn crossed the dais to the altar and bowed low before the queen.

No.

The floor seemed to fall out from under her as he offered the Dark Queen the amulet with a shaking hand, his sightless eyes fixed on the floor. "My Queen."

His voice was a reverent whisper twined with terror. Never had two words struck fear in Haven as they did now. *My Queen.*

Stolas did the same, bending the knee and uttering the same two piercing words.

No. She had been betrayed. Her heart felt ready to split wide open, the pain a double-edged blade rammed into her chest.

The Shade Queen plucked the ruby from Bjorn's palm and held it up. If before it had flickered with light, now it was a blinding star sending red prisms dancing over her onyx armor. They cast all the way to the high ceiling of the chamber.

"Foolish, stupid girl," the queen purred. "How could you not recognize the Solis I had steal you from your home years ago? The one who sold you to the Devourer who worships me?"

Haven's knees buckled, and she barely managed to keep from falling to her knees as the true extent of the betrayal sunk in. "That was . . . that was Bjorn?"

Images of the man who took her that day by the riverbank danced inside her head, flickering and blurry. But whenever she tried to focus on the face, a shadow passed over it, making the features hard to make out.

It couldn't be him. Impossible. They rode into battle together. They ate from the same cauldron and slept at the same fire.

Bjorn couldn't be the man who kidnapped her from her family. Her home.

"Oh!" The queen clapped her hands together, her armor grating with the movement. "This is too good. He must have bound your memory with magick. Clever Solis. I taught him well."

Haven's heart rammed her sternum as she tried to make sense of everything. "But, why? Why would he take me?"

"For your magick," the queen said, still admiring the amulet.

"Why else? It was to keep you safe and protected until your magick was ready, but then you escaped, stupid girl. Yes, you ran straight into the arms of the foolish Penrythian king, who would have killed you if he'd known what hid inside your mortal flesh."

A wild rage overtook Haven as she faced the traitor. "You knew they were coming last night and you didn't warn us. Rook died because of you."

Her body shook with need as she searched for her dark magick, her fury begging to be unleashed. But it was gone.

Instead, she plucked a throwing knife from her breast and sent it flying. The dagger spun end-over-end toward Bjorn, but a split second before it would have sunk deep into his neck, Stolas waved his hand and froze it midair.

Tears stung Haven's eyes as her dagger transformed into a raven. It was the same trick he'd performed when they first met. As the dark bird took to the air, a horrifying thought hit her.

Did Stolas betray them, too?

She didn't think she could handle such a blow. Not now. Not with everything that had happened.

She tried searching his face, but he refused her stare.

Bjorn was still bowed on his knees, his face partially hidden. But a flicker of pain had broken through his emotionless mask, his lips twitching. Lifting to his knees, his face once again smoothed into a remorseless look as he turned his back on them.

"Bjorn!" Surai cried, her voice breaking. "Bjorn! You killed her, you bastard! Your friend. The warrior princess who nursed you back to health, who trusted you like family."

For a breath, Bjorn froze, and Haven thought she might have heard him murmur, "I am sorry."

A ragged exhale shuddered his body as Surai whispered curses across the divide between them. Each one seemed to enter his flesh and reverberate, and he flinched as if taking the end of a whip.

When Surai finally went quiet, he seemed to sag. Then he rushed across the dais to a beautiful girl of dark skin.

They looked alike. Both with high cheekbones and fine features.

Except, while he was healthy and well fed, she was a skeleton draped in ragged silk that must have once been fine but now barely covered her shriveled body.

From her mess of hair, the emaciated girl stared at them with glossy, faraway eyes, hardly seeming to notice as Bjorn slipped a shoulder beneath her armpit for support.

Haven watched them flee the dais, caught in her own sort of daze. Everything had gone wrong. Everything. And she didn't know how to stop it.

"Traitor!" Archeron bellowed, loud enough for Bjorn to hear even on the other side of the cavern. "I promise you, there will be nowhere safe for you to travel. Nowhere for you to hide. Forever, your name will be known as traitor! And if Surai's curses don't kill you, I will."

Bjorn halted, turning back once to look at them. Perhaps remorse flickered across his face, perhaps not. But one thing was clear even from here.

His eyes were no longer white.

Part of his price to betray them. His sight. The other one being the girl, whoever she was to him.

The Shade Queen laughed and slipped the amulet over her head. The stone clinked against her armor. "Did you not notice your power draining? Or were you too caught up in the killing? Each time you murdered one of my creatures, I heard your heart shiver with pleasure. Heard your bones sigh with gratitude. This is what you were born for, Mortal. A weapon of light and dark.

A god killer."

Haven glared at the queen, swallowing down the kernels of truth in her words. "Was all of this to take my magick?"

"Take? I cannot take from you what is an eternal spring of magick given by the Goddess herself. Your powers will come back. And when they do, I will rip them from you again and again until I have enough amulets for my entire army."

"The runestones and the ceremony?"

"Bjorn knew you would ask for the marks eventually. He just had to convince the others."

She'd done that. Had forced Archeron to use his magick for this. She felt like vomiting, bile hot and sticky inside her throat. "Why?"

The queen's neck cracked as she glanced greedily down at the amulet pulsing light at her chest. "Because, foolish girl, without the runemarks, I could not access your powers. You are the conduit, the key that opens the door to their precious light magick, but the runes harness that power into something that can be possessed."

"You mean stolen," Haven snapped.

Rage flared inside those ancient, cruel eyes. "Stolen? A mortal dare talks of thievery when it was your kind who stole light magick that is rightfully ours? Your kind, who thought you were deserving of endless power while we have to beg and scrape for every bit of magick, siphoning it from the earth and the Solis like scavengers. Your kind, who helped throw us into the Netherworld pits while you danced over our eternal prison. You know nothing of having what's rightfully yours stolen."

A hollow feeling had taken over, and Haven pressed a fist into her chest. She'd done this. And now it would be her that gave the Shade Queen and her army the magick to conquer her lands.

Somehow, she had to make it right.

"What's the bargain?" Haven's voice rang out in the quiet, strong despite everything.

The madness drained from the queen's face, a triumphant smile twisting her lips. "Come with me. Willingly allow me access to your magick. Become the weapon you were always meant to be. Become *my* weapon. And you can kill and kill to your heart's delight."

"If I do?"

Archeron snarled beside her, but Haven ignored him.

"I will let your friends go free."

Haven's mouth went dry. "Even Prince Bellamy?"

The queen tilted her head, the shadows pooling inside her hollow cheekbones as she considered the request. "He may go as well."

From the corner, Ravenna hissed her displeasure. Bell arched his back, straining against his binds. "No, Haven! Not like this."

Surai said, "Please, Haven. We will find another way."

"Now," the queen rasped in that horrible, slithering voice. She lifted her hand and beckoned Haven closer. "Come to me. Or I can simply take you and make you watch while I rip out your friends' bones one by one. Perhaps I will make you do it."

"No!" Archeron roared.

His sword glinted as it lifted—but the Shade Queen flicked her long fingers, and his sword shattered into pieces. Twisting her hand, she forced him to his knees. He groaned as he fought her, but she was too powerful.

The Dark Queen could do anything she wanted. Haven was powerless. They all were.

Haven stepped forward as her friends' cries faded into the background. Already, she felt a thousand miles away.

There was no more fear. No more doubt.

She would trade herself for her friends, for Bell.

And when the time came, she would either kill the queen or plunge a dagger into her own heart before anyone could use her as a weapon.

The decision was suddenly simple. Her life was over. But they could live.

She was nearly to the altar, the queen's hand still out, when a flash of gray caught her eye.

Haven turned to face the movement, shock shooting through her as her brain made sense of the skeletal monster with round, milky eyes a few feet away.

Not a shadowling.

Not a Noctis.

Vorgrath. The name clicked just as the vorgrath's mate leapt. The impact knocked Haven flat on her back, her head cracking the floor. The vorgrath's mate slammed its full weight onto Haven's body, pinning her to the stone.

The queen screeched with rage while Archeron growled and leapt to his feet. From her periphery, she saw Stolas lunge toward them.

But it was all too late. The vorgrath had her.

Their eyes met. Monster and prey. Haven nearly laughed at the absurdity of it all—

Pressure and pain roared across her chest, searing waves of agony, and she looked down in disbelief to see the vorgrath's long fangs plunging through her flesh and sternum with a sickening crack.

Straight into her heart.

FORTY-ONE

The beast lunged for Haven, and Bell writhed against the altar. *Vorgrath*. An image of the creature from his book popped into his head, spiking his body with adrenaline. By its size and pearlescent coloring, it was probably a female.

What was it doing here?

"Haven," he shouted, but she seemed to be in some kind of fog; she didn't even try to fight as the vorgrath took her down. Didn't move as it bared its dagger-length fangs and—

Goddess Above. He whipped his head away as the monster sunk its fangs into his friend's chest.

"No!" Bell bucked, feeling the sharp stone edges gouging his back. The crunch of the vorgrath's incisors piercing her sternum twisted his gut, and a surge of vomit flooded his mouth. "Haven!"

The room descended into chaos around him. Gremwyrs swarmed the vorgrath, tearing it to pieces in seconds. Bell watched in shock as they fought over the pieces, screeching and thrashing.

All the while, Haven lay perfectly still.

She can't be dead. The thought sounded stupid and naïve in his head. He opened his mouth to breathe, but the air wouldn't come.

The Shade Queen was completely still. She appraised Haven lying on her back, her face still twisted in a grimace of pain and surprise.

A pool of blood darkened the stone around her. She was dead. His friend was dead. *Dead. Gone.*

There was no denying it this time. No surprise revelation to make him whole again.

Bell blinked as another surge of vomit seared his throat.

He felt caught in a dream as he watched his father's Sun Lord, Archeron, tear himself away from the Noctis soldiers holding him and approach Haven. A soft cry fled his lips as he fell to his knees beside her. Carefully, he slipped his cloak beneath her head.

His beautiful face was a ragged mask of agony as he leaned down to whisper something in her ear, wiping the blood from her cheeks. A slender Solis female with long, dark hair pulled into a braid joined him, crying silently.

In his grief, Bell had almost forgotten about Renault near the back of the dais. When they'd first arrived, Magewick had personally guarded Renault, forcing him to stay and watch the sacrifice.

Now, he was unguarded.

Bell heard Renault's gasp of pain and surprise when the man who betrayed Haven stepped forward. He was handsome in the way of all Sun Lords, his skull shaved clean and dark skin reminding Bell of his mother's.

The traitor's face seemed familiar, and after Renault's reaction, Bell thought he knew who the Sun Lord was. Renault's lover from the other-world garden, the one with a sister.

Any doubt Bell had died the moment he saw Bjorn embrace his sister, Ephinia. How strange that the Sun Lord who stole Haven all those years ago was this same Solis—and that he ended up traveling with her again.

Then betraying her once more.

"Traitor," Bell growled, struggling with his binds. If he had been free, he would have thrown himself at the cowardly Sun Lord.

Twisting his body against his binds, Bell cast a look back at Renault, who was using the moment of confusion to make his way to Bell.

Silver flashed, and his body lightened as the rope around his wrists fell away.

"You must go now," Renault whispered, helping Bell from the altar.

Bell's knees nearly buckled as his feet made contact with the floor. "But Haven—"

"There's nothing you can do for your friend now."

But Bell couldn't just leave. Instead, he froze, as if he could simply wait and his hesitation would bring Haven back to life.

That's when he noticed the Shade Lord, the one who helped them earlier, slip behind the distracted Shade Queen. He was in and out of focus, a flash of darkness, so that Bell thought he might be a manifestation of his shock.

Except for the raven's cloak Stolas wore, he wouldn't have even recognized it was him, he moved so quickly.

A flicker of shadows, and the Shade Lord was gone.

But somewhere in that split-second, Bell could swear he saw the red hilt of a dagger, and it was odd enough to make Bell watch the Shade Lord as he crossed through the riled shadowlings and found Archeron still tending to Haven.

"This feels familiar." Stolas's words cut through the din, and silence fell as the Dark Queen and her creatures watched to see what the Shade Lord would say.

"What do you want?" The Sun Lord's ragged, defeated tone hinted that he had cared for Haven. More than even Bell would have guessed possible.

"It seems you fail to protect those you love, Archeron. Except, then it was your soulbrother. What was his name, again? Oh, right. Remurian."

Bell had never heard the name, but as soon as it left the Shade Lord's sneering lips, Archeron snarled and attacked him. They spilled across the dais, a violent vortex of light and dark.

The shadowlings shrieked and flapped their wings, but the fight ended almost before it began.

Two Noctis grabbed Archeron, and the Shade Lord pulled back, ruffling the feathers of his wings and cracking his neck. Then he leaned forward and whispered something into Archeron's ear.

Bell's fists curled at his sides. Bastard! Why was he taunting Archeron? Especially after he had helped them?

Archeron strode back to Haven and said something in Solissian to the Solis girl. For a second, she froze, her strange purple eyes going wide. Then she pulled something out of her pocket and dropped it into Archeron's palms.

The Shade Queen slithered across the stage to the Solis, her lips bared in a jagged smile. "Such a shame." She made a flippant gesture over Haven. "Her magick was unique. But now she's dead, and any bargain I had died with her."

Ravenna joined her mother. Together, they were twin shadows of wrath and ruin. Their sharp, twisted wings glittering with talons. Their primordial eyes and curved, predatory fangs.

Every part of their bloodless bodies were angular and unyielding as the broken end of a bone.

An inky mist began swirling from their flesh as their dark magick seeped out, cold and terrifying.

"Which one would you like first?" the Shade Queen asked Ravenna.

By the way Ravenna's gaze scraped over Archeron, she'd already decided. "He's nearly too pretty to eat, Mother."

Archeron stood tall, seemingly unfazed. In fact, a glimmer of arrogance had returned to him, his lips curled into a lazy smile as he regarded the two creatures with disdain. It was the same loathsome look he gave Bell's father.

All at once, he held out his hands palms up. As the room fell silent and the Noctis gathered closer, Bell instinctively drew forward to see.

Five items rested inside those broad hands: A glass vial, some type of bone, a golden scale shaped like a teardrop, and what looked to be a dried fruit, perhaps a fig.

And the smooth black tip of . . . of a horn.

"Queen Morgryth Malythean," Archeron boomed. "I am Archeron Halfbane, and I present you with the Curseprice."

The queen went quiet and still in a way that terrified Bell. Slowly, she brought her hand up and felt along the tip of her massive horns. From here, it looked as if one horn was slightly shorter than the other, and blunter.

The skin around her mouth tightened as she dropped her hand and turned her head. Bell followed her frightful gaze to the Shade Lord who had helped them, Stolas.

The darkness that passed between them could dim the Penrythian sun. Bell felt Renault come up behind him.

"You need to go," he hissed, pressing something into Bell's

open palm. The dagger was cold and heavy in Bell's hand. "If you leave now, they may be distracted long enough for you to escape."

Bell blinked at him. "Can't you see? They've broken the Curse."

"I'm sorry, but they have not."

Renault's solemn tone pitted Bell's gut, and he clutched the knife tighter. "What do you mean?"

Renault shook his head, his eyes downcast. "They must not know about the last item on the Curseprice. The sacrifice of two lovers torn."

Bell's breath hitched inside his chest, his heart an icy fist.

A cold laugh split the air, and the Shade Queen waved her hand. The items inside Archeron's palm erupted in flame. "Foolish Sun Lord."

But Archeron was already dropping to his knees. His arms slipping beneath Haven's neck. Her back. He was lifting her up. Her beautiful riot of rose-gold hair spilling from his arms, free at last.

"My one wish," Archeron said, his steady voice echoing across the cavern, "is to bring Haven Ashwood back to life."

The Shade Queen's head snapped to Archeron. "What did you say?"

"Bring her back."

A silence like Bell had never known fell over the cavern. The Shade Queen leaned forward, using one bony, clawed, and crooked finger to lift Archeron's chin so he couldn't avoid her stare. "I know what you want, Sun Lord. Freedom. Your homeland, Effendier. That is what you desire."

Bell's hands were squeezed so tight around the handle of the dagger that his fingernails carved crescents inside his palm. There must have been truth to her words because Archeron's face twisted with pain as he peered down at Haven, pale and limp inside his arms. Her blood smeared his cheek.

"Your heart calls for the land of your ancestors." The Shade Queen's voice was a soft, slithering snake of persuasion. "For the sea that flows in your veins, the shores that haunt your dreams. What would you care for the short life of a mortal girl? A few blinks, and she will be nothing more than bones and dust."

A faraway look flickered inside Archeron's eyes. Bell wondered if he could see his homeland, if it danced in front of him the same way Penryth did for Bell.

Then the Sun Lord's torn and weary gaze rested on Haven, and peace settled across his face. "This mortal haunts my dreams; her laughter flows in my veins. And I would gladly sacrifice my homeland to hear her call me arrogant and pretty just one more time. A few hours longer with her or a few years, it matters not. Just that I would hear her voice again."

The Shade Queen's body went rigid; she bared her fangs in a hiss.

"Bring her back to me." His voice carried a righteous finality. "That is my one wish."

The breath caught behind Bell's sternum. *The sacrifice of two lovers torn . . .*

The queen shrieked as a sound like two rocks smashing together rumbled the air. A wave of hot, blinding light blasted through the cavern. As the tongues of golden flame touched the shadowlings and Noctis, they screamed and fell, writhing on the ground.

Cracks appeared over their flesh, as if molten fire spewed from their marrow and swelled their skin to bursting. Howling, they dragged themselves across the stone to try and get away, but the magick was everywhere. Bell could feel it surging all around him, a pulse of the most radiant light he'd ever experienced.

It was so bright, so pervasive that he threw an arm over his eyes to shield them.

In a sickening whoosh, the queen's wings caught fire, a golden miasma of flames that licked at her flesh. She raked at the inferno with her claws as her screams shredded the air.

A gasp fled Bell's lips as the reality hit him.

The Curse that had raged for centuries, that had killed countless mortals and destroyed kingdoms and lives, was broken.

Meaning he was free.

Ravenna stumbled beside her mother, a dazed look on her face. Unlike the others, she remained untouched. And then, as Bell watched, her body began to restore itself. The cadaverous hollows beneath her cheeks filled in. Her sagging, bloodless flesh became plump and pink with life. The opaque film misting her eyes disappeared.

But, if she was happy the Curse keeping her in-between life and death had been severed, she didn't show it. And she certainly wasn't overjoyed at Bell's newfound freedom.

Her furious gaze scoured the room until she found Bell. Rage to match her mother's twisted her lips into a horrible sneer.

Before he could move, she lunged for him.

The dagger Renault had given him was still held firmly between his fingers. He'd been trained for over half his life on how to hold a blade. Yet as she neared, his only thought was *pointy side up, Bell.*

She was upon him before he could get in a proper stance. His eyes shut as he flinched backward, blindly thrusting the dagger out . . .

He opened his eyes in time to see the tip of his blade nick her forearm.

The moment the steel point broke the skin, surprise jerked her eyes wide. With a ragged cry, she yanked her arm away, cradling it against her chest.

Both Ravenna and Bell watched the flesh where his weapon made contact. Angry serpents of gold wriggled outward from the tiny wound, snaking beneath the skin and wrapping up her arm.

The dagger was tipped with the thorn-paste poison.

She screamed again, a nauseating mixture of shock and agony.

Then she fled.

Bell stole a deep breath and turned to Renault—except any trace of the creature was gone. In his place was the prince from the other-world. No scales. No claws or reptilian eye.

Overwhelmed with happiness, Bell slid his arms around the prince's waist and pulled him close, surprised at how lithe Renault was. "We did it."

Renault leaned back to face Bell. Goddess Above, his face was beautiful. His eyes were amber-lit, his sensuous lips grinning. "Bellamy . . ." His voice was nothing like the creature's rumble. "Prince, I . . ."

Bell went stiff as Renault leaned forward, brushing his lips over his. But instead of the interrupted kiss from earlier, this one was long and drawn out. A bold declaration of their feelings.

"I've wanted to do that for a while, now," Renault murmured. "I didn't dare until now, for I fear we are out of time."

One second, Renault was in his arms.

The next, he was sliding to the ground.

"Renault!" Bell grasped at his arms and tried to lift him, but he was too heavy.

A ragged sigh slipped from Renault's lips. His eyes were fluttering. "My name. Say it once more. I have not heard it in so long."

Bell dropped beside him, cradling his head in his lap. "What's happening?"

"I'm tired, Bellamy. The Curse . . . it kept me alive for centuries, preserving my mortal flesh for its depravity. Centuries of horror and shame. But now that it has been broken . . . now I can finally rest." His fingers were shaky as he reached up and took Bell's hand in his.

A deep ache filled Bell's chest. "I wanted more time with you."

The fallen prince's body went limp, but his eyes, his warm mortal eyes held onto Bell. "You have a beautiful soul, Prince Bellamy of Penryth. I wish I'd met you earlier. Perhaps your goodness would have made me a better man. Perhaps . . ."

A few seconds, a few breaths, a few beats of Bell's broken heart—that's all the time it took for the creature, the fallen prince and Cursemaker, to slide from this world to the other.

Tears staining his vision, Bell held the dead prince in his arms as the world around him descended into chaos.

FORTY-TWO

Flowers—there were flowers everywhere. And stars dashed across the heavens. Haven ran her hand through the meadow that spread out around her, rubbing the silky petals between her fingers before something made her touch her chest.

The vorgrath.

She should be dead.

She *was* dead—and inside her meadow dreamscape.

"You are indeed," came a purring male voice she recognized. The sound sent shivers rippling through her as Stolas appeared, prowling across the field of flowers.

For a heartbeat, she took in the sight of the Lord of the Netherworld stalking through daisies and phlox. He was no longer clad in his dark regalia but instead a thin tunic and black leather pants, his pale hair messy and wings splayed. In fact, he looked for all the world a young man enjoying an afternoon walk.

Except, he wasn't a young man—he was a monster. A traitor.

Fury propelled her toward him. There were no weapons in this realm, but she would use her fists. She was inches from raking out his eyes when he grabbed her wrists. His fingers wrapped tightly around her bones, gentle but firm.

"Bastard," she snarled, baring her teeth. "You betrayed us."

He tsked, a sad smile lifting his high cheekbones. "Why do you always assume the worst about me?"

"You bowed before her. *Willingly.*"

"Yes," he admitted in a soft voice. "And when I refuse, she breaks every bone in my body until I can no longer stand. If she's in a particularly sour mood, she rips out my spine, then pieces me back together so she can repeat the lovely process."

"I trusted you." Tears wet her eyes. For some reason, the idea that he betrayed them was intolerable.

As soon as he glimpsed her unshed tears, he released her arms and took a step back. "I promise you, Beastie, I did not betray you. I would never."

She swallowed, trying to gauge the truth in his words. "Then why am I here?"

"Your spirit is trapped inside your dreamscape."

"Why?"

"Because," he said, the yellow ring around his pupils flaring, "once it enters the Netherworld, there is no coming back. You will be mine, and I will be forced to torture you."

"No," she clarified. "Why help me at all? I'm dead and therefore no longer useful to you."

He grinned. "Oh, you will always be useful to me. But I need you here now so we can negotiate."

She quirked an exasperated eyebrow. Even dead, it seemed, she couldn't escape his cryptic talk. "Negotiate what, exactly?"

"Your life." Stolas rubbed two fingers over his sharp chin. "I'm about to do something for your precious Sun Lord. If he is as smitten with you as I think he is, he will demand your life back."

Haven shifted on her feet. "In return?"

"In return, all I ask is for you to find your way to my hidden home inside the Netherworld and take something back with you to Penryth. Keep it safe. Protect *it* . . . from itself. Mainly. Although you may need to protect others from *it* at times."

She clenched her jaw. *More cryptic talk.* "It?"

His eyes narrowed. *"Her."*

Her curiosity flared. "And I assume this deal is bound with magick?"

"All the good ones are." Stolas blinked at her with those strange, ever-changing eyes, now tawny and flecked silver. "So, do we have a deal?"

Perhaps death had made her soft, but she reached out and put a hand on Stolas's cold, hard shoulder, the ropy muscles beneath his shirt reminding her of the few times he wrapped that godlike body around her, protected her.

His flesh flinched beneath her touch, but this time, he didn't remove her hand. In fact, for a crazy moment, she thought he might have leaned into her palm.

"Will whatever you do get you in trouble with the Shade Queen?"

A sad smile tugged at his lips. "Yes."

"Then why do it?"

"For the same reason you gave your life to save the prince." He lifted an ash-white slash of eyebrow. "What, did you think me entirely heartless? We all love something beyond reason or comprehension. Beyond survival, even."

Her heart wrenched as she imagined all the things the Shade Queen would do when she found out he was complicit. "Can't you escape somehow?"

Pain flickered across his face. "I'm afraid that I'm bound by dark magick to the Netherworld and the Shade Queen for eternity. My life is over, and daring to hope otherwise is a fool's torment. But I hope, very soon, someone I love will be safe."

His voice was a rasping whisper that hinted at agony and loss. A loss so deep she swore, for a moment, her entire dreamscape trembled with his grief. His longing for freedom. For the life he had before he became the monster of the Netherworld.

Haven understood that emotion only too well, and she nodded, a soft, defeated dip of her chin. "I'll do it."

His tense brows lifted with relief. "Thank you. There is a portal near the chasm that will take you into the Netherworld. Ravius will find you when you are near and guide you the rest of the way. If it's not too much to ask, take care of him as well."

Giving away his pet? That didn't bode well for Stolas. Her throat clenched. "Will I ever see you again?"

He held her gaze for what felt like minutes beneath those beautiful, fathomless stars. "Thankfully not. Your dreams will go back to the boring mortal trivialities. Try not to celebrate too hard at my absence."

She opened her mouth to protest just as he disappeared, a wisp of black smoke evanescing on the breeze. A single feather drifted in his wake. She plucked the inky-black quill from the air, surprised by its downy softness.

As she glanced at the stars, she heard his voice whisper across the meadow, "Goodbye, Beastie."

And standing alone inside that glorious meadow, she felt her own strange, inexplicable loss.

FORTY-THREE

Haven awoke in Archeron's arms, feeling as if she'd just come from someplace very far away. Someplace she couldn't name or quite remember.

"What happened?" she asked, even as the memories came flooding back. The vorgrath's mate. Its wicked fangs, the crunch of bone scraping against her eardrums.

She clawed at her chest, expecting blood and pain. Instead, her flesh was mended—but the dried blood of her tunic was evidence she'd been bitten. "How?"

There was a sadness to Archeron's eyes as he set her down, gently. "I brought you back."

She blinked, not understanding at first. "You . . . the Curse is broken?"

"Yes."

It was true, she realized as she glanced around. The pungent reek of burned flesh was masked with the sweet scent of cinnamon and roses left by the light magick. The shadowlings not injured or dead had fled, the Shade Queen and Ravenna nowhere in sight. And the dark, scathing magick that had permeated this place was gone. Scrubbed clean.

A part of her shivered with grief at its absence—*no.* She pushed the feeling away.

Promise you will never rely on dark magick again, Ashwood. Even now, as she steadied herself against Archeron, the memories of her bloodlust filled her with shame. She splayed her fingers to grip Archeron's shoulder and noticed something dark emerge from her hand.

A midnight-black feather, dampened with her sweat.

Stolas.

Before Archeron could see, she shoved the hand-length plume into her pocket and headed for Bell.

Night-creatures scuttled beneath her boots. Black and green beetles, moon-white scorpions, and all manner of spiders. Bats swooped toward the exits, their squeaks bouncing off the walls. A red centipede as long as her arm scampered over her boot, and she kicked it away.

They were fleeing the light magick.

"Bell?" As soon as she said his name, she saw him lying over someone's chest. A handsome young man with an aristocratic face and a thin, regal nose.

Her heart stuttered as she realized the man's body was slowly crumbling into ash.

Bell hardly seemed to notice. His head was bowed, his shoulders trembling with silent sobs. His springy curls had grown long and disheveled, and they eclipsed his brow, hiding much of his eyes. But Haven could imagine the tears pooling there, the way his eyelashes clumped.

Before she could go to him, Archeron stopped her. "Give him a moment to grieve. Whoever he cries over, they were friends."

She nodded, ripping her gaze from Bell. "What about Effendier?"

Archeron wasn't quick enough to hide the flash of pain that rippled across his face, but he covered it with a tender smile. "What is my home without you, Little Mortal, reminding me of my arrogance?"

Knowing how much he wanted to go home, that sacrifice struck her to the core. "How did you get the Shade Queen's horn?"

A blur flashed in Haven's periphery, and then Surai wrapped Haven in a tight hug. "He didn't," Surai breathed as if it was a secret. "The Shade Lord did."

"Stolas?" Haven blurted, remembering how she nearly raked out his eyes.

Archeron's mouth tightened. "Yes. I don't know how he took part of the horn without her knowing—"

"I do," Haven said, squirming from her friend's grip.

Surai and Archeron gave her questioning stares as she grinned, recalling the magickal dagger she'd nearly lost when she fought the vorgrath. The one that cut without pain.

Archeron arched an eyebrow. "And do you happen to know *why* he helped us?"

It was then she remembered making a promise to Stolas, and she found herself toying with the feather in her pocket. But how to explain that to them?

"We can talk about it after we leave," she said. She would need time to come up with a response that didn't sound outright insane.

Resting a hand on Archeron's chest, she reveled in the firm muscles pressed into her fingertips. The strong heartbeat beneath.

"Thank you, Archeron Halfbane. I'll always be grateful."

He held her gaze for a few breaths. A Sun Lord and a mortal, once enemies and now . . . something more.

Haven slipped past Archeron and rushed to Bell. Up close, she hesitated, appalled at his condition.

Beneath the slick varnish of tears, his cheeks jutted sharply. Ash coated his fingertips and knees. Lack of sunlight colored his skin a greenish-tallow color, bruises flecking his body and pooling beneath his once bright blue eyes. And dirt wedged beneath his too-long fingernails.

But it was the agony wrenching his face that hurt the most.

Hardly able to believe this moment was real, she wrapped him in her arms and whispered, "Let's go home."

"Home," he repeated, the sound raspy and near-imperceptible. Then he hugged her back, his fingers clawing into her flesh as if he thought she might disappear. "You are my home, Haven."

EPILOGUE

As they left Spirefall, the darkness that had shrouded the land bled away, replaced by the soft gaze of the sun. Parts of the castle were crumbling, massive slabs of obsidian breaking off with a *crack* to reveal the white walls of the fallen prince's castle beneath.

But as gilded turrets and domes peeked from the broken walls of the Shade Queen's lair, it was hard to imagine anything beautiful ever existing here again. Especially with the tang of ash clinging to their throats and the reek of blood on the wind.

Still, the thick crust of snow beneath their boots had already begun to melt, rivers of water bubbling and tinkling from the valleys carved into the rocks.

Already, the land was trying to heal itself, to purge the evil that had ruled it for so long. As they ventured away from the Shadow Kingdom and into the Ruinlands, the air was light and full of life, and a shadow lifted from Haven's mind.

Her mood further improved when Archeron explained, now that dark magick's hold on the land was broken, they could invoke horses and gear.

Haven's power had yet to recover, so she had Surai invoke Lady Pearl. Rook's horse, Aramaya, would have been more practical, but after everything that had happened, Haven needed something familiar, something good, to try to bring back a semblance of her old life.

Life before so much horror and loss.

Afraid Bell would tumble from his horse due to exhaustion, Haven sat behind him and held him in place. Ignoring the way her already fatigued arms shook, she whispered reminders of all the things from home he loved.

Sticky buns. Panels of sunlight slanting across the dusty library floor as he read. Taking lunch in the meadow beneath the ancient oak.

It would all be waiting for them when they returned to Penryth, she promised, choking back the false promise of normalcy. Even in her hopeful optimism, she knew that was too much to ask.

But he was limp inside her arms. A quiet, unmoving ghost of the prince she remembered. Just like the land around them, it would take time to heal his wounds.

And she would be there with him however long it took.

The oath she'd made, what seemed like centuries ago, to protect him wasn't over—it had just taken on new meaning.

When they found the steep, winding cliffs that led to Rook's body, Surai froze, her shoulders slumping and eyes glassy.

The decision was made to leave her while Haven and Archeron retrieved Rook.

They left the others at the cliff base and made the winding trek to where the Morgani Princess lay, still interred by an iridescent shell of magick. As her tawny hair came into view, trussed into an elaborate set of braids, a pang of sadness shot straight to Haven's core.

She missed Rook's strength, her unflinching honesty. Her straightforward humor and fearsome love for everyone in her tiny circle.

The fact that Rook had placed Haven inside that sacred circle meant the world, and she wished she could have told her that before she passed.

Archeron hesitated beside Haven. The muscles around his shoulders drew taut, his lips twisting into a grimace as he struggled to hide his grief from her.

Reaching out, she took his h [illegible] s he tried to yank it away. "You don [illegible]"

Averting his gaze, he let out a dark laugh. "My kind do not see displaying emotions in the same honorable way you do. For a male Solis to openly grieve is a weakness."

"Then your kind is wrong," Haven said, jutting out her chin. "I told you I want all of you. Everything, even the parts of you that are wounded and hurt and ugly. There's nothing cowardly about exposing the shattered parts of yourself to someone you love, Archeron. It takes courage for that sort of trust."

A ragged sigh spilled from his lips as he turned to face her. Pain stiffened his face. Pain and rage and agony, making him appear, for a moment, like a stranger. "Haven, you do not want the burden of my demons upon your shoulders."

She closed the distance between them. He was rigid as she swept her arms around his waist, whispering, "I'm stronger than I look, Sun Lord, and I want *all* of you."

Another breath tore from his mouth, and this time, the tears fell. The muscles of his back and chest leapt beneath her fingertips as his entire body seemed to convulse. "I should have saved her," Archeron said, his voice a frayed whisper. "I should have known Bjorn was corrupted. I should have . . . done more."

She could almost feel him breaking inside. This strong, beautiful Solis, sobbing quietly in her arms.

"It's not your fault," she insisted.

His body softened, and it was his turn to tangle his arms around her. "Thank you for trying to comfort me, but I must carry this guilt until I have ended Bjorn's life."

"Where do you think he went?"

"I don't know. The only thing I can be sure of is that he'll stay close to the Shade Queen. He is her creature, and if she survives the onslaught of light magick, she'll keep him near."

"When will you leave to find him?" She willed him to say never, that there had been enough bloodshed to last a century.

"As soon as we return, I will ask the king for leave to hunt him down."

Because he would need the king's permission. A pang of guilt lanced through her, and she disentangled herself from his arms. "Do you regret using your wish to bring me back?"

"Never." He held her stare, forcing her to believe him. "If I hadn't made such a sacrifice, the curse would not be broken. I do not wish to return to the king as a slave . . ." His gaze wavered for a moment, the muscles of his temple popping. "There was no other way, and I will never regret saving your life. Do you understand?"

She nodded, her throat aching with emotion.

"We should get back." Composing himself, he looked over at Rook. "There was no one else like you in this realm, my friend, and I will feel your absence until the day I die. But I swear on the Goddess and everything holy that I will avenge you and kill the traitor, no matter the cost."

Haven shivered at his words. Hadn't they already paid enough? Talk of killing and cost settled darkly inside her, and she busied herself preparing Rook for travel so she wouldn't have to think about what more they could lose.

They lifted the Morgani Princess and carried her down the mountainside. At the bottom, they invoked a makeshift sled to lay her upon. Rook's horse, Aramaya, was given the honor of carrying her master one last time.

As if the beautiful creature knew the importance of her charge, she lifted her head high, antlers shimmering beneath the sun, and carefully began to trot after the group.

Even with the Curse lifted, no one wanted to stay in the Ruinlands longer than necessary. Somewhere along the way, Haven told the others about her promise to Stolas, although she kept out her previous relationship with the Shade Lord and only revealed their current deal.

She spent two frustrating hours trying to convince them to go through with it, and Archeron especially hadn't taken it well.

Still, in the end, she'd made a deal bound in magick, and they all agreed she had to follow through.

It was a two-day ride to the forest near the rift where Haven remembered the portal being. Even with her memory, they would have never found it if Ravius didn't appear. He landed on Haven's shoulder, big as a cat, squawking as Surai pointed an arrow at his ruffled breast.

Haven barely kept Surai from killing the poor bird. And when he led them to the wavering circle of magick hidden behind a thick copse of alders, Haven was the first to enter, drawn by her curiosity.

Something told her she was finally about to discover the owner of that brush.

The others hesitated. Archeron sighed heavily before urging his horse into the portal. She shied away, nickering in fear, and he had to dismount and gently coax her through. Surai managed to make her horse enter but only with the promise of freshly conjured raisins.

As Surai passed from the living realm to the dead, she made the sign of the Goddess.

The Netherworld was exactly as Haven remembered, a monochromatic realm hewn with silver and black and the occasional indigo. Something about the crystalline skies and delicate shadows made Haven smile . . . before she remembered that the Netherworld was supposed to be a horrible place.

And she was supposed to hate it.

The others obviously did. Their faces were grim, their breathing rapid and hands at their weapons. They felt the dark magick permeating the air, but Haven thought it seemed different than the twisted magick inside Spirefall.

It was cold, yes, and eerily sentient. But instead of malevolent, it felt . . . curious.

"Let us hurry and be done with this blasted realm," Archeron grumbled.

Surai hissed in agreement, and they spurred their horses into a gallop through the gnarled mirror-forest, the snap of branches matching the sharp crack of hoof beats.

Ravius led them straight there. Once the charcoal peak of Stolas's secret mountain home appeared, Ravius landed on the saddle horn in front of Haven, feathers puffing out proudly, and began preening his beautiful wings.

The ridge was nestled inside a crescent flank of taller bluffs. Unlike last time, there were no gremwyrs circling the sky. No signs of life at all. The sun was a faded star as she squinted at the only visible balcony, from here, barely a smudge of white against the dark mountain.

Night would fall in a couple of hours. And none of them wanted to discover what the Netherworld was like after sundown.

"How will we get up there?" Surai mused beside her, shielding her eyes with her hand against the stifled sun.

"Only the Goddess knows," Haven answered.

It seemed odd that Stolas would tell her to come here but not give her a way up, especially if whoever was inside the house was important enough for him to sacrifice himself to the Shade Queen.

Once again, the brush came to mind. Did Stolas have a lover? The thought was unsettling, if only because she couldn't imagine anyone putting up with his mercurial temper and sour moods.

What would the Lord of the Netherworld's lover be like? As wild and savage as him, surely. With horns and wings and a sardonic smile.

"Perhaps it is Stolas's final joke," Archeron mused.

He hardly bothered hiding his contempt for the Shade Lord. Even if that particular Shade Lord had helped them break the Curse—and would now pay dearly.

"No." Haven wiped a bead of sweat from her forehead and opened her mouth to speak—when something caught her eye. A flicker just above the balcony.

Archeron must have seen it too because he unsheathed his sword a few inches, and his eyes sharpened as they followed the shadow.

As the form grew closer, it became clearer. There were . . . wings. Lovely, feathered wings that seemed to reflect every shade of blue and purple beneath the setting sun.

Surai's mouth fell open. "Is that . . .?"

"A Noctis," Haven finished. "A female."

A twinge of jealousy nestled beneath Haven's ribs as she watched the female Noctis float on the wind toward them in graceful, ever-tightening circles.

The horses shifted on their feet and neighed as the winged shadow flickered across the grass. Watching the predatory creature draw closer, Haven wasn't sure if she should pull her bow or wave.

Had Stolas prepared whoever this was for Haven's arrival? If not, the Noctis might just as easily kill them as say hello.

Between the broad sweep of wings, Haven caught glimpses of fine marble cheekbones and full lips, the palest of blue eyes fringed black, and a tangle of ashen-white hair that desperately needed brushing.

A gold dress of gossamer clung to the female Noctis's body, blowing wildly in the breeze she drifted on. She couldn't be over fourteen or fifteen years of age.

All at once, the girl dove straight for them, sending Haven's heart into a frenzy. Seconds before she might have slammed into Haven, she folded her wings and dropped, landing with cat-like precision on her bare feet in front of Haven's horse.

Silvery-blue eyes peered at Haven above a long, straight nose and pillowy lips. Her heart-shaped face was strikingly beautiful, hewn with a savagery Haven recognized; the girl's feral gaze darted over Haven's companions before landing back on her.

The girl canted her head to the side. "Hello, Haven Ashwood."

"Hello," Haven said, her voice soft and movements slow. She

couldn't help but feel fast movements would scare her or incite the wildness simmering beneath her child-like features.

The nightgown. The hairbrush. Haven's mind whirred as she tried to recall her conversation with the Shade Lord. He'd said his kind lived for centuries. That one-hundred mortal years equaled five of his.

"I'm Nasira, Stolas's sister."

Sister? But that's . . . impossible.

Nasira's eyes once again trailed over the others, but this time, hunger lingered in her gaze. "What are these creatures?"

Haven thought she was talking about the Solis, but Archeron understood, and he huffed a laugh. "Horses. Did your brother never show you the mortal kingdoms?"

Brother. Haven couldn't get used to it, the idea that Stolas was a brother with a sister he obviously adored. Especially because Stolas had said his sister died trying to escape.

A ruse, of course. To hide her from Morgryth.

Nasira's full lips crumpled into a pout. "Stolas never let me out. He said it was too dangerous." Suddenly her face brightened. "Do we eat them?"

Silence reigned. Archeron found Haven and gave her a serves-you-right look while Surai stared open-mouthed at the girl, and Bell looked off in the distance, lost in his world of grief.

"Yep," Archeron said. "She's definitely Stolas's sister."

Haven swallowed down a groan. Goddess Above. What sort of bargain had she made?

"No," she said, carefully. "Nasira, we don't eat the horses. That's how those of us without wings travel."

"Oh." Disappointment tinged her voice. "I am famished. Is this one you hold your slave?" She indicated Bell with a jerk of her bird-boned shoulder. "Can I drink from him?"

Drink? "No!" Haven snarled, too fast. Her arms tightened around Bell. If Stolas had been around, Haven would have decked him in his beautiful, smirking face.

Haven's aggressive tone sparked something predatory inside Nasira, and she grinned. "I do not need your permission, Mortal. But . . . since Stol made me promise to behave, I won't force the issue." A pout darkened her face. "I do need to eat, you know."

Shadeling's shadow! They didn't have time for this.

Archeron chuckled, obviously enjoying the predicament Haven had gotten herself into.

Haven nodded slowly at Nasira, hiding her annoyance behind a tight smile. "Stolas failed to mention that particular detail, but we can figure something out. Just not right *now*."

Nasira's lips quivered. Haven thought she might throw a tantrum, but then her eyes brightened. "I've never left the Netherworld before—at least, not that I remember. Perhaps there will be creatures to hunt while I fly."

"Fly?"

"As I follow you back to your mortal kingdom. Stolas said you would come to collect me. That . . ." Her lips twisted as she tried to remember. "That you would have strange hair and be rude but that I shouldn't kill you."

Nasira beamed at this last part, as if they should all thank her for being so magnanimous as to not slaughter them all.

Archeron shot Haven another smirk before turning his attention on Nasira. "Of course. And Haven cannot wait to introduce you to the mortal king. He will love you, Nasira." He flashed his teeth in a wry smile as he urged his horse into a trot, calling over his shoulder, "Feel free to kill *him* whenever the mood strikes."

Runes! Haven hadn't even thought that far. How the Netherworld would she explain an adolescent Noctis to King

Horace? Especially one that feasted on mortals—*thanks for excluding that part, Shade Lord*—and, by the looks of her, was half wild and had never been properly introduced to the world?

There was no time to rethink anything. Nasira was already shadowing Archeron's horse in the sky, and so Haven urged Lady Pearl into a slow trot.

Ravius regarded her from his lazy perch on her saddle horn, his sharp, beady eyes too curious for her comfort. Occasionally, as if she did something to annoy the bird, he would peck at her fingers and caw shrilly at her.

Bell didn't seem to notice any of it. He was quiet in her arms, half-asleep by the look of his loose shoulders and his soft breathing. She couldn't imagine the horrors he had witnessed, and she was careful not to jostle him as she urged her mare into a smooth canter.

Sleep was the best thing for him now.

Surai's lavender eyes, a soft mauve in the silvery light, were wide as she pulled up beside Haven on her horse. "You do know who Stolas tasked you with safekeeping, don't you?"

Haven shrugged even as her stomach tangled in knots. "His feral, bloodthirsty sister?"

"Haven, the Noctis have Shade Lords, but only one true Shade Queen, the oldest Seraphian female descended from the royal line. With only Stolas alive and married to Ravenna, that title went to Ravenna and Morgryth. But if the Noctis knew his sister wasn't actually dead . . ."

"Stolas said his sister died trying to escape." Haven's breath caught, and she ran her sweaty palms over her pants. "Surai, what have I gotten myself into?"

"Congratulations." Surai flashed a wry smile. "You are now bound as protector to the last true queen of the Noctis."

Ravius cawed in what almost sounded like delight, and Haven groaned, sinking into her saddle. One of these days, she would let Stolas know what she thought of their deal. If she ever saw him again.

Despite her current annoyance, a part of her hoped.

As they galloped after Archeron, Bell swinging unsteadily in Haven's arms, she sucked in calming breaths, trying hard not to look at the shadow circling above—the one occasionally diving to scare the horses while cackling.

If Morgryth knew . . .

No, she could never find out. Wherever she and her shadowlings had fled, wherever they went to regroup and lick their wounds, they could never learn of the royal Seraph Haven was bound by magick to protect.

If they were lucky, the Dark Queen would decide to ignore Haven and her friends. And if they were truly blessed by the Goddess, the queen would slither away to die from her wounds.

But Haven would only believe the Shade Queen was gone when she saw her rotting corpse with her own eyes. Until then, they would never truly be safe.

Eventually, when the sun sank into the earth and the air cooled, Nasira grew tired of teasing the horses and found a breeze to glide on, her wings carving dark shadows across the moonlit ground.

At this pace, it would take just over a week to reach Penryth. The kingdom would already be aware that the Curse was broken; perhaps they would send out an envoy to greet them.

After all, King Horace would want to claim all the glory.

Glory—the word seemed wrong.

Undoubtedly, they would be immortalized for breaking the Curse. Their names written in fables and sang in songs, their story passed from generation to generation. Mortals would tell their tale in reverent tones around campfires or drunkenly at banquets.

Perhaps their yarn would become a bedtime story for children, a watered-down myth for the masses to believe good always defeats evil.

And somewhere along the way, the details would be lost to history until some idealized version was all that remained of their journey, their sacrifice.

Their names would be forgotten, their losses and heartbreaks glossed over, their truth lost forever. The world would never truly understand what they gave up for it—and a bitter part of her thought the realm wasn't worth the things they lost.

If they could go back to their old lives, would they?

If Haven could have Bell, unbroken, and Rook could live. If Surai could get married to the love of her life, and Archeron would have never tasted freedom only to have it dashed from him. They would have never felt the cruel blade of Bjorn's betrayal, and Haven would have never understood the wicked, inescapable allure of dark magick.

Haven released a heavy sigh. There was no turning back, their fates were written. All she could do was try to make up for it somehow. They wouldn't return to Penryth the same—but they would return.

Sometimes, that was all you could ask for. Another chance.

Bell stirred in her arms then settled against Lady Pearl's glossy neck, his fingers twined around her white mane. As Haven brushed back his hair from his face, moonlight danced inside the runes snaking along her arms, highlighting muscles and scars.

Even now, her fleshrunes burned with gathering power.

Begging to be used. Tested.

Limitless magick, both dark and light. Fire and ice. *Forbidden.*

As if reading her thoughts, Archeron came up beside her and brushed his warm fingers down her arm. A tender gesture that said what words could not.

I'm here.

Surai joined on the other side, and they traveled in silence, all of them vastly different from the people who had entered the Ruinlands what felt like years ago. All of them fractured and grieving in their own way.

But they had each other. They had tomorrow and all the days after.

To cry. To mourn. To heal. To hope.

And, perhaps, if they were lucky, to love.

THE END

Book three, KING MAKER, will release February 2020. You can pre-order it on Amazon.

In the meantime, you can keep up with Haven and Archeron's world and all things Kingdom of Runes by signing up for my monthly author newsletter!

WWW.KINGDOMOFRUNESSAGA.COM

GLOSSARY

- **The Bane** – The central region of Eritrayia and a barren wasteland, it acts as the buffer between the Ruinlands destroyed by the Curse and the untouched southern kingdoms protected by the runewall

- **Curseprice** – The items that must be collected and presented to the Shade Queen to break the Curse

- **Dark magick** – Derived from the Netherworld, it cannot be created, only channeled from its source, and is only available to Noctis. Dark magick feeds off light magick.

- **Darkcaster** – One who wields dark magick

- **Devourers** – Mortals with Noctis blood who practice demented dark magick and worship the Shade Queen; live in the bane and guard the rift/crossing into the Ruinlands

- **The Devouring** – The dark magick-laden mist that descends when the Curse hits and causes curse-sickness and death in mortals

- **Donatus Atrea** – All-Giver, or runetree of life where all light magick springs from

- **Eritrayia** – Mortal realm

- **Fleshrunes** – Runes Solis are born with; the markings tattoo a

Solis's flesh and channel their many magickal gifts

- **The Goddess** – Freya, mother of both Solis and Noctis, she is a powerful and divine being who gifted mortals with magick and fought on their side during the Shadow War.

- **Heart Oath** – Oath given before an engagement to marry. Can only be broken if two parties agree to sever the oath and at great cost

- **House of Nine** – Descendants of the nine mortals given runeflowers from the Tree of Life

- **Houserune** – Rune given to each of the Nine Houses and passed down from generation to generation

- **Light Magick** – Derived from the Nihl, it cannot be created, only channeled from its source, and is only available to Solis and royal mortals from the House Nine.

- **Lightcaster** – One who wields light magick

- **Mortalrune** – Runes mortals from the House Nine are allowed to possess/use

- **Netherworld** – Hell, where immoral souls go, ruled over by the Lord of the Netherworld

- **Nihl** – Heaven, ruled over by the Goddess Freya

- **Noctis** – Race of immortals native to Shadoria and the Netherworld who possess dark magic, they have pale skin, dark wings, and frequently horns

- **Powerrune** – Powerful type of rune forbidden to mortals

- **The Rift** – Chasm in the continent of Eritrayia caused by the Curse that leads to the Netherworld and allowed the Shade Queen and her people to escape

- **Ruinlands** – Northern half of Eritreyia, these lands are enchanted with dark magick and ruled by the Shade Queen

- **Runeday** – The eighteenth birthday of a royal child of the Nine Houses, where he or she receives their house runestone and potentially come into magick.

- **Runemagick** – Magick channeled precisely through ancient runes

- **Runestone** – Stones carved with a single rune—usually—and imbued with magick

- **Runetotem** – Tall poles carved with runes, they are used to nullify certain types of magick while enhancing others

- **Runewall** – A magickal wall that protects the last remaining southern kingdoms from the Curse

- **Sacred Heart Flower** – Given to the Solis at birth, this sacred bud is kept inside a glass vial and worn around the neck of one's intended mate

- **Shade Lord** – A powerful Noctis male, second only to the Shade Queen

- **The Shadeling** – Odin, father of both Solis and Noctis, he once loved Freya but became dark and twisted after fighting against his lover in the Shadow War. He now resides in the deepest pits of the Netherworld, a terrifying monster even the Noctis refuse to unchain.

- **The Shadow War** – War between the three races (mortals, Noctis, Solis,) sparked by the Goddess Freya giving mortals magick
- **Shadowlings** – Monsters from the Netherworld, under the control of the Lord of the Netherworld and the Shade Queen
- **Solis** – Race of immortals native to Solissia who possess light magick, they are more mortal-like in their appearance, with fair eyes and hair
- **Solissia** – Realm of the immortals
- **Soulread** – To read someone's mind
- **Soulwalk** – To send one's soul outside their body
- **Soulbind** – To bind another's will to yours/take over their body
- **Sun Lord** – A powerful Solis male who enjoys special position in the Effendier Royal Sun Court under the Effendier Sun Sovereign
- **Sun Queen** – A powerful Solis female who enjoys special position in the Effendier Royal Sun Court under the Effendier Sun Sovereign

SOLISSIAN WORDS AND PHRASES

• **Ascilum Oscular** – Kiss my ass (maybe)

• **Carvendi** – Good job (more or less)

• **Droob** – Knob/idiot

• **Paramatti** – Close the door to the Nihl, used during a light magick spell

• **Rump Falia** – Butt-face

• **Umath** – You're welcome

• **Victari** – Close the door to the Netherworld, used during a dark magick spell

THE NINE MORTAL HOUSES

• **Barrington** (Shadow Kingdom, formerly Kingdom of Maldovia)

• **Bolcvick** (Kingdom of Verdure)

• **Boteler** (Kingdom of Penryth)

• **Courtenay** (Drothian)

• **Coventry** (Veserack)

• **Halvorshyrd** (unknown location)

• **Renfyre** (Lorwynfell)

• **Thendryft** (Dune)

• **Volantis** (Skyfall Island)

KINGDOM OF RUNES PLAYERS

Mortal Players

- **Haven Ashwood** – orphan
- **Damius Black** – Leader of the Devourers
- **Prince Bellamy (Bell) Boteler** – House Boteler, crown prince, second and only surviving heir to the king of Penryth
- **King Horace Boteler** – House Boteler, ruler of Penryth
- **Cressida Craven** – King Horace Boteler's mistress
- **Renk Craven** – half-brother to Bell, bastard son of Cressida and the King of Penryth
- **Eleeza Thendryft** – Princess of House Thendryft of the Kingdom of Dune, House Thendryft
- **Lord Thendryft** – House Thendryft of Dune Kingdom
- **Demelza Thurgood** – Haven Ashwood's Lady's Maid

Noctis Players

- **Stolas Darkshade** – Lord of the Underworld, husband to Ravenna, son of the last true Noctis Queen
- **Avaline Kallor** – Skeleton Queen, Ruler of Lorwynfell, half Noctis half mortal, promised to Archeron Halfbane
- **Remurian Kallor** – Half Noctis half mortal, brother of Amandine, died in the last war
- **Malachi K'rul** – Shade Lord, Shade Queen's underling

- **Morgryth Malythean** – Shade Queen, Cursemaker, queen of darkness, ruler of the Noctis
- **Ravenna Malythean** – Daughter of the Shade Queen, undead

Solis Players

- **Bjorn** – Sun Lord of mysterious origins
- **Archeron Halfbane** – Sun Lord and bastard son of the Effendier Sun Sovereign
- **Surai Nakamura** – Ashari warrior
- **Brienne "Rook" Wenfyre** – Sun Queen, outcast princess, daughter of the Morgani Warrior Queen

GODS

- Freya – the Goddess, ruler of the Nihl, mother of both Noctis and Solis
- Odin – the Shadeling, imprisoned in the Netherworld pits, father of both Noctis and Solis

ANIMALS

- Aramaya – Rook's temperamental horse
- Lady Pearl – Haven's loyal horse
- Ravius – Stolas's raven
- Shadow – Damius's wyvern

WEAPONS

- Haven's Sword – Oathbearer
- Stolas's Dagger – Vengeance

ABOUT THE AUTHOR

AUDREY GREY lives in the charming state of Oklahoma surrounded by animals, books, and little people. You can usually find Audrey hiding out in her office, downing copious amounts of caffeine while dreaming of tacos and holding entire conversations with her friends using gifs. Audrey considers her ability to travel to fantastical worlds a superpower and loves nothing more than bringing her readers with her.

Find her online at:

WWW.AUDREYGREY.COM

DON'T MISS MY NEW ACADEMY SERIES!

Welcome to Evermore Academy where the magic is dark, the immortals are beautiful, and being human SUCKS.

After spending my entire life avoiding the creatures that murdered my parents, one stupid mistake binds me to them for four years.

My penance? Become a human shadow at the infamous Evermore Academy, finishing school for the Seelie and Unseelie Fae courts.

All I want is to keep a low profile, but day one, I make an enemy of the most powerful Fae in the academy.

The Winter Prince is arrogant, cruel, and apparently also my Fae keeper. Meaning I'm in for months of torture.

But it only gets worse. Something dark and terrible looms over the academy. Humans are dying, ancient vendettas are resurfacing, and the courts are more bloodthirsty than ever.

What can one mortal girl do in a world full of gorgeous monsters?

Fight back with everything I have—and try not to fall in love in the process.

CPSIA information can be obtained
at www.ICGtesting.com
Printed in the USA
LVHW091721171219
640801LV00005B/73/P